AF118398

THE STORMBOUND DIVIDE

The World-Song Saga, Book 4

Written by Diane Kann

Brought to you by Volans Galaxy Press

© 2026 Diane Kann

All rights reserved.

No part of this publication may be reproduced, stored in a retrieval system, or transmitted in any form or by any means—electronic, mechanical, photocopying, recording, or otherwise—without prior written permission of the publisher, except in the case of brief quotations for review or educational use.

Published by Kannceptual Creations LLC

An imprint of Volans Galaxy Press

ISBN: 978-1-971356-77-8

Printed in the United States of America

First Edition, January 2026

CONTENTS

Author's Biography	V
Dedication	VI
1. Whispers of the Unraveling	1
2. The Accord's Shadow	33
3. Echoes of Rebellion	57
4. The Song Silenced	86
5. Whispers from the Deep	112
6. The Listener's Journey	143
7. The Guardian's Gambit	172
8. The Skybound's Game	206
9. The Voice of the World	236
10. The Gathering Storm	259
11. Symphony of Conflict	290
12. The Abyssal Climax	321
13. The Quiet After the Song	353
Glossary	381

Reference

AUTHOR'S BIOGRAPHY

Diane Kann writes eco-science fantasy that explores the intersections of technology, nature, and hope. Drawn to mysterious worlds, sentient ecosystems, and the quiet strength of unlikely heroes, she crafts stories that imagine not just what humanity might survive, but how it might heal.

A believer in environmental stewardship and deeply fascinated by the natural world, Diane weaves themes of conservation and interconnected life throughout her work. When she's not writing, she can be found exploring the diverse ecosystems of Central Florida with her family and dogs—dreaming up strange futures rooted in compassion and the resilience of nature.

DEDICATION

For you, the reader—
who stepped into this world with an open heart.
Thank you for listening to its storms and silences,
for caring about what trembles beneath the sky,
and for believing that even when harmony frays,
it is still worth protecting.

May this story stay with you long after the last page,
like a quiet song reminding us that hope,
once heard, is never truly lost.

Chapter One
Whispers of the Unraveling

The air hung thick with an almost palpable stillness, a breathless pause that precedes a violent exhalation. For Mara Lysenne, the quiet was not one of peace, but of a low, resonant hum that vibrated with a wrongness she felt not just in her ears, but in the marrow of her bones. The world, or rather, the planet, possessed a song, an intricate tapestry of atmospheric currents, magnetic fields, and the subtle energetic whispers of every living thing. Mara, as a Listener, was attuned to this cosmic symphony, able to perceive its harmonies and dissonances with an intimacy that was both a gift and a burden. Lately, the symphony had begun to fray.

It started subtly, like a single misplaced note in an otherwise perfect aria. A tremor in the usual flow of the sky-currents, a momentary hesitation in the predictable dance of the wind. Mara had dismissed it at first, attributing it to a particularly turbulent season, a fleeting atmospheric anomaly. But the disturbances persisted, growing in frequency and intensity. The air, usually a predictable medium for travel and life, began to feel... sluggish, resistant. It was as if the very sky was sighing, its breath catching in its throat.

The implications rippled outward, touching even the smallest, most insignificant lives. Mara noticed it in the erratic flight paths of the sky-moths, their delicate wings beating with a frantic, almost panicked rhythm, their usual migration patterns dissolving into chaotic zigzags.

Schools of shimmering aether-fish, once predictable in their silvery shoals, scattered like startled dust motes, their bioluminescent trails flickering erratically through the twilight. These were not isolated incidents; they were symptoms of a deeper malaise, a pervasive discord that was slowly but surely unraveling the intricate weave of the planet's song.

Mara walked along the edge of the Whispering Cliffs, the wind that usually caressed her face now tugging at her cloak with an aggressive impatience. Below, the Obsidian Sea churned, its waves crashing against the ancient rock with a sound that felt less like the ocean's roar and more like a guttural groan. She closed her eyes, focusing her senses inward, seeking the familiar pulse of the planet. It was there, undoubtedly, but it was no longer pure. It was overlaid with a static, a low-frequency thrum that felt like grinding stone against a delicate instrument. This was the discord. It was a dissonance that spoke of imbalance, of a fundamental cosmic flaw that was slowly, inexorably, beginning to reveal itself.

The atmospheric flow, once a predictable series of currents that guided both natural and artificial flight, had become turbulent. Pilots spoke of sudden downdrafts and inexplicable headwinds, of instruments that flickered and died without warning. Trade routes, once reliably charted, were becoming perilous. Even the weather, usually subject to a degree of predictability, was becoming erratic. Gentle rains turned into flash floods, and periods of calm were punctuated by sudden, violent squalls that appeared out of nowhere, tearing through settlements and flattening crops.

Mara felt this disturbance not just as an external phenomenon, but as an internal tremor. It resonated deep within her, a psychic echo of the planet's distress. It was a constant, low-grade ache, a feeling of being out of sync with the world around her. She found herself more easily agitated, her usual calm replaced by a simmering anxiety. Sleep offered little respite, her dreams often filled with fractured melodies and the sensation of falling, of being lost in a sky that no longer held its shape.

THE STORMBOUND DIVIDE

She recalled a conversation with Elder Maeve, the former Listener, who had spoken of the planet's song as a living entity, a conscious force that maintained the delicate equilibrium of their world. "The song is life, Mara," Maeve had said, her voice raspy with age and wisdom. "And when the song falters, so too does life itself." Mara had understood the words then, but now, she *felt* them. The faltering was undeniable, a palpable decay that was leaching the vibrancy from the world.

The implications were profound, reaching far beyond mere atmospheric inconvenience. The planet's song was intricately linked to the life cycles of its inhabitants, to the very stability of its ecosystems. The erratic migration patterns of the lesser aerial creatures were just one visible sign. Deeper within the oceans, the ancient coral cities pulsed with a weakened luminescence, their symbiotic relationships strained. Even the plant life seemed to exhibit a subtle lethargy, their leaves less verdant, their growth slowed. It was a creeping sickness, an unraveling that threatened to pull apart the very fabric of existence.

Mara's sensitivity, her ability to perceive these subtle shifts, made her acutely aware of the scale of the unfolding crisis. While others might dismiss the odd weather patterns or the unusual behavior of animals, Mara understood that these were merely the visible ripples of a much larger disturbance. The cosmic imbalance was not a distant theoretical concept; it was a tangible force, a creeping darkness that was beginning to eclipse the familiar light of their world.

She sat by her window, tracing the condensation that formed on the cool glass. Outside, the sky was a bruised purple, a color that spoke of an impending storm, but one that felt unnatural, forced. The usual gentle currents that guided the high-flying skyships were absent, replaced by a churning, chaotic wind that tossed even the sturdiest vessels about like leaves in a gale. It was a terrifying spectacle, a visible manifestation of the disharmony Mara felt singing in her very soul.

The Whispers of the Unraveling. That was what the Elders called this period, this creeping unease that had settled over the world. They spoke of ancient prophecies, of times when the planet's song had been threatened by forces beyond mortal comprehension. Mara had always dismissed these as old wives' tales, comforting fictions for times of uncertainty. But now, with the discord thrumming in her bones, the ancient stories felt chillingly real.

The familiar patterns of nature were breaking. The seasonal migrations of the luminous sky-whales, once a majestic and predictable spectacle, had become erratic, their vast forms appearing in unusual locations, their mournful songs distorted and pained. Even the humble moss-grazers, creatures of habit and instinct, were venturing into unfamiliar territories, their usual foraging grounds now seemingly devoid of the subtle energetic signatures they relied upon. It was as if the very earth beneath their feet was no longer whispering the familiar guidance, replaced by a confused, stuttering murmur.

Mara felt a responsibility, a weight that settled upon her shoulders with each passing day. As a Listener, she was meant to be a conduit, a bridge between the world and its song. But what could one person do against such a pervasive, cosmic imbalance? Her ability was one of perception, not of control. She could feel the sickness, but she could not yet articulate a cure. The tone of unease that had settled over the land was more than just a feeling; it was a prelude, a quiet before a storm that promised to be unlike any they had ever witnessed. The planet's song was unraveling, and Mara was one of the few who could truly hear its mournful lament.

The air crackled with an unseen energy, a static charge that prickled the skin and set the nerves on edge. It was a feeling Mara had come to know intimately in recent weeks, an externalization of the discord she felt thrumming within her own being. The planet's song, the intricate symphony of atmospheric currents, magnetic fields, and the subtle energetic whispers of all life, was no longer a harmonious melody. It was a fractured, discordant symphony, each errant note a testament to a growing imbalance that threatened the very fabric of their world.

THE STORMBOUND DIVIDE

She stood on the precipice of the Sky-Ridge, a place usually known for its serene vistas and gentle breezes. Today, the wind was a capricious bully, whipping her cloak around her and tugging at her hair with an almost malicious force. The familiar currents, the invisible pathways that guided the graceful flight of skyships and the migratory routes of aerial creatures, were erratic, unpredictable. It was as if the sky itself was drunk, its celestial currents stumbling and swaying with no regard for the established order.

Mara closed her eyes, focusing her unique sensitivity. She felt the dissonance not just in the air, but deep within the earth. It was a low hum, a grating sound that vibrated against the very foundations of her being. The planet's song, once a clear, resonant melody, was now overlaid with a disturbing static, like the sound of a thousand voices crying out in pain. This wasn't just a seasonal anomaly; it was a profound disturbance, a cosmic imbalance that was slowly but inexorably unraveling the delicate tapestry of life.

The migration patterns of the lesser aerial creatures were the most obvious manifestation of this decay. Mara had spent years observing them, their synchronized flights a beautiful testament to the planet's inherent order. Now, the sky-moths, tiny bioluminescent sparks that usually traced predictable paths through the twilight, darted and weaved with a frantic, almost desperate energy. They scattered like dropped jewels, their internal compasses seemingly broken, their collective dance dissolving into chaos. Similarly, the schools of aether-fish, which normally moved as one shimmering entity through the upper atmosphere, now broke apart into smaller, disoriented groups, their luminous trails flickering like dying embers.

This breakdown in natural order was deeply unsettling. It suggested that the very forces that governed life on their world were faltering. The planet's song was not merely a pleasant background noise; it was the lifeblood of their ecosystem, a complex system of energetic vibrations that influenced everything from weather patterns to the instincts of even the smallest creatures. When the song faltered, so too did the harmony of existence.

Mara walked along the edge of the Whispering Cliffs, the wind whipping around her with an unusual ferocity. Below, the Obsidian Sea, usually a majestic expanse of deep blues and greens, churned with an unsettling grey froth. The waves crashed against the ancient rocks with a sound that was less a roar and more a guttural groan, as if the ocean itself was in distress. The air was thick with the scent of ozone and something else, something metallic and acrid that Maya couldn't quite place, but which set her teeth on edge.

She reached out a hand, feeling the invisible currents of the air. They were no longer smooth, predictable channels. Instead, they felt choppy, turbulent, like a river choked with debris. This turbulence wasn't confined to the edges of the land; reports were already filtering in from the skyship captains, tales of sudden downdrafts that threatened to send vessels plunging from the sky, of inexplicable headwinds that brought journeys to a grinding halt. The sky, once a reliable highway, was becoming a treacherous, unpredictable domain.

The implications of this atmospheric chaos were far-reaching. Agriculture, reliant on predictable weather patterns, was already suffering. Unseasonal frosts nipped at young crops, and sudden downpours washed away precious topsoil. Trade routes, both by skyship and by land, were becoming increasingly hazardous, disrupting the flow of goods and creating anxieties among the populace. The subtle decay Mara felt was manifesting in tangible ways, threatening the stability and prosperity of their civilization.

Mara felt the discord not just as an external phenomenon, but as an internal vibration. It was a constant, low-grade ache in her bones, a feeling of being out of sync with the world. Her senses, usually sharp and clear, felt dulled, as if a fine layer of dust had settled over them. Sleep offered little respite, her dreams often filled with fractured melodies and the sensation of falling, of being lost in a sky that no longer held its shape. She felt the planet's distress as if it were her own, a profound empathy that was both a blessing and a curse.

THE STORMBOUND DIVIDE

She recalled the words of Elder Maeve, the former Listener, who had spoken of the planet's song as a living, breathing entity. "It is the heart of our world, Mara," she had said, her voice thin as parchment. "And when the heart falters, all of life suffers." Mara had understood the words then, but now, she *felt* them. The faltering was undeniable, a palpable decay that was leaching the vibrancy from the world, leaving behind a hollow echo of what once was.

The subtle shifts were more than just an inconvenience; they were a harbinger. They hinted at a deeper, more profound cosmic imbalance that was slowly but inexorably manifesting itself. The planet's song was unraveling, note by painful note, and Mara, as a Listener, was one of the few attuned enough to truly hear its mournful lament. The eerie calm before the storm was a deceptive façade, masking a growing disquiet that was poised to erupt into something far more tumultuous. The stage was being set, not just for a storm of wind and rain, but for a tempest of existential consequence.

The wind, usually a predictable caress against the ancient stones of the Sky-Ridge, now clawed and buffeted, a wild thing unnerved by unseen forces. Mara Lysenne, a Listener attuned to the planet's very breath, felt the discord deep within her bones. It wasn't the sharp, sudden pain of injury, but a dull, pervasive ache, a resonance that spoke of something fundamentally *wrong*. The world's song, the intricate, invisible symphony of atmospheric currents, magnetic fields, and the energetic whispers of all living things, was fraying at the edges.

Her sensitivity, a gift honed through years of dedicated practice and innate connection, allowed her to perceive this unraveling with an intimacy that was both terrifying and profound. The sky, usually a vast, predictable ocean of air, felt... thick. Stagnant in places, and in others, violently agitated, as if something within it was struggling to break free. The familiar sky-currents, the invisible pathways that guided the graceful arc of skyships and the journeys of migrating creatures, were no longer reliable. They twisted and broke, faltering like a dying breath.

Mara watched, her gaze fixed on a flock of cloud-swallows, their usually elegant aerial ballet dissolving into a panicked scramble. They darted and swooped with an erratic energy, their synchronized movements replaced by a chaotic thrashing. It was a small detail, perhaps, but to Mara, it was a scream from the planet itself. These lesser aerial creatures, so finely tuned to the planet's song, were faltering. Their innate compasses, guided by the subtle ebb and flow of atmospheric energies, were failing them.

The disquiet wasn't confined to the sky. The familiar hum of the earth, a grounding vibration that always settled Mara's spirit, felt subtly altered. It was deeper, more resonant, and laced with a low-frequency thrum that felt like grinding stone against the delicate strings of a celestial harp. This was the discord. It was a dissonance that spoke not of a storm's passing fury, but of a deeper, more insidious decay, a creeping imbalance that was beginning to erode the very foundations of their world.

She walked down from the ridge, the wind tugging at her cloak as if trying to pull her back, to keep her from venturing further into this unsettling new reality. The trees, their branches usually swaying in a gentle, rhythmic dance, seemed to shiver, their leaves rustling with a dry, anxious sound. Even the sunlight filtering through the canopy felt different, somehow less warm, less vital.

Mara's mind turned to the ancient texts, to the hushed legends of Listeners who had felt the planet's song falter before. They spoke of a time when the sky had wept fire, and the earth had convulsed in a paroxysm of rage. These were tales meant to inspire caution, to remind them of the immense power of the natural world and the delicate balance that sustained their existence. But they had always felt like distant echoes, like stories from a forgotten age. Now, they resonated with a chilling immediacy.

The atmosphere, this vast expanse that cradled their world, was the lifeblood of so much. It carried the seeds, the rain, the very breath of life. For it to be so disrupted, so filled with a chaotic, dissonant energy, was a grave omen. The predictable patterns that governed their lives, from the turning of the seasons to the simple act of a bird's flight, were being subtly, yet fundamentally, undermined.

Mara felt the implications pressing in on her. This wasn't just about inconvenient weather or confused wildlife. This was about the deep, intrinsic interconnectedness of all things. The planet's song was the melody that bound them all together. And when that melody began to break, so too did the bonds that held their world in cohesive existence. The unease she felt was not a personal affliction; it was a reflection of a world out of tune, a planet groaning under the weight of an encroaching cosmic imbalance.

The air itself seemed to vibrate with a low, insistent hum, a sound that Mara felt more in her bones than heard with her ears. It was the planet's song, and for weeks now, it had been discordant. The familiar, comforting melody that had always underscored her existence as a Listener had become a jarring, uneven rhythm, like a lute with strings snapped and slack. This dissonance was more than just an auditory phenomenon; it was a deep, visceral wrongness that unsettled the very core of her being.

Mara stood on the edge of the Sky-Ridge, a place usually alive with the predictable flow of atmospheric currents, and felt only chaos. The wind, normally a gentle, guiding hand, was now a capricious entity, whipping and tearing with an unpredictable fury. It tossed aside the normally graceful flight of the skyships, turning their majestic journeys into desperate struggles for survival. She watched, her heart tightening, as a smaller scout vessel, caught in an unseen downdraft, spiraled erratically towards the jagged peaks below. It was a sight that was becoming far too common.

The disruption wasn't confined to the immediate vicinity. Reports trickled in from across the continent: flocks of luminescent sky-whales, usually following ancient migratory paths with unerring precision, were scattering, their mournful songs replaced by cries of confusion. The delicate atmospheric balance that governed weather patterns was faltering. Gentle rains had become flash floods, and periods of calm were shattered by sudden, violent squalls that appeared from nowhere, devastating villages and farmlands alike.

Mara, as a Listener, felt these shifts acutely. The planet's song was her lifeblood, the intricate tapestry of energies that connected her to the world. Now, that tapestry was unraveling, thread by agonizing thread. The discord was a constant companion, a low-grade ache in her bones, a psychic static that dulled her senses and frayed her nerves. Sleep offered little solace, her dreams filled with fragmented melodies and the unsettling sensation of falling through a sky that no longer held its shape.

She remembered Elder Maeve, the former Listener, her voice a dry rustle like autumn leaves, speaking of the song's importance. "It is the pulse of the world, Mara," she had whispered, her eyes clouded with ancient knowledge. "And when the pulse falters, so too does all of life." Maeve's words, once a wise caution, now felt like a prophecy being fulfilled. The pulse was faltering, and the signs of sickness were everywhere.

The predictable migration patterns of the smaller aerial fauna were breaking down. Sky-moths, usually a shimmering river of light through the twilight, now darted and weaved in disorganized clusters, their bioluminescent trails flickering erratically. Schools of aether-fish, creatures that typically moved with a unified grace, scattered like startled dust motes. These were not isolated incidents, but symptoms of a profound, pervasive imbalance. The very energetic pathways that guided life were becoming corrupted, twisted by the pervasive discord.

The implications were vast. The planet's song was not merely atmospheric acoustics; it was the underlying harmony that dictated the health of ecosystems, the fertility of the soil, the very rhythm of life. For it to be so disrupted suggested a cosmic imbalance of immense proportions, a slow decay that threatened to unravel the intricate web of existence. The eerie calm that seemed to pervade the land was deceptive, a breath held before a storm of unprecedented magnitude. The planet's song was unraveling, and Mara was one of the few who could truly hear its lament, a harbinger of the turbulent times to come.

THE STORMBOUND DIVIDE

The sky dragons, those magnificent, iridescent titans of the upper atmosphere, were no longer the serene guardians they had always been. For millennia, their presence had been a silent promise of stability, their immense wingspans carving predictable, elegant paths through the celestial currents. Their migratory journeys were not mere flights of fancy, but a vital part of the planet's atmospheric regulation, their powerful movements subtly guiding the wind, their very exhalations shaping the clouds. But now, a tremor ran through their ancient lineage, a disquiet that mirrored the growing discord in the planet's song.

Whispers, carried on the increasingly agitated winds, spoke of unease amongst the dragons. Once, their flights were synchronized, a majestic ballet performed across the vast sapphire stage of the sky. Now, their formations were fractured, their movements jerky and uncertain. Reports, often dismissed by the pragmatic as mere sailor's tales, began to surface with alarming frequency. Tales of dragons veering from their ancestral routes, their roars, once resonant with calm power, now laced with a raw, untamed ferocity. The air, once their dominion, now felt like a battlefield in the making, the sky dragons themselves the first, most terrifying heralds of the unraveling.

Mara listened to these fragmented accounts, piecing them together with the gnawing anxiety that had become her constant companion. The dragons, she knew, were intrinsically linked to the planet's energetic hum. Their very existence was a testament to the harmonious interplay of atmospheric forces. If they were disturbed, if their ancient instincts were thrown into disarray, it was a sign that the disturbance ran deeper than any casual observer could comprehend. It suggested that the very pacts, the unspoken agreements that had governed the relationships between species and the planet, were beginning to fray.

The ancient pacts. The term itself was steeped in myth and legend, tales passed down through generations of how the first beings to walk the earth, the dragons amongst them, had forged an understanding with the nascent planet. It was a pact of mutual respect, of balance, a promise that the powerful would protect the fragile, and that the planet would provide for all. Now, it seemed, the terms of that ancient agreement were being questioned, or worse, utterly forgotten.

The first signs of territorial disputes were subtle, easily explained away by unusual weather patterns or the general increase in atmospheric turbulence. A dragon's shadow falling too close to a traditionally protected nesting ground, a roar of warning that lingered too long, carrying an edge of aggression that had never been heard before. But soon, these subtle shifts escalated. Reports began to emerge of clashes, of brief, violent encounters between dragons who had previously coexisted peacefully, or even migrated together. These were not playful sparring matches; they were battles born of fear, of territorial imperative, and perhaps, of a primal instinct to lash out at a world that no longer felt stable.

The sky dragons, creatures of immense power and ancient wisdom, were not inherently malicious. They were beings of instinct and energy, their actions dictated by the health of their environment and the clarity of the planet's song. The disarray that had seized them was a direct reflection of the disharmony that Mara felt so keenly. Their ancient minds, so attuned to the subtle shifts in the atmospheric currents, were now receiving distorted signals, fragmented commands that their primal natures interpreted as threats.

Mara's thoughts drifted to the Great Migration, a spectacle that had drawn watchers from across the land for centuries. Thousands of dragons, their scales shimmering with every hue imaginable, would ascend into the heavens, forming a breathtaking river of life that flowed across the sky for weeks. It was a testament to their unity, to the enduring strength of the pacts that bound them. The thought of that spectacle being replaced by fragmented, warring factions sent a shiver down Mara's spine.

The formation of factions was the logical, terrifying progression. If the dragons were no longer acting as a unified force, if their ancient instincts were driving them to protect their own perceived interests, then divisions would inevitably form. Some dragons, perhaps those older and more attuned to the planet's song, might cling to the old ways, trying to maintain order and understand the disturbance. Others, younger and more impulsive, or perhaps those whose territories were more immediately impacted by the atmospheric chaos, might react with aggression, seeing conflict as the only solution.

These factions, Mara mused, would likely be defined by their elemental affinities, or by the regions they traditionally patrolled. There would be the Sunscale dragons, their scales burning with golden light, who ruled the high altitudes, and the Shadowwing dragons, their forms cloaked in twilight hues, who preferred the cooler, lower reaches. Perhaps the Stormborn dragons, who thrived in the volatile skies, would see the current chaos as an opportunity, while the Sky-Reef dragons, who nested amongst the floating islands, would be more inclined to defend their established domains.

The implications of these burgeoning divisions were dire. The sky dragons were not just beautiful creatures; they were keystone species, their presence essential to the delicate atmospheric balance. Their coordinated flights helped to dissipate destructive storms, their energy currents were vital for the growth of certain high-altitude flora, and their very passage through the skies seemed to calm the restless winds. Without their stabilizing presence, the atmospheric chaos would surely escalate, impacting the world below in ways that were becoming increasingly evident.

The skyships, once symbols of safe and efficient travel, were now more vulnerable than ever. Pilots spoke of unexpected aerial predators, of dragons no longer indifferent to their passage but actively hostile, their roars shaking the very hulls of the vessels. The predictable trade routes were becoming death traps, the skies a warzone where ancient, powerful beings clashed with a ferocity that belied their usual grace. The loss of the dragons' unifying presence was a gaping wound in the fabric of the world's stability, a wound that was widening with every passing day.

Mara envisioned the sky as a canvas, once painted with the serene, flowing strokes of dragon flight. Now, that canvas was becoming a chaotic smear, a violent clash of colors and forms. The once-familiar silhouette of a dragon against the setting sun was no longer a comforting sight, but a potential harbinger of danger. The majesty of their forms was now tinged with a terrifying unpredictability, their power, once a force for balance, now a source of immense, volatile potential.

The stories of broken pacts were particularly troubling. These were not just abstract concepts; they were the foundational principles that had ensured relative peace and stability for ages. If the dragons, the oldest and most powerful of the planet's inhabitants, were reneging on these agreements, it signaled a breakdown at the most fundamental level. It suggested that the very forces that had once maintained order were now actively working against it.

Mara imagined a grand council of dragons, a meeting that had not occurred for centuries, where representatives from each lineage would convene. But instead of solemn deliberation, there would be accusations, threats, and the chilling realization that their shared heritage was no longer enough to bind them. The primal instincts, amplified by the planet's distress, were overriding the ancient wisdom.

The concept of "differing interpretations of the planet's distress" was particularly poignant. Some dragons might perceive the unraveling as a natural cycle, a phase that would eventually pass, and thus seek to endure it with stoic patience. Others might see it as an attack, an external force that needed to be confronted and vanquished, leading to aggressive territorial expansion and preemptive strikes. And then there were those driven purely by instinct, their minds clouded by the dissonant frequencies, their actions simply reactive to the chaos they felt.

The visual of the dragons clashing was burned into Mara's mind. The sheer scale of such battles would be catastrophic. Imagine two titans, their wingspans wider than any skyship, locking in aerial combat, their roars echoing like thunder across the land, their powerful claws tearing at each other, their fiery breath scorching the very air. These were not mere skirmishes; they were elemental forces colliding, their impact rippling outwards to affect weather, ecosystems, and the lives of all who dwelled beneath them.

The loss of their stabilizing presence would be felt most acutely by those who lived in close proximity to the sky dragons' traditional territories. Villages nestled in mountain valleys, communities built on the floating islands of the Sky-Reefs, all relied on the unseen beneficence of these creatures. Their sudden absence, or worse, their active hostility, would leave these settlements exposed to the full fury of an increasingly volatile atmosphere.

Mara's heart ached for the inherent tragedy of it all. These magnificent beings, once the embodiment of the sky's serene majesty, were being drawn into the same chaos that was plaguing the planet. Their majestic flight, once a symbol of unity and natural order, was becoming a terrifying display of fractured power. The sky dragons were not just victims of the unraveling; they were becoming active participants, their discord amplifying the very disharmony that was tearing their world apart. The fractured heavens were no longer just a poetic descriptor; they were becoming a literal reality, a domain now ruled by the turbulent clashes of its former guardians. The silence of their former harmony was being replaced by the deafening roar of conflict.

The unease that had gripped the sky dragons, once a subtle tremor, was now a seismic shift. Their fractured flights, their territorial skirmishes, were no longer isolated incidents. They were symptoms of a deeper malady, a cosmic fever that was beginning to reshape the very fabric of the sky. It was amidst this burgeoning chaos, this grand unraveling of the celestial order, that a new entity began to stir, an entity whose existence had previously been relegated to the hushed whispers of myth and the hushed reverence of ancient lore. This was the Skybound Conclave.

No one could pinpoint the exact moment of their emergence. There was no singular proclamation, no grand announcement etched in starlight. Instead, their presence was felt, a subtle but undeniable pressure in the upper atmosphere, a coalescing of power that seemed to draw sustenance from the very discord it observed. The Conclave was not solely comprised of dragons, though their number and influence were undeniable. It was a gathering of beings that held dominion over the aerial realms, entities whose origins were as varied as the winds themselves. Some were ancient dragons, yes, but others were beings of pure elemental air, sentient storm fronts, and creatures born from the aurora borealis, their forms shifting and ethereal. There were also whispers of celestial navigators, beings who charted paths through the astral sea, and entities that seemed to be extensions of the planet's own atmospheric consciousness.

Their motives remained shrouded in the same ambiguity that defined their genesis. Were they saviors, poised to restore the fractured harmony? Or were they opportunists, seeking to exploit the prevailing chaos for their own inscrutable ends? The ambiguity was, perhaps, their most potent weapon. They did not overtly declare allegiance, nor did they openly condemn the escalating dragon conflicts. Instead, they observed, their collective gaze seemingly sweeping across the planet's atmospheric tapestry, assessing the unraveling threads.

The first concrete signs of the Conclave's involvement were indirect, yet profoundly impactful. Certain regions of the sky, previously prone to violent storms or unpredictable turbulence, began to exhibit an unusual calm. It wasn't the serene stillness of a clear day, but a controlled quietude, as if a powerful hand had simply smoothed out the atmospheric wrinkles. Trade routes, once perilous due to the rogue dragon attacks, started to see a tentative resurgence of safety. Skyships, navigating these now strangely placid air currents, reported encountering no aggression, no territorial disputes. It was as if an invisible cordon had been established, an unspoken decree that the skies within these designated zones were no longer open to the free-for-all of dragon conflict.

This imposition of order was unsettling. For millennia, the sky had been a domain of wild, untamed beauty, its movements dictated by natural forces and the ancient, instinctual rhythms of its aerial inhabitants. The idea of an external force, however powerful, unilaterally deciding the fate of these atmospheric currents felt like a profound violation. It raised a host of questions. Who were these beings? By what right did they presume to regulate the skies? And what was their ultimate agenda?

The dragons themselves reacted in a spectrum of ways. Those who had been most aggressive, their primal instincts amplified by the planet's distress, found themselves subtly, yet firmly, redirected. Warnings, not of roars but of an immense, silent pressure, would descend upon them, nudging them away from newly "protected" zones. For some, this felt like an affront, an unwelcome curtailment of their newfound freedom to assert dominance. They would test these boundaries, their roars of defiance echoing against an unseen barrier, only to be met with an overwhelming, yet non-violent, force that compelled them to retreat.

Other dragons, particularly the older and more wise, seemed to regard the Conclave with a mixture of apprehension and reluctant respect. They understood, perhaps better than most, the sheer scale of the unraveling. Their own attempts to restore balance had been met with confusion and escalating conflict. The Conclave, with its seemingly effortless ability to impose order, represented a power that dwarfed even the mightiest dragon. Some might have seen them as a necessary evil, a force capable of restoring a semblance of peace, even if that peace came at the cost of absolute freedom.

The implications for human settlements were equally complex. For the skyfarers, those who lived and worked among the clouds, the Conclave's interventions brought a much-needed respite. Trade began to flourish once more, and the terror of aerial transit lessened. Yet, this newfound safety was a double-edged sword. It created a dependence on an unknown entity, a reliance on powers that operated beyond human comprehension or control. The old gods, the primal forces that had always governed their world, were being overshadowed by this new celestial bureaucracy.

The floating island cities, like Aeridor, found themselves in a particularly unique position. These were not mere settlements; they were ancient ecosystems, intertwined with the very currents of the sky. The Conclave's presence was undeniable here. The swirling mists around Aeridor, once unpredictable and often hazardous, became remarkably predictable, the air currents that sustained the city's buoyancy becoming more stable. However, the Aeridorians, known for their deep understanding of atmospheric phenomena and their intricate relationship with the sky dragons, felt the shift acutely. Their shamans and elders spoke of a "silencing" of the natural winds, a loss of the vibrant, untamed song that had always permeated their lives.

Mara, observing these developments from her remote observatory, felt a chilling premonition. The Skybound Conclave was a manifestation of a new order, one that seemed determined to impose its will upon the chaotic symphony of the planet. But order, imposed rather than earned, was often fragile. It masked the underlying issues, suppressing the symptoms without addressing the root cause. The dragons' unrest, the atmospheric dissonance, these were not merely random acts of rebellion. They were the planet's cries of distress, its desperate attempts to reassert its equilibrium. If the Conclave merely silenced these cries without heeding their message, the unraveling would only take on a different, perhaps more insidious, form.

She began to study the patterns of the Conclave's influence. They seemed to favor areas of critical importance: major trade routes, vital atmospheric regulators, and regions known for their dense dragon populations. Their interventions were precise, almost surgical. They did not seek to eradicate the dragons, but rather to channel their energies, to confine their conflicts to designated, less impactful zones. It was a grand, celestial management strategy, one that hinted at a long-term plan, a vision for the skies that extended far beyond the immediate crisis.

This ambition, this desire to orchestrate the heavens, was what most concerned Mara. The planet's song was not meant to be a monotone, dictated by a single conductor. It was a complex, polyphonic composition, its beauty lying in its diversity, its dynamism. The Conclave, in its quest for order, risked silencing the very voices that made the song so rich.

She also noted the subtle shifts in the dragon territories. While the Conclave imposed its own boundaries, there were also regions where the dragon factions seemed to be solidifying. The Sunscale dragons, once a unified force, were now reported to be aligning themselves with certain aerial currents, their territories expanding and contracting with the seasonal atmospheric shifts. Similarly, the Shadowwing dragons were becoming more insular, their domains in the perpetually twilight regions of the upper atmosphere becoming heavily guarded. The Sky-Reef dragons, with their unique dependence on the floating islands, were forging alliances with these islands' sentient flora, creating a defensive network of symbiotic relationships.

The Conclave seemed to be aware of these emergent dragon alliances. Instead of disrupting them, they appeared to be *integrating* them into their broader strategy. It was as if the Conclave were not merely imposing order from above, but were also weaving a new tapestry of aerial governance, incorporating the existing, albeit fractured, power structures into their grand design. This was a far more complex and dangerous game than a simple suppression of conflict. It suggested a deep understanding of the planet's ecological and energetic systems, an ability to manipulate not just the physical forces of the atmosphere, but the very essence of its inhabitants.

Mara's concern grew when she considered the possibility that the Conclave might be more than just an external force. What if they were, in part, a product of the unraveling itself? Could these beings of air and light have been summoned, or even created, by the planet's desperate struggle for equilibrium? The thought was both terrifying and strangely hopeful. If they were born of the planet's need, then perhaps their ultimate goal was indeed to heal, to restore balance. But the methods they employed, the cold, calculated imposition of order, still felt alien to the natural world Mara understood.

She spent days poring over ancient texts, searching for any mention of such a conclave. There were fragmented myths, tales of "sky shepherds" and "celestial weavers," beings who were said to mend the fabric of the heavens. But these were often allegorical, their meanings lost to time and mistranslation. None described a coherent organization, a deliberate political entity like the Skybound Conclave. This suggested their emergence was something novel, something unprecedented in the planet's known history.

The most pressing question remained: what was their relationship with humanity? Were they benevolent overseers, ensuring the safety of human endeavors in the skies? Or were they merely using human skyships as convenient tools, their routes and movements integrated into a larger, more alien agenda? The lack of direct communication was a significant barrier. The Conclave communicated through its actions, through the subtle redirection of winds and the silent pressure of its presence. There were no ambassadors, no negotiations, only the undeniable reality of their influence.

Mara's own isolation became a poignant symbol of this communication gap. She was a lone observer, a scholar attempting to decipher a cosmic language spoken through atmospheric shifts and the silent pronouncements of powerful, unseen entities. She felt a growing sense of urgency. The dragons were in disarray, their ancient pacts broken, their instincts warped. The planet was groaning under an unseen strain. And now, a new power, the Skybound Conclave, had emerged, its intentions as vast and unreadable as the sky itself.

The implications of this new power structure were far-reaching. If the Conclave succeeded in imposing its will, it would fundamentally alter the relationship between all beings and the sky. The wild, unpredictable beauty of the heavens would be tamed, its raw power harnessed and controlled. This might bring stability, but at what cost? The spirit of the sky, the very essence of its untamed freedom, could be lost forever.

Mara imagined the Conclave as a vast, invisible network, its tendrils reaching into every gust of wind, every whisper of cloud. They were not just directing the flow of air; they were shaping the very consciousness of the skies. The dragon factions, the human skyships, even the nascent elemental spirits of the storms, were all becoming part of this grand, celestial orchestration. It was a symphony of control, and Mara feared that the natural melody of the world was being drowned out.

THE STORMBOUND DIVIDE

The silence that followed a Conclave intervention was often more telling than the intervention itself. It was a void where the natural cacophony of the skies once existed. The absence of a dragon's territorial roar, the sudden stillness of a previously turbulent air current – these were the signs of the Conclave's hand at work. And with each instance of this imposed silence, Mara felt a growing sense of dread. The unraveling was not just about chaos; it was also about the dangerous allure of control, the seductive promise of order that could ultimately stifle the very life it sought to preserve. The Skybound Conclave had emerged, not as a savior, but as a new, formidable force in a world already teetering on the brink, its ambiguous presence a stark indicator of the profound transformations that lay ahead.

Cael Thornevale's gaze swept across the undulating expanse of the sky, not with the awe or wonder of a poet, but with the grim calculus of a strategist. From his vantage point atop the aerie of Skywatch Citadel, the shifting atmospheric patterns were not merely visual spectacles; they were tactical considerations, each eddy and surge a potential threat or an exploitable weakness. The sky dragons, once predictable forces of nature, now moved with a frantic, discordant energy that sent ripples of unease through the meticulously maintained defenses of the human kingdoms. The once reliable trade winds had become fickle tricksters, prone to sudden, violent shifts that could tear a skyship apart or drive it leagues off course. And beneath these turbulent skies, the dragons themselves were no longer monolithic entities. Their territorial disputes, once contained and understood within ancient, if often bloody, hierarchies, had escalated into a free-for-all, a maddening unraveling of their primal instincts.

He traced the path of a rogue storm front, a bruised purple behemoth churning with unnatural ferocity, its edges rimmed with crackling lightning that looked less like a natural phenomenon and more like a deliberate weapon. This was no longer merely weather; it was an expression of the planet's fever, a symptom of the deep-seated disquiet that was beginning to infect every level of existence. His fingers, calloused from years of handling both the reins of his war-lizard and the weighty tomes of strategy, tapped a restless rhythm on the polished obsidian of his command console. Each tap was a silent question, a desperate plea for clarity in a world increasingly shrouded in chaos.

The weight of his office, the mantle of Guardian, pressed down on him with an almost physical force. He was the shield of the Northern Reach, the bulwark against the encroaching wild, and the sky was his primary battlefield. Unlike Mara, whose connection to the sky was woven from intuition and ancient lore, Cael's understanding was forged in the crucible of discipline and rigorous training. He saw the world in terms of strategic advantages, logistical nightmares, and the chilling efficiency of calculated risk. While Mara might feel the pulse of the planet, Cael felt the strain on his supply lines, the strain on his soldiers, and the ever-present threat of a breach in his carefully constructed defenses.

The reports filtering in from the patrols were a constant barrage of disquieting news. Skyship captains spoke of spectral presences in the upper atmosphere, of currents that seemed to guide them with an unseen hand, and of dragons whose roars were now tinged with a strange, almost sorrowful resonance. The Skybound Conclave, a name spoken in hushed tones by the aerie's mystics and scribes, was becoming an undeniable factor in their strategic calculations. Cael, however, viewed their intervention with a deep-seated skepticism. Order imposed was not true order, and this new celestial bureaucracy, whatever its true nature, felt like a cage being built around the wild heart of the sky.

His mind, trained to anticipate enemy movements, to predict the flow of battle, struggled to grasp the Conclave's motives. They were neither overtly hostile nor demonstrably benevolent. Their actions were precise, surgical – rerouting storms away from vital trade routes, creating pockets of unnerving calm amidst the growing turbulence, and subtly but firmly redirecting aggressive dragon flights away from populated areas. It was undeniably effective, a swift and potent solution to the immediate crisis. But Cael, ever the pragmatist, saw the inherent danger in such absolute control.

"Captain," he addressed his second-in-command, a grizzled veteran named Torvin, who stood a respectful distance away, his own gaze fixed on the swirling skies. "The wind patterns over the Serpent's Tooth mountain range are becoming increasingly erratic. Patrols are reporting anomalous energy signatures within the storm cells. Have the mages confirmed the nature of these signatures?"

Torvin consulted a tablet, his brow furrowed. "They're inconclusive, Commander. The energies don't match any known elemental manifestation. Some suggest it's a form of atmospheric resonance, others... something else entirely. The shamans are calling it 'sky-song interference'."

Cael grunted, a sound that held the frustration of a man facing an enemy he couldn't fully comprehend. Sky-song interference. It was a poetic term, one that Mara might embrace. For Cael, it translated to an unknown variable in an already volatile equation. "Interference implies intent. Who or what is interfering?"

"The Conclave's presence is felt most strongly in these areas," Torvin ventured, his voice low. "Their influence seems to be... smoothing out the rough edges. But perhaps in doing so, they are also silencing the natural song, as the shamans put it."

Cael's jaw tightened. Silencing. That was precisely his fear. The dragons' discord, the planet's fever – these were outward manifestations of something deeper, something that needed to be understood, not merely suppressed. If the Conclave merely masked the symptoms, the underlying disease would fester, growing stronger in the shadows until it erupted in a form far more destructive than any dragon's rage. His duty was to protect the kingdom, to maintain the fragile peace, but he was acutely aware of the ethical tightrope he walked. Every decision carried the potential for unforeseen consequences, for a ripple effect that could reshape the world in ways he couldn't predict.

He thought of the young dragon riders, their youthful exuberance and unwavering loyalty, now grappling with the unsettling reality of their mounts' increasingly erratic behavior. The bond between rider and dragon was sacred, a partnership forged in trust and mutual respect. But that bond was being tested, strained by forces beyond their comprehension. A rider's courage was useless against an unseen hand that could twist the very air around them, or against a dragon whose primal instincts were being subtly warped.

Cael remembered the last council meeting, the hushed pronouncements of the Grand Vizier, his pronouncements laced with a desperate hope that the Conclave's interventions would restore balance. But Cael had seen the calculations behind the Vizier's eyes, the pragmatic assessment of immediate threats and the willingness to accept any solution that offered respite, regardless of its long-term implications. They were focused on the immediate danger, the visible chaos, while Cael felt the gnawing certainty that the true threat lay in the unseen, in the subtle shift of power and the erosion of the natural order.

He turned his attention to a detailed map of the Northern Reach, its surface marked with strategic points, patrol routes, and known dragon territories. The Sky-Reef dragons, once a reliable, if sometimes unpredictable, presence, were now confining themselves to the immediate vicinity of the floating islands, their alliances with the islands' flora growing stronger, almost defiant. The Sunscale dragons, their fiery scales shimmering even in the dim light of the aerie, were becoming more territorial, their movements increasingly dictated by the subtle ebb and flow of atmospheric currents. And the Shadowwing dragons, masters of the twilight realms, were becoming even more reclusive, their domains in the upper atmosphere seemingly impenetrable.

The Conclave's influence was evident here too. Instead of dismantling these emergent dragon factions, they seemed to be *integrating* them, subtly guiding their movements, their conflicts, their very existence, into a new, overarching structure. It was a grand design, a meticulous weaving of power that made Cael's own efforts to maintain order feel like mere patching of holes in a rapidly disintegrating dam. He was a soldier, a defender, but the Conclave operated on a scale that dwarfed any military campaign. They were not fighting a war; they were redesigning the battlefield itself.

"Commander," a young lieutenant, barely out of his academy days, approached with a nervous tremor in his voice. "A message from the south. The Obsidian Peaks are reporting increased dragon activity, but not aggressive. They... they seem to be moving in unison, following a specific aerial path. Like a migration."

Cael's eyes narrowed. Unison. Following a path. This was not the chaotic discord they had been experiencing. This was... coordinated. "Towards what?"

"Towards the Eye of the Storm, sir," the lieutenant replied, his voice barely a whisper. "The place where the Conclave's influence is strongest."

The Eye of the Storm. A region of the sky notoriously difficult to navigate, prone to unpredictable shifts and home to ancient, powerful elemental forces. If the dragons were gathering there, drawn by the Conclave's unseen hand, it signaled a profound shift in their natural behavior. It was a move that could either lead to a catastrophic confrontation or a chilling, unprecedented union.

Cael felt a wave of cold dread wash over him, a sensation that had nothing to do with the biting wind. He was a Guardian, sworn to protect his people, to maintain the established order. But the very nature of that order was being rewritten by forces beyond his control, beyond his comprehension. He was expected to adapt, to strategize, to defend, but against what? An enemy that operated through subtle suggestion, through the manipulation of natural forces, through the very air his people breathed?

He understood Mara's perspective, her deep connection to the natural world, her concern for the planet's song. He respected it, even if he couldn't fully emulate it. His own burden was different. It was the burden of responsibility, of knowing that a single misstep, a single moment of hesitation, could lead to the annihilation of everything he had sworn to protect. He felt the crushing weight of command, the isolation of knowing that the ultimate decisions rested solely on his shoulders, and that the stakes had never been higher.

He returned his gaze to the horizon, to the vast, inscrutable canvas of the sky. The dragons were moving, the winds were shifting, and a new power was asserting its dominion. He was a Guardian, tasked with holding the line, but he was also a man caught in a tempest, struggling to find his footing as the very foundations of his world were being remade. The disquiet was no longer a whisper; it was a roar, and Cael Thornevale, for all his training and strategic acumen, could only brace himself for the storm. He knew that his duty was to restrain, to observe, to understand, before he could act.

But the accelerating pace of the unraveling, the growing presence of the Conclave, felt like a relentless tide, threatening to sweep away all that he held dear before he could even comprehend its source. The pressure to act was immense, a constant hum beneath his skin, yet the fear of acting wrongly, of exacerbating the very chaos he sought to quell, held him in a state of agonizing paralysis. He was a dam against a flood, and he could feel the water rising, pressing against him with an ever-increasing force, and he could only hope that his foundations would hold.

The unease was a creeping shadow, first felt in the hushed whispers of market traders whose ships returned empty, their holds gnawed by storms that seemed to materialize from nothing. Then it bloomed into a gnawing anxiety in the bellies of farmers whose fields lay parched or drowned by rains that fell with the fury of a dragon's wrath, not the gentle sustenance of nature. For generations, the human kingdoms, nestled in the valleys and perched on the plateaus, had enjoyed a hard-won, but nonetheless tangible, peace. They had their ancient pacts with the earth, their rituals to appease the sky, and a general understanding of the world's rhythms. Now, those rhythms were broken, shattered into a thousand discordant notes that echoed in the uneasy silences between the growls of thunder and the mournful cries of wind-torn banners.

THE STORMBOUND DIVIDE

In the coastal city of Port Caladon, the salt-laced air, usually a balm to the soul, carried a new, acrid tang – the scent of fear mixed with the metallic tang of desperation. Fishing fleets, once a reliable source of sustenance, found themselves battling currents that dragged their nets towards unknown depths or returned them shredded, empty save for the clinging tendrils of kelp that seemed to writhe with an unnatural life. The bounty of the sea, a cornerstone of their economy and diet, was drying up, replaced by unsettling sightings: phosphorescent algae that painted the waves with an eerie glow, and schools of fish that swam with a frantic, disoriented panic, their scales dull and their eyes vacant.

One grizzled fisherman, old Manius, his face a roadmap of sun and sea, claimed he'd seen a pod of leviathans, creatures of myth usually slumbering in the abyssal trenches, breach the surface near the city's harbor, their ancient eyes filled with a sorrow that chilled him to the bone. He spoke of a low, resonating hum that vibrated through the very timbers of his boat, a sound that felt less like a call of nature and more like a lament for a world in pain. His words, dismissed by many as the ramblings of an old man addled by the sun, found fertile ground in the hearts of those already feeling the pinch, adding another layer to the encroaching dread.

In the fertile heartlands of the Verdant Marches, the disruption was even more profound. The agrarian calendar, a system honed over centuries of observation and tradition, was now a jester's almanac. Seeds sown in hope withered under a sky that refused to weep, or were swept away by torrential downpours that turned fields into muddy lakes. The seasons themselves seemed to have lost their compass. Spring arrived with a biting frost that killed nascent blossoms, and summer brought heatwaves so intense they cracked the earth and baked the soil to the consistency of pottery.

The crops that did manage to survive often bore the marks of the world's disquiet. Grains were stunted, their kernels shriveled, and fruits ripened with strange, dark blemishes that spread like contagion. Whispers began to circulate of animals acting strangely – livestock refusing to graze, their udders running dry, and birds migrating in erratic patterns, their songs replaced by an unnerving silence. The usually robust harvests of wheat and barley, the lifeblood of the inland kingdoms, were dwindling, forcing granaries to be opened far earlier than planned and leading to rationing in towns that had never known hunger. The bread, once a symbol of prosperity, was becoming a luxury, its price soaring with each passing week.

Beyond the tangible hardships of food and weather, the sky itself became a source of growing terror. The predictable dance of the celestial bodies, the comforting passage of sun and moon, was now punctuated by unsettling anomalies. For weeks, the moon seemed to hang in the sky longer than it should, casting an unnaturally pallid light that seeped into dreams and fueled anxieties. Eclipses, once rare and awe-inspiring events, occurred with unsettling frequency, each one a stark reminder of celestial mechanics gone awry.

The stars, too, appeared to flicker with an erratic intensity, some winking out altogether, leaving behind vast, empty voids that felt like gaping wounds in the fabric of the night. Those who dared to gaze upwards reported seeing strange lights, not the familiar glint of distant constellations, but shimmering, ethereal forms that moved with an intelligence that defied natural explanation. Children, more attuned to the subtle shifts in the world's energy, began to experience nightmares filled with falling skies and monstrous shadows, their innocent slumber disturbed by the growing cosmic unrest.

The omens were no longer confined to the lore of ancient texts or the pronouncements of isolated mystics. They were seeping into the collective consciousness, manifesting in the anxieties of the common folk. The sudden, unprovoked anger of children, the uncharacteristic melancholy of the elderly, the fleeting moments of profound dread that would descend upon a bustling marketplace – these were the subtler manifestations of humanity's unease. People began to attribute meaning to every odd occurrence: a flock of crows circling a town square three times before dispersing, a sudden gust of wind that extinguished every lamp on a street, the recurring dream of a crumbling tower. These were not mere coincidences; they were signs, portents of a world unraveling.

THE STORMBOUND DIVIDE

The fear was compounded by the growing disconnect between the natural world and human understanding. The ancient animistic beliefs, once a source of comfort and a framework for interacting with the spirits of the land, seemed insufficient to explain the current chaos. The forest spirits, once benevolent guardians, now felt capricious and unpredictable. Rivers that had flowed pure and life-giving now occasionally ran sluggish and thick with an unknown sediment. The mountains, once symbols of immutable strength, seemed to groan and shift in their slumber. It was as if the very soul of the world was in flux, and humanity, so long accustomed to its place within that order, found itself adrift.

This pervasive sense of helplessness bred a desperate yearning for control. The established authorities, from the King's Council in the capital city of Aethelgard to the village elders in remote hamlets, struggled to provide answers or solutions. Their pronouncements, once met with respect and trust, now carried a hollow ring. Reports of military patrols finding no sign of the alleged atmospheric disturbances, or of royal surveyors dismissing crop failures as simple bad luck, only served to deepen the suspicion that those in power were either ignorant or willfully blind to the encroaching darkness. The common people, left to fend for themselves against an invisible enemy, began to look for a different kind of leadership, a different kind of protection.

In the taverns and town squares, conversations, once filled with the mundane chatter of daily life, now revolved around the unsettling changes. The tales of sky dragons were no longer just stories told to frighten children; they were increasingly cited as a potential cause, or at least a symptom, of the unraveling. But the dragons themselves were shifting, their ancient patterns disturbed, their movements no longer predictable. And the whispers of the Skybound Conclave, a mysterious entity whose influence seemed to be growing in the upper reaches, added a new and unsettling dimension to the unfolding crisis. Were these celestial beings, with their uncanny ability to manipulate weather and redirect dragon flights, a force for good, or something far more insidious? The uncertainty gnawed at people, fueling a desire for a power that could impose order, that could *force* the world back into a semblance of predictability.

This growing desperation began to manifest in more extreme ways. Fringe cults, promising divine intervention or arcane solutions, gained traction, attracting those who felt abandoned by conventional wisdom. Offerings to forgotten deities, once relegated to dusty tomes, were resurrected with fervent intensity. The desire for a savior, for someone or something to halt the descent into chaos, was palpable. It was a dangerous cocktail of fear, uncertainty, and a nascent yearning for a power that could offer a firm hand to guide them through the storm. This, more than anything, was the true fertile ground for the seeds of change, the soil in which more drastic solutions, however unpalatable, might eventually take root. The peace they had known was gone, and in its place was a gnawing dread, a primal fear that humanity's place in the grand cosmic tapestry was not as secure as they had once believed. The world was unraveling, and they were caught in the threads.

This profound unease was not confined to the common folk. Even within the hallowed halls of power, a subtle shift was occurring. The nobles, accustomed to their comfortable lives and predictable political machinations, found themselves increasingly preoccupied with matters beyond the usual squabbles over land and influence. Their advisors, men and women of learning, spoke of strange atmospheric phenomena, of unsettling omens in the celestial bodies, and of the growing disquiet among the populace. The usual routines of courtly life felt increasingly out of step with the palpable tension that seemed to permeate the very air. Balls and banquets, once grand affairs, were now often marred by hushed conversations and worried glances towards the windows, as if expecting the sky itself to breach the castle walls.

The whispers of the Skybound Conclave, initially dismissed as fanciful tales from isolated communities, began to gain an unwelcome legitimacy as their interventions became more frequent and noticeable. A sudden, localized calm descending over a region plagued by perpetual storms, a precisely timed redirection of a rogue weather system that would have devastated a vital trade route – these were not the actions of chance. They were calculated, deliberate, and undeniably effective. Yet, they also instilled a deep-seated unease. For millennia, humanity had navigated the world's chaos, adapting and enduring. The idea of an external force, however benevolent its immediate actions, dictating the course of nature, was a profound disruption of their established order. It was a usurpation, not of power in the traditional sense, but of the very elemental forces that had shaped their lives for so long.

In the bustling city of Silverstream, renowned for its intricate canal system and thriving merchant guilds, the impact of the disrupted trade routes was keenly felt. The usual steady flow of goods – exotic spices from the southern kingdoms, finely crafted silks from the eastern realms, precious ores from the northern mines – had dwindled to a trickle. Skyships, once a common sight dotting the horizon, were now a rare commodity, their captains often returning with harrowing tales of navigational hazards and unsettling encounters. The marketplaces, once overflowing with a dazzling array of wares, now displayed a starker selection, with prices climbing to unprecedented heights. Staple goods like grains and salt became luxuries, and the common citizens found themselves stretching their meager resources thinner with each passing market day. The vibrant hum of commerce was replaced by a low murmur of anxiety, punctuated by the sharp exclamations of traders lamenting their lost fortunes.

The impact on agriculture was equally dire. The farmers of the central plains, the breadbasket of the kingdom, watched in despair as their fields succumbed to the capricious weather. Unseasonably harsh frosts withered nascent crops, while sudden, violent hailstorms shredded delicate shoots. The predictable cycles of planting and harvesting, a rhythm that had guided their lives for generations, were thrown into disarray. Some farmers, desperate to salvage something from their ruined lands, turned to increasingly unorthodox methods, including appeasing spirits of the earth and sky with offerings that bordered on the blasphemous. Their plight was mirrored in the highlands, where shepherds found their flocks falling prey to predators that seemed bolder and more cunning than ever before, or succumbing to strange, wasting illnesses that defied any known remedy.

Even the normally predictable patterns of the wild had begun to falter. Hunters reported encountering game that behaved with unnatural fear or aggression. Birds, usually reliable indicators of the changing seasons, migrated at odd times or in confused flocks. The forests, once perceived as places of wild beauty and occasional danger, now seemed to hold a more pervasive, unsettling aura. The rustling of leaves could be mistaken for whispers, the snap of a twig for a predatory footfall, and the deepening shadows seemed to hold an almost sentient malice.

This pervasive sense of instability fueled a growing desire for order, for a return to a world where cause and effect were clear, and where the future, while not entirely predictable, was at least comprehensible. The very fabric of human society, built on millennia of understanding and adaptation to the natural world, was being strained to its breaking point. The grand cosmic struggles, the machinations of ancient beings, were no longer abstract concepts confined to prophecies and legends. They were manifesting in the empty larders, the failed harvests, the unsettling silence of the skies, and the growing fear in people's hearts.

This tangible impact of the mythic chaos on everyday human life was the true catalyst for a deeper, more profound unease, a feeling that humanity was no longer in control of its own destiny, but rather a pawn in a game played by forces beyond their comprehension. The desire for a strong hand, a decisive power that could impose order and provide safety, was becoming an overwhelming chorus, a desperate plea echoing through the increasingly tumultuous world. They looked to the skies, not with wonder, but with apprehension, and a nascent hope that somewhere, someone, or something, could bring back the lost stability, no matter the price.

Chapter Two

THE ACCORD'S SHADOW

The whispers of the Skybound Conclave and the growing unrest among the populace were not the only forces shaping the new, uncertain world. Beneath the veneer of tradition and the ancient pacts with nature, a different kind of society was emerging, one forged in the crucible of necessity and driven by a relentless pursuit of control. These were the Accord Cities, bastions of human ingenuity and pragmatism, a stark counterpoint to the encroaching mythic chaos. They represented a conscious, deliberate choice to wrestle power back from the unpredictable whims of fate and to impose order through the sheer force of applied intellect and engineering.

The genesis of the Accord Cities lay not in a shared cultural heritage, but in a shared, existential dread. As the storms raged with increased ferocity, as the skies defied their ancient patterns, and as the very earth seemed to conspire against the established ways of life, a consensus began to form among the more forward-thinking leaders of humanity's more technologically inclined settlements. They saw the old rituals, the fervent prayers, and the appeasement of spirits as increasingly futile gestures against a force that seemed both indifferent and utterly alien. What was needed, they argued, was not supplication, but understanding. Not reverence, but analysis. Not surrender, but mastery.

The first city to truly embody this new philosophy was Aethelgard, not the ancient royal capital already mentioned, but a newer, purpose-built metropolis nestled in the strategically advantageous confluence of three major rivers, a nexus of trade and innovation. Here, under the guidance of a council of engineers, alchemists, and strategists, the foundations of the Accord were laid. They began by pooling resources, sharing knowledge, and committing to a unified approach to the growing environmental instability. Their initial efforts were focused on observation. Vast networks of atmospheric sensors, crafted from intricate clockwork and alchemically treated metals, were deployed across their territories. Sky-watchers, not for omens, but for data, meticulously charted wind patterns, temperature fluctuations, and atmospheric pressure, feeding a colossal, ever-growing repository of information.

This data was then fed into calculating engines, complex mechanical marvels that, while lacking the sentience of true magic, could process information with a speed and accuracy that astonished even their creators. These engines began to reveal patterns within the chaos, subtle correlations between disparate phenomena that had previously been invisible. They predicted storm fronts with an unnerving precision, not through divination, but through the cold, hard logic of atmospheric dynamics. They identified the tell-tale signs of unusual celestial alignments that preceded extreme weather events, not because the stars willed it, but because their gravitational and energetic influences were measurable.

The success of Aethelgard soon attracted other like-minded settlements. Cities like Veridian, built on the precipitous cliffs overlooking a volatile coast, and Ironhold, a sprawling industrial hub nestled within mineral-rich mountains, joined the Accord. Each brought its unique strengths: Veridian, with its expertise in hydrodynamics and tidal prediction, and Ironhold, with its mastery of metallurgy and the construction of durable, weather-resistant structures. Together, they formed a formidable bloc, bound by a shared vision of a future where humanity was not a passive victim of nature's fury, but an active participant in its management.

The infrastructure of the Accord Cities was a testament to their philosophy. Their buildings were not adorned with carvings of benevolent spirits or protective wards, but were instead feats of engineering designed to withstand the harshest conditions. Massive windbreaks, constructed from reinforced stone and interwoven with alchemically treated timbers, shielded their inhabitants from gale-force winds. Sophisticated drainage systems, a labyrinth of channels and reservoirs, managed the unpredictable deluge of rainfall, channeling excess water to underground cisterns for later use or safely away from populated areas. The very air within their walls was often carefully regulated, filtered and circulated through intricate systems of vents and conduits, a stark contrast to the wild, untamed air of the outside world.

The most striking innovation, however, was their attempt to actively *influence* the atmosphere. The Accord Cities invested heavily in what they termed "Atmospheric Regulators." These were not magic staffs or shamanic drums, but towering structures of polished metal and resonating crystals, powered by immense geothermal energy sources or carefully harnessed lightning. These regulators, strategically placed within and around the cities, could emit specific frequencies and energy pulses, designed to subtly alter localized weather patterns. They were not intended to conjure sunshine from a clear sky, or to quell a hurricane in its nascent stages – such ambitions were deemed wildly unrealistic, even by the Accord's forward-thinking leaders. Instead, their purpose was to nudge, to guide, to mitigate. They could weaken the intensity of a hailstorm, disrupt the formation of deadly ice patches on crucial roads, or subtly redirect a particularly destructive gust of wind away from vulnerable settlements.

The effectiveness of these regulators was a matter of intense debate. To the inhabitants of the Accord Cities, they were tangible proof of their progress, a shield against the encroaching chaos. They saw firsthand how a predicted storm seemed to lose some of its bite as it approached their cities, how the intensity of a blizzard was noticeably blunted. They took pride in their ability to maintain a degree of normalcy, to keep trade routes open, and to ensure the steady flow of essential resources, all thanks to the tireless efforts of their engineers and the hum of their atmospheric regulators.

However, this pursuit of control came at a significant cost, both to the environment and to the Accord's relationship with the wider world.

The immense energy required to power the regulators placed a heavy strain on the earth. Deep mining operations, often in already unstable regions, became commonplace, leading to increased seismic activity and further disruption of natural underground currents. The emission of specific energy pulses, while seemingly localized in their immediate effect, had unforeseen consequences on the broader atmospheric and perhaps even the subtle, mythic currents of the world. Some argued that these interventions, in their attempt to impose order, were merely creating new, unpredictable forms of chaos elsewhere, pushing the already strained balance of nature even further out of kilter.

Furthermore, the Accord Cities' philosophy of tangible, scientific solutions bred a distinct arrogance, a subtle disdain for those who still clung to older, more mystical ways of understanding the world. To the Accord's leaders, the farmers who offered prayers to the rain gods, the fishermen who consulted sea spirits, and the shamans who communed with the forest were simply indulging in superstition, clinging to the past in the face of irrefutable evidence. They saw themselves as the enlightened ones, the vanguard of human progress, burdened with the responsibility of saving their species from its own ignorance and the capricious nature of the cosmos.

This ideological divide created a growing rift between the Accord Cities and the traditional kingdoms. While the Accord offered pragmatic solutions, their methods were often alien and their motives suspect to those outside their influence. The Kings and Queens of the older realms, while grappling with the same environmental challenges, were hesitant to embrace the Accord's radical approach. They feared the unknown consequences of meddling with forces they didn't fully understand, and they bristled at the implicit critique of their own ancient traditions and beliefs. The Accord's success in mitigating localized disasters was undeniable, but it came with a growing sense of unease, a feeling that these cities were not just protecting themselves, but were perhaps actively exacerbating the problems faced by others, creating an imbalance that would eventually demand a reckoning.

THE STORMBOUND DIVIDE

The Accord Cities, with their gleaming metal towers and their humming regulators, stood as a testament to humanity's capacity for innovation and its deep-seated fear of the unknown. They represented a bold, and perhaps reckless, attempt to impose order on a world that seemed determined to remain wild and untamed. Their rise was not just a response to the chaos, but a deliberate act of defiance, a statement that humanity would not be a passive victim. Yet, as their influence grew, so too did the questions surrounding their methods, and the unsettling suspicion that in their quest for control, they were playing with forces that could ultimately prove far more dangerous than the storms they sought to tame. The Accord was a beacon of human resilience, but also a harbinger of a future where old ways and new clashed with an intensity that threatened to shake the very foundations of the world.

The hum was a constant, almost subliminal thrum that permeated the very stone and steel of the Accord Cities. It was the pulse of their ambition, the audible manifestation of their determined defiance against the capricious whims of the encroaching chaos. For years, the architects of the Accord had toiled, not merely to build walls against the storm, but to craft instruments that could actively engage with the very forces that threatened to consume them. These were the Resonance Towers, colossal structures of alchemically treated alloys and precisely cut crystals, their spires piercing the turbulent skies like accusatory fingers. They were the physical embodiment of the Accord's core tenet: that humanity, through intellect and ingenuity, could not only withstand the planet's song, but could also learn to conduct it, to harmonize it to their own rhythm.

The conceptualization of the Resonance Towers had been born from the data harvested by the calculating engines, from the painstaking analysis of atmospheric phenomena. The Accord scientists, obsessed with quantifying the unquantifiable, had observed recurring patterns in the planet's energetic emissions, subtle shifts in the aetheric currents that seemed to precede meteorological upheaval. They theorized that the planet, in its vast and ancient existence, possessed a form of inherent resonance, a subtle vibration that influenced the very fabric of weather.

It was this 'planet's song' that they aimed to tap into. Their initial goal was ostensibly one of understanding and mitigation. By identifying the natural frequencies of atmospheric stability, they believed they could amplify them, creating localized zones of calm. By detecting the dissonant chords that heralded storms, they hoped to introduce counter-frequencies, disrupting the build-up of destructive energy before it could fully manifest.

The construction of these towers was an undertaking of staggering scale and complexity. Each tower was a symphony of engineering and arcane metallurgy. The foundational cores were sunk deep into the earth, anchoring the structures to ley lines and geothermal vents, drawing power and stability from the planet's molten heart. The main shafts, often exceeding a thousand feet in height, were constructed from a proprietary alloy of iron, copper, and rare earth minerals, chosen for their exceptional conductivity and their ability to withstand extreme thermal and kinetic stresses.

Within these shafts, a matrix of resonating conduits pulsed with controlled energy. But the true heart of the Resonance Tower lay in its apex. Here, vast, geometrically perfect crystals, meticulously grown and enchanted by Accord alchemists, were suspended within intricate scaffolding. These crystals, often clear quartz or deep amethyst infused with powdered meteoritic iron, were the focal points, the emitters. They were designed to vibrate at specific frequencies, responding to the ambient energies of the world and, crucially, to the commands of the Accord's central control arrays.

The process of 'tuning' a Resonance Tower was a delicate and perilous ritual. It involved carefully calibrating the energy output, the frequency modulation, and the harmonic convergence of the tower's components. Teams of specialized technicians, known as Harmonizers, worked in shifts within the control chambers, their hands dancing over complex arrays of levers, dials, and alchemical conduits. They monitored the subtle shifts in the tower's resonance, correlating them with real-time atmospheric readings and the input from the ever-vigilant atmospheric sensors scattered across the Accord territories. When a storm front was detected, the Harmonizers would initiate a sequence, gradually increasing the tower's energy output, coaxing the crystals to emit specific harmonic frequencies. The aim was not to create a deafening roar, but a subtle, pervasive hum, a gentle nudge to the atmospheric currents. Imagine a musician carefully adjusting the pitch of a single note to correct a discordant chord in an orchestra; that was the Accord's ambition on a planetary scale.

The immediate effects were, for many, nothing short of miraculous. Within the shadow of a fully operational Resonance Tower, the ferocity of storms seemed to diminish. Gale-force winds often found themselves inexplicably blunted, their destructive potential seemingly diffused before reaching the city walls. Torrential rains, while still heavy, would sometimes dissipate into less damaging showers, their intensity modulated by the tower's pervasive influence. The inhabitants of the Accord Cities, accustomed to the constant threat of elemental fury, found a new sense of security.

They could see the towers standing sentinel, their crystalline heads gleaming in the stormy sunlight, and feel a tangible difference in the air. Children played in courtyards that would have previously been evacuated, trade caravans moved along crucial routes with a degree of confidence unseen for generations, and the steady flow of resources that underpinned their pragmatic society was less frequently interrupted by the wrath of nature.

This success, however, was not without its disquieting undertones. The very concept of 'harmonizing' with the planet's song inherently implied a degree of manipulation, a redirection of its natural cadence. While the Accord spokesmen spoke of balance and protection, the underlying engineering was undeniably an attempt to impose human will upon the natural world. The 'song' they sought to harmonize with was not merely a series of weather patterns; it was the fundamental energetic signature of the planet itself, a complex interplay of geological forces, aetheric flows, and, some whispered, the very consciousness of the earth. To actively modulate this song, to introduce their own frequencies, was to risk more than just altering the weather. It was to tamper with the fundamental essence of the world.

The Accord's scientific cadres, driven by their relentless pursuit of empirical proof, tended to dismiss such concerns as sentimental mysticism. They argued that the planet's song was, in essence, a complex set of physical and energetic interactions, and that any 'consciousness' attributed to it was anthropomorphism. Their focus was on measurable outcomes, on data points and statistical probabilities. They saw the Resonance Towers as sophisticated tools, akin to a surgeon's scalpel, capable of precise intervention without necessarily understanding the full depth of the patient's biology.

Yet, even within their own ranks, a quiet unease sometimes surfaced. The sheer power channeled through these towers, the immense energy required to alter atmospheric dynamics on such a scale, raised questions about long-term consequences. The deep geothermal taps, while providing vital power, were causing localized tremors and altering subterranean water flows. The emission of modulated energy pulses, though intended to be precise, often created complex interference patterns, the full extent of which was still being charted.

The Accord's rhetoric, however, remained steadfastly focused on progress and control. They presented the Resonance Towers as the ultimate expression of human triumph over the primal forces that had held humanity hostage for millennia. They were not just safeguards; they were symbols of dominance. And in this pursuit of dominance, they began to inadvertently, or perhaps deliberately, create a new form of dissonance. The very act of imposing their amplified harmonies on a localized area created energetic vacuums or imbalances in surrounding regions. While Aethelgard might enjoy a calm sky, the neighbouring valleys, not protected by such towering edifices, might experience an intensification of the storms, as the displaced energy sought a new outlet. The planet's song, when forced into a new key, was bound to produce unpredictable echoes.

THE STORMBOUND DIVIDE

The visual impact of the Resonance Towers was also a potent statement. Unlike the more organic or traditionally architectural styles of the older kingdoms, these were stark, almost brutalist monuments to human ambition. Their polished metal surfaces reflected the turbulent skies, seeming to absorb and then re-emit the very chaos they sought to control. They stood as defiant beacons against the natural order, their crystalline apexes often shimmering with an unnatural, internal light. From a distance, they were awe-inspiring, testaments to what humanity could achieve. Up close, however, they exuded an almost unnerving aura, a sense of immense, barely contained power. The air around their bases often carried a faint metallic tang, and the constant hum, amplified at ground level, could induce a subtle, disorienting resonance in the human mind.

The Accord's control over the Resonance Towers was absolute and centralized. The data from every tower, every sensor, every calculating engine, flowed back to the central Accord Conclave, a shadowy council of engineers, strategists, and industrial magnates. They were the conductors of this planetary symphony, and their decisions were final. They meticulously planned the 'performance' of the towers, adjusting their frequencies and power outputs based on a complex matrix of predicted threats and desired outcomes. This level of centralized authority, while efficient, also bred a dangerous myopia. The Conclave's perspective was inherently urban, focused on the immediate needs and safety of the Accord Cities. The needs of the rural communities, the nomadic tribes, the natural world beyond their heavily regulated zones, were often secondary, if considered at all.

The very naming of the towers – 'Resonance Towers' – was a carefully chosen piece of propaganda. It implied a cooperative effort, a mutual understanding between humanity and the planet. But the underlying function was anything but cooperative. It was an assertion of primacy, a technological declaration that humanity's needs and desires superseded the natural rhythms of the earth. The 'planet's song,' once a mystery and a force to be respected, was now reduced to a dataset, a series of frequencies to be manipulated and, if necessary, silenced. The Accord's brilliance lay in their ability to disguise their ambition as salvation, their quest for control as an act of preservation. They built their towers to protect themselves, but in doing so, they were weaving a complex web of unintended consequences, a tapestry of amplified storms and displaced energies that threatened to unravel the very world they claimed to be saving. The hum of the Resonance Towers was not just the sound of human ingenuity; it was also the ominous whisper of a planet struggling to be heard beneath the weight of imposed control.

The hum of the Resonance Towers was a palpable thing, a low thrum that vibrated not just in the air but in Mara's bones. It was a constant reminder of the Accord's relentless push, their audacious attempt to bend the very will of the planet to their own. For years, she had listened to the world's song, not as a series of data points or atmospheric disturbances to be cataloged and controlled, but as a living, breathing entity. And now, that song was faltering, its ancient melodies fractured by the discordant chords the towers broadcasted. It was a sound of distress, a subtle, agonizing plea that echoed in the depths of her being, a plea that the Accord, in their arrogance, refused to acknowledge.

Her role as a Listener was a solitary one, a sacred trust passed down through generations. It was a gift, or perhaps a burden, that allowed her to perceive the subtle currents of the planet's energetic flows, to feel the earth's heartbeat, to understand the nuanced language of the wind and the rain. From her secluded vantage point, high in the craggy peaks that overlooked the sprawling Accord Cities, she had watched the crystalline spires ascend, a forest of metallic ambition against the bruised twilight sky. Each tower was a wound, a point of invasive surgery on the planet's delicate anatomy. The Accord claimed they were harmonizing, creating order from chaos. But Mara heard only a forced silence, a drowning out of the natural world's voice.

The reports, filtered down to her by hushed voices and furtive glances, spoke of success. Storms were blunted, winds gentled, rains less destructive. The citizens of the Accord Cities slept soundly, lulled by the illusion of control. But Mara knew the cost. She felt the displacement, the churning of energies that were being pushed, unceremoniously, into less guarded territories. The mountains themselves seemed to groan under the strain, their ancient rocks resonating with a deep, troubled vibration. The very air, once alive with the planet's wild, untamed spirit, now carried a sterile, manufactured quality, a faint metallic tang that spoke of tampering, of interference.

Her mind replayed the council meetings, the hushed debates amongst the elders of her small community. They spoke of alliance, of shared defense against the encroaching 'chaos' that the Accord so readily defined. They spoke of the Accord's power, of their ability to protect. But Mara saw only a gilded cage, a comfortable prison built on a foundation of stolen harmony. She saw a society that had traded its connection to the wild for a semblance of security, a people who had forgotten how to listen to the very earth that sustained them.

The dissonance wasn't just external; it churned within her. She possessed a unique understanding, a deep empathy for the planet's plight. As a Listener, she had been trained to discern the subtle shifts, the underlying currents of the world's song. She could feel the planet's pain as if it were her own. Yet, the thought of stepping into a leadership role, of actively challenging the Accord's dominion, filled her with a profound hesitation. Her strength lay in listening, in understanding, not in commanding or controlling. The Accord's modus operandi was the antithesis of her own philosophy. They sought to impose order through force of will and technological might, while she believed in the power of connection, of mutual understanding, of finding harmony by listening, not by dictating.

Her days were spent in quiet contemplation, tracing the veins of energy that flowed through the land. She would sit for hours, eyes closed, her senses attuned to the subtle frequencies that emanated from the earth, from the whispering pines, from the distant, mist-shrouded peaks. She would trace the flow of the planet's song, feeling its ebb and surge, its moments of vibrant crescendo and its periods of quiet repose. And with each passing day, the distress became more pronounced. It was a low-grade fever, a constant ache that permeated the planet's being. The Resonance

Towers, with their insistent, artificial hum, were like a relentless, irritating noise that prevented her from hearing the finer, more delicate nuances of the planet's true voice.

She remembered her training, the ancient teachings of the Listeners. They were not warriors, nor politicians. They were custodians of knowledge, interpreters of the world's unspoken language. Their power lay in their ability to guide, to advise, to remind humanity of its place within the grand tapestry of existence. To confront the Accord directly, to actively oppose their monumental endeavors, felt like a betrayal of that lineage. It was a leap into a realm she had always observed from a distance, a realm of open conflict and direct confrontation.

"They are deaf to the deeper harmonies," she murmured to the wind, the words barely a whisper against the omnipresent thrum of the towers. "They mistake obedience for harmony. They believe they are conducting an orchestra, when in reality, they are simply silencing the instruments they do not understand."

The weight of her knowledge pressed down on her. She saw the potential for catastrophic imbalance. The energy that was being so forcibly contained within the Accord's protected zones had to go somewhere. It was like damming a mighty river; the water would inevitably find a new path, often with destructive force. She had seen subtle signs, localized disturbances in regions far from the towers, where the weather seemed to have become more erratic, more volatile, as if the displaced energies were lashing out in their confinement. The Accord, however, conveniently ignored these anomalies, dismissing them as natural fluctuations or blaming them on the 'unruly' elements beyond their sophisticated reach.

Mara traced the rough bark of an ancient pine, its needles sighing in the wind. This tree, this forest, had weathered countless storms. It had swayed, bent, and endured, but it had always maintained its connection to the earth, its inherent rhythm. The Resonance Towers, by contrast, were rigid, unyielding. They imposed their will, rather than seeking to understand and flow with the planet's natural inclinations. It was a fundamental difference in philosophy, a chasm between two opposing worldviews.

The Accord's leaders, the men and women of the Conclave, were brilliant engineers, master strategists, and formidable industrialists. They had achieved what many believed was impossible: creating pockets of relative stability in a world teetering on the brink. But their brilliance was myopic, focused solely on the quantifiable, the measurable. They saw the planet as a complex machine to be repaired, not as a living being to be respected. They dealt in power, in control, in the imposition of order. Mara dealt in empathy, in understanding, in the quiet wisdom of observation.

She yearned for a different approach, one that honored the planet's inherent wisdom. She envisioned a future where humanity worked *with* the planet's song, not against it. A future where the Listeners' guidance was sought, not dismissed as superstition. A future where the Resonance Towers, if they had to exist at all, were tools of understanding, not instruments of dominance. But how could she, a solitary figure dwelling in the wilderness, possibly influence the monolithic power of the Accord? The very thought of confronting them, of demanding they halt their grand experiment, felt like asking a tidal wave to recede.

Her hesitation was not born of cowardice, but of a deep-seated understanding of her own limitations, and a profound respect for the forces she sought to influence. She knew that brute force, even intellectual force, would likely be met with the same rigidity that defined the Accord. Her path had always been one of subtle persuasion, of gentle redirection, of guiding others toward a deeper understanding. But the current situation demanded more than gentle nudges. It demanded a roar, a challenge that would shake the very foundations of the Accord's authority.

She closed her eyes, trying to filter out the omnipresent hum of the towers, to find the fainter, more ancient melody beneath. She felt the planet's weariness, the subtle tremors of its unrest. It was a song of resilience, still, but tinged with a growing sorrow. The Listeners had always spoken of balance, of the delicate equilibrium that sustained all life. The Accord, in their pursuit of absolute control, were tipping that balance with a reckless abandon that chilled Mara to the core.

Could she articulate this to the Accord? Could she make them understand that their 'solutions' were merely exacerbating the underlying problem? She doubted it. Their minds were set, their path forged in the crucible of their own perceived necessity. They saw the natural world as a chaotic force to be tamed, not as a partner to be understood.

And so, Mara remained a watcher, a listener. Her heart ached with the planet's distress, her mind churned with the implications of the Accord's actions. She was a guardian of a secret language, a keeper of a fading wisdom, torn between the urge to protect the world she loved and the deep-seated hesitation to step into a role she felt ill-equipped to play. The Accord built their towers to impose their will; Mara listened to the planet's song, and in its troubled melody, she heard a warning that few others seemed willing to acknowledge. Her struggle was not against the Accord's power, but against her own internal conflict, a quiet battle between her core values and the desperate need for someone, anyone, to speak for the silenced earth. The hum of the towers was a constant assault on her senses, a physical manifestation of the discord she felt so keenly, and a persistent question mark hovering over her own future role in this increasingly fractured world.

The crystalline spires of the Accord Cities pierced the sky like shards of solidified lightning, a testament to human ingenuity and, Cael Thornevale suspected, human folly. From his observatory, nestled within the ancient stone ramparts of Silverwood Citadel, the distant glow of the Accord's metropolitan heart was a constant, almost mocking presence. It represented a paradigm shift, a bold declaration that humanity, through sheer force of will and technological prowess, could bend the very fabric of the world to its needs. Cael, however, saw not progress, but a dangerous overreach. His perspective was not one of outright opposition, but of calculated caution, a deep-seated understanding that true strength lay not in dominion, but in equilibrium.

THE STORMBOUND DIVIDE

He traced the delicate lines of a star chart projected onto a polished obsidian table, the constellations an ancient language he understood far better than the pronouncements of the Accord's Conclave. For generations, the Thornevale line had been stewards of the human territories, guardians of a delicate peace forged through diplomacy and a profound respect for the natural world. They had learned to read the subtle shifts in the earth's humors, to anticipate the temper of the winds, to understand the delicate dance between the celestial bodies and the terrestrial realm. The Accord, in their relentless pursuit of control, seemed determined to ignore these fundamental truths, to sever the very threads that bound their civilization to the planet's pulse.

Cael's apprehension stemmed from a lifetime of observing the cyclical nature of power. Empires rose and fell, driven by ambition and the hubris of believing their reign was eternal. The Accord, with its gleaming towers and its promise of absolute stability, felt like a new iteration of an age-old trap. They spoke of taming the wild, of eradicating the unpredictability that had always been an intrinsic part of existence. But Cael knew that the wild was not something to be conquered, but understood. It was a force of immense power, and to attempt to stifle it completely was to invite a backlash of devastating proportions. The Resonance Towers, which he had heard whispered about in hushed tones by traders and scouts, were the most egregious example of this reckless ambition. Their purpose, as he understood it, was to impose a synthetic order, to dampen the planet's natural energetic flows. It was a crude and dangerous solution, like attempting to silence a symphony by smashing the instruments.

"They mistake control for harmony," he mused aloud, his voice echoing softly in the hushed chamber. His advisors, a seasoned group of scholars and strategists, exchanged knowing glances. They understood Cael's reservations. They had witnessed the Accord's rapid expansion, their assimilation of smaller enclaves, their increasingly assertive stance in regional affairs. While the Accord's citizens lived in a manufactured peace, the surrounding territories, the ones Cael felt a sacred duty to protect, were increasingly vulnerable. The Accord's success was built on a foundation of what others were forced to sacrifice.

Cael's strategy was not one of outright war, a prospect he found both wasteful and ultimately futile. The Accord's technological advantage was undeniable. Instead, his focus was on containment and influence. He envisioned a multi-pronged approach, one that leveraged the Thornevale's established network of alliances, their deep understanding of local ecologies, and their reputation for measured diplomacy. The Accord, for all its power, was still a relatively young entity, and its leaders, while undoubtedly brilliant, were also untested in the face of true, sustained opposition. They operated within a carefully constructed reality, one that prioritized measurable outcomes and immediate results. Cael's strength lay in his ability to play the long game, to exploit the inherent weaknesses in their seemingly impenetrable facade.

He gestured towards a detailed topographical map spread across the table, its surface intricately etched with rivers, mountain ranges, and the subtle outlines of ley lines that pulsed with unseen energy. "The Resonance Towers," he explained, his finger tracing a line from the Accord's heartland towards the untamed eastern territories. "They are suppressing the planet's natural rhythms here. But energy, like water, always finds a way to flow. When it is dammed in one place, it builds pressure and seeks an outlet elsewhere." He tapped a cluster of remote mountain ranges on the map, regions known for their unpredictable weather patterns and their resistance to external influence. "This is where the Accord's hubris will manifest. They believe they are controlling the elements, but they are merely redirecting their fury."

His advisors nodded. They had received fragmented reports from their scouts in those regions. Unseasonal blizzards, sudden, violent storms that appeared with little warning, localized seismic activity that defied conventional explanation. These were not the chaotic outbursts of a wild world, but the strained groans of a planet pushed beyond its limits. The Accord, naturally, dismissed these incidents as isolated anomalies, the predictable unpredictability of the 'uncivilized' territories. Cael, however, saw a pattern, a predictable consequence of the Accord's attempts to impose their will.

"Our primary objective," Cael continued, his gaze sweeping over the faces of his advisors, "is to ensure that the Accord's ambition does not destabilize the entire continent. We cannot allow their quest for absolute order to plunge the rest of us into absolute chaos." He paused, allowing the weight of his words to settle. "This means fostering resilience in our own territories, strengthening our alliances, and, where necessary, subtly undermining the Accord's narrative of benevolent control. We need to remind the world that true strength comes not from dominance, but from interdependence."

One of his advisors, a shrewd woman named Lyra who oversaw their intelligence network, spoke up. "The Accord's propaganda is pervasive, Lord Thornevale. They paint themselves as saviors, as the bringers of light in a world shrouded in darkness. Their citizens are convinced that their ordered lives are a direct result of the Accord's wisdom."

Cael steepled his fingers. "And that is precisely where we must begin our counter-offensive. Not with weapons, but with truth. We must highlight the sacrifices being made, the natural wonders being suppressed, the subtle erosion of the planet's vitality that their 'progress' entails. We need to empower those who, like Mara, can *feel* the changes, and give them a voice. The Accord thrives on manufactured ignorance. We will combat it with awareness."

He envisioned a carefully orchestrated campaign of information dissemination, utilizing the vast network of independent traders, nomadic tribes, and secluded communities that lay beyond the Accord's direct influence. These groups, often overlooked by the Accord's centralized command, were the lifeblood of the wider continent. Their stories, their observations, their lived experiences of the Accord's impact would become the seeds of dissent. Cael understood that public opinion, even in a world increasingly reliant on technological marvels, could still be a potent force.

"We will also focus on strategic alliances," Cael declared, his voice firm. "The Freeholds of the North, the Mountain Clans of the West, even some of the more independent enclaves within the Accord's nominal sphere of influence. We need to present a united front, a testament to the fact that there is an alternative to the Accord's rigid, centralized control. An alternative that values diversity, adaptability, and a deep respect for the natural order."

His thoughts then turned to the more direct implications of the Resonance Towers. He had commissioned detailed studies, utilizing the most advanced arcane instruments available to his people, to monitor the energetic shifts. The reports were alarming. The suppression of natural atmospheric phenomena, while seemingly beneficial in the short term, was creating massive energy build-ups in the planet's deeper, less understood layers. These were not just meteorological effects; they were akin to the build-up of tectonic stress, the slow, inexorable pressure that preceded seismic events.

"Imagine, if you will," Cael explained, his voice taking on a more somber tone, "that the Accord's towers are like enormous plugs, forced into the earth's natural circulatory system. They are preventing the natural release of energy, the vital ebb and flow that keeps the planet healthy. What happens when a vessel containing such immense, pent-up force is suddenly ruptured? The resulting explosion would dwarf any storm they have ever 'controlled'."

He pointed to a region on the map, far from the Accord's current influence, a vast expanse of untamed wilderness known for its ancient forests and its reclusive inhabitants. "This is where the pressure is building. The Accord believes they are safe within their shielded cities, their amplified order. But they are dangerously naive if they believe they can insulate themselves from the consequences of their actions. The planet will not be silenced. It will find its voice, and when it does, it will be a roar that will shatter their illusion of control."

THE STORMBOUND DIVIDE

Cael's strategy was not about direct confrontation, but about fostering a long-term awareness of the Accord's dangerous path. He understood that the Accord's power was rooted in their perceived efficacy, their ability to provide a stable, predictable environment. His task was to expose the fragility of that promise, to demonstrate that their pursuit of control was, in fact, sowing the seeds of future catastrophe. He aimed to weaken their narrative, not by force, but by revealing the hidden costs of their technological salvation.

"We must prepare," Cael concluded, his gaze steady and resolute. "Not for an immediate war, but for a future where the Accord's unchecked ambition may force our hand. We will strengthen our defenses, diversify our energy sources, and cultivate our understanding of the planet's true rhythms. We will be the custodians of balance, the guardians of a world that the Accord seems determined to forget exists."

His advisors understood. Cael's approach was not one of passive observation, but of active, strategic preparation. He was not simply reacting to the Accord's rise; he was anticipating its consequences, calculating the potential fallout, and developing a measured, long-term plan to safeguard the wider human civilization. His apprehension was tempered by a deep sense of responsibility, a conviction that the true strength of humanity lay not in its ability to dominate nature, but in its capacity to live in harmony with it. And in that harmony, he saw not weakness, but the ultimate form of resilience. The Accord might build towers of steel and glass, but Cael Thornevale was building something far more enduring: a legacy of wisdom, foresight, and a profound respect for the living world. He knew that the shadow cast by the Accord's ambition was long, but he was determined to ensure that it did not eclipse the light of a sustainable future.

The hum of the Accord's meticulously engineered environment, a constant thrum of controlled energy, had always grated on Mara's senses. Now, standing on the precipice of the Great Sky-Reach, a colossal natural amphitheater carved by millennia of wind and rain, the hum felt more like a prelude to a storm. Below, the city of Aethelburg, a jewel-like cluster of crystalline spires and gleaming metallic domes, pulsed with a manufactured luminescence, a stark contrast to the raw, untamed beauty of the surrounding peaks. Aethelburg was the heart of the Accord, and from its core, the proposal had rippled outwards, a proposal that threatened to irrevocably alter the delicate equilibrium between their world and the sky.

"The First Sky Accord," Elder Sorin's voice, a dry rustle like autumn leaves, echoed across the vast expanse. He stood beside her, his ancient eyes, pools of shadowed wisdom, fixed on the distant city. He was one of the few who remembered the world before the Accord, a world where the sky was not a territory to be claimed, but a realm to be respected, a domain shared with beings of immense power and ancient lineage. "They speak of peace, of regulation. But I hear the clang of chains in their words."

Mara nodded, her hand instinctively going to the smooth, cool surface of the Sky-Stone amulet that rested against her skin. It pulsed faintly, a silent reassurance, a connection to the very essence of the world the Accord seemed so eager to dominate. "They call it an accord, Elder, but it feels more like a decree. A demand for submission." She'd seen the projections, the intricate legalistic texts that had been disseminated throughout the human territories. The language was deliberately couched in terms of mutual benefit, of shared responsibility for the world's recovery from the devastating events of the Great Sundering. But beneath the veneer of conciliation lay a chilling assertion of human primacy.

The Accord, in its relentless pursuit of order, had identified the sky dragons – the Aeridons, as they were known in the ancient tongues – as a key variable. For centuries, these magnificent creatures had been guardians, their presence a symbol of the world's wild, untamed spirit. They soared on currents unseen by human eyes, their roars echoing through the heavens, a natural force that had, in its own way, maintained a crucial balance. But the Accord, with its ambition to control every facet of existence, saw them as an uncontrollable element, a potential threat to their meticulously constructed dominion.

THE STORMBOUND DIVIDE

The Sky Accord, as proposed, was designed to formalize the relationship, to bring the Aeridons under human jurisdiction. It outlined protocols for flight paths, designated zones for their interaction with human settlements, and, most disturbingly, established a framework for their 'management.' This management, Mara knew, was a euphemism for subjugation. It spoke of 'guidance,' of 'training,' of ensuring their actions were 'aligned with the greater good' – the Accord's definition of the greater good, naturally.

"They forget," Sorin murmured, his gaze distant, as if conjuring memories of a sky teeming with dragons, "that the Aeridons were not created to serve us. They are as old as the mountains, as primal as the storms. They are not beasts to be tamed, but spirits of the wind and sky, woven into the very fabric of this world." He turned to Mara, his expression grave. "You have a gift, Mara. You can feel their presence, their moods, their ancient sorrow. You understand that the Accord's approach is not merely misguided; it is a profound act of disrespect."

Mara felt a familiar ache in her chest, a sympathetic resonance with the creatures the Accord sought to control. She had encountered them on rare occasions, fleeting glimpses of their majestic forms against the vast canvas of the sky. Each encounter left her breathless, humbled by their power and their serene detachment from human affairs. There was a wisdom in their ancient eyes, a knowledge of the world that far surpassed anything the Accord's scholars could ever glean from their data streams and theorems.

"The Accord believes they are acting out of necessity," Mara said, her voice barely above a whisper. "They point to the instability, the lingering effects of the Sundering, and say that order must be imposed. They claim the Aeridons are unpredictable, a danger to recovering territories. They conveniently ignore the fact that the Aeridons were often the ones who *protected* us during those chaotic times."

She remembered the stories her grandmother used to tell, of Aeridons who had shielded settlements from rogue elemental forces, who had guided lost travelers through treacherous storms, not out of any obligation, but seemingly out of a primal instinct for balance. The Accord, however, framed these actions as chaotic interventions, as dangerous deviations from a predictable norm. Their proposals suggested that all aerial beings, not just the Aeridons, would be subject to these new regulations. This included the smaller, more ephemeral sky-folk, the Sylphs and Zephyrs, creatures of pure air and light, who had always existed in a state of delicate symbiosis with the natural world. The Accord saw no difference between them and the great dragons, classifying all as potential threats to their meticulously crafted order.

"They are trying to erase the wild," Mara continued, her voice growing stronger, fueled by a growing sense of urgency. "They want a world that is predictable, controllable, devoid of the very forces that make it alive. The Sky Accord is not just about regulating dragons; it's about solidifying their control over *everything* that doesn't fit into their sterile, ordered vision."

Sorin sighed, a sound heavy with the weight of ages. "The Conclave, the governing body of the Accord, is blinded by its own success. They have built a gilded cage and convinced themselves it is a paradise. They believe that by imposing their will, they can prevent another Sundering. But they fail to see that the true cause of the Sundering was not the wildness of the world, but the hubris of those who sought to dominate it."

He gestured towards the city below. "Aethelburg, and the other Accord Cities, are marvels of engineering, I will not deny that. They have brought comfort and security to many. But that security is bought at a price. They have severed their connection to the earth, to the rhythms of nature. They have outsourced their resilience to machines and algorithms. And now, they seek to do the same with the sky."

Mara understood the implications. The Aeridons were a powerful, sentient species. Forcing them into rigid flight paths and controlled territories would not only be an act of cruelty, but it would disrupt the natural flow of energies that the dragons, through their very existence, helped to maintain. The Sky Accord was not just a political maneuver; it was an ecological disruption of the highest order, dressed up in legalistic jargon.

"And the other territories?" Mara asked, her gaze sweeping across the rugged landscape that lay beyond the Accord's immediate sphere of influence. "The Freeholds, the Nomadic Enclaves, the wilder regions that still remember the old ways?"

"Their voices are being drowned out," Sorin admitted grimly. "The Accord's propaganda machine is relentless. They present the Sky Accord as a fait accompli, a necessary step for global stability. Many in the smaller territories, those who suffered most during the Sundering and its aftermath, are desperate for any form of order. They are susceptible to the Accord's promises, failing to see the strings attached."

He paused, his eyes narrowing as he focused on a distant point in the sky, a faint shimmer that hinted at movement. "The Aeridons themselves are divided. Some have always been reclusive, content to dwell in the highest reaches, indifferent to human affairs. Others, though, remember the pacts, the ancient understandings between their kind and ours. They see this Accord for what it is: a betrayal."

Mara felt a surge of hope, a flicker of defiance. "Then there is still a chance. If they understand the Accord's true intentions, they will resist."

"Resistance is not always met with understanding, child," Sorin cautioned. "The Accord has its instruments of enforcement. Their Sky-Wardens, equipped with sonic emitters and energy dampeners, are formidable. They have the technological might to impose their will, even on creatures as powerful as the Aeridons. What they lack, however, is the wisdom to understand the true cost of their actions."

He then spoke of the deeper implications, the energetic imbalances that the Accord's enforced order would create. "The Aeridons, in their natural flight, circulate vital energies across the planet. They carry spores, seeds, even subtle atmospheric charges that are essential for ecological balance. By restricting their movement, the Accord is not just controlling dragons;

they are disrupting the planet's natural systems. They are creating pockets of stagnation, areas where the natural flow of life will falter."

Mara thought of the ancient forests, the deep, verdant places that still thrummed with an untamed magic, places that the Accord's influence had not yet fully penetrated. These were the places where the Aeridons often congregated, where their presence seemed to invigorate the very air. If their movements were curtailed, these sacred places would suffer.

"The First Sky Accord," Sorin continued, his voice resonating with a profound sadness, "is more than a treaty. It is a declaration of war. A war against the wild, against the natural order, against the very spirit of the world. The Accord believes they are bringing peace and order, but they are, in truth, sowing the seeds of a far greater chaos. They are attempting to shackle forces they do not understand, and the backlash, when it comes, will be terrible indeed."

He turned his gaze back towards the Accord City, the glittering monument to human ambition. "They have built their towers to the sky, believing they can command the heavens. But the sky has its own laws, its own ancient guardians. And when those guardians are threatened, the very foundations of the earth will tremble."

Mara clutched the Sky-Stone tighter. She could feel the subtle tremors of dissent, not just from the Aeridons, but from the earth itself. The Accord's pronouncements, so confident and absolute, felt hollow against the ancient pulse of the world. They spoke of control, but Mara knew that true strength lay in balance, in respect, and in the understanding that some forces were not meant to be mastered, but to be coexisted with. The First Sky Accord was a test, a crucible for the planet's future, and Mara knew, with a certainty that settled deep within her bones, that she could not stand idly by and watch the sky be chained. The age of imposed order was upon them, but the age of wild harmony was not yet extinguished. It was merely waiting for its moment to roar.

Chapter Three
ECHOES OF REBELLION

The murmurs began as whispers among the peaks, carried on the same thermals that the Aeridons rode. News of the First Sky Accord, disseminated with the Accord's characteristic efficiency, had reached the ancient aeries, stirring a potent cocktail of confusion, anger, and, for a desperate few, a flicker of hope. The proposal, couched in the language of mutual benefit and global stability, was a poison chalice to most, its glittering promise of order masking a bitter draught of control.

Within the vast, cathedral-like caverns that served as the council chambers for the Skybound Conclave, the heart of Aeridon society, the air crackled with a tension that rivaled any nascent storm. Elder Kaelen, his scales the color of a twilight sky, his horns spiraling towards the vaulted ceiling like ancient, petrified lightning, presided over the gathering. His voice, a deep rumble that vibrated through the very stone, carried the weariness of centuries, but beneath it pulsed a current of fierce resolve.

"They presume to dictate our skies," Kaelen boomed, his gaze sweeping across the assembled dragons. There were hundreds present, their forms ranging from the colossal, mountain-like frames of the Elder Drakes to the more lithe, agile forms of the younger generations. Each bore the markings of their lineage, their scales a testament to generations of flight and territorial dominion. "They, who have only recently clawed their way back from the brink of their own self-destruction, now seek to impose their will upon us, the ancient custodians of this world's breath."

A chorus of agreement rippled through the conclave. Grumbles of indignation, sharp exhales of fire-tinged air, the restless shifting of immense bodies – all spoke of a unified outrage. This was their domain, their birthright, a sacred trust passed down from the dawn of time. The idea that ephemeral, short-lived beings, prone to squabbles and fleeting passions, could presume to regulate beings as old as the mountains themselves was an affront of unimaginable magnitude.

Yet, amidst the roiling discontent, a different current of thought was beginning to surface. A scarred, obsidian-scaled dragon named Vorlag, his wing membranes bearing the ragged marks of countless battles, spoke with a raspy, guttural voice that commanded attention. He represented a faction that had been increasingly pushed to the fringes, their ancestral hunting grounds encroached upon by the expanding Accord cities, their food sources dwindling as human settlements cleared the wild lands.

"Elder Kaelen," Vorlag began, his voice strained with desperation, "we cannot afford to dismiss this Accord outright. The Accord cities grow. Their reach extends further with each passing cycle. Our young starve while their machines devour the land. This treaty, for all its indignity, offers a chance. It speaks of designated territories, of regulated hunting grounds. It promises an end to the constant fear of aerial patrols and their sonic deterrents."

A wave of disquiet swept through the conclave. Vorlag's words were a heresy to many, a betrayal of their inherent pride and autonomy. The younger dragons, those who had known relative peace and abundance, hissed their disapproval. But the older, more weathered dragons, those who remembered the harsh realities of the post-Sundering world and the aggressive expansion of human civilization, felt a grim understanding dawn in their ancient eyes.

"Survival is not a betrayal, Vorlag," Vorlag continued, his voice gaining strength as he saw the flicker of comprehension on some faces. "It is necessity. They offer us a gilded cage, yes, but a cage that might shield us from the gnawing hunger and the constant threat of annihilation. Their 'management' may be an insult, but what is our alternative? To be hunted to extinction in the skies they now claim as their own?"

A powerful, sapphire-scaled dragon, her movements fluid and graceful despite her immense size, rose to counter Vorlag. Lyra, a descendant of a long line of dragons who had acted as intermediaries and diplomats in ancient times, spoke with a clear, resonant voice that carried an air of authority.

"Vorlag, you speak of survival, but at what cost? To accept their terms is to surrender our very essence. They do not seek to coexist; they seek to dominate. Their 'designated territories' will be prisons. Their 'regulated hunting grounds' will be barren reserves, where they dictate what we may eat and when. They will clip our wings not with chains, but with laws and regulations, and in doing so, they will break our spirits."

Lyra's gaze then shifted, her eyes, like chips of a summer sky, piercing the assembled dragons. "And what of the Sylphs and Zephyrs? What of the other sky-dwellers who share our realm? The Accord makes no distinction between us. They see us all as elements to be controlled, to be cataloged, to be made subservient to their grand design. They have already begun to test their sonic deterrents on the lesser air spirits, driving them from their ancient nesting grounds. Do we stand by and watch as our world is systematically stripped of its wild magic, all for the sake of human order?"

The mention of the Sylphs and Zephyrs resonated deeply. These ethereal beings, woven from wind and light, were not merely inhabitants of the sky; they were integral to its very breath, their playful dances and migratory patterns essential for the distribution of vital atmospheric energies. Their displacement was a symptom of a deeper ecological sickness, a disruption that the Aeridons, in their wisdom, understood all too well.

Kaelen listened, his ancient mind weighing the arguments, the desperate pragmatism of Vorlag's faction against the fierce idealism of Lyra and her supporters. He understood the allure of Vorlag's words. The Accord's cities, with their seemingly inexhaustible resources and their advanced technology, represented a power that even the mightiest Aeridon could not easily dismiss. Some of the younger dragons, particularly those whose families had suffered significant losses during the recent skirmishes with Accord patrols, were swayed by the promise of safety, however illusory. They saw the Accord's proposal as a lifeline, a way to preserve their lineage in a world that was increasingly hostile to their existence.

"There are whispers," Kaelen said, his voice now softer, more contemplative, "that some of the more isolated clans, those who have long eschewed contact with human settlements, are considering a different path. They speak of aligning themselves with certain human factions who resist the Accord's dominion, of seeking alliances with those who still remember the ancient pacts, the symbiotic relationship that once existed between our peoples."

This revelation sent a fresh ripple of consternation through the conclave. The idea of dragons allying with *humans* against other humans was an unprecedented notion. For millennia, the Aeridons had maintained a careful neutrality in human affairs, observing their rise and fall, their triumphs and their follies, from a distance. But the Accord's ambition had forced a reckoning, a realization that their ancient detachment was no longer a viable option.

"The Shadow Peaks clan," Lyra stated, her gaze fixed on Kaelen, "has always been fiercely independent. They remember the pacts made with the Starfall Nomads, before the Nomads were scattered by the Sundering. They believe that true balance can only be achieved through a united front, dragon and human, against the encroaching control of the Accord."

Vorlag scoffed. "The Starfall Nomads are a ghost of a memory. The Accord has systematically dismantled their traditions, absorbed their territories. What strength can a fragmented people offer us?"

"They offer knowledge," Kaelen countered, his voice steady. "They offer understanding of the Accord's weaknesses, their internal divisions. They offer a network of allies beyond the Accord's immediate grasp, in the

Freeholds and the distant, untamed territories. And they offer a shared desire for freedom, a rejection of the Accord's sterile, imposed order."

The schism within the dragon community was becoming more pronounced with each passing moment. Vorlag's faction, driven by pragmatism and the immediate threat of starvation, saw the Accord as a necessary evil, a means to endure. They spoke of compromise, of accepting reduced sovereignty for the sake of continued existence. Their arguments, though born of desperation, held a grim logic that resonated with those who had seen their kin fall prey to the Accord's ever-expanding influence.

Conversely, Lyra's faction, and indeed the majority of the Conclave, viewed the Accord's proposal as an existential threat, a fundamental assault on their nature. They feared that any compromise, however small, would inevitably lead to complete subjugation, to the erosion of their ancient connection to the planet, to the silencing of the wild heart of the world. Their arguments were fueled by pride, by a deep-seated love for their freedom, and by a profound understanding of the ecological devastation that the Accord's enforced order would unleash.

"The Ancient Accord," a wizened, moss-green dragon named Roric chimed in, his voice a dry whisper like leaves skittering across stone, "was a pact of mutual respect, of shared guardianship. It recognized our intrinsic value, our role in the world's natural rhythms. The First Sky Accord is a perversion of that ideal. It seeks to reduce us to mere tools, to cogs in their grand, mechanical design."

"And what of the elders who have been 'integrated'?" Vorlag's voice was sharp, laced with a bitterness that hinted at personal loss. "The Elder Drakes who were captured and subjected to the Accord's 'training'? They are said to be docile now, their roars replaced by programmed calls. Are we to suffer the same fate, or worse, to stand by and watch it happen to our brethren?"

The question hung heavy in the air, a stark reminder of the Accord's capacity for ruthlessness. The 'integration' of recalcitrant dragons was a closely guarded secret, but the rumors that filtered out were chilling: tales of forced sedation, of painful neurological modifications, of the shattering of ancient minds. This was the reality behind the Accord's claims of benevolent management.

Kaelen's gaze darkened. He knew of the dragons Vorlag spoke of. He had felt their absence, the hollow space they left in the collective consciousness of their kind. "The Sky-Wardens," he stated, his voice regaining its rumble, "are a formidable force. Their technology is advanced, their resolve unyielding. They have the means to impose their will. But they lack understanding. They cannot comprehend the intricate web of life that we are a part of, the essential role we play in maintaining the world's vitality. They see only a threat to their order, not the disruption of a fundamental life force."

He paused, his ancient eyes scanning the faces of his kin, seeing the fear, the anger, the dawning realization that this was more than just a political dispute; it was a battle for their very soul, for the future of their world. "We are divided," Kaelen admitted, his voice heavy with the weight of his responsibility. "And in our division, lies the Accord's greatest strength. Vorlag's faction seeks survival, and their desperation is a powerful motivator. Lyra's faction seeks freedom, and their conviction is a potent weapon. But neither path alone may be enough."

He spread his immense wings, the leathery membranes catching the faint light filtering from high above. "We must find a third way. A way that honors our pride without inviting destruction. A way that acknowledges the dangers we face without surrendering our essence. The Sky Accord is not merely a proposal; it is a test. A test of our unity, of our wisdom, and of our resolve. The dragons of this world have always been masters of the sky, but now, we must prove ourselves masters of our own destiny, even in the face of a power that seeks to bind us."

The debate raged on, the cavern filled with the cacophony of ancient voices, each vying to be heard, each fighting for the future of their species. Alliances were being forged in the crucible of this dissent, old animosities momentarily forgotten in the face of a common, existential threat. Some spoke of a unified, defiant roar, a challenge to the Accord's dominion. Others, however, whispered of clandestine negotiations, of seeking out the fractured human resistance, of forging a fragile, desperate alliance. The dragons, once a singular force of nature, were fracturing, their society facing a schism that threatened to redefine their ancient lineage for all time to come. The First Sky Accord had not brought peace; it had ignited a firestorm within the heart of the dragon community, a dissension that would echo through the ages.

The oppressive weight of the Sky Accord, a physical manifestation of human ambition, pressed down on Mara's very soul. It wasn't just the decree itself, nor the machinations of the council chambers she had left behind. It was the insidious hum of the Resonance Towers, newly erected sentinels of control, that grated against the delicate symphony of the planet. Each pulse of their arcane energy was a discordant note, a wrenching of the very fabric of the world's song. Mara felt it acutely, a psychic resonance that vibrated in her bones, a lament of an earth struggling to breathe.

The dragons' council, a maelstrom of pride, desperation, and ancient wisdom, had merely amplified the dissonance. Vorlag's grim pragmatism, Lyra's defiant idealism, Kaelen's weary diplomacy – each voice, though born of genuine concern, added another layer of complexity to the already strained melody. They spoke of dominion, of territory, of survival, all within the framework of human-imposed order. But they, like so many humans, seemed to miss the fundamental truth: the planet itself was singing, and its song was one of distress.

Mara knew, with a certainty that transcended logic, that she had to speak. Not just to the humans, the architects of this burgeoning tyranny, but to those who still embodied the wild heart of the sky – the Aeridons, the Sylphs, the Zephyrs. Her message was not one of treaties or territories, but of reverence, of listening, of understanding the profound interconnectedness of all living things. It was a plea for the planet's song, a desperate attempt to remind all sentient beings of what they stood to lose.

Her path, however, was fraught with peril. The political currents she had navigated within the human council were treacherous enough, filled with veiled threats and self-serving agendas. Now, she had to venture beyond those familiar confines, seeking an audience with beings of myth and legend, beings who had long retreated from the clamor of human civilization. The very act of seeking them out was an invitation to danger, a transgression of unspoken boundaries.

Mara found herself drawn to the fringes, to the places where the Accord's influence was less absolute, where the wild still held sway. She walked through hushed forests, her feet treading softly on moss-laden earth, listening to the rustling leaves and the chirping insects, the quiet orchestra of the natural world. She sought out ancient groves, places rumored to be thin between worlds, where the veil separating the mundane from the magical was said to be most permeable. Her hope was that if she could attune herself to the deeper frequencies of the planet, she might find a way to project her voice, her plea, beyond the cacophony of human discourse.

She remembered the tales her grandmother had told her, stories of the Sylphs, ephemeral beings woven from the very air, their laughter like chimes carried on the wind, their tears like morning dew. The Sylphs were said to dance in the high currents, their movements orchestrating the subtle shifts in weather, their presence a blessing to the wild places. If anyone could understand the planet's song, it would be them.

Mara's first attempt to connect was an act of pure faith. She climbed to the highest accessible peak in the region, a windswept promontory that offered an unobstructed view of the vast, cerulean expanse. She stood there for hours, her eyes closed, her mind a blank canvas onto which she projected her thoughts, her anxieties, her fervent hope. She imagined the planet's song as a great, vibrant tapestry, woven from countless threads of life, and she pleaded for the threads to be strengthened, not frayed.

"Hear me," she projected, not with sound, but with an intensity of will that felt like a physical force. "Hear the earth's lament. The Resonance

THE STORMBOUND DIVIDE

Towers... they are a wound. They are silencing the ancient melodies. We are drowning out the world's breath."

The wind howled around her, a wild, untamed symphony that seemed to mock her solitary efforts. She felt the subtle shifts in air pressure, the gentle caress of unseen currents, but no direct response. It was like shouting into a hurricane, her words lost in the immensity of the elements. Disappointment gnawed at her, but the urgency of her mission propelled her onward. She could not afford despair.

Her journey led her to a secluded valley, a place untouched by human development, where the trees grew ancient and gnarled, their branches reaching towards the sky like supplicating arms. Here, she found a crystalline stream, its waters so pure they seemed to hold the light of the stars. As she knelt to drink, she felt a subtle shift in the air, a presence that was both there and not there. It was a delicate, ethereal vibration, a whisper of sound that seemed to originate from the very molecules of water and air.

"Who are you?" Mara thought, her heart leaping with a mixture of fear and exhilaration.

A series of shimmering, almost imperceptible movements caught her eye. The air above the stream began to coalesce, forming indistinct shapes that danced and swirled like motes of dust in a sunbeam. They were the Sylphs, or at least, their nascent form.

"We hear the song," a voice, or rather, a chorus of delicate, bell-like tones, echoed in her mind. It was not a single voice, but a symphony of ephemeral beings communicating as one. "We feel the strain. The sky weeps."

Mara's breath hitched. She had reached them. "The Resonance Towers," she projected, her thoughts a torrent of concern. "They are disrupting the planet's harmony. They are a force of control, not balance. And the Accord... it seeks to cage the wildness, to silence the ancient voices."

The Sylphs swirled more rapidly, their forms brightening and dimming like distant stars. "Control," the chorus echoed, a hint of sadness in their ethereal tones. "The humans forget. They seek to own what cannot be owned. The song is life. To silence it is to invite stillness, and stillness is death."

"But they do not listen!" Mara pleaded, her own voice, her internal voice, filled with a desperate urgency. "They are deafened by their own ambition. The dragons, too, are divided. Some seek to survive by submitting, others by defying, but few seem to grasp the true nature of the threat."

"The great scaled ones," the Sylphs' voices resonated, tinged with a hint of ancient knowledge. "They too are bound by the earth's song, but their understanding is of a different key. They feel the tremors of change, but the melody of the sky... that is our domain. Your plea is heard, Listener. Your heart beats in time with the world's rhythm."

Mara felt a wave of gratitude wash over her. To be called a 'Listener' by these beings of pure spirit was an honor she hadn't dared to imagine. "What can be done?" she asked, her voice imbued with the hope they had rekindled. "How can we make them understand before it is too late?"

The Sylphs pulsed with a soft, luminous light. "Understanding comes not from decree, but from resonance. The song must be amplified, not muted. The Aeridons listen to the wind. The Zephyrs dance with the currents. Their ears are open, though their minds are troubled. Your words must reach them, through the conduits they understand. The highest peaks, the most ancient winds."

Their message was cryptic, but Mara understood. She had to find a way to speak to the dragons, not with words of political strategy, but with the language of the planet, a language she was only beginning to truly comprehend. The Sylphs, having delivered their counsel, began to dissipate, their forms melting back into the shimmering air, leaving only the gentle murmur of the stream and the rustle of leaves in their wake.

Her resolve hardened. The Sylphs had confirmed her fears, but they had also offered a sliver of hope, a direction to pursue. She turned her gaze towards the distant, snow-capped peaks, the ancestral homes of the

THE STORMBOUND DIVIDE

Aeridons. She knew it would be a perilous journey, a climb into a realm few humans dared to tread. But the fate of the world, its very song, depended on it.

As she journeyed, Mara began to practice her projection, honing her ability to imbue her thoughts with emotional resonance. She thought of the ancient forests, the vibrant coral reefs, the teeming life within the earth's crust – all parts of the planetary symphony. She focused on the pain she felt when the Resonance Towers pulsed, the crushing weight of control, the stifling of natural expression. She wove these feelings into her projected messages, hoping to convey a truth that mere words could not.

She encountered the Zephyrs during her ascent, ethereal beings of pure air currents, their forms constantly shifting, like living gusts of wind. They played in the updrafts, their movements a chaotic ballet that seemed to follow an unseen rhythm. Mara sent out her plea, focusing on the feeling of freedom, of unimpeded flow, of the joy inherent in natural movement.

"We feel the discord," a multitude of whisper-soft voices, like the sigh of the wind through reeds, brushed against her consciousness. "The sky is... heavy. The balance shifts. The humans build walls against the wind."

"They build walls against life itself," Mara projected, pouring her conviction into the thought. "The song is being silenced. The great flying ones... they are at a crossroads. They need to hear the true melody, not the echoes of human ambition."

The Zephyrs seemed to swirl in contemplation, their forms momentarily solidifying into shimmering, translucent shapes that mimicked the flight of birds. "The Listener's heart sings a true note," they seemed to convey, a ripple of understanding passing through their ephemeral collective. "The song reaches the highest aeries. It reaches the ancient ones. The wind carries it. The wind remembers."

Mara pressed on, the wind her constant companion, the whispers of the air spirits her guide. She saw evidence of the Accord's reach even here, in the occasional glint of metal on distant crags, the faint, unnatural hum that sometimes accompanied the wind's song. These were the encroaching tendrils of control, the attempts to tame the untamable.

She reached a treacherous pass, the air thin and biting, the wind a relentless force that threatened to tear her from the mountainside. It was here, amidst the roaring gale, that she finally felt the distinct, powerful presence of an Aeridon. It was a young dragon, its scales a vibrant emerald green, its eyes the color of a stormy sea. It was perched on a rocky outcrop, its magnificent wings tucked close against its body, observing her with an intensity that made her skin prickle.

Mara knew this was her chance. She didn't approach directly, understanding the inherent power imbalance. Instead, she sat on a sheltered ledge, drew a deep breath, and projected her message, not as a plea, but as a statement of truth, infused with the echoes of the planet's song she had learned to feel.

"Great flyer," she began, her projected thoughts resonating with the wind's keen edge. "You who ride the currents and feel the pulse of the world from above. I am Mara, a Listener. I come not to bargain or to plead for human concerns, but to speak of the song that binds us all."

The young dragon shifted, its head tilting as if to better catch her thoughts. Its eyes narrowed, a flicker of curiosity battling with caution.

"The Accord," Mara continued, her thoughts flowing like a clear stream, "and the Resonance Towers they erect... they are a discord. They are a deliberate silencing of the planet's voice. The earth groans. The ancient harmonies are being strained. The magic that flows through all things... it is being choked."

She projected the feeling of the Resonance Towers' pulse, the unnatural vibration that grated against her soul. She showed the young dragon, through shared imagery, the vibrant tapestry of life being threatened by the sterile lines of control. She spoke of the Sylphs and Zephyrs, their distress at the disruption.

The dragon remained silent for a long moment, its gaze fixed on some unseen point beyond Mara. Then, a thought, surprisingly clear and direct, echoed in her mind. "You speak of a song? We hear the wind, the calls of our kin, the rumble of the earth. We feel the shifts in the atmosphere. But a song... a song of the world itself?"

"It is a symphony of life," Mara projected, her hope surging. "It is the rhythm of growth and decay, of creation and renewal. It is the very breath of this planet. And it is being threatened. The Accord seeks to impose its own rhythm, a sterile, predictable beat that will eventually extinguish the wilder, more vital melodies."

She projected the memory of the Elder Drakes, their proud spirits broken by the Accord's 'integration.' She showed the young dragon the fear in Vorlag's voice, the desperate pragmatism that was born of genuine suffering. She also conveyed Lyra's fierce idealism, the understanding that true freedom was not merely survival, but the preservation of essence.

"Your kind," Mara projected, addressing the dragon directly, "are the custodians of the sky. You know its moods, its currents, its hidden pathways. You are woven into its song more deeply than any of us who walk the earth. You can feel the strain, can you not? The unnatural stillness that sometimes falls, the way the air seems to hold its breath?"

The young Aeridon shifted again, a low rumble emanating from its chest. It was not a growl of aggression, but a sound of contemplation. "The air has been... unsettled. The currents sometimes feel... forced. We have attributed it to the shifting seasons, the unpredictable nature of the world. But you speak of a deliberate imposition."

"It is a sickness," Mara stated, her projected voice firm. "And the Accord, in its blindness, is the carrier. They seek to control what they do not understand, to impose order where nature's own intricate balance should prevail. You must make your elders hear this. Not just the pragmatism of survival, nor the pride of defiance, but the fundamental truth of the song.

The Accord is not just a political threat; it is an ecological and spiritual one."

The young dragon extended one of its immense claws, tapping it against the rocky outcrop. A faint tremor ran through the stone, a subtle vibration that Mara felt in her own bones. It was a gesture, she realized, of acknowledgment, of a connection being forged.

"The Listener's words resonate," the Aeridon projected, its voice now carrying a deeper, more resonant quality. "They echo what many have felt but could not articulate. The elders... they are besieged by many voices, many fears. But the song of the world... that is a language older than any accord, any decree. I will carry your message, Listener. I will try to make them hear, not with their ears, but with their ancient hearts."

With a powerful beat of its emerald wings, the young dragon launched itself into the air, soaring into the turbulent currents. Mara watched it go, a fragile sense of hope blooming within her. She had spoken. She had reached one of the sky-dwellers. And she had planted a seed, a seed of understanding that, with luck, would grow into a chorus that could drown out the discord of the Resonance Towers and the suffocating ambition of the First Sky Accord. Her plea, she realized, was not just for her own world, but for all the worlds that sang the same, vital song.

The biting wind whipped at Cael Thornevale's cloak, a constant, abrasive reminder of his precarious position. He stood on the parapet of the Sky Court, a fortress carved into the sheer face of Mount Aeridor, a place that had once been a symbol of neutrality, now a gilded cage for his increasingly untenable mandate. Below, the Accord Cities sprawled like a geometric disease, their polished towers glinting under the perpetually overcast sky, each one a monument to human ambition and, increasingly, human oppression. The Resonance Towers, those accursed obelisks of sonic control, hummed their insidious song, a low thrum that vibrated not just in the air, but deep within his very bones.

THE STORMBOUND DIVIDE

He was Cael Thornevale, First Minister of Accord Diplomacy, a title that felt more like a brand than an honor. His task was to bridge the chasm between the burgeoning dominion of the Sky Accord and the ancient, proud realms of the aerial beings. Peace. That was the watchword. A fragile, enforced peace, built on a foundation of increasingly aggressive mandates and the subjugation of natural order. The dragons, those magnificent, tempestuous creatures who were the very soul of the skies, were not merely restless; they were a coiled spring, their patience wearing thinner with each passing cycle of the twin moons.

His council chamber, usually a space of measured debate and calculated compromises, had devolved into a tempest of conflicting desires. Elder Valerius, his face a roadmap of ancient grief and simmering resentment, argued for direct military intervention. "These Sylphs and Zephyrs," he'd declared, his voice raspy with age and disdain, "they are a blight upon our ordered world. Their unpredictable movements, their resistance to the Towers' influence... they are a threat to the stability we have so painstakingly achieved." Stability. The word tasted like ash in Cael's mouth.

On the other side, Lyra, her eyes blazing with a fire that mirrored the planet's struggling lifeblood, pleaded for restraint. "Stability at what cost, Elder? We are not taming a wild beast; we are dissecting a living heart. The Accord's methods are brutal, Cael. They are deafening the world's song, not harmonizing it. And the dragons... they feel it too. Their ancient bonds are fraying under the strain."

Cael felt the truth in Lyra's words like a physical blow. He saw it in the strained whispers of the Aeridon scouts, their reports detailing unusual flight patterns, unexplained tremors in the atmospheric currents, a growing unease that even their stoic nature could not entirely mask. He heard it in the fragmented, almost panicked messages that had recently filtered back from the lower regions, tales of strange sonic disruptions that drove even the most placid creatures into a frenzy. The Resonance Towers were not merely tools of control; they were instruments of psychic warfare, designed to homogenize thought and suppress any deviation from the Accord's rigid doctrine.

His mandate was clear: maintain peace. But peace, Cael was beginning to understand, was a fluid concept, its definition shifting with the ambitions of those in power. Was peace the silence of subjugation, the absence of overt conflict achieved through overwhelming force? Or was it a more profound, intrinsic harmony, a state of being where all creatures, in their myriad forms and expressions, could coexist without the imposition of artificial constraints? The Sky Accord championed the former, a sterile, manufactured order that prioritized efficiency and control above all else. But Cael, raised in the hushed reverence of the mountain monasteries, had been taught a different kind of peace, one that was intertwined with the natural world, with the subtle symphony of life that pulsed through every leaf, every wingbeat, every whispered breath of the wind.

He walked the battlements, the vast expanse of the sky stretching out before him, a canvas of swirling clouds and distant, jagged peaks. The very air seemed to thrum with an unspoken tension. He could almost feel the planet's song, a melody that was growing increasingly strained, a lament sung in a thousand different voices, from the deepest earth tremors to the highest atmospheric currents. And at the heart of this dissonance were the Resonance Towers, their unholy hum a physical manifestation of the Accord's hubris.

The dragons, in particular, were proving to be a volatile element. Their ancient pacts with the early human settlers, forged in an era of mutual respect and shared stewardship, were being eroded by the Accord's unilateral decrees. The Elder Drakes, those venerable beings who had once been the guardians of the sky's wisdom, were now divided. Some, like Vorlag, harbored a grim pragmatism, believing that appeasement and strategic submission were the only paths to survival in the face of humanity's overwhelming technological and political might. They saw the Accord's iron fist as an unavoidable force, a storm to be weathered rather than defied.

Others, like Lyra's faction, were fueled by a fiery defiance, a refusal to yield the inherent freedom and dignity of their kind. They spoke of ancient rights, of the sacred duty to protect the wild heart of the world, and they viewed the Accord's expansion as an existential threat. Their arguments, though impassioned, often bordered on recklessness, a dangerous pride that Cael feared could lead to a catastrophic escalation.

And then there were those who, like himself, were caught in the agonizing middle, torn between the perceived necessity of order and the growing awareness of the moral cost. Cael's own internal struggle was a constant, gnawing ache. He had sworn an oath to uphold the Accord, to maintain peace. But what if that peace was a lie? What if the very stability he was tasked with preserving was a slow poison, designed to extinguish the vibrant essence of the world?

He thought of Mara, the young woman who had dared to challenge the council, her voice a clear, unwavering note in the cacophony of self-interest. Her words, though dismissed by many as idealistic folly, had resonated deeply within him. She spoke of a planet that sang, of a song being silenced. At the time, he had seen her as a symbol of the very chaos he was meant to control. But now, standing here, feeling the oppressive weight of the Accord's influence, he wondered if she hadn't been speaking a profound truth that he, blinded by his duty, had failed to grasp.

The Sylphs and Zephyrs, those ephemeral beings of wind and air, were the Accord's most immediate irritants. They flitted through the upper atmosphere, their movements seemingly random, their existence an affront to the ordered grid of the Resonance Towers. The Accord viewed them as pests, as glitches in the system, and there were whispers, growing louder each day, of a new initiative: a 'purification' campaign, designed to cleanse the skies of these wild, untamed entities.

Cael had received reports of aerial patrols being dispatched with sonic emitters, devices designed to disorient and scatter the Sylphs. He had seen schematics for atmospheric containment fields, meant to corral and neutralize any aerial presence that resisted the Accord's influence. Each report, each schematic, felt like another nail in the coffin of the natural world.

He closed his eyes, trying to filter out the oppressive hum of the Resonance Towers, trying to find a different frequency, a quieter song. He pictured the Sylphs, their forms like shimmering veils, dancing on the wind currents. He imagined the Zephyrs, their playful gusts and swirls. They were not enemies; they were manifestations of the planet's breath, its spirit made visible. To silence them would be to silence a part of the world itself.

His own conscience was a battlefield. Duty warred with morality, pragmatism with idealism. If he enforced the Accord's latest directives, if he sanctioned the further aggression against the aerial realms, he would be securing a fragile peace, yes, but he would also be complicit in the destruction of something ancient and beautiful. The dragons would grow more restless, their alliances with the Accord would fracture irrevocably, and the planet's song would be reduced to a mournful dirge.

But if he resisted, if he chose diplomacy over enforcement, he risked igniting open rebellion. The Accord's power was immense, its reach extending into every facet of human society. To defy them was to invite ruin, not just for himself, but for all those who relied on the stability, however flawed, that the Accord provided. The cities, the infrastructure, the very systems that kept millions alive... they were all dependent on the Accord's iron grip.

He thought of his mentors in the mountain monasteries, their quiet wisdom, their understanding that true strength lay not in domination, but in balance. They had taught him to listen, to observe, to understand the intricate interconnectedness of all things. Had he forgotten those lessons? Had he become so enamored with the trappings of power that he had lost sight of the true purpose of his office?

He looked out at the horizon, where the sky met the distant mountains, the ancestral homelands of the Aeridons. He knew that Mara had sought them out, that she had spoken of the planet's song. Had she reached them?

THE STORMBOUND DIVIDE

Had she managed to bridge the divide in a way that he, bound by his oath, could not? He desperately hoped she had. He hoped that somewhere, in the wild heart of the sky, a different kind of understanding was taking root, a melody that could eventually drown out the discordant hum of human ambition.

The weight of his decisions pressed down on him, a physical burden. The mandate of peace was a heavy one, but the responsibility for defining that peace, for deciding what constituted true harmony, was even heavier. He could feel the tremors of impending conflict, not just in the skies, but within the very fabric of his own being. He was Cael Thornevale, the diplomat, tasked with maintaining a peace that was rapidly becoming a tyranny. And he was Cael Thornevale, the man, struggling to reconcile his duty with the increasingly undeniable truth that the Accord's path was leading not to lasting peace, but to a profound and devastating silence.

The question that haunted his every waking moment, and stalked his dreams, was no longer *if* the Accord's methods were wrong, but rather, what was he willing to sacrifice to stand against them? Could he find a way to uphold his oath without sacrificing his soul, and the very essence of the world he was sworn to protect? The path forward was shrouded in mist, and every step felt like a gamble with the fate of existence itself. He knew, with a chilling certainty, that the time for passive observation was over. The time for a choice, a definitive, perilous choice, was upon him.

The air crackled with an unnatural energy, a symphony of dissonance that clawed at the very foundations of the Sky Court. Cael Thornevale, his face a mask of grim determination, stood beside Mara at the edge of the precipice. The Resonance Tower, a stark obsidian needle piercing the bruised heavens, hummed with a malevolent intensity, its sonic waves a palpable force against their skin. This was not the controlled thrum of regulation; this was a frantic, desperate pulse, as if the tower itself was in pain, or worse, actively inflicting it.

"It's too much," Mara whispered, her voice barely audible above the rising cacophony. Her hands, usually so steady, trembled as she clutched a smooth, unadorned stone, its surface cool and unyielding against her palm. "The song... it's being torn apart. Not just suppressed, Cael, but *shredded*." Her eyes, wide and luminous, were fixed on the tower, and Cael saw a profound sorrow blooming within them, a reflection of a world in agony. He felt it too, a visceral ache that resonated in his bones, a disquiet that the Accord's sterile pronouncements of order had never managed to quell.

Suddenly, the tower's hum surged, a piercing shriek that seemed to rip through the very fabric of reality. The sky above them churned, not with the familiar, swirling patterns of atmospheric currents, but with a violent, chaotic maelstrom. Colors unseen in any natural storm bled into the clouds – sickly greens, bruised purples, and an unsettling, phosphorescent blue. The wind became a tormented beast, not merely whistling, but howling with a thousand tormented voices, each one a distinct cry of pain and terror.

Mara cried out, stumbling back. The stone in her hand pulsed with a faint, internal light, mirroring the growing distress of the world. "It's not just the Sylphs or the dragons," she gasped, her breath ragged. "It's... it's deeper. The planet itself is screaming."

Cael felt a cold dread seep into his heart. He had always understood the Accord's actions as a form of control, a brutal but ultimately human-driven attempt to impose order on a chaotic world. But Mara's words, the raw terror in her eyes, the undeniable wrongness of the storm brewing before them, suggested something far more ancient, far more fundamental. This wasn't just about human dominion; it was about a fundamental rupture in the planet's very being.

"What do you mean, Mara?" Cael demanded, his voice strained against the rising sonic assault. "Screaming about what?"

"The... the Deep Song," she stammered, her gaze unfocused, as if seeing beyond the immediate storm. "It's an old song. Older than the mountains, older than the first breath of wind. It's the song of creation, Cael. The resonance that binds everything together. The Towers... they're not just jamming the planet's song; they're trying to *replace* it. They're trying to impose their own discordant rhythm onto the very core of existence."

As she spoke, a wave of pure, raw energy washed over them, not sound, but a sensation that bypassed their ears and vibrated directly in their souls. It was a memory, or perhaps a premonition, of a world vibrant and interconnected, where the very air pulsed with a life force that human technology had forgotten, or perhaps, deliberately ignored. Cael saw fleeting images: vast, luminous oceans teeming with bioluminescent life, colossal forests that breathed with a collective consciousness, and skies alive with creatures of myth and wonder, all moving in a harmonious dance.

Then, the vision fractured, replaced by a stark, terrifying emptiness. A void, vast and consuming, where the Deep Song had once echoed. And from that void, a cold, insidious whisper began to emerge, a sound that promised not peace, but an eternal, sterile silence. Cael understood with horrifying clarity that the Accord's desire for order was not a quest for balance, but a desperate, misguided attempt to fill an ancient emptiness, a void that their actions were only widening.

"The Abyss," Mara breathed, her voice hollow. "They've awakened it. The Accord's relentless pursuit of control... it's not just silencing life; it's cracking the very foundations of reality. The Deep Song was the shield against the void. And they are shattering it."

The ground beneath Cael's feet vibrated with an alarming intensity. It wasn't the rumble of distant seismic activity; it was a deep, primal shudder, as if the planet itself was convulsing. He looked down at his hands, expecting to see them tremble, but instead, they felt strangely steady, grounded by a new, terrible understanding. The peace he had sworn to uphold was a lie, a fragile veneer over a chasm of oblivion.

"They believe they are creating order," Cael murmured, his voice heavy with the weight of this revelation. "But they are only hastening the return of chaos. A chaos that predates us, that lies dormant, waiting for the world's song to fade."

The Resonance Tower pulsed again, this time with a sickening, rhythmic *thump*, like a diseased heart struggling to beat. The storm above intensified, the winds screaming in a language of pure despair. Cael saw a flock of Sylphs, their ethereal forms usually so graceful, now flailing in the turbulent air, their luminescence dimmed, their movements erratic and desperate. They were not merely being scattered; they were being *unmade*.

"The storm routes," Mara said, her voice gaining a desperate urgency. "They're not just weather patterns, Cael. They're tears in the world's fabric, pathways for the Abyssal energies to seep through. The Accord's 'disruptions' are widening those tears, weakening the barriers."

Cael's mind raced, trying to reconcile this terrifying truth with the mandates he had been sworn to uphold. Elder Valerius's calls for dominance, Lyra's pleas for harmony, his own desperate attempts at diplomacy – all of it seemed so tragically small in the face of an existential threat that reached back to the dawn of creation. The Accord's ambition, once a source of concern, now appeared as a fatal hubris, a reckless dance on the edge of annihilation.

"The dragons," Cael said, his gaze sweeping across the tumultuous sky. "Vorlag... he believed in submission, in appeasing the Accord to survive. But he couldn't have known this. He couldn't have foreseen that survival meant *this*." He gestured towards the roiling, chaotic sky. "If the Deep Song is fading, their own ancient songs, their connection to the world... it will be severed too."

"And they will be just as lost as we are," Mara finished, her voice barely a whisper. "Stripped of their purpose, their ancient wisdom, left to drift in an empty sky. The Accord doesn't just want to control us; it wants to erase what makes us *us*. What makes any of us alive."

A sudden, sharp crackle of energy erupted from the Resonance Tower, followed by a blinding flash of violet light that momentarily bleached the world of color. When their vision returned, a section of the tower, directly above the control spire, seemed to shimmer and distort, as if the very material of its construction was unstable. Through this distortion, Cael saw a glimpse of something vast and horrifying – not a place, but an absence, a churning, infinite darkness that seemed to drink in all light and sound.

He recoiled, a primal fear gripping him. This was no mere atmospheric anomaly. This was the edge of the Abyss, a tangible manifestation of the void that the Deep Song had once held at bay. The Accord, in their blind pursuit of absolute control, had not just disrupted the planet's natural harmony; they had torn a hole into the very fabric of existence.

"They're not just silencing the song," Cael rasped, his throat tight with a mixture of terror and a dawning, righteous fury. "They're inviting the silence to consume us." He looked at Mara, her face pale but resolute. "This changes everything. My oaths, my duties... they are meaningless if the world itself is collapsing."

The wind howled, and for a terrifying moment, Cael thought he heard a whisper from the void, a seductive promise of an end to all struggle, all pain, all existence. But then, the small stone in Mara's hand pulsed again, a warm, steady glow that pushed back against the encroaching darkness. It was a fragile ember, but it was there, a testament to a deeper, more resilient song that still lingered, however faintly, beneath the surface.

"We have to find a way to mend it," Mara said, her voice firm, though her eyes still held the reflection of the void. "We have to help the planet sing again. If the Towers are tearing it apart, perhaps... perhaps they can also be used to amplify what's left. To help the Deep Song resurface."

Cael looked at the Obsidian needle, no longer just a symbol of the Accord's oppressive power, but a wound, a gateway to annihilation. The truth was terrifying, a burden that threatened to crush him. But in Mara's quiet determination, in the faint glow of the stone, he found a flicker of hope. The Abyssal truth had been revealed, a horrifying testament to the Accord's folly, but it was not the end. It was a new beginning, a desperate race against the encroaching darkness, a chance to fight for the song of a dying world.

He gripped his cloak, the biting wind now a reminder of the battle that raged not only above them, but within the very heart of their world. The path forward was shrouded in a terror he had never imagined, but for the first time, he felt a clarity of purpose. He would not be a cog in the Accord's destructive machine. He would find a way to sing, however feebly, against the encroaching silence. He would fight for the Deep Song, for the soul of the world, and for the chance to rebuild what had been so carelessly broken. The fight for peace had always been a fight for harmony, but now, that harmony was the only thing standing between existence and the Abyss.

The crackle of energy from the Resonance Tower, once a disquieting hum, had escalated into a constant, grating assault on the senses. It was a sonic plague, designed not to soothe, but to subdue, to overwrite the planet's ancient symphony with a metallic, artificial cadence. For weeks, the Sky Court had engaged in hushed negotiations, their words like delicate whispers against a brewing storm, while below, in the untamed reaches of the world, the storm had already broken. The Accord, the supposed pinnacle of interspecies accord, was already proving to be a brittle shield against the ancient forces it sought to control.

The first tremor of defiance wasn't a roar, but a guttural, earth-shaking *crack*. It emanated from the Obsidian Peaks, a jagged scar across the northern plains where the great Elder Wyrms, guardians of the mountain's heart, had nested for millennia. Elder Vorlag, pragmatic and weary, had initially bowed to the Accord's stringent regulations. He had believed that submission, even to a flawed human-centric agreement, was the only path to the survival of his kind. He had reasoned that the Accord's Resonance Towers, while unpleasant, were a lesser evil than outright war. He was wrong.

The Accord City of Veridian, perched on the foothills of the Peaks like a parasitic growth, had begun its own Resonance deployment. Not in the sterile, controlled zones designated by the Sky Court, but directly at the base of the mountains, closer than any human settlement had dared to venture in centuries. Their objective, according to the hushed whispers that reached Cael's ears through his network, was to "stabilize migratory patterns" and "discourage unauthorized aerial incursions" – euphemisms for disrupting the dragons' natural flight paths and potentially their egg-laying cycles. The Sylphs, whose delicate forms were exquisitely sensitive to sonic manipulation, reported the dragons' agitation. Their luminescence flickered with distress, their normally graceful aerial ballets replaced by anxious patrols and sharp, warning cries.

Mara, her senses attuned to the planet's subtle vibrations, felt the intrusion as a physical blow. "They are pressing too close," she had told Cael, her voice tight with a familiar fear. "The earth beneath the Peaks is trembling with a deeper anger than I've ever felt. The Wyrms... their song is laced with a primal fury. They are not merely annoyed, Cael. They are being *threatened*." She had shown him visions, fragments of dragon consciousness: the cool, damp earth of the nesting caverns, the scent of ozone and ancient rock, the instinctive rhythm of gestation and birth. And then, overlaid with this primal serenity, the jarring, alien pulse of Veridian's Resonance emitters, a sound that felt like shards of glass grinding against the very bones of the world.

The Wyrms' retaliation was not a calculated act of aggression, but an instinctive, territorial defense. It began with a low, resonant growl that rumbled through the Obsidian Peaks, a sound that shook the very foundations of Veridian. The city's crystalline spires, designed to refract and amplify the Accord's ordered frequencies, began to vibrate erratically. The carefully orchestrated sonic fields that protected Veridian faltered, then collapsed. A wave of pure, untamed draconic resonance, amplified by the very mountainside, washed over the city. It wasn't a destructive force of fire or claw, but a sonic wave of such immense power that it shattered glass, cracked stone, and sent tremors through the city's core. Buildings designed to withstand hurricanes buckled. The sky above Veridian, usually a canvas of regulated azure, fractured into a maelstrom of dust and displaced air.

The Accord's response was swift and predictable. Lyra, her face etched with a new severity, declared it an act of unprovoked aggression, a direct violation of the Sky Accord's tenets of peaceful coexistence. She authorized immediate retaliatory measures, focusing on neutralizing the source of the draconic resonance. This, of course, meant targeting the dragons themselves. Cael, witnessing the escalating bloodshed, felt a hollow ache in his chest. He had believed in the Accord, in the possibility of bridging the chasm between species, but he now saw the inherent flaw: the Accord was built on the assumption of shared values, of a common understanding of order and peace. But what if the very definition of those terms differed so fundamentally?

The dragons, particularly the ancient Wyrms, did not perceive the world through the lens of political treaties. They understood territory, lineage, and the sacredness of their ancestral grounds. Veridian's encroachment was not a diplomatic infringement; it was an invasion. Their retaliation was not an act of war; it was a desperate, primal scream of defiance.

Meanwhile, in the Sunken Mire, a region of ancient, bioluminescent swamps far to the south, a different kind of violation was unfolding. This area was home to the Fenfolk, a reclusive, amphibious species whose existence was intimately tied to the delicate balance of the Mire's ecosystem. They were masters of camouflage and subtle magic, their lives a slow, quiet rhythm dictated by the ebb and flow of the tides and the pulse of the bioluminescent flora. The Accord, in its relentless pursuit of mapping and controlling all of the world's resources, had identified the Mire as a prime location for rare alchemical ingredients and a potential source of geothermal energy.

A contingent from the Accord City of Aethelgard, under the guise of scientific exploration, had established a research outpost on the Mire's fringes. Cael had received hushed reports from the Sylphs who patrolled the southern skies: strange lights in the swamp, unnatural silence where there should have been the hum of insect life, and a faint, acrid scent tainting the usually pure air of the Mire. Mara confirmed these anxieties. The Mire's Deep Song, usually a gentle, life-affirming melody, was now interspersed with discordant notes, a subtle but persistent dissonance that spoke of distress.

"They are altering the water's flow," Mara explained, her brow furrowed in concentration as she studied a shimmering map woven from moonlight and mist. "The alchemical properties are shifting. The luminous mosses are dimming, and the amphibious creatures are moving deeper into the swamp, away from the human presence. The Fenfolk... they are becoming ghosts in their own home."

The Fenfolk, unlike the dragons, did not possess the raw power to shatter cities. Their strength lay in their intricate understanding of their environment, in their ability to manipulate its very essence. Their response to Aethelgard's intrusion was a slow, deliberate unraveling of the human presence. The outpost's water purification systems began to fail, the water tasting inexplicably bitter. Their communication devices sputtered and died, plagued by phantom interference. The very air around the outpost grew heavy, oppressive, filled with a subtle miasma that induced lethargy and unease. It was a silent, insidious resistance, a testament to the Mire's ancient power turning against its unwelcome guests.

Then came the more overt actions. One night, the ground beneath the Aethelgard outpost liquefied. Not a sudden sinkhole, but a slow, deliberate dissolution of the soil, drawing the prefabricated structures into the swamp's embrace. The Fenfolk, emerging from the depths like shadows, did not attack the retreating humans. Instead, they carefully harvested the discarded equipment, the metal components slowly corroding, the synthetic materials biodegrading at an unnaturally rapid pace, reabsorbed back into the Mire's embrace. They were not destroying; they were reclaiming.

These were not isolated incidents. Throughout the vast territories, the Accord's attempts to impose its sterile order were meeting with a quiet, but firm, resistance. A Sylph enclave, meticulously cataloged and designated for observation, had simply vanished, their ethereal homes dissolving into the mist, leaving behind only the faintest echo of their song. A nomadic tribe of beastfolk, whose migratory routes were deemed disruptive to agricultural expansion, had altered their path so drastically that they had disappeared into the uncharted wilderness, their existence now a rumor.

The Sky Court, once a beacon of potential unity, was fracturing under the strain. Lyra, ever the pragmatist, saw these as acts of defiance that needed to be quashed with decisive force. She argued for increased patrols, for stricter enforcement of the Accord's mandates, for the swift and brutal suppression of any group that dared to deviate from the imposed order. Elder Valerius, predictably, supported her, his pronouncements echoing the human desire for dominance, for a world neatly cataloged and controlled.

But Cael, standing beside Mara at the precipice of the Obsidian Peaks, watching the dust settle over the damaged city of Veridian, felt a growing despair. He saw the futility of Lyra's approach. The Accord wasn't a shield; it was a gauntlet thrown down. The dragons' response, born of primal instinct, was not a political statement but a guttural roar of pain. The Fenfolk's silent reclamation was not rebellion but a desperate act of self-preservation.

"They don't understand," Cael murmured, the wind whipping his cloak around him. "They think 'order' is about control, about drawing lines on maps and dictating behavior. But the world doesn't work that way. It breathes. It sings. And when you try to silence that song, it finds another way to be heard. A louder way."

Mara nodded, her gaze fixed on the distant, wounded city. The stone in her hand was warm, pulsing with a steady, comforting rhythm, a stark contrast to the chaos unfolding around them. "The Accord is trying to force a single note onto a symphony of infinite complexity," she said, her voice soft but firm. "They are trying to make the planet sing *their* song. But the Deep Song is too ancient, too powerful to be erased. It will resist. And in its resistance, it will break everything the Accord has built."

THE STORMBOUND DIVIDE

The violations were no longer whispers in the wind; they were a cacophony of defiance, a testament to the inherent fragility of any agreement that sought to impose a singular will upon a world teeming with diverse life and ancient power. The Accord's dream of order was dissolving into the harsh reality of an awakening world, a world that refused to be silenced. The era of political maneuvering was over. The era of active confrontation had begun, and the echoes of rebellion were only just starting to be heard. The first cracks in the Accord's foundation were widening, revealing the volatile, untamed forces that lay beneath, forces that the Accord had underestimated, and now, desperately, feared. The conflict was no longer theoretical; it was visceral, undeniable, and it was spreading like wildfire across the land. The Accord had sought to impose a reign of predictable harmony, but in doing so, they had inadvertently ignited the very chaos they sought to suppress.

Chapter Four
The Song Silenced

The twin cities, Veridian and Aethelgard, bastions of the Accord's ambition, pushed their Resonance Towers to the brink of their designed capacity. It was a desperate gamble, a frantic attempt to drown out the burgeoning dissonance with an overwhelming tide of manufactured harmony. The air above these meticulously planned metropolises, usually a testament to the Accord's control with its regulated atmospheric currents and predictable weather patterns, began to shimmer with an unnatural tension. The Towers, monolithic structures of polished obsidian and humming crystal, pulsed with an aggressive, throbbing light, their sonic output amplifying to a deafening crescendo. This was not the subtle, underlying hum of previous deployments; this was a direct assault, a blunt instrument wielded against the very fabric of the world's song.

Mara, miles away in the relative quietude of a secluded forest grove, recoiled as if struck. The resonant frequencies, now operating at their peak, didn't just reach her ears; they vibrated through her bones, a dissonant chord struck deep within her being. It felt like being plunged into freezing water, a shock that stole her breath and left her gasping. She clutched her head, her vision blurring as the planet's natural melody, the one she had spent her life attuning to, was violently fractured, splintered into a thousand shards of jarring noise. The gentle earth-song, the rustling of leaves, the murmur of the wind – all were being systematically overwritten by a relentless, metallic screech.

"They are overcharging," she managed to choke out, her voice strained. Cael, beside her, felt the same psychic assault, though his sensitivity was less acute than Mara's. He saw it not as a sound, but as a wave of pure, suffocating pressure, a crushing weight that pressed in on his mind, seeking to obliterate thought. The very air felt thick, viscous, as if the atmosphere itself was struggling to breathe under the strain. "They are not trying to harmonize," he added, his brow furrowed. "They are trying to *break* it."

This was not the nuanced manipulation of migratory patterns or the subtle discouragement of flight paths that had characterized the Accord's earlier efforts. This was a full-scale sonic war, waged with the planet's own resonant frequencies as the weapon. The Resonance Towers, designed to harmonize with and subtly guide the world's song, were instead being overloaded, their carefully calibrated mechanisms pushed beyond their intended limits. The result was not the creation of a new, ordered melody, but a chaotic explosion of raw, unfiltered sonic energy.

In Veridian, the effects were immediate and terrifying. The crystalline spires, those elegant symbols of human achievement, began to groan under the strain. The perfect angles, designed to refract and amplify the intended frequencies, now seemed to vibrate with a frantic energy, shedding dust and small fragments of glass. The carefully manicured gardens, the meticulously aligned avenues, the very foundations of the city – all were subjected to this sonic bombardment. Plants wilted and died, their chlorophyll leaching out as if drained by an invisible force. The artificial streams, designed to mimic the gentle flow of nature, churned with an unnatural turbulence, their waters frothing with an agitated energy.

The inhabitants of Veridian, those not shielded by specialized sonic dampeners in their homes and public buildings, experienced a terrifying descent into sensory chaos. Migraine headaches, the kind that felt like ice picks driven into the skull, became commonplace. Sleep offered little respite, haunted by nightmares filled with screeching metal and collapsing structures. Even the simplest tasks became Herculean efforts, requiring immense concentration to overcome the pervasive sonic disruption that gnawed at the edges of their consciousness. Those with a natural sensitivity to the planet's song – children, the elderly, and those who had spent their lives in close communion with nature – suffered the most. They were incapacitated by the sheer dissonance, their minds and bodies overwhelmed by the cacophony. Reports of spontaneous weeping, of catatonic states, and of violent outbursts began to filter out of the city, hushed whispers of a growing crisis.

The Elder Wyrms, whose initial defiant roar had been the catalyst for Veridian's current predicament, found themselves in the heart of a sonic maelstrom. The amplified resonance of the Towers, far from being suppressed, seemed to resonate with the very rock of the Obsidian Peaks, creating a feedback loop of devastating proportions. The ancient dragons, creatures whose very existence was woven into the planet's deep song, were experiencing an agony that transcended mere physical discomfort. Their immense forms, usually radiating a calm, ancient power, were wracked with tremors.

Their roars, no longer sounds of defiance, were cries of pure, unadulterated pain. The earth beneath them, the solid, unyielding bedrock that had cradled their ancestors for millennia, began to crack and fissure under the relentless sonic pressure. The nesting caverns, sacred sites of generation and life, were vibrating so violently that delicate eggs were shattering, the nascent life within them extinguished before it had a chance to begin. Elder Vorlag, once stoic and resolute, was seen thrashing in his lair, his scales dull, his usually piercing eyes clouded with agony. The very essence of his being, his connection to the earth, was being torn asunder by the artificial dissonance.

In the Sunken Mire, the effects were more insidious, a slow poisoning of an already delicate ecosystem. Aethelgard, while not employing the same brute force as Veridian, was equally ruthless in its application of Resonance technology. Their Towers, disguised within the dense foliage and cloaked by holographic projections, emitted a subtler, yet equally destructive, frequency. This was not a blunt assault, but a targeted disruption, designed to unravel the Mire's intricate biological symphony.

THE STORMBOUND DIVIDE

The bioluminescent flora, the source of the Mire's ethereal glow, began to dim, their light fading as if their life force was being systematically siphoned away. The amphibious creatures, their senses attuned to the subtlest shifts in water pressure and sonic vibrations, grew agitated and disoriented. Their natural migratory patterns were thrown into disarray, their breeding cycles disrupted.

The Fenfolk, whose very existence was a testament to the Mire's unique resonance, suffered profoundly. The water, their medium of life, began to carry the taint of the foreign frequency. It felt thick and sluggish in their gills, a constant, irritating buzz that frayed their nerves and clouded their minds. Their innate ability to communicate through subtle pulses of bioluminescence and low-frequency hums became distorted, their messages garbled and lost in the pervasive interference. They found themselves unable to perform the ancient rituals that maintained the Mire's delicate balance, their connection to the water's song weakened, their ability to manipulate its flow and properties severely hampered. The subtle miasma that had plagued the Aethelgard outpost now intensified, seeping into the very heart of the Mire, a creeping lethality that choked the life out of the swamp.

Mara witnessed this degradation through her empathic connection with the Mire's flora and fauna. She felt the dimming of the luminous mosses as a personal loss, a fading of her own inner light. She felt the distress of the amphibious creatures as a growing anxiety within her own chest. The Fenfolk's plight was a particularly sharp pang, a sense of helplessness as she felt their struggle to maintain their home against an unseen enemy.

"It's like a poison," she whispered to Cael, her voice trembling. "Not a physical poison, but a corruption of the very essence of life. They are forcing the Mire to forget its song, to sing a song of sickness."

Cael, seeing the broader implications, felt a cold dread settle in his stomach. The Accord's strategy was backfiring on a catastrophic scale. They had sought to impose order, to control the natural world through technological dominance, but in their hubris, they had unleashed forces they could not comprehend. The overload of the Resonance Towers wasn't a localized problem; it was a global phenomenon, a planetary fever that was now spreading, infecting every corner of the world.

The Sylphs, whose ethereal nature made them acutely susceptible to sonic manipulation, were vanishing. Not fleeing, but dissolving. The resonant frequencies, amplified to such an extreme, were tearing at their very forms, their existence too delicate to withstand the sonic onslaught. Their once vibrant aerial dances, their shimmering trails of light, were replaced by an unnerving stillness, a void where their presence had once been. The Accord had designated their nesting grounds for "atmospheric research," a sterile euphemism for intrusive study. Now, those grounds were silent, devoid of any trace of the Sylphs, their song silenced not by decree, but by annihilation.

Even the nomadic beastfolk, who had sought refuge in the uncharted wilderness, were not entirely safe. While the wildlands offered a buffer, the amplified Resonance still permeated the atmosphere, causing tremors of unease among the herds, disrupting their instinctual migratory routes even in the most remote regions. The planet's song, even in its wildest corners, was being distorted, its ancient rhythms thrown into disarray.

The Sky Court, once a symbol of reasoned diplomacy, was teetering on the edge of collapse. Lyra, clinging to her belief in control, doubled down. She authorized the deployment of more Resonance Towers, faster and more powerful, in an attempt to regain the upper hand. Her pronouncements grew increasingly strident, painting the natural world's resistance as outright rebellion, a threat to civilization that must be met with overwhelming force. Elder Valerius, ever the loyal proponent of human dominance, echoed her sentiments, his pronouncements laced with a righteous fury.

"This is not a matter of differing perspectives," Valerius declared in a Sky Court address, his voice amplified to reach every corner of the city. "This is a challenge to our very existence. The Accord provides order, stability. These creatures, driven by primal instinct and chaos, seek to drag us back into barbarity. We must not yield. We must assert our dominance, for the future of all ordered societies."

But Cael, standing with Mara on a windswept ridge overlooking the fractured plains, saw only the burgeoning disaster. He saw the Accord's attempt to force the planet's song into a single, rigid key as an act of profound arrogance. The dissonance wasn't just an inconvenience; it was a symptom of a deeper illness, a planetary scream of pain.

"They don't understand the concept of overload," Cael said, his voice grim. "They think more power means more control. But this isn't about power; it's about resonance. They've pushed the Towers past their harmonic point. They're not amplifying the planet's song; they're shattering it. And in doing so, they're creating a feedback loop of chaos that will consume them too."

Mara nodded, her gaze distant, her hand resting on a moss-covered stone that vibrated with a faint, struggling warmth. "The Accord is like a deaf man trying to conduct an orchestra," she murmured. "He hears only noise, so he demands that the musicians play louder, faster, more aggressively, hoping to drown out the perceived cacophony. But he only creates more discord. The planet's song is not a single note, Cael. It is an infinite symphony. And when you try to force it into a single, dissonant chord, it will break. And what follows will be a deafening silence, broken only by the screams of those who tried to silence it."

The Resonance Overload was not a weapon of war; it was a self-inflicted wound, a desperate gamble that had spiraled into catastrophe. The Accord's pursuit of absolute control had led them to unleash a force that was actively dismantling the very world they sought to govern. The natural processes of life, the delicate balance of ecosystems, the intrinsic connections between beings and their environment – all were being frayed and torn by the unceasing sonic assault.

The world was not just resisting the Accord; it was breaking under the strain of its misguided technological might, its very song distorted into a death knell for the harmony it was meant to embody. The consequences of this sonic deluge were only just beginning to manifest, a terrifying testament to the fragility of order when it sought to extinguish the vibrant, untamed symphony of life itself. The Accord's dream of a controlled paradise was dissolving into a nightmare of their own making, a discordant symphony of destruction.

The agony was not a sound, not precisely. It was a physical tearing, a brutal eviction from a sacred space. Mara doubled over, her hands clamped to her temples as if to physically contain the shattering within her skull. The world's song, her lifeblood, the intricate tapestry of whispers and roars, rustles and flows, had been brutally ripped asunder. It was a violation so profound, so deeply personal, that it felt like a violation of her very soul. The Resonance Towers, those arrogant monoliths of human control, were not merely broadcasting noise; they were performing a surgical excision, attempting to sever the planet's voice from its being.

Her own voice was a strangled gasp. She felt the vibrant thrum of the earth beneath her feet, once a comforting lullaby, now a frantic, jangling discord. The wind, usually a playful companion, was a shriek of metallic friction. Even the slow, patient pulse of the ancient trees, a rhythm she knew as intimately as her own heartbeat, was distorted, their life-force writhing under the sonic assault. It was as if every cell in her body was screaming in protest, a symphony of pain that mirrored the planetary agony. Cael, his face a mask of shared torment, could only offer a silent, commiserating grip on her arm. He felt the pressure, the psychic inundation, but Mara felt the *absence* more acutely. It was the silence where the song used to be, a void that threatened to swallow her whole.

She retreated inward, a desperate act of self-preservation. The cacophony was too much, a tidal wave of unnatural frequencies threatening to drown her. She closed her eyes, focusing on the remnants, the echoes of what had been. She sought the deep, resonant hum of the ancient stones, the soft murmur of the hidden springs, the soaring melodies of the migrating birds. But the Accord's manufactured noise was a suffocating blanket, muffling every delicate note, crushing every gentle cadence. It was like trying to hear a whispered secret in the midst of a roaring inferno.

Yet, in the desperate quiet of her inner world, something stirred. Beneath the harsh, grating layers of artificial sound, there was a faint, almost imperceptible tremor. It wasn't the raw, unfiltered power of the Accord's broadcasts; it was something far more subtle, far more resilient. It was the earth's song, not silenced, but *suppressed*. Like a seed buried deep beneath frozen soil, it was waiting. It was a stubborn refusal to be erased, a tenacious whisper against the roar of technological dominance.

Mara focused on that tremor, a fragile thread in the overwhelming darkness. She imagined herself as a single, pure note, a tuning fork in the midst of chaos. She hummed, a low, almost inaudible sound that resonated in her chest. It was a pure tone, stripped of all complexity, a single assertion of existence. She directed this inner sound outward, not to combat the noise, but to seek out its suppressed counterpart. She felt the vibrations of her own voice, a physical manifestation of her will, and sent it down, deeper into the earth, searching for that faint, resilient tremor.

It was an excruciating process. Each attempt to connect felt like pushing through a wall of razor wire. The Accord's sonic weapon was designed to overwhelm, to obliterate, to leave no room for the natural world to breathe, let alone sing. But Mara's connection was not a brute force endeavor. It was an act of listening, of empathy, of profound understanding. She wasn't trying to fight the dissonance; she was trying to find the harmony hidden within it. She was looking for the places where the Accord's sonic influence faltered, where the natural song still managed to seep through the cracks.

She felt the pain of the Elder Wyrms, not as a roar of agony, but as a deep, seismic tremor of pure suffering. Their ancient hearts, attuned to the planet's core, were being battered by the same disruptive frequencies. But beneath that suffering, she sensed their ancient resilience, the deep, primal song of the earth that flowed through their very beings. It was a song of granite and lava, of immense patience and unyielding strength. It was a song that had weathered eons of change, and it would weather this, too.

Then, she felt it. A faint echo, a ghostly whisper, from the Sunken Mire. The Fenfolk's unique bioluminescent communication, usually a silent language of pulsing light, was being distorted, their messages garbled. But Mara, with her attuned senses, could still pick up the fragmented pulses. It was a song of water, of mist, of life thriving in the shadowed depths. It was a song that spoke of adaptation, of finding beauty in the obscured, of a vibrant existence even in the face of encroaching darkness. The Accord was trying to silence the Mire's song, but they were failing to understand that the Mire's song was not just heard; it was *felt*, a deep, organic resonance that permeated the very water itself.

She felt the Sylphs, not as dissolving entities, but as shimmering fragments of light that were being buffeted by the sonic storm. Their ethereal dance, their aerial ballet, was being disrupted, their delicate forms struggling against the unseen forces. But Mara saw that their song was not tied to their physical form; it was the song of the wind, of the atmosphere, of the spaces between things. And the wind, though distorted, still blew. The atmosphere, though strained, still held. The Sylphs' song was a melody of air and freedom, and the Accord's attempts to silence it were merely forcing it to take a different, more elusive form.

The agony of the Resonance Overload was a constant companion, a dull ache that never fully receded. But within that ache, Mara discovered pockets of persistent, defiant melody. She found the raw, untamed song of the wildlands, the instinctual rhythms of the beastfolk herds, their journeys disrupted but not erased. She found the deep, abiding song of the ancient forests, their roots holding firm against the sonic onslaught, their leaves still rustling with a muted, determined whisper. The Accord's towers broadcasted a single, oppressive chord, but the planet's song was a million different melodies, each one fighting for its existence.

She realized the Accord's mistake. They believed they could simply overwrite the world's song with their own. They thought dominance was about volume, about force. But the planet's song was not a competition to be won; it was a complex, interconnected web of existence. And the very act of trying to silence it with such brute force was, ironically, creating new pathways for its expression. The dissonance wasn't destroying the song; it was forcing it to adapt, to mutate, to find new ways to be heard.

Mara began to focus her efforts, not on resisting the noise, but on amplifying these pockets of resistance. She imagined herself as a beacon, a receiver tuning into these faint signals. When she felt the deep, primal song of the Elder Wyrms, she would hum in response, a low vibration that traveled through the earth, a silent acknowledgement of their suffering and their strength. When she sensed the fragmented pulses of the Fenfolk, she would visualize the bioluminescent patterns, piecing them together in her mind, reconstructing their lost messages. She was not creating new music; she was helping to restore the old, to amplify the faint whispers until they could become a chorus once more.

It was a draining endeavor. Each connection, each attempt to resonate with a suppressed song, took a toll. The searing agony of the Resonance Overload would flare up, threatening to overwhelm her. But each time, she would find that fragile tremor again, that stubborn seed of life, and she would nurture it with her own inner song. She began to understand that her role was not to silence the Accord's noise, but to find the true song that lay beneath it, and to amplify its resilience.

She saw that the 'silence' the Accord imposed was a deception. The planet's song wasn't gone; it was merely struggling to be heard. It was in the desperate tremors of the Elder Wyrms, in the distorted pulses of the Fenfolk, in the rustling of leaves against a screaming sky. It was in the very act of survival, the desperate struggle to maintain existence against an overwhelming force. And Mara, the Listener, was beginning to understand that her purpose was not to fight the silence, but to become the amplifier for the song that refused to be silenced. She was the conduit, the one who could hear the planet's faint, defiant melody and, in her own way, give it strength. The cacophony was the Accord's power, but the quiet, resilient song was the planet's enduring soul.

And Mara, in her desperate listening, was finding the strength to help that soul endure. The effort was immense, a constant battle against the encroaching sonic void, but with each flicker of the Mire's bioluminescence she managed to perceive, with each deep rumble of the Wyrms' pain she could translate into a resonance of their strength, she felt a spark of hope ignite within the overwhelming darkness. The Accord had sought to impose a singular, sterile order, but life, in its myriad forms, was proving far more adaptable, far more persistent, than their rigid technology could ever comprehend. The song had not been silenced; it had merely learned to whisper in the storm. And Mara was learning to listen to the storm, to find the music within its fury.

The cacophony hammered at Cael, a physical manifestation of the Accord's hubris. He watched Mara, her face etched with a pain that transcended his own immediate discomfort, and a cold dread began to settle in his gut. The resonant frequencies, designed to pacify and control, were instead fracturing the very world they claimed to protect. The air vibrated with a discordant whine, a sound that grated against his teeth and made his vision swim. He felt the tremor in the earth beneath his boots, not the steady pulse of life, but a frantic, irregular tremor, like a dying heartbeat. This was not the promised dawn of order; this was the prelude to chaos.

He had championed the Accord, had believed in their vision of a unified world, a world free from the unpredictable whims of nature and the messy inefficiencies of disparate cultures. He had seen the logic, the cold, hard data that pointed to a future of stability and progress under their monolithic guidance. But Mara's agony, so raw and visceral, was a truth that no amount of data could refute. The "song" she spoke of, the interconnectedness he had dismissed as esoteric folklore, was clearly something vital, something the Accord's sonic assault was brutally severing. The Elder Wyrms' suffering, the Fenfolk's garbled messages, the Sylphs' erratic dance – these were not abstract problems; they were symptoms of a deeper illness, an illness his Accord had inflicted.

Cael pulled away from the window of the small observation post, the panoramic view of the ravaged landscape suddenly unbearable. The once vibrant hues of the ancient forest now seemed muted, the leaves listless, as if drained of their very lifeblood. The air, usually alive with the buzz of unseen insects and the calls of distant birds, was unnervingly quiet, punctuated only by the persistent, grating hum of the Resonance Towers. It was a silence that screamed of absence, a void where life's symphony had once played. He had seen the reports of the blight spreading from the Accord Cities' perimeter, the unnatural storms that lashed the farmlands, the disquiet among the beastfolk herds. He had attributed them to natural cycles, to the usual friction of progress. But now, standing beside Mara, feeling the phantom ache of the world's disrupted song within himself, he knew better. He had been blind, a willing participant in a grand delusion.

The Accord's promises of stability felt like ash in his mouth. He had believed they were bringing order, but they were merely imposing a sterile, suffocating uniformity. Their control was not the benevolent guidance of a shepherd, but the iron fist of a conqueror, crushing the vibrant diversity of the world under its weight. He thought of the treaty negotiations he had overseen, the carefully worded clauses that subtly eroded local autonomies, the assurances of protection that masked a creeping dominion. He had been a craftsman of this system, a builder of its gilded cage. The realization was a bitter draught.

He ran a hand through his hair, the sleek, controlled lines of his Accord-issued uniform suddenly feeling like a costume. He was a Thornevale, a name synonymous with pragmatism, with shrewd negotiation, with a lineage of leaders who understood the levers of power. His life had been a calculated ascent, each step a carefully considered move on the geopolitical chessboard. He had always prioritized efficiency, stability, and the long-term prosperity of the Accord's vision. But the Accord's vision was proving to be a nightmare.

He remembered the early days, the passionate debates, the scientists and strategists who spoke of harnessing the planet's energies, of creating a harmonious coexistence between technology and nature. They had painted a picture of a world revitalized, of sustainable cities powered by clean, unobtrusive energy sources. He had been swayed by their vision, by the undeniable allure of progress. But somewhere along the line, the vision had been corrupted, twisted by ambition and a hunger for absolute control. The subtle manipulation of the Resonance frequencies, the gradual suppression of natural cycles – it had all been incremental, insidious, until they had reached this cataclysmic point.

Mara stirred beside him, a soft groan escaping her lips. Cael turned his attention back to her, his heart clenching. Her eyes were still closed, her brow furrowed in concentration, but there was a subtle shift in her posture, a faint tremor that seemed to emanate from deep within her. She was still connected, still listening to the silenced song, but the effort was clearly immense. He wanted to offer comfort, a steadying hand, but he felt a profound inadequacy, a crippling sense of his own ignorance. He had been so focused on the mechanics of power, on the tangible assets of cities and armies and resources, that he had entirely neglected the intangible, the vital, the very soul of the world.

He had always considered himself a man of reason, of logic. He dealt with facts, with quantifiable outcomes. The spiritual and the ecological, while acknowledged as factors, had always been secondary to the immediate needs of governance and expansion. He had seen the prophecies of the ancient peoples, the warnings etched into the very landscape, as quaint folklore, charming but ultimately irrelevant to the practical realities of the modern world. Now, he wasn't so sure. If Mara's perception was accurate, if the world truly possessed a song, a consciousness, then the Accord's actions were not just destructive; they were sacrilegious.

He looked back out at the desolate landscape, the skeletal remains of trees clawing at the bruised sky. The Resonance Towers, gleaming like malevolent needles against the horizon, seemed to mock him. They were monuments to his failure, to the Accord's catastrophic miscalculation. He had believed they were building a sanctuary, a bulwark against the wilderness. Instead, they had created a wound, a festering sore that was poisoning everything around it.

A memory surfaced, unbidden, of his father, Thornevale the Elder, a man who had ruled their ancestral lands with an iron will and a deep, almost superstitious reverence for the old ways. He had often spoken of the balance, of the symbiotic relationship between civilization and nature. Cael had dismissed it then as sentimental nonsense, the ramblings of an old man clinging to the past. But now, those words echoed with a terrifying prescience. His father had understood something that Cael, in his pursuit of modern efficiency, had completely overlooked.

He found himself walking away from the observation post, his steps uncertain, drawn by an impulse he couldn't articulate. He moved through the sterile, functional corridors of the Accord outpost, the familiar hum of its machinery now sounding hollow and artificial. He passed by soldiers, their faces impassive, their armor gleaming, but their eyes held a subtle unease, a reflection of the disquiet that was beginning to ripple through the Accord's ranks. They were trained for conflict, for external threats, but this enemy was internal, a creeping rot that gnawed at the foundations of their authority.

He needed to think, to re-evaluate everything he had ever believed. The Accord's promises of progress had become a deceptive veil for destruction. Their pursuit of control had devolved into an act of brutal suppression. He had been a key architect of this system, and the weight of that realization was crushing. He had always operated on the principle of necessary sacrifices for the greater good, but the "greater good" the Accord was pursuing was rapidly becoming indistinguishable from a global catastrophe.

He found himself in the small, sparsely furnished private quarters assigned to him. The walls were bare, the furniture functional and unadorned, a reflection of the Accord's utilitarian ethos. He sank onto the edge of the bed, the crisp, synthetic fabric feeling alien against his skin. He closed his eyes, trying to block out the pervasive hum of the towers, the phantom ache in his skull. He tried to conjure the image of Mara, her face a mask of empathy and pain, and the image solidified his growing unease. He had underestimated the resilience of the natural world, and in doing so, he had underestimated the true cost of the Accord's ambitions.

He was no longer convinced that the Accord's path was the only one, or even the right one. The conflict he had once viewed as a necessary evil, a clash between order and chaos, now seemed like a struggle between a suffocating, artificial control and the wild, vibrant pulse of life itself. He had always believed in making difficult choices, in the cold calculus of leadership. But now, the choices he faced were no longer about balancing economic growth or strategic advantage. They were about fundamental ethics, about the very survival of the world as he knew it.

The idea of distancing himself from the Accord's authority, a concept that would have been unthinkable mere days ago, began to take root. It was a dangerous thought, a path fraught with peril. He was Cael Thornevale, a prominent figure within the Accord's hierarchy. To question their methods, to suggest an alternative approach, was to invite suspicion, to risk ostracization, perhaps even worse. But the alternative – continuing to blindly follow a path that was demonstrably leading to ruin – was no longer an option.

He thought of the stories his father used to tell, tales of ancient pacts between humans and the spirits of the land, of the respect that was owed to the earth and its myriad inhabitants. He had always dismissed them as myth, as remnants of a primitive past. But what if they held a truth that the Accord, in its arrogance, had completely forgotten? What if the "song" Mara heard was not just a metaphor, but a literal aspect of the world's existence, a force that could not be commanded, only respected?

The pragmatic calculations that had always guided him were beginning to crumble, replaced by a dawning, unsettling understanding. The Accord's focus on control, on imposing their will, was a fundamental flaw. True stability, he was starting to realize, came not from dominance, but from harmony. It came from understanding the intricate web of life, from respecting its delicate balance, from listening to its inherent rhythms.

He stood up, a new resolve hardening within him. He couldn't undo what had been done, but he could refuse to be a part of it any longer. He needed to find Mara, to understand what she was experiencing, and perhaps, just perhaps, to find a different way forward, a path that didn't involve silencing the world's song. The Accord had promised order, but they had delivered devastation. It was time to seek a different kind of strength, a strength born not of control, but of connection. The sterile silence of the Accord Cities now felt like a tomb, and Cael Thornevale, for the first time in his life, felt an overwhelming urge to escape it, to find the melody that still dared to whisper beneath the deafening roar.

He looked at his reflection in the polished metal of a nearby console. The face staring back was still that of Cael Thornevale, the strategist, the diplomat, the man of order. But beneath the surface, something fundamental had shifted. The foundations of his carefully constructed world were cracking, and a new, uncertain path was beginning to emerge from the rubble. He knew, with a chilling certainty, that his days of unquestioning adherence to the Accord were over. The cost of their vision was simply too high.

The sky, once a canvas of shifting blues and whites, had become a maelstrom of primal, untamed energy. The discordant hum of the Resonance Towers, a sound that had begun as an irritant, had now escalated into a visceral assault, a sonic plague infecting the very air. For the Sky Dragons, ancient beings whose lives were intrinsically woven into the atmospheric currents and the subtle melodies of the world, this was not merely an annoyance. It was a violent tearing of their essence, a desecration of their very being.

Cael, standing in the observation post, his own senses still reeling from the unnatural frequencies, could see the initial signs of the disaster unfolding above. It wasn't a uniform reaction. The dragons, he now understood with a sickening clarity, were not a monolithic entity. They were a complex ecosystem of individuals, of clans, of ancient rivalries and alliances, all now subjected to the Accord's brutal symphony of discord.

A shudder ran through the immense form of a Sky Dragon passing in the distance, its usual graceful silhouette contorted by an internal agony. Its scales, meant to shimmer with the captured light of the sun, now seemed to pulse with an unhealthy, feverish glow. Instead of the confident, sweeping arcs that marked its passage, its movements became jerky, erratic. It banked sharply, not in a display of aerial mastery, but in a desperate attempt to escape an invisible tormentor. Its roar, usually a sound that resonated with power and territorial dominion, was now a ragged, choked cry, a sound of pure, unadulterated pain.

Then, the madness truly began. From the north, a formation of crimson-scaled dragons, known for their fierce territoriality and their almost blinding pride, descended like a storm of fury. Their usual hunting patterns, their calculated dives and soaring patrols, were abandoned. They flew in a chaotic swarm, their roars not calls to each other, but guttural screams of rage. They attacked anything that moved, their powerful claws tearing through the corrupted atmosphere, their fiery breath, usually a controlled weapon, now erupting in uncontrolled bursts of plasma that scorched the very air, leaving trails of acrid smoke and a lingering smell of ozone.

They were no longer hunters; they were instruments of destruction, driven by a primal fury that the Resonance had unleashed. Cael watched, horrified, as one of the dragons, in a blind fit of rage, slammed its massive body into another, the impact echoing with a sickening crunch that even from this distance, seemed to vibrate through the reinforced glass of the observation deck. The sky became a battlefield, not just against the Accord, but against their own fractured minds.

But not all dragons succumbed to fury. Further south, a different kind of suffering was evident. A majestic elder dragon, its scales the color of twilight and its wingspan vast enough to cast a shadow over a small village, was struggling to maintain altitude. Its powerful wings beat with a desperate, uncoordinated rhythm, its body listing precariously. It was disoriented, its ancient senses overwhelmed by the cacophony. The subtle shifts in wind currents, the faint scent of approaching storms, the distant calls of its kin – all the sensory input that guided its flight and its life had been drowned out, replaced by a maddening, ceaseless drone. It spiraled downwards, its immense body a tragic testament to the Accord's disregard for the natural order. Cael saw it dip below the horizon, a silent, terrifying question hanging in the air: would it crash? Or would its weakened form be claimed by the very atmosphere it had once commanded?

The corrupted atmosphere itself seemed to be a weapon. The air, thick with the Resonance's unnatural vibrations, was no longer a medium for flight, but a tangible obstacle, a viscous, choking substance. Where the dragons' fiery breath met this corrupted air, there were not clean explosions of flame, but violent, sputtering reactions, spitting sparks of green and purple that dissipated into noxious fumes. The dragons that attempted to fly through these areas found their wings buffeted by invisible currents, their bodies pulled and twisted in unnatural ways. The sky, their domain, had turned against them.

Cael's mind raced, trying to process the sheer scale of the devastation. He had seen the reports of increased seismic activity, of erratic weather patterns, of the growing unease among the beastfolk. He had dismissed them as predictable side effects of the Accord's ambitious projects, minor tremors in the grand edifice of progress. But this... this was a cataclysm. This was the world fighting back, and the dragons, as the sky's most prominent inhabitants, were bearing the brunt of its agony.

He watched as a group of smaller, serpentine dragons, known for their agility and their role as messengers between dragon aeries, attempted to navigate the chaos. They were like tiny sparks trying to evade a wildfire. Their usual rapid, darting movements were hampered by the turbulent air, their communication calls, once clear and distinct, were lost in the overwhelming sonic assault. They dodged and weaved, their bodies contorting in impossible ways, trying to find a pocket of calm, a sliver of clear sky, but it was a futile endeavor. The Resonance was everywhere, an invisible, all-encompassing predator. Some of them, overwhelmed by the disorientation, flew directly into the path of the rampaging crimson dragons, their screams of terror swallowed by the din. Others simply lost altitude, their energy depleted, their will to fly broken.

The visual spectacle was as terrifying as it was beautiful, in a twisted, horrifying way. The sky, normally a clear expanse, was now a canvas of roiling, unnatural colors. Patches of the atmosphere glowed with an eerie luminescence, the result of the Resonance interacting with unseen energies. Lightning, not the natural, jagged bolts of a storm, but shimmering, almost crystalline arcs of energy, crisscrossed the sky, seemingly independent of any cloud formation. These ethereal displays were often the harbingers of a dragon's descent into madness or its final, broken fall.

Cael gripped the railing of the observation deck, his knuckles white. He had always viewed the Sky Dragons as magnificent, awe-inspiring creatures, symbols of untamed power and freedom. He had seen their aerial displays during Accord celebrations as a sign of the world's enduring grandeur, a backdrop to humanity's ascendance. Now, he saw them as victims, their magnificence shattered, their freedom extinguished by the Accord's hubris. He saw the fear in their contorted movements, the agony in their roars, the sheer terror of being unable to control their own bodies, their own minds, in the very element that defined them.

He remembered reading an old text, dismissed by Accord scholars as superstitious ramblings, that spoke of the Sky Dragons as guardians of the upper winds, their songs dictating the flow of atmospheric currents. It spoke of a delicate balance, a symbiotic relationship between the dragons and the sky, a harmony that, once disrupted, could lead to widespread atmospheric instability. He had scoffed at it then, a relic of a bygone era. Now, standing here, witnessing the utter chaos unfolding before him, those words resonated with a chilling prophetic truth. The Accord hadn't just silenced the world's song; they had shattered the very instruments that played it.

He saw a dragon, its scales the iridescent blue of a summer sky, attempting to dive bomb one of the distant Resonance Towers. It was a desperate, suicidal act, a futile strike against the source of its torment. The dragon was clearly driven by a desperate, primal urge to end the source of its pain, to silence the infernal noise that was tearing it apart. It gathered speed, its wings tucked, its body a missile aimed at the metallic spire. But as it neared the tower, the Resonance field intensified, a localized surge of sonic energy. The dragon's dive became a death spiral. Its wings flailed uselessly, its body twisted as if caught in an invisible vise. It didn't explode; it simply crumpled, its magnificent form dissolving into a cloud of shimmering dust that was then instantly dispersed by the chaotic winds, leaving no trace of its existence. It was a stark, brutal illustration of the Accord's overwhelming power, and the dragons' horrifying vulnerability.

The air around the observation post seemed to vibrate with the collective suffering of the dragons. Cael could almost feel the phantom ache in his own bones, the phantom disorientation in his own mind. It was as if the world itself was in convulsions, and he, a part of this world, was experiencing its pain. He thought of Mara, of her sensitivity to the natural world's song. What must she be feeling? What must she be hearing amidst this deafening symphony of destruction? Her pain, he realized, was likely amplified tenfold, a direct conduit to the suffering of these majestic creatures.

He looked at the faces of the Accord soldiers manning the perimeter defenses. Their expressions were a mixture of awe and fear. They were trained to combat conventional threats, to face tangible enemies. But this was beyond their comprehension, beyond their training. They were witnessing the unraveling of the natural order, the primal forces of the world unleashed in a terrifying, uncontrollable display. Some of them shifted nervously, their gazes darting towards the sky, as if expecting the chaos to descend upon them next. The Accord's narrative of control and order was crumbling before their eyes, replaced by a raw, terrifying reality.

The sheer spectacle of destruction was overwhelming. Dragons, once symbols of power and grace, were now falling from the sky like broken toys. Their roars of fury and pain mingled with the infernal whine of the Resonance Towers, creating a terrifying cacophony that echoed Cael's own growing despair. He had been a part of this. He had believed in the Accord. He had helped build the infrastructure that was now unleashing this horror upon the world. The realization was a bitter, burning poison.

He turned away from the panoramic view, the beauty of the shattered sky now an unbearable torment. He couldn't unsee what he had seen, couldn't unhear the dying cries of the Sky Dragons. His faith in the Accord, already fractured, had been irrevocably shattered. They had promised progress, stability, a perfected world. Instead, they had unleashed a nightmare, transforming the heavens into a celestial abattoir. The very air seemed to weep with the sorrow of these magnificent creatures, their songs silenced, their spirits broken, their reign over the skies reduced to a reign of terror. The sky was no longer a domain of freedom, but a testament to the Accord's devastating, unforgiving power, a realm where even the mightiest of creatures could be brought to their knees by the unseen force of technological hubris. The spectacle was a brutal, undeniable refutation of everything the Accord claimed to stand for, a horrifying testament to the profound, devastating consequences of silencing the world's song.

The cacophony from the sky, a symphony of screeching metal and agonizing roars, had spilled beyond the atmospheric veil, seeping into the polished halls of the Accord Cities. It was a sound that had been designed to impose order, to harmonize the world's erratic energies, but it had instead ripped open the very fabric of governance. In the gleaming council chambers, where decisions were once made with sterile precision, a palpable disquiet had taken root. The unwavering certainty that had propelled the Accord's grand designs was now eroded, replaced by a gnawing apprehension.

High Councilor Valerius, his face etched with a weariness that went beyond mere sleepless nights, paced the polished obsidian floor of his private study. The reports that had landed on his desk in the last cycle were not of diplomatic victories or technological advancements, but of dissent, of alarm, of outright rebellion brewing in the less regulated sectors of the city. The Sky Dragons' plight, once a distant concern, a mere data point in their grand equation, had become a tangible, terrifying reality that even the most insulated citizen could no longer ignore. The visual feed from the observation posts, though filtered and redacted by Accord censors, had still managed to sow seeds of doubt. Whispers of the dragons' suffering, of their uncharacteristic madness, had spread like a contagion, finding fertile ground in the hearts of those who had always harbored a quiet unease about the Accord's relentless pursuit of progress.

"It's not just the dragons, Valerius," Anya Petrova, the pragmatic head of the City's resource allocation, had stated with grim finality during an emergency session that had devolved into chaos. Her voice, usually measured and authoritative, had cracked with frustration. "The agricultural zones are reporting unprecedented crop failures. The atmospheric regulators are failing in sectors seven and nine. We're seeing increased seismic activity not just near the Resonance Towers, but across the entire continent. This isn't a localized anomaly; it's a systemic collapse."

Valerius had countered with familiar rhetoric, a desperate attempt to cling to the Accord's established narrative. "These are temporary setbacks, Anya. The towers are adjusting to new energy thresholds. The dragons' reactions are unfortunate, but predictable given their primitive connection to the biosphere. We must maintain our focus."

But Anya's sharp gaze had betrayed her doubt. "Predictable? Valerius, we are witnessing the systematic destruction of the world's most majestic creatures. And it's not just them. The very air we breathe is becoming... volatile. People are afraid. They're looking at us, and they don't see leaders anymore; they see architects of this disaster."

The fracture within the Accord's leadership was no longer a subtle hairline crack; it was widening into a chasm. The architects of the Resonance Towers, primarily the ambitious and the rigidly pragmatic, found themselves increasingly at odds with those who prioritized stability and considered the ecological ramifications. Councilman Thorne, a staunch advocate for expanded Resonance implementation and a vocal critic of Anya's cautious approach, had openly dismissed the concerns as alarmist hysteria.

"The dragons are a noble species, I grant you," Thorne had declared, his voice booming with an almost theatrical gravitas during a televised address, the image of a suffering dragon still fresh in the public consciousness. "But their primal instincts cannot dictate the pace of our civilization's advancement. We have unleashed a new era of control, and with it, inevitable growing pains. The Accord will not falter. We will adapt, we will overcome, and the world will sing our praises for ushering in an age of unparalleled prosperity."

His words, however, rang hollow. The very act of suppressing the unrest – the increased patrols, the tighter information controls, the subtle silencing of dissenting voices – only served to fuel the growing suspicion. The Accord's promise of transparency and progress was beginning to feel like a carefully constructed facade, hiding a desperate scramble for control.

Within the labyrinthine corridors of power, new factions began to coalesce, drawn together by shared anxieties and burgeoning ambitions. There were those who, like Anya, believed the Accord's current trajectory was unsustainable and advocated for a significant recalibration of their technological agenda, even proposing a temporary shutdown of the Resonance Towers until a more thorough understanding of their impact could be achieved. This group, though vocal, was largely marginalized by the entrenched power structures.

Then there were the hardliners, led by Thorne, who saw the current chaos not as a sign of failure, but as an opportunity to consolidate power. They argued for increased surveillance, for the deployment of advanced suppression technologies, and for a more forceful integration of the Resonance into every facet of life, believing that total control was the only antidote to the escalating instability. Their rhetoric resonated with a segment of the population desperate for a return to order, however authoritarian it might be.

But a third, more subtle, faction was emerging. These were individuals who understood that the Accord's monolithic authority was cracking, and that this very instability presented a unique window for influence.

They were not necessarily opposed to the Accord's ultimate goals, but they recognized the need for a more nuanced approach, one that acknowledged the world's intrinsic complexities and the inherent dangers of unchecked technological hubris. It was within this nascent, unaligned group that Mara and Cael found themselves operating, their actions now imbued with a new urgency and a delicate precision.

Mara, her senses still raw from the sonic assault on the Sky Dragons, found herself increasingly attuned to the subtle shifts in the human political landscape. The discordant hum of the Resonance Towers was a constant, agonizing thrum against her very being, but now, the cacophony of human ambition and fear was a new, unsettling layer to the chaos. She could feel the fear radiating from the ordinary citizens, a low-frequency vibration of anxiety that pulsed beneath the Accord's veneer of control. She also sensed the desperate scramble for power among the factions, a discordant chord of self-interest that grated against her innate desire for harmony.

"They're afraid, Cael," she had whispered to him, her voice barely audible above the distant, unnatural whine of a nearby tower. They were observing a clandestine meeting in a dimly lit sector of the city, a meeting between individuals who had previously been staunchly loyal to the Accord's mandate but were now openly questioning its efficacy. "Not just of the dragons, but of what this means for them. For their livelihoods, their safety. They see the Accord's promises dissolving like mist."

Cael, his gaze fixed on the hushed, furtive exchange between the figures below, nodded grimly. "Thorne is consolidating his power. He's using this crisis to justify more draconian measures. He's spinning the narrative, blaming the instability on 'external influences' and 'unforeseen variables,' but never on the Accord's fundamental flaws."

"But Anya's faction is growing," Mara insisted, her eyes alight with a flicker of hope. "They see the truth. They understand the damage. They're cautious, yes, but they're not blinded by ambition. They're willing to listen, to consider a different path."

The political fallout was not confined to the upper echelons. In the bustling marketplaces and the shadowed alleyways, the Accord's authority was being subtly challenged. Citizens who had once lauded the Accord's advancements now muttered their grievances, their fear of the sky's collapse mirrored by their growing distrust of their leaders. The illusion of infallibility had been shattered, replaced by a gnawing awareness of human fallibility, amplified by the Accord's catastrophic miscalculation. Propaganda efforts, once a seamless flow of reassuring messages, now felt disjointed and desperate. Attempts to downplay the dragons' suffering were met with open derision, as the horrifying images, however censored, had already imprinted themselves upon the collective consciousness.

Cael found himself navigating this new, treacherous terrain with a growing sense of urgency. His previous role as an enforcer of Accord policy now felt like a betrayal of his own burgeoning understanding. The line between right and wrong, between progress and destruction, had blurred into a chaotic spectrum, and he found himself increasingly drawn to the dissenting voices, to those who dared to question the prevailing dogma.

"Thorne is pushing for a complete lockdown of Sector Gamma," Cael reported to Mara after a tense infiltration into an Accord security briefing. His voice was low, laced with a grim urgency. "He wants to use it as a testing ground for enhanced suppression fields. He claims it will 'stabilize' the atmospheric anomalies, but Anya believes it's a thinly veiled attempt to exert absolute control and silence any further dissent that might emerge from that sector, which has been a hotbed of uneasy whispers."

Mara's brow furrowed. "Sector Gamma? That's where the old natural reserves are. If they deploy those fields there... the impact on the remaining wildlife, on the very soil... it would be devastating. We have to warn Anya. And we need to find a way to expose Thorne's true intentions before he can act."

The Accord's internal divisions were a double-edged sword. While they offered a sliver of hope for dissent and the possibility of course correction, they also created an environment of profound instability. The human response to the ecological crisis was becoming as fractured and unpredictable as the dragons' descent from the heavens. Each faction acted with its own agenda, its own interpretation of the unfolding disaster, and its own vision for the future, often at cross-purposes with the others. This fragmentation presented an opportunity for Mara and Cael, allowing them to maneuver through the cracks in the Accord's armor, but it also meant that any unified, effective response to the broader crisis was becoming increasingly unlikely.

The specter of the Sky Dragons' suffering served as a constant, potent reminder of the stakes involved. Their agonizing shrieks and chaotic falls were not just an ecological tragedy; they were a stark warning of what could happen to humanity if their own internal conflicts led to further disarray. The Accord, built on a foundation of unwavering control and technological supremacy, was now unraveling from within, its leaders caught in a web of their own making. The song of the world had been silenced, and in its place, a discordant chorus of fear, ambition, and a desperate, fracturing quest for power had begun to echo through the heart of the Accord Cities. The very foundations of human governance were being tested, not by an external enemy, but by the internal rot of its own unchecked hubris, a chilling parallel to the celestial chaos unfolding above.

Chapter Five
Whispers from the Deep

The shattering roar of the Resonance Overload still echoed in Mara's bones, a phantom limb of pain that throbbed with every beat of her heart. It wasn't just the physical trauma, the jarring assault on her senses, but the profound, shattering realization that followed. The Accord, in its relentless pursuit of dominion, had not only inflicted immense suffering upon the Sky Dragons but had also deafened itself to the very song of the world it claimed to govern. Brute force, the imposition of technological will, had proven to be not a solution, but a catalyst for deeper despair. Her previous path, one of direct resistance and counter-force, now felt like a futile gesture, akin to shouting at a hurricane.

The cacophony of the Accord Cities, once a symphony of ordered progress, now sounded like a dying gasp. The hum of the Resonance Towers, that omnipresent, invasive drone, no longer registered as a symbol of control, but as a persistent ache, a wound in the planet's very soul. Mara had spent so long fighting against the outward manifestations of this control, focusing on the metal and energy that bound the world. But the overload had ripped away that illusion, revealing the deeper, more insidious corruption: a disconnect, a deafness at the core of their civilization.

She found herself walking through the city, the usual bustling crowds a blur of anxious faces. Their fear was a tangible thing, a low-frequency hum that resonated with her own newfound disquiet. They looked to the Accord for answers, for salvation, but Mara knew, with a certainty that chilled her to the marrow, that the Accord had no answers left to give. They had broken the instrument, and now they were trying to force the silence into a melody.

Her gaze drifted upwards, towards the bruised and turbulent skies where the Sky Dragons, her kin, had once soared. Their suffering had been a brutal, undeniable testament to the Accord's hubris. But it was more than just their pain; it was the disruption of a balance so ancient, so fundamental, that its unraveling threatened to pull the world into an abyss. The whispers of the deep, the subtle vibrations that had always guided her, had been drowned out by the roar of technology. Now, in the aftermath, those whispers were all she could hear, a desperate plea for attention, for understanding.

"It's not about fighting them anymore, Cael," she murmured, her voice barely a breath against the wind whipping through the narrow streets. Cael walked beside her, his usual stoic demeanor now tinged with a shared apprehension. "It's about listening."

He glanced at her, his eyes mirroring her own dawning understanding. "Listening to what, Mara? The Accord's lies? The fear in their voices?"

"No," she replied, her gaze fixed on the horizon, a place where the artificial glow of the city met the uncertain twilight. "To the world. To what's left of its song. The overload... it broke the Accord's control, but it also cracked open the silence. It's given the planet a chance to speak, if only we have the ears to hear."

This was the new path, a radical departure from her previous convictions. The instinct to lash out, to dismantle, was still present, a primal urge born of witnessing such profound injustice. But it was now tempered by a deeper understanding. The Accord's power lay not in its might, but in its ability to sever the connection between humanity and the natural world. To truly heal, they needed to reforge that connection, to find the pure, uncorrupted frequencies that had been buried beneath layers of technological arrogance.

Her mind drifted to the ancient lore, the fragmented tales of the First Times, when the world pulsed with a vibrant, untamed energy. Stories of places where the veil between the physical and the spiritual was thin, where the planet's true voice could be heard, unadulterated by the clamor of progress. These were not mere myths to Mara; they were echoes of a forgotten reality, a truth she now desperately needed to find.

"The old texts speak of the Deep Places," she explained to Cael, her voice gaining a quiet intensity. "Sanctuaries, born from the heart of the earth itself. Places where the Resonance of life is still pure. Where the planet sings its own song, unmarred by Accord interference."

Cael frowned, his pragmatic mind grappling with the abstract nature of her quest. "Deep Places? Where are these places? And how do we even begin to look for them in a world choked by Accord infrastructure?"

"That's the journey," Mara replied, a sense of purpose, sharp and clear, cutting through the lingering confusion. "I don't have the answers, not yet. But I know where to start. The fragments of vision I've had since the overload... they're not about destruction, Cael. They're about seeking. They're about a place beneath the surface, a place of profound stillness, where the water runs true and the earth remembers its original hum."

She felt a strange pull, a subtle resonance guiding her thoughts towards the forgotten corners of the world, the places the Accord had deemed too insignificant, too wild, to warrant their sterile touch. These were the places that held the planet's memory, the places where its song might still endure.

The shift in Mara's focus was more than just a change in strategy; it was a profound internal transformation. She was no longer the warrior fighting against the chains of the Accord. She was becoming a seeker, a listener, a conduit for a voice that had been systematically silenced. This path was fraught with uncertainty. It required patience, introspection, and a willingness to embrace the unknown. It demanded that she shed the armor of anger and don the mantle of humility, to approach the world not as an enemy to be conquered, but as a wounded entity to be understood.

Her connection to the Sky Dragons, once a source of shared struggle, now became a poignant reminder of what was at stake. Their suffering was a manifestation of the world's broken harmony. And if that harmony could not be restored, then humanity, too, was destined to fall. The image of a dragon, its magnificent form twisted in agony, would forever be etched in her mind, not as a symbol of the Accord's cruelty, but as a lament for a world out of tune.

The Accord's very existence, built upon the principle of absolute control, had inadvertently created the conditions for its own potential undoing. By suppressing the natural world, they had also suppressed the truth. And now, that truth, like a subterranean river, was seeking its own path to the surface, carving new channels through the hardened earth of Accord doctrine.

Mara felt a surge of resolve. She would venture into the forgotten spaces, the places that existed beyond the Accord's gaze. She would follow the faint echoes of the planet's song, seeking out the remnants of its ancient melody. This was not a quest for vengeance, but for restoration. It was a desperate attempt to reawaken the world, and in doing so, to find a new path for humanity, one that was not defined by dominion, but by reverence.

The city, with its towering structures and suffocating order, suddenly felt alien. She yearned for the wild places, the untamed corners where the earth still breathed freely. The Accord had built its empire on the ruins of the natural world, and in doing so, they had built it on a foundation of sand. Mara knew, with an unshakeable conviction, that the true strength of any civilization lay not in its ability to control, but in its capacity to coexist, to listen, and to harmonize with the intricate, vital song of life.

Her journey would not be one of grand battles and strategic maneuvers. It would be a pilgrimage of the spirit, a descent into the quiet heart of the world. She would seek out the hidden springs, the ancient groves, the deep caverns where the earth's memory still whispered. It was a path that offered no guarantee of success, no clear-cut victory. But it was the only path that offered hope, the only path that could lead to genuine healing.

The weight of her new mission settled upon her, not as a burden, but as a profound responsibility. She looked at Cael, and in his steady gaze, she saw a reflection of her own burgeoning hope. They were moving from the reactive, the defiant, to the proactive, the seeker. They were leaving the war for control behind, and embarking on a quest for understanding. The world was wounded, its song fractured, but Mara Lysenne was determined to find the lost notes, to piece together the melody, and to help the planet, and humanity, sing again. The whispers from the deep were calling, and she was finally ready to answer.

The gnawing disquiet that had settled in the Accord Cities after the Resonance Overload had begun to manifest in Mara in a far more profound way. It was no longer a question of how to dismantle the Accord's oppressive systems, but of how to heal the very essence of the world they had so carelessly damaged. The jarring, violent symphony of the overloaded Resonance Towers had been a brutal revelation. It had not only sent shockwaves through the Sky Dragons, but had also reverberated through Mara's own being, shattering her long-held beliefs about the efficacy of direct confrontation. The path of brute force, she now understood, was a dead end, a cycle of destruction that only perpetuated the very discord she sought to quell.

The cacophony of the city, once a symbol of humanity's progress, now felt like a discordant dirge, a mournful testament to a lost harmony. The omnipresent hum of the Resonance Towers, a constant physical reminder of the Accord's grip, had transformed from an irritant into a persistent ache, a deep-seated wound in the planet's very soul. Mara found herself re-evaluating everything. Her previous focus on resisting the outward manifestations of control – the metallic structures, the energy fields –

now seemed superficial. The true corruption lay deeper, in the Accord's fundamental severance of humanity from the natural world, a deafening silence that had replaced the planet's vibrant, intrinsic song.

She found herself drawn to the fringes of the city, the less polished sectors where the Accord's veneer of perfection was thinner. The anxiety emanating from the populace was a palpable wave, a low-frequency tremor that mirrored her own internal turmoil. They craved answers, a return to the certainty the Accord had once promised, but Mara knew, with a chilling clarity, that the Accord had lost its way. They had broken the instrument, and now they were attempting to force a broken song upon a suffering world.

Her gaze was no longer drawn to the towering structures of the Accord, but upwards, towards the bruised and tumultuous skies. The suffering of the Sky Dragons, her kin, was a wound that would never fully heal. Their agonizing descent was not just an ecological catastrophe; it was a stark, undeniable manifestation of a broken planetary balance. The ancient whispers, the subtle currents of life that had always guided her, had been drowned out by the relentless roar of progress. Now, in the suffocating silence that followed the overload, those whispers were returning, a desperate plea for recognition, for understanding.

"It's not about fighting them anymore, Cael," she murmured, the words barely audible above the urban din. Cael, ever her steadfast companion, walked beside her, his usual composed demeanor now shadowed by a shared sense of dread.

"Fighting whom, Mara?" he questioned, his voice laced with concern. "The Accord? Or the fear that's gripping everyone?"

"Neither," she replied, her eyes sweeping across the cityscape, a longing for something more pure, more authentic, surfacing within her. "It's about listening. Listening to what's left of the world's song. The overload... it didn't just break the Accord's control; it fractured the silence. It's given the planet a voice again, if only we have the courage and the stillness to hear it."

This marked a profound turning point, a radical departure from the path of direct action she had always known. The ingrained instinct to resist, to dismantle, still flickered within her, a primal response to the injustice she had witnessed. But it was now tempered by a deeper, more profound realization. The Accord's power, she understood, was not derived from its technological might, but from its ability to sever the innate connection between humanity and the natural world. To achieve true healing, that connection needed to be reforged, the pure, uncorrupted frequencies of life re-discovered beneath the layers of technological hubris.

Her thoughts turned to the ancient lore, the fragmented narratives of the First Times, when the world pulsed with an untamed, vibrant energy. Tales of places where the veil between the physical and the spiritual was gossamer-thin, where the planet's voice resonated with an unadulterated clarity, free from the clamor of human ambition. These were not mere bedtime stories to Mara; they were echoes of a forgotten reality, a truth she now felt compelled to seek.

"The ancient texts speak of the Deep Places," she explained to Cael, her voice resonating with a newfound sense of purpose. "Sanctuaries, born from the very heart of the earth. Places where the Resonance of life remains pure, where the planet sings its original song, unmarred by the Accord's interference."

Cael, ever the pragmatist, struggled to grasp the ethereal nature of her quest. "Deep Places? Where are these places, Mara? And how do we find them in a world so thoroughly encased by Accord infrastructure?"

"That," Mara stated, a determined glint in her eyes, "is the journey. I don't have all the answers, not yet. But the fragmented visions I've experienced since the overload... they're not about destruction. They're about seeking. They speak of a place beneath the surface, a place of profound stillness, where the waters run true and the earth remembers its original hum."

She felt a subtle, almost imperceptible pull, a guiding resonance drawing her thoughts towards the forgotten corners of the world, the wild spaces the Accord had deemed too insignificant, too unruly, to warrant their sterile attention. These were the places that held the planet's memory, the places where its song might still endure.

Mara's transformation was more than a strategic shift; it was a deep internal recalibration. She was no longer the warrior fighting against the chains of oppression. She was becoming a seeker, a listener, a conduit for a voice that had been systematically silenced. This new path was shrouded in uncertainty, demanding patience, introspection, and a willingness to embrace the unknown. It required her to shed the armor of her anger and don the mantle of humility, to approach the world not as an adversary to be subdued, but as a wounded entity in need of understanding.

The specter of the Sky Dragons' suffering served as a constant, potent reminder of the stakes involved. Their agonizing shrieks and chaotic falls were not just an ecological tragedy; they were a stark warning of what could happen to humanity if their own internal conflicts led to further disarray. The Accord, built on a foundation of unwavering control and technological supremacy, was now unraveling from within, its leaders caught in a web of their own making. The song of the world had been silenced, and in its place, a discordant chorus of fear, ambition, and a desperate, fracturing quest for power had begun to echo through the heart of the Accord Cities. The very foundations of human governance were being tested, not by an external enemy, but by the internal rot of its own unchecked hubris, a chilling parallel to the celestial chaos unfolding above.

Mara's journey would not be one of overt conflict or strategic maneuvers. It would be a pilgrimage of the spirit, a descent into the quiet, often overlooked, heart of the world. She would venture into the hidden springs, the ancient groves, the deep caverns where the earth's memory still whispered its ancient truths. This path offered no guarantee of tangible success, no clear-cut victory to be claimed. But it was the only path that offered a glimmer of hope, the only path that could lead to genuine, lasting healing for both the planet and its inhabitants. The gnawing unease had finally coalesced into a clear, albeit daunting, purpose. The world was wounded, its song fractured, but Mara Lysenne was resolved to find the lost notes, to painstakingly piece together the melody, and to help the planet, and by extension humanity, sing again. The whispers from the deep were calling, and she was finally ready to answer their urgent summons.

Cael Thornevale found himself adrift in a sea of doubt, the rigid doctrines of the Accord no longer a beacon, but a suffocating fog. The Resonance Overload had been a watershed moment, not just for Mara, but for him as well. He had witnessed firsthand the brutal efficacy of the Accord's control, the sterile order imposed at the cost of life itself. The screams of the Sky Dragons, a sound that clawed at his sanity, had been a testament to the Accord's blindness, a chilling prelude to the world's potential demise. His role as a guardian, once a source of pride, now felt like a complicity he could no longer bear.

He walked through the meticulously manicured gardens of the Accord's lower sectors, the air thick with the scent of genetically engineered flora that seemed to mock the wilting spirit of the planet. Each perfectly sculpted bloom, each precisely pruned shrub, was a monument to the Accord's pursuit of control, a control that had proven to be not mastery, but a desperate attempt to stifle the wild, untamed heart of existence. His thoughts, usually sharp and decisive, were now a tangled mess of conflicting loyalties. He had sworn an oath to uphold the Accord's mandate, to protect its citizens from the perceived chaos of the outside world. But what if the greatest threat to the world wasn't chaos, but the suffocating embrace of order?

Mara's newfound conviction to "listen" to the world, to seek out the forgotten Deep Places, resonated with a part of him that had always felt the disconnect, the hollowness at the core of their technologically advanced society. He had always been a man of action, of tangible solutions, but Mara's quest felt different, more elemental. It spoke of a truth that lay beneath the polished surfaces, a truth that the Accord had systematically eradicated in its relentless march of progress. He understood the pragmatic necessity of his previous role, the need to maintain stability in a world teetering on the brink. But the cost of that stability was becoming unbearable, a burden on his conscience that grew heavier with each passing day.

He remembered the hushed conversations in the dimly lit corridors of the Accord's administrative buildings, the whispers of dissent that were quickly silenced, the careers of those who dared to question the Grand Design. These were the individuals, the forgotten voices, who might now be his only hope. They were the ones who had seen the cracks in the Accord's facade long before the Resonance Overload, who had understood, on an intellectual level, the inherent flaws in a system built on absolute dominion. He had dismissed them as idealistic fools, unable to comprehend the harsh realities of governance. Now, he saw them as prophets, their warnings tragically unheeded.

The idea of seeking out such individuals was a dangerous one. The Accord's surveillance was pervasive, its agents adept at sniffing out any deviation from the prescribed path. To make contact would be to risk everything – his standing, his safety, his very life. Yet, the alternative, to continue as a cog in the Accord's destructive machinery, was becoming increasingly unthinkable. The image of the Sky Dragons, their magnificent forms broken and falling from the sky, was seared into his mind, a constant reminder of the Accord's catastrophic hubris.

He began to subtly probe, to test the waters. During his routine patrols, he would linger a moment longer at certain informational kiosks, feigning interest in public service announcements while discreetly scanning for keywords that hinted at dissatisfaction. He paid closer attention to the hushed conversations in the marketplaces, the coded language used by those who operated on the fringes of Accord society. It was a delicate dance, a game of calculated risks, where a single misstep could lead to his swift and brutal removal from the equation.

One evening, while reviewing a standard supply manifest for a remote Accord outpost, he noticed an anomaly. A significant quantity of energy cells, far beyond what the outpost's operational requirements would dictate, had been diverted to a sector known for its extensive cave systems and its proximity to what were once considered "unsettled territories." The official explanation cited research into rare mineral deposits, a common justification for unusual resource allocation. But Cael's instincts, honed by years of navigating the Accord's labyrinthine bureaucracy, screamed foul play. Such a large expenditure of resources suggested something more significant, something the Accord was either actively concealing or exploiting.

He began to cross-reference the energy cell allocation with other data streams. He discovered that the outpost had also recently requested an unusual number of atmospheric processors, devices typically used to mitigate the effects of high concentrations of airborne toxins – or, perhaps, to mask other atmospheric anomalies. He traced the requisition orders back to a specific research division, one that had a history of controversial experiments involving bio-engineering and atmospheric manipulation. This division, known only as "Xenobiology Annex 7," had been officially disbanded years ago, its projects deemed too volatile and ethically questionable. Yet, here it was, resurfacing under the guise of mineralogical research.

Driven by a growing sense of unease, Cael decided to take a calculated risk. He used his administrative access to divert a small, untraceable maintenance drone towards the general vicinity of the remote outpost. He programmed it with a broad spectrum sensor suite, designed to detect energy signatures, atmospheric composition, and even subtle seismic activity. The drone's data stream was routed through a series of encrypted relays, masking its origin and destination.

The drone's initial findings were perplexing. The outpost itself was operating normally, its energy consumption within expected parameters. However, a few kilometers away, nestled deep within the network of caves, the drone detected a massive, localized energy surge, far exceeding anything that could be attributed to natural geological phenomena. The atmospheric readings from that location were also highly anomalous, registering trace elements that were not cataloged in any Accord database, and a significant depletion of oxygen that was being artificially replenished.

This confirmed his suspicions. Xenobiology Annex 7 was not only active, but was conducting experiments on a scale that demanded a considerable power supply and sophisticated environmental controls. The energy cells and atmospheric processors were not for mineral research; they were for whatever was happening within those caves. The Accord, in its relentless pursuit of dominance, was clearly dabbling in forces it did not fully understand, or perhaps, was actively trying to weaponize.

The thought of the Accord engaging in such clandestine activities, especially after the recent catastrophic failure of the Resonance Overload, filled him with a cold dread. It suggested a desperate, potentially dangerous, escalation. If these experiments were related to the very forces that had caused the overload, then the Accord was not learning from its mistakes; it was doubling down, risking another, perhaps more devastating, cataclysm.

Cael knew he couldn't confront the Accord directly about this. Any attempt to do so would be met with immediate suppression. He needed proof, undeniable evidence, that he could use to expose their reckless agenda. But more than that, he needed to understand what they were doing, and why. Was this an attempt to replicate or control the very energies that had driven the Sky Dragons mad? Or was it something else entirely, something even more alien and dangerous?

His mind turned to the Skybound Conclave, the loose confederation of indigenous tribes and nomadic groups who lived in the outer territories, beyond the Accord's direct influence. They had always been wary of the Accord, their traditions deeply rooted in a respect for the natural world that the Accord had so cavalierly disregarded. While they had their own internal conflicts and power struggles, they were united by a common opposition to the Accord's encroachment. Cael had always viewed them with a degree of suspicion, their ways alien to his ordered upbringing. But now, he saw them as potential allies. They possessed knowledge of the land, of its hidden pathways and ancient secrets, that the Accord's engineers could never comprehend. They might even have insight into the very energies the Accord was so carelessly manipulating.

Contacting them would be a delicate undertaking. The Accord had propagated a narrative of barbarism and savagery regarding these groups, designed to justify their subjugation and isolation. Cael would have to overcome his own ingrained prejudices, his upbringing in the sterile, controlled environment of Accord society. He would have to find a way to approach them not as an agent of the Accord, but as someone seeking genuine understanding, someone who recognized the Accord's destructive path.

He began to research the Conclave's known territories, their migratory patterns, their historical interactions with Accord outposts. He learned of their shamanistic traditions, their deep connection to the earth and its rhythms, their reverence for the ancient spirits of the land. He saw in their ways a stark contrast to the Accord's relentless pursuit of technological advancement, a contrast that spoke of a wisdom he had previously dismissed as superstition.

His investigation into Xenobiology Annex 7 continued in parallel. He discovered fragmented reports, heavily redacted, of experiments involving sonic frequencies and atmospheric resonance, hinting at a disturbing connection to the very forces that had caused the Sky Dragons' suffering. One particularly disturbing entry spoke of "controlled harmonic disruption" and its potential applications in "terraforming and population management." The implications were chilling. The Accord wasn't just seeking control; it was seeking to fundamentally alter the planet's natural frequencies, to impose its will on the very song of life.

This revelation solidified Cael's resolve. He could no longer stand by and watch. The Accord's path was not one of stability, but of escalating destruction. He had to find a way to disrupt their plans, to expose their recklessness, and to forge alliances with those who understood the true meaning of balance.

His thoughts then turned to the Sky Dragons themselves. While the Accord had inflicted terrible suffering upon them, they were not a monolithic entity. There were factions within the dragon population, ancient lineages with their own histories and motivations. Some had been aggressively resistant to the Accord, while others, perhaps more pragmatic or desperate, had sought accommodation. Mara, with her innate connection to them, was already on the path to understanding their plight. But Cael wondered if there were dragons, perhaps older, wiser ones, who understood the dangers of the Accord's experiments. Could they be convinced to join a united front, a desperate alliance to protect their world?

He began to discreetly explore the possibility of communicating with dragon enclaves, using his access to deep-network communication channels that were theoretically secured against unauthorized use. He sent out encrypted probes, veiled inquiries disguised as environmental monitoring requests, searching for any sign of intelligent, non-Accord communication patterns emanating from known dragon habitats. It was a long shot, a shot in the dark, but he felt a growing imperative to explore every avenue.

The shift within Cael was not a sudden one, but a gradual erosion of his ingrained loyalties, replaced by a burgeoning sense of moral responsibility. He was no longer just a guardian of Accord law; he was becoming a guardian of a larger truth, a truth that transcended the narrow confines of their ideology. He understood the risks, the potential for severe reprisal. But the alternative, the continuation of the Accord's destructive trajectory, was a future he refused to accept. He was moving from a position of conflicted adherence to one of active dissent, a silent rebellion that would soon need to find its voice, and its allies. The whispers of the deep, once dismissed as the ramblings of the unenlightened, now seemed to hold the key to a different kind of future, a future where survival was not about domination, but about harmony. And Cael Thornevale, the disillusioned guardian, was ready to listen.

The Skybound Conclave, a tapestry woven from the diverse and often disparate threads of the planet's sky-dwelling peoples, had long observed the escalating conflict below with a mixture of apprehension and calculated detachment. For generations, their interactions with the ground-bound Accord had been marked by a wary distance, a silent acknowledgment of shared territory but fundamentally different philosophies of existence. They had witnessed the Accord's relentless technological advancement, its sterile pursuit of order, and the growing unease that pulsed beneath the veneer of their manufactured peace. The recent discord, however, the shrieking agony of the Sky Dragons and the subsequent fracturing of Accord unity, had shifted the Conclave's posture from passive observation to active deliberation. The sky, their domain, was now tainted by the planet's discord, and the resonant hum of the world, the very song that underpinned their existence, was growing ragged and strained.

Within the echoing chambers of their aeries, carved into the colossal, wind-scoured peaks that pierced the upper atmosphere, the Conclave's elders convened. These were not leaders in the Accord's rigid, hierarchical sense, but rather individuals whose wisdom was as ancient as the mountains themselves, whose connection to the sky-winds and the celestial currents was profound and undeniable. Their council was a complex negotiation of perspectives, each elder representing a distinct lineage, a unique facet of the Conclave's collective consciousness. Among them were the Kestrel Lords, swift and decisive, their strategies often involving rapid aerial maneuvers and precise strikes; the Roc Matriarchs, keepers of ancestral knowledge and the guardians of vast sky-territories, their influence slow and pervasive, like the inexorable drift of cloud banks; and the Sylph Chroniclers, whose ethereal forms allowed them to commune with the very breath of the atmosphere, recording the subtle shifts in the planet's song and the emotional echoes of its inhabitants.

"The groundlings," rasped Elder Aerion, his voice like the grating of stone on stone, the Kestrel Lord's feathers ruffled in agitation, "they tear themselves apart. Their machines scream, their dragons weep. This is not the balance we have striven to maintain." His gaze, sharp as a raptor's, swept across the assembled faces, each reflecting a different facet of the Conclave's deep-seated concern. "The Song grows discordant. The very air we breathe carries the taint of their strife."

THE STORMBOUND DIVIDE

Elder Lyra, her presence serene and grounding, her Roc-like features etched with the patience of centuries, inclined her head slowly. "Discord is but a phase, Aerion. The Song has known many rhythms, many silences and many crescendos. What concerns me is not the discord itself, but the nature of its origin. The Accord's hubris, their arrogant belief that they can command the very essence of life, has unleashed something they cannot control. And now, it spreads, like a blight upon the sky." Her voice, a deep, resonant murmur, seemed to carry the weight of ages. "The dragons' agony... it is a wound in the heart of the world."

"A wound that festers," chimed in Sylph Weaver, a being of shimmering light and mist, whose form pulsed with the gentle rhythm of the planet's atmospheric currents. "I feel it. The resonance... it is not merely a product of their machines. It is a perversion of something ancient, something elemental. The Accord seeks to harness it, to weaponize it, but they understand nothing of its true nature. They are like hatchlings playing with lightning."

The chambers fell silent, the weight of these pronouncements settling heavily upon the Conclave. The Accord's actions had always been a source of irritation, a constant encroachment upon the skies, but this was different. This was an existential threat, not just to the Conclave, but to the planet's very soul. The Resonance Overload, as the Accord termed it, was more than a technological mishap; it was a symptom of a deeper illness, a symptom that threatened to unravel the delicate balance that the Conclave had tirelessly sought to preserve.

"We have observed," Aerion continued, his voice regaining its edge, "their internal schisms. The question arises, do we intervene? Do we descend and impose our own order upon their chaos? The Sky-song is our birthright, our responsibility. The Accord has proven itself incapable of stewardship."

Lyra's gaze remained steady, her disapproval a palpable force. "Intervention? And become what, Aerion? Another Accord, dictating terms from above? Our strength lies not in imposition, but in guidance. We are the keepers of the deep places, the whisperers to the winds. Our power is not in chains, but in connection. To descend with force would be to mirror their own failings, to embrace the very path that has led them to this precipice."

"But what if the precipice is now theirs, and ours by extension?" Weaver's voice was a soft lament, a sigh carried on an invisible breeze. "The dragons are suffering. Their ancient spirits are being twisted. If the Accord succeeds in their endeavor, if they truly learn to control this resonance, this... song... then the very essence of our world will be held captive. And then, what of us? We who live by the Song, who are woven from its very threads?"

This was the crux of their dilemma. The Conclave was not a unified military force, nor a monolithic political entity. It was a confluence of distinct peoples, each with their own territories, their own traditions, their own ways of interacting with the world. Direct military intervention was fraught with peril, risking alienating potential allies among the groundlings and drawing the full, unyielding wrath of the Accord's remaining forces. Furthermore, many within the Conclave believed that their true strength lay not in brute force, but in a subtler, more pervasive influence. They were the custodians of ancient knowledge, the navigators of the planet's unseen currents, the interpreters of its primal melodies.

"Perhaps," Aerion mused, his sharp features softening slightly, "our strategy must evolve. We cannot simply watch and wait. The Accord's experiments are accelerating. They are not merely seeking to understand the Resonance; they are seeking to master it, to bend it to their will. This is a violation of the natural order, a transgression against the very heart of existence."

"Mastery is not our path," Lyra stated, her voice firm. "We seek harmony. But harmony requires balance. And the current balance is irrevocably shattered. The Accord has tipped the scales with their arrogance, and the dragons' pain is the seismic tremor of that imbalance. We must find a way to restore it, not by dominating, but by influencing. By guiding."

"Guiding how?" Aerion pressed. "The Accord will not listen to our pleas. They see us as primitives, as obstacles to their progress. And the dragons... they are broken, their will fractured by the Accord's machinations."

"The dragons are not entirely broken," Weaver murmured, their form swirling like a nascent nebula. "I have felt echoes, faint at first, but growing stronger. Whispers of defiance, of a will to endure. They are wounded, yes, but their spirit is not extinguished. They remember the old ways, the true song. And there are those among the groundlings, the Cael Thornevales, the Mara's, who are beginning to hear it too. They are the cracks in the Accord's facade, the seeds of a different future."

This was the nascent strategy, not of direct assault, but of subtle redirection. The Conclave recognized that their power was not in commanding legions, but in shaping the narrative, in nurturing the flicker of dissent, in subtly steering the course of events. They would become the unseen architects of change, their influence like the slow erosion of a mountain by the wind, imperceptible but inexorable.

"Our strategy," Lyra declared, her gaze now fixed on a point beyond the cavern walls, as if gazing out at the planet itself, "must be one of calculated influence. We cannot defeat the Accord through force, but we can undermine their legitimacy, their narrative. We will amplify the whispers of dissent, both among the groundlings and within the dragon communities. We will provide aid, not in the form of weapons, but in the form of knowledge, of forgotten wisdom that speaks to the heart of the world's true song."

"And what of the Resonance itself?" Aerion inquired, his gaze sharp, ever the strategist. "If the Accord seeks to control it, should we not seek to understand it, perhaps even to reclaim it?"

"Understanding, yes," Weaver responded, their voice tinged with caution. "But reclamation? That is a dangerous path, Aerion. The Resonance is a force of nature, not a tool to be wielded. To attempt to control it is to court disaster. Our role is not to control, but to harmonize. To ensure that the planet's song is sung with balance, not with subjugation. We can guide those who seek to understand it, those who respect its power. We can warn against those who would seek to exploit it."

The Conclave began to weave their intricate web of influence. Through the Sylphs, they sent ethereal messages, woven from atmospheric currents and charged with empathic resonance, to the scattered dragon enclaves, reminding them of their ancient strength, of their connection to the world's primal song, and of the Accord's dangerous ambition. These messages were not calls to arms, but whispers of remembrance, of a shared heritage that transcended their current suffering. They spoke of the Resonance not as a weapon, but as a vital force, a part of the planet's living song that the Accord was attempting to silence.

Simultaneously, the Kestrel Lords, ever vigilant, began to monitor the Accord's movements with renewed intensity. They gathered intelligence on the clandestine operations of Xenobiology Annex 7, tracking the energy signatures and atmospheric anomalies emanating from the remote outposts. Their role was not to engage in direct confrontation, but to provide crucial information to those who might be able to act upon it – individuals like Cael Thornevale, whose growing disillusionment was a beacon in the Accord's sterile landscape. The Kestrel Lords would ensure that the evidence of the Accord's recklessness reached the right hands, subtly nudging events towards a confrontation that would expose the Accord's dangerous agenda.

The Roc Matriarchs, in their own way, began to influence the flow of information and resources. They subtly redirected migratory routes of sky-creatures that carried seeds of ancient, potent flora towards the desolate regions where the Accord was experimenting, allowing nature itself to reassert its presence, to offer an alternative to the Accord's sterile interventions. They also provided sanctuary and guidance to those who sought to escape the Accord's reach, their vast sky-territories becoming havens for those who heard the dissonance and sought a different path. Their influence was slow, profound, and deeply rooted in the planet's natural cycles.

THE STORMBOUND DIVIDE

The Conclave's strategy was a multi-pronged approach, a symphony of subtle actions designed to create a cascade of change. They understood that direct confrontation was likely to fail, that the Accord's might, though fractured, was still formidable. Instead, they would work from the periphery, nurturing the seeds of rebellion, amplifying the voices of the marginalized, and ensuring that the true song of the planet was not silenced. Their enigmatic motives, often perceived as aloofness by the groundlings, were in fact a deep-seated understanding of the interconnectedness of all life, a recognition that the fate of the dragons, the Accord, and the Conclave itself were inextricably bound to the health of the planet's song.

They were not seeking to impose their will, but to restore a lost harmony, to guide the world back from the brink of self-destruction, and to ensure that the sky realms, and the planet below, could once again sing with clarity and balance. Their power, though less overt than the Accord's technological might, was rooted in the very essence of existence, a force as old as the stars and as enduring as the wind. They were the silent guardians, the unseen weavers of fate, and their strategy was to ensure that the planet's song, though currently discordant, would ultimately find its truest, most balanced melody. They would not conquer, but cultivate; not command, but inspire. The chaos below was an opportunity, not for dominion, but for restoration, for a reawakening of the ancient rhythms that the Accord had so carelessly disrupted. And in this delicate dance of influence, the Skybound Conclave would play their part, ensuring that the planet's song, in its grand and complex harmony, would ultimately prevail.

The tremors that rippled through the planet were no longer confined to the seismic shifts accompanying the Resonance Overload. They had become subtler, more insidious, manifesting in ways that defied Accord science and shook the foundations of the Conclave's understanding. The sky, once a predictable canvas of winds and currents, now pulsed with an unseen energy, a disquiet that even the most detached Sylph Chroniclers could no longer ignore. It was as if the planet itself was sighing, a deep, weary exhalation that carried with it the echoes of an ancient, forgotten truth.

Elder Weaver, their translucent form shimmering with an agitated luminescence, brought forth images from their communion with the atmospheric currents. They were not visions of the Accord's gleaming fortresses or the dragons' shattered aeries, but something far more primal. They depicted vast, oceanic abysses where light had never touched, where pressures unimaginable had sculpted life into forms that defied conventional biology. And within these abysses, a consciousness, ancient and immense, stirred. It was a truth that predated the Skybound Conclave, a truth that predated the Accord, a truth that whispered of the planet's origins not as a cradle of life, but as a prison.

"The Resonance," Weaver's voice, usually a gentle murmur, now held a tremor of dread, "is not merely a force that can be manipulated. It is a reflection. A siren song that draws attention to the deeper currents, to the truth that has been buried beneath the strata of our world." They projected another image, a vast, intricate network of bioluminescent veins pulsing beneath the planet's crust, each pulse resonating with the very heartbeat of the world. "The Accord believes they are tapping into power. They are, but not in the way they comprehend. They are disturbing the slumber of something far older than any dragon, something that predates even the oldest mountains."

Elder Lyra, her weathered face etched with a new kind of gravity, considered these visions. The Roc Matriarchs had always held oral traditions that spoke of the 'Deep Song,' a resonance that emanated from the planet's core, a melody that shaped its very existence. For generations, it had been seen as the lifeblood of the world, a benevolent force. Now, Weaver's visions suggested a far more complex, and perhaps terrifying, reality.

"The abattoirs," Lyra murmured, her gaze distant, "the places where the Accord extracts the dragon's essence... they are not merely sites of technological advancement. They are points of entry. Points where the abyssal truth can bleed into the surface world. The dragons' suffering, the Resonance Overload, is not just a consequence of the Accord's hubris. It is a symptom of the planet's fundamental wound, a wound that festers because we have ignored its true nature for millennia."

The 'abyssal truth' was a concept that had been whispered in hushed tones among the most ancient members of the Conclave, a forbidden lore often dismissed as myth or the ramblings of those whose minds had been too long steeped in the sky-winds. It spoke of a time when the planet was not a vibrant, living entity, but a vessel, created or perhaps even *imprisoned* by beings from the void between stars.

These creators, or captors, had imbued the planet with a core of immense, primal energy – the Resonance – to contain something else, something even more terrible, something that lay dormant in the deepest abysses. The dragons, with their innate connection to the planet's deeper energies, had always been sensitive to this duality, their songs a reflection of both the vibrant life on the surface and the unsettling currents from below. The Accord, in their blind pursuit of power, had stumbled upon this ancient mechanism, not realizing they were not unlocking a source of energy, but rather weakening the very containment that held the true abyss at bay.

Elder Aerion, the Kestrel Lord, bristled. His natural inclination was towards direct action, towards identifying a threat and neutralizing it. But this... this was a threat that defied conventional understanding. How does one fight a truth that was woven into the very fabric of existence? "A prison?" he rasped, his voice rough with disbelief. "You speak of cosmic jailers and captive entities. These are tales for hatchlings, Weaver. We are facing a technological threat, a political conflict, not the nightmares of a slumbering world."

"And yet," Weaver countered, their ethereal form coalescing into a more defined, almost melancholic shape, "the environmental shifts speak otherwise. The tides are turning with a ferocity unknown to our oldest records. The auroras, once a celestial ballet, now writhe with a disturbing intelligence, mimicking the patterns of the dragons' agony. And the flora... the ancient trees in the Elderwood, they are weeping sap that is not of this world. It is viscous, dark, and carries the chill of unfathomable depths. The

Accord's machines are merely the catalyst; the underlying truth is the true source of the disturbance."

Lyra nodded slowly, her gaze unwavering. "The Deep Song is not just a melody of creation, Aerion. It is also a song of containment. The dragons, by their very nature, are attuned to both. When the Accord disrupts their connection to the surface song, they inadvertently expose them to the abyssal song, the song of what lies beneath. And what lies beneath is not benevolent. It is a primal hunger, a void that seeks to consume." She paused, her voice dropping to a whisper that nonetheless filled the cavern. "The Resonance Overload is not an explosion. It is a tear. A rent in the veil that separates our world from the Abyss. And the Accord, in their arrogance, are widening it with every experiment."

The implications were staggering. The Conclave, with its focus on maintaining balance and harmony, had always operated under the assumption of a world that was fundamentally alive and benevolent, albeit subject to natural cycles of growth and decay. The idea that their planet was, in essence, a cosmic cage, a containment system for a primordial horror, shattered this foundational belief. Their struggle against the Accord, their efforts to protect the dragons, were no longer simply about preserving their way of life or the planet's natural order. They were about holding back an existential threat that could unmake reality itself.

"If this 'abyssal truth' is as you describe," Aerion stated, his voice tight with a dawning apprehension, "then the Accord's goals are not just misguided; they are catastrophically ignorant. They seek to control a force that is not meant to be controlled, a force that is, in fact, a cosmic warden. And by disturbing it, they are not only endangering themselves and us, but potentially unleashing a doom that would make their wars and rivalries seem like fleeting skirmishes."

"Precisely," Weaver affirmed, their luminescence intensifying. "The ancient prophecies, the ones dismissed as folklore, speak of the 'Great Devouring,' when the Deep Song would become a hunger, and the world would be consumed from within. They speak of the 'Silent Masters' who forged the world as a sanctuary, and of the 'Whispers from the Void' that seek to break free. The Accord's Resonance Overload is the first echo of those whispers, amplified by their crude technology. It is not a flaw in their design; it is a consequence of their tampering with a force they cannot even begin to comprehend."

Lyra closed her eyes, her mind reaching out, not to the sky-winds, but to the deeper currents of the planet. She felt it then, a subtle thrumming beneath the surface, a bass note that had always been there, usually a steady, grounding rhythm. Now, it was irregular, punctuated by unsettling silences and sharp, discordant stabs. It was the sound of a great beast stirring in its slumber, disturbed by the incessant, irritating noise of the surface dwellers.

"The dragons' agony," Lyra said, her voice a low, resonant hum, "is not just a response to pain. It is a primal scream of warning. They are the planet's natural guardians, its ancient sentinels. Their connection to the Deep Song has always been about maintaining the balance, about reinforcing the containment. When the Accord tortures them, when they try to extract and weaponize their essence, they are not merely harming individual creatures; they are weakening the very integrity of the planet's defenses. They are driving the wedges deeper into the prison walls."

The Conclave had always prided itself on its understanding of the planet's intricate ecosystems, its ability to read the subtle signs of nature. But this... this was beyond anything they had ever conceived. Their mythologies, their lore, had always centered around the living world, the cycles of life and death. The concept of their world being a construct, a mechanism for containing something truly inimical, was a terrifying paradigm shift.

"So, our enemy is not just the Accord," Aerion stated, his voice grim, "but the very ignorance that drives them, and perhaps, the ancient power they are inadvertently awakening. How do we fight a truth that is the foundation of our existence? How do we defend against a force that could consume us all?"

"We do not fight it directly," Lyra replied, her gaze now fixed on the cavern floor, as if tracing the lines of the planet's subterranean arteries. "We fortify. We reinforce the containment. The Accord seeks to control the Resonance, to wield it as a weapon. We must seek to understand its true purpose – its role in maintaining the separation. We must find ways to strengthen the natural barriers, to mend the tears. And we must find a way to communicate this truth, not through pronouncements, but through actions that resonate with the planet's deepest song. We must remind the dragons, and any among the groundlings who are willing to listen, of the true nature of their world, and the ancient pact that binds it."

Weaver's ethereal form pulsed with a newfound purpose. "The ancient trees... they are not merely weeping. Their roots are attempting to anchor themselves deeper, to reinforce the planet's structure. The bioluminescent veins... they are not just energy pathways; they are reinforcement lines, holding back the pressure. We must learn to read these signs, to work with them, rather than against them. The Accord is focused on the surface, on the immediate power. We must look to the depths, to the ancient foundations."

The weight of this revelation settled heavily upon the Conclave. Their mission, which had once seemed clear – to counter the Accord's reckless ambition and protect the natural order – now expanded into a struggle for the very survival of existence as they knew it. They were not merely guardians of the sky, but custodians of a cosmic prison, tasked with maintaining a delicate, precarious balance that had been threatened by the hubris of a single faction. The whispers from the deep were no longer just echoes of conflict; they were the first stirrings of a cosmic awakening, a testament to the profound and terrifying abyssal truth that lay at the heart of their world.

And the Conclave, with its ancient wisdom and its profound connection to the planet's hidden melodies, was now the only hope of preventing the prison from breaking open and unleashing its ancient horrors upon the stars. Their struggle was no longer one of dominion or influence, but of preservation on a scale that dwarfed any prior conflict, a silent war waged against an enemy as old as time itself, an enemy that resided not in the ambitions of men, but in the very core of their world.

The tremors no longer felt like the planet's groans of pain, but rather like a subtle, insistent knocking at a forgotten door. Mara found herself attuned to them in a way that baffled even her own burgeoning senses. It wasn't a physical sensation, not like the rumble of collapsing earth or the shriek of stressed metal. It was a resonance within her bones, a whisper that bypassed her ears and settled directly into her consciousness. These were not the grand, sweeping pronouncements of the Elders, nor the stark, logical pronouncements of the Accord. These were fragmented glimpses, like shards of a shattered mirror reflecting a world that was both achingly familiar and utterly alien.

She first experienced them in the quiet of her own chambers, a small, sparsely furnished space within the relative safety of a dwindling Sky-Haven settlement. She'd been tracing the intricate patterns on a piece of ancient parchment, a relic passed down from her mother, a scholar of forgotten lore. Her fingers brushed over a symbol, a spiral etched in faded ochre, and suddenly, her vision fractured. The rough-hewn walls of her room dissolved, replaced by the impossibly smooth, iridescent surface of what looked like living stone.

The air grew heavy, not with the scent of dust and decay, but with the primal fragrance of earth and rain and something else... something wild and untamed. She saw colossal, serpentine trees, their bark glowing with a soft, internal light, their roots delving deep into a soil that pulsed with a slow, deliberate beat. It was a world teeming with life, a life that flowed in intricate, interconnected currents, a stark contrast to the fractured, hyper-specialized existence she knew. This was not the world shaped by the Accord's relentless progress, nor by the ancient dragons' tragic fall. This was a world *before*. Before the whispers became shouts, before the deep song became a dirge.

These visions were fleeting, disorienting. They would flicker into existence without warning, triggered by an unexpected touch, a particular scent, or even the peculiar slant of light. One moment, she might be observing the hurried, anxious faces of refugees, the next, she'd be immersed in a tableau of beings whose forms were fluid, their movements an extension of the very air around them, their eyes holding the depth of ancient seas. These beings, she sensed, were not of the Accord's sterile cities or the Conclave's sky-bound aeries. They were connected to the very fabric of the world, their existence interwoven with its rhythms.

She struggled to articulate these experiences to anyone. The Elders spoke of the planet's deep song, of containment and abyssal truths, but their words, while profound, felt like theoretical frameworks. Mara's visions were visceral, experiential. When she tried to describe the glowing trees or the beings of pure energy, her words fell flat, sounding like the fanciful imaginings of a child. Elder Lyra, in her quiet way, listened with a knowing sadness, recognizing the nascent stirrings of a deeper communion. "The planet remembers, Mara," she had said, her voice like rustling leaves. "And sometimes, it chooses to share its memories with those who are willing to listen, even when those memories are painful, or bewildering."

The Accord Cities, with their gleaming chrome and humming energy conduits, became anathema to her. Their sterile efficiency, their relentless dissection of natural processes, felt like an offense against the primal world her visions revealed. She found herself drawn to the fringes, to the forgotten places, the spaces that the Accord had deemed too insignificant, or too wild, to conquer. It was in these liminal zones that her fragmented insights began to coalesce, not into a clear map, but into a series of breadcrumbs, each one pointing her further away from the familiar and towards the unknown.

One vision, particularly potent, occurred when she was observing a group of Accord engineers attempting to extract a fragment of what they called 'Resonance Core' from a petrified forest, a place where the very trees had turned to stone, their forms twisted in silent agony. As the brutal machinery whirred and ground, Mara saw not stone, but flesh. The trees writhed, their spectral forms weeping a viscous, bioluminescent sap that mirrored the light pulsing from the Accord's contraptions. And within the deepest roots, she perceived a network, not of wood and earth, but of shimmering threads, intricately woven, connecting everything. This network, she understood, was the planet's true circulatory system, its nervous system, and the Accord's reckless extraction was not just damaging the petrified trees; it was tearing at the very heart of the world. This vision instilled in her a deep aversion to the Accord's methods, a visceral understanding that their pursuit of power was a form of desecration.

Another recurring glimpse involved a massive, ancient structure, half-buried in the earth, its surface covered in swirling glyphs that seemed to shift and reform with the light. It radiated a profound sense of stillness, a quiet power that contrasted sharply with the chaotic energies of the Accord's technological heart. This structure was not built; it felt *grown*, an organic part of the planet's geological tapestry. She sensed that within its silent chambers lay not answers, but keys – keys to understanding the deeper currents, to interpreting the fragmented visions that now plagued her waking and sleeping hours. The glyphs, when she focused, seemed to hum with a forgotten language, a language of resonance and form that spoke of creation and containment.

Her intuition began to guide her physical movements. While the Conclave debated the strategic implications of the Accord's latest technological surge, Mara felt an undeniable pull towards the vast, untamed wilderness that lay beyond the Accord's established territories. It was a call to the wild, a yearning for the places where the planet's natural rhythms were still dominant, where the Accord's sterile influence had not yet fully encroached. She felt a growing certainty that the answers she sought, the path towards true harmony, lay not in the machinations of politics or the advancements of technology, but in the ancient, forgotten heart of the world itself.

She began to compile these fragmented insights, not in written words, but in sketches, in abstract patterns drawn on scraps of salvaged material. A spiral for the flow of primal energy, a series of radiating lines for the interconnectedness of life, a dark, swirling vortex for the abyssal presence, and a strong, anchoring root for the world's foundational strength. These were not scientific diagrams, but intuitive representations, attempts to map the unseen forces that were now so vividly manifesting within her. The act of creation, of translating these ethereal experiences into tangible forms, helped to solidify her understanding, to give them a semblance of order.

The whispers from the deep became her compass. They led her away from the predictable routes, away from the safety of known paths, and towards the wilder, more unpredictable expanses of the planet. She felt a growing urgency, a sense that time was running short. The Accord's ambition was a wildfire, spreading its destructive influence across the land, and the planet's fragile containment was being stretched to its breaking point. Her journey was not just a personal quest for understanding; it was becoming a race against oblivion.

One day, while seeking refuge in a hidden cavern behind a waterfall, a place where the air was thick with the scent of damp earth and mineral-rich water, she experienced a particularly vivid vision. The cavern walls seemed to dissolve, revealing a vast, subterranean landscape illuminated by shimmering fungi and veins of glowing ore. Strange, phosphorescent creatures, unlike any she had ever seen, swam through unseen currents in the darkness. And at the heart of this hidden realm, she saw a colossal crystal, pulsing with a soft, blue light. This crystal, she understood, was a nexus, a point where the planet's deepest energies converged.

It was a source of great power, but also of great balance. The vision conveyed a profound sense of peace, of harmony, a stark contrast to the agitated state of the surface world. The crystal seemed to hum a silent song, a melody of pure existence, and Mara felt an echo of it within her own being. It was a glimpse of what the world was meant to be, a vision of true balance that resonated with the deepest parts of her soul.

The vision was accompanied by a sudden, intense feeling of sorrow. It was as if the crystal itself was weeping for the imbalance, for the pain inflicted upon the world. This sorrow was not a passive emotion; it was a powerful, almost physical force, urging Mara to act, to seek out this place of deep harmony and understand its connection to the planet's plight. The fragmented visions were no longer just glimpses of the past or abstract concepts. They were becoming active directives, guiding her toward a tangible goal, a place where she might find the strength and understanding to counter the destructive forces at play.

She began to notice recurring symbols in her visions that she had previously overlooked. A stylized representation of a dragon's wing, not in flight, but folded protectively over a glowing orb. A cluster of celestial bodies arranged in a specific, non-random pattern. These symbols, she instinctively felt, were not mere decorations; they were clues, encoded messages left by those who understood the true nature of the world, perhaps even by the 'Silent Masters' the Elders spoke of. They pointed towards ancient sites, places where the veil between worlds was thin, where the planet's deeper currents were most accessible.

Her journey took on a new dimension. It was no longer solely about evading the Accord or seeking out wild places. It was a conscious pursuit of these cryptic clues, a quest to decipher the planet's hidden language. She found herself drawn to the desolate plains where ancient ruins, dismissed by the Accord as insignificant, lay scattered. She spent days sifting through rubble, her hands raw, her body aching, guided by the faint echoes of resonance that only she seemed to perceive. It was in one such ruin, a crumbling edifice of obsidian-like stone, that she found a small, intricately carved amulet.

It depicted a serpent coiled around a star, its scales shimmering with an inner light. The moment her fingers closed around it, a wave of understanding washed over her, clearer and more potent than any vision before. It was as if the amulet amplified the whispers, sharpening her focus, and providing a rudimentary map of sorts, a directional pull towards a significant location.

This artifact, she sensed, was a key. Not to a physical lock, but to a deeper understanding of the Resonance, of the balance it was meant to maintain. It pulsed with a gentle warmth, and when she held it close, she could feel the faint, steady beat of the planet's heart, a rhythm that was being violently disrupted by the Accord's relentless machinations. The amulet seemed to resonate with the 'Deep Song' the Elders spoke of, but it was a song that was currently distorted, marred by discordant notes of pain and conflict.

Mara knew that her path would not be easy. The Accord's reach was extensive, their patrols frequent. The wild places, while offering a semblance of sanctuary, were fraught with their own dangers – unpredictable weather, scarce resources, and the ever-present threat of discovery. But the fragmented visions, the cryptic clues, and the growing conviction that she was on the right path fueled her resolve. She was no longer just a survivor; she was a seeker, driven by a profound, intuitive understanding that the fate of her world, its very existence as a sanctuary rather than a prison, depended on her ability to unravel the ancient mysteries and help restore the broken harmony.

The whispers from the deep were no longer just fragments; they were becoming a symphony of guidance, leading her towards a destiny she was only just beginning to comprehend. She understood that the Accord's technological marvels were a distraction, a garish veneer masking a profound ignorance of the world's true nature. Her path lay in the opposite direction, towards the untamed, the ancient, the places where the planet's deepest truths were still sung, albeit in a fractured, mournful key.

Chapter Six
The Listener's Journey

The world outside the Sky-Havens was a tapestry of muted greens and browns, a landscape that felt both weary and resilient. Mara Lysenne, cloaked in salvaged, earth-toned fabrics, moved through it with a quiet purpose. The clang of Accord machinery, the sterile hum of their cities, the anxious murmurs of displaced populations – these were sounds she had deliberately left behind. Her departure had been as silent as the falling of ancient leaves, a conscious severing from the known, driven by an internal compass that pulsed with a rhythm far older than any technology. She was seeking not just a place, but a frequency, a primal song that she felt resonating deep within her bones, a melody she believed held the key to the planet's ailing heart.

Her initial steps were tentative, the ground beneath her boots a mix of yielding soil and sharp, scattered stones. The air, stripped of the recycled sterility of the Sky-Havens, was a revelation. It carried the scent of damp earth after a forgotten rain, the sharp tang of pine needles, and the subtle, sweet perfume of unseen wildflowers. It was a symphony of natural aromas, a stark contrast to the metallic tang and chemical undertones that had become the norm. Each breath felt like a rediscovery, a reawakening of senses dulled by artificiality. The sun, when it broke through the lingering haze, felt warmer, more vital, its rays painting the world in hues that seemed to hum with life.

She walked for days, guided by an intuition that felt as natural as breathing. The Accord's influence, while diminished, was still a subtle presence. The skeletal remains of their failed outposts, rust-eaten hulks of metal half-swallowed by encroaching flora, served as stark reminders of their relentless, and often destructive, expansion. Mara avoided these scars on the landscape, her path veering away from any sign of their intrusion. She sought places where nature had begun to reclaim its own, where the wild edges of the world still held sway, untouched by the brutal logic of progress.

Her journey led her into the embrace of an ancient forest, a place where the trees stood as colossal sentinels, their trunks gnarled and thick with centuries of growth. Sunlight filtered through the dense canopy in dappled shafts, illuminating a forest floor carpeted with moss and fallen leaves. The silence here was profound, broken only by the rustling of unseen creatures, the distant call of a bird, or the sigh of wind through the upper branches. It was a silence that was not empty, but teeming with the quiet hum of existence. Mara felt a kinship with these ancient trees, their deep roots anchoring them to the earth, their branches reaching towards the heavens. They seemed to exude a patient wisdom, a testament to endurance and continuity.

Within this forest, she encountered a stream, its waters crystal clear, flowing over smooth, grey stones. She knelt beside it, not to quench her thirst, but to listen. The water's gentle murmur, its constant, soothing flow, felt like a lullaby, a simple, pure expression of the planet's vitality. She closed her eyes, letting the sound wash over her, trying to discern if it held a deeper resonance, a hint of the primal song she sought. It was pure, uncorrupted, a single note in a vast, complex composition. It was beautiful, but it was not the full symphony.

As she ventured deeper, the terrain began to shift, the forest giving way to the rugged ascent of a mountain range. The air grew cooler, thinner, carrying the sharp scent of rock and hardy alpine flora. The silence here was even more absolute, broken only by the occasional skitter of scree or the mournful cry of a hawk circling in the vast, blue expanse above. The mountains, like the ancient trees, possessed a timeless quality, their stone forms weathered by eons of wind and rain. Mara found herself drawn to the caves that honeycombed their slopes, dark openings that promised both shelter and mystery.

She chose one such cave, a deep fissure in the mountainside, its entrance shrouded by a curtain of cascading vines. Inside, the air was cool and still, carrying the faint, mineral tang of damp rock. Darkness enveloped her, a velvety blackness that pressed in on all sides. Yet, as her eyes adjusted, she began to perceive subtle variations in the gloom. Veins of quartz shimmered faintly, catching the scant light that filtered in from the entrance. And then, she felt it. A subtle vibration, a low thrumming that seemed to emanate from the very heart of the mountain. It was not a sound she heard with her ears, but a sensation she felt in her bones, a deep, resonant pulse that echoed the tremors she had felt before, but with a newfound clarity.

This was closer. This was a fundamental note, a foundational rhythm. She spent hours in the cave, sitting in the quiet darkness, focusing on the sensation. It was like a slow, deliberate heartbeat, a steady, unwavering rhythm that seemed to ground her, to connect her to the very mass of the planet. She imagined the immense pressure, the geological forces at play deep within the earth, and this vibration was their song, their silent declaration of existence. It was a song of immense power, of raw, untamed energy, but it was also a song of immense patience, of enduring strength.

Her internal landscape began to mirror her external journey. The fragmented visions that had once been disorienting now felt like pieces of a puzzle, each new experience in the wild adding a crucial element. The memory of the petrified forest, of the Accord's desecration, sharpened her resolve. The glimpse of the subterranean crystal, a nexus of pure energy and harmony, provided a vision of what the planet *could* be. The amulet, with its serpent and star, felt like a key, a guide that hummed with forgotten knowledge. She began to understand that the planet's song was not a single melody, but an intricate composition, a symphony of interconnected frequencies, each representing a different aspect of its being.

She realized that the Accord's technology, in its relentless pursuit of control and extraction, had been attempting to *replicate* or *manipulate* these frequencies, rather than to understand or harmonize with them. Their fragmented approach, their dissection of natural processes, had only succeeded in creating dissonance, in drowning out the subtler, more profound notes of the world's true song. Her own burgeoning abilities, her sensitivity to these resonances, were not a product of her own unique biology alone, but a reflection of a natural attunement that existed within all living things, an attunement that had been systematically suppressed.

Her journey continued, leading her away from the mountains and towards the coast, where the vast, restless expanse of the ocean stretched out to the horizon. She found herself on a secluded stretch of beach, the sand warm beneath her bare feet, the rhythmic crash of waves a constant, powerful presence. Here, the planet's song took on a new dimension, a liquid cadence, a pulse that seemed to echo the tides, the very breath of the ocean. She felt the immense energy contained within the water, the primal force that shaped coastlines and sustained countless forms of life.

She watched as a pod of ancient, sleek creatures, their forms perfectly adapted to their aquatic realm, breached the surface, their movements fluid and graceful. They were an intrinsic part of the ocean's symphony, their calls, though inaudible to her, undoubtedly a part of its deep, resonant chorus. The ocean, she understood, was not merely a body of water; it was a vast, living entity, its depths holding secrets and energies that dwarfed even the mountains. Its song was one of constant motion, of life and death, of immense power held in delicate balance.

One evening, as the sun bled fiery hues across the western sky, casting long shadows on the sand, Mara sat at the water's edge, the salt spray misting her face. She focused on the rhythmic push and pull of the waves, the deep, resonant rumble that vibrated through the earth and into her very core. It was a song of immense scale, a grand, sweeping melody that spoke of creation, of forces beyond human comprehension. It was both exhilarating and humbling. She felt herself dissolving into it, her individual consciousness merging with the vast, ancient consciousness of the planet.

THE STORMBOUND DIVIDE

In this state of deep communion, the fragmented visions began to coalesce further. She saw not just individual elements of the planet's song, but their interconnectedness. The deep thrum of the earth, the gentle murmur of the stream, the rustling whisper of the ancient forest, the powerful cadence of the ocean – they were all facets of a single, overarching melody. The glyphs on the half-buried structure, the stylized dragon's wing, the celestial patterns – they began to resolve into a coherent language, a symbolic representation of these frequencies and their relationships. The amulet, warm against her skin, pulsed in time with this emergent understanding.

She understood that the "primal song" was not just a sound, but a state of being, a harmonic resonance that had once permeated the planet. It was the underlying truth of existence, a fundamental vibration that maintained balance and fostered life in its purest form. The Accord, in their ignorance, had been attempting to build their civilization on a foundation of broken notes, creating a cacophony that was slowly tearing the world apart.

Her journey was no longer about simply finding a quiet place. It was about actively listening, about deciphering the planetary symphony, and about finding the points of convergence, the places where the song was strongest, where its original purity could still be perceived and potentially amplified. These places, she suspected, were not merely geographical locations, but conduits, nexus points where the veil between the physical and the mythic was thinnest.

She began to seek out these convergence points, guided by an increasingly sophisticated internal map woven from her visions, her intuition, and the subtle guidance of the amulet. Her path led her to remote islands, forgotten atolls where the only sounds were the cries of seabirds and the ceaseless song of the ocean. On one such island, a place of stark, volcanic rock and resilient, wind-swept flora, she found a network of ancient, submerged caves, accessible only during the lowest tides.

Venturing into these caves was an act of faith. The water was cold, the darkness absolute, but the amulet pulsed with a steady warmth, guiding her through the submerged passages. Within the deepest chamber, far from any surface light, she encountered a phenomenon that transcended mere sensory experience. The water itself seemed to hum with a luminous energy, casting an ethereal glow. Strange, bioluminescent creatures, like living constellations, drifted through the water, their movements weaving intricate patterns of light. And at the center of the chamber, suspended in the water, was a colossal, crystalline structure, pulsing with a soft, internal light, a nexus of pure, unadulterated resonance.

This was a place where the planet's song was not just heard, but *felt* in its entirety. It was the symphony in its purest form, a harmonious convergence of all the frequencies she had encountered – the deep thrum of the earth, the gentle flow of water, the whispering life of the forests, the vastness of the oceans. The crystal seemed to be the source, the conductor of this grand orchestra, its light a visual manifestation of the planet's fundamental vibration. Here, Mara felt a profound sense of peace, an overwhelming feeling of belonging. She was not just a listener; she was a participant in this cosmic melody.

She realized that the "primal song" was the planet's true language, a language of energy, of vibration, of interconnectedness. The Accord's technology was a crude, clumsy imitation, a forced translation that had lost all nuance and beauty. Her own journey was not merely an escape, but a homecoming, a return to the fundamental truths of existence that had been buried beneath layers of technological ambition and societal disconnect. The path ahead would be to understand how to amplify this song, how to restore its harmony, and how to perhaps, through her own growing attunement, help others to hear it again. The solitary journey was far from over; it was merely leading her to the heart of the world's deepest mysteries.

The journey had led Mara to places that existed in the quiet spaces between the Accord's pronouncements, realms where the planet's song was not just audible, but palpable. She had learned to read the land not through maps or sensor readings, but through the subtle shifts in the air, the unique vibrations that resonated through stone and soil. It was in one such place, a secluded valley cradled by mist-shrouded peaks, that she encountered her first true guardian.

The valley was a tapestry of emerald and sapphire, a riot of vegetation that seemed to thrum with an intensified life force. Ancient trees, their bark etched with the calligraphy of ages, formed a living cathedral, their canopy a mosaic of dappled sunlight. The air was thick with the scent of damp earth, wild herbs, and something else, something primal and untamed. It was here, beside a waterfall that plunged into a crystal-clear pool, that she saw him.

He was old, impossibly old, his skin like weathered parchment stretched over bone, his eyes holding the deep, calm wisdom of millennia. He wore simple, undyed robes woven from what appeared to be spun moonlight and moss, and his silver hair was braided with dried wildflowers. He was seated on a moss-covered stone, his hands resting on a staff carved from a single piece of ancient wood, its surface alive with intricate, swirling patterns that seemed to shift and reform as she watched.

Mara approached with a reverence that went beyond mere politeness; it was a recognition of a presence that was as much a part of the valley as the water and the stone. The old man looked up as she drew near, his gaze not of surprise, but of patient expectation. There was no fear in his eyes, only a profound stillness.

"You hear it," he stated, his voice a low, melodious rumble, like pebbles shifting in a slow-moving stream. It wasn't a question.

Mara nodded, her throat tight. "I do. I'm trying to understand it."

A faint smile touched his lips, creasing the ancient landscape of his face. "Understanding is a journey, not a destination. Many seek to grasp it, to quantify it, to bend it to their will. They are the ones who hear only noise." He gestured to the land around them. "This is a place of resonance. A place where the planet breathes deeply, and its song is clearest."

He introduced himself as Kaelen, a listener, a guardian of these ancient places. He spoke of his lineage, of those who had tended to these sacred sites for uncounted generations, acting as conduits and protectors of the planet's harmonic frequencies. They were not warriors, nor sorcerers in the common sense, but keepers of a delicate balance, ensuring that the world's song was not drowned out by the clamor of discord.

"The Accord," Kaelen said, his gaze distant, as if peering through the mists of time, "they sought to silence the song. To replace it with their own sterile hum. They are like a child who finds a perfectly tuned instrument and decides to smash it, believing they can create a grander sound from the broken pieces."

He explained that the "song" was not merely an auditory phenomenon, but a fundamental energetic vibration that underpinned all of existence. It was the pulse of life, the interconnectedness of all things, the harmonious dance of creation and decay. When this song was disrupted, the world itself began to sicken, its systems thrown into disarray.

Kaelen began to teach Mara, not through lectures, but through shared experience. He guided her to different points within the valley, each with its own subtle, yet distinct, resonance. He showed her how to attune herself to the deep, grounding hum of the earth beneath their feet, how to feel the vibrant, life-affirming pulse of the ancient trees, how to hear the clear, pure note of the waterfall's cascade.

"The trees," he explained, touching the gnarled bark of an ancient oak, "they are the planet's memory. Their roots delve into the deep earth, drawing up its wisdom, and their branches reach for the stars, carrying its dreams. They are the silent librarians of our world."

He led her to a cluster of smooth, grey stones by the riverbank. "These stones have been shaped by the water's constant caress for epochs. They have learned patience, resilience, and the beauty of yielding. Listen to their silence. It is not an emptiness, but a fullness of acceptance."

THE STORMBOUND DIVIDE

Mara found that with Kaelen's guidance, her own innate sensitivity was amplified. She could feel the subtle energies of the valley weaving around her, a complex symphony that resonated with the nascent understanding blooming within her. She saw that the "song" was not a single melody, but an intricate harmony of countless voices, each playing its part in the grand composition.

Her lessons were not without their tests. Kaelen would sometimes pose riddles, veiled in metaphor, that challenged her perception and forced her to look beyond the obvious. One such riddle involved a wilting flower.

"This blossom," Kaelen said, pointing to a bloom that had begun to fade, "is reaching the end of its cycle. Is its song fading? Or is it transforming into a new melody?"

Mara observed the flower, its petals curling inward, its vibrant color softening. She felt the subtle energy shift within it, a diminishment of its immediate, outward-facing song, but a new, deeper resonance emerging from within, a whisper of the seeds it held, of the life that would continue.

"It is transforming," Mara replied, her voice gaining confidence. "Its song is not ending, but changing. It is returning its energy to the earth, to nourish what will come next."

Kaelen smiled, a genuine warmth radiating from him. "You listen with more than your ears, Listener. You listen with your spirit."

Her time with Kaelen was a period of profound growth, a deepening of her connection to the planet and its ancient rhythms. He spoke of other guardians, of isolated enclaves and hidden sanctuaries scattered across the world, places where the planet's song remained pure, protected by those who understood its sacred nature. He warned her that not all such guardians would be as welcoming as he. Some, scarred by the intrusion of the Accord and others who sought to exploit the world's natural energies, were fiercely protective, their wariness a hardened shell around their profound connection.

One evening, as a twilight mist began to weave its way through the valley, Kaelen spoke of the Elder Dragons. These were not the fire-breathing beasts of legend, but ancient, wise beings who had chosen to retreat from the conflicts of the younger races, their immense lifespans allowing them to perceive the world on a scale that few could comprehend. They were beings of immense power, tied to the very foundations of the planet, and their presence was often a silent, watchful guardianship of places of profound energetic significance.

"There are those," Kaelen murmured, gazing into the swirling mist, "who still slumber in the deep places, their dreams woven into the planet's own. They have seen empires rise and fall, watched stars ignite and fade. They are the oldest listeners, their awareness a vast ocean upon which the currents of our world flow."

He described one such dragon, rumored to reside in the crystalline caverns beneath a perpetually snow-capped mountain range far to the north. This dragon, named Aethelgard by the few who dared to whisper its name, was said to be a keeper of the planet's deep earth energies, its slumber a form of silent vigilance. Kaelen cautioned that approaching such a creature was a perilous undertaking, for their awakening could be as cataclysmic as their slumber was peaceful.

"They are not to be commanded, nor cajoled," Kaelen warned. "Their wisdom is a force of nature itself. One can only hope to be found worthy of their notice, and even then, their guidance will be as cryptic as the shifting of tectonic plates."

Before Mara departed the valley, Kaelen presented her with a small, intricately carved wooden bird. "This is a gift from the valley itself," he said. "It will sing when you are close to a place of strong resonance, its melody a sweet harbinger of the planet's song. But remember, Listener, the greatest songs are often found not in the places of loudest resonance, but in the quiet spaces between. The song is everywhere, for those who truly learn to listen."

THE STORMBOUND DIVIDE

As Mara walked away from the valley, the wooden bird nestled in her palm, she felt a newfound resolve. Her journey was no longer a solitary quest for a lost melody. She was now a student of a much grander symphony, guided by ancient wisdom and the subtle harmonies of a living planet. She knew the path ahead would be fraught with challenges, that the guardians of these ancient places might not always be as benevolent as Kaelen, and that the true understanding of the planet's song required not just sensitivity, but a deep and unwavering respect for the natural order.

Her next destination, guided by a subtle shift in the amulet's pulse and a faint, almost imperceptible hum from the wooden bird, led her towards a region known for its vast, ancient forests, a place rumored to be largely untouched by the Accord's influence. The journey there was long, taking her through rolling hills and across wide, untamed plains where herds of wild grazers moved like living rivers across the landscape. She learned to move with the rhythms of the wild, to find sustenance from the earth, and to sleep under the star-dusted canvas of the night sky, her senses now acutely attuned to the subtle shifts in the nocturnal chorus.

The forest, when she finally reached its edge, was unlike anything she had encountered before. The trees were colossal, their trunks so wide that it would take several people to encircle them, their branches interlaced so tightly that they formed an unbroken canopy, filtering the sunlight into a perpetual twilight. The air was cool and moist, smelling of rich, decaying earth, ancient wood, and the sweet, cloying scent of unseen blossoms. A profound silence reigned here, broken only by the rustle of unseen creatures and the gentle sigh of the wind through the impossibly high branches.

As she ventured deeper, the wooden bird in her hand began to emit a soft, resonant chirp, a melody so pure and clear it seemed to hang in the air like spun crystal. It was a signal, a confirmation that she was on the right path. The chirp grew stronger, guiding her through the dense undergrowth, past ferns as tall as a person, and over fallen logs that had long since become part of the forest floor.

Her path eventually opened into a hidden clearing, a place bathed in an ethereal glow that seemed to emanate not from the sky, but from the very heart of the forest. In the center of the clearing stood a single, ancient tree, its bark shimmering with an iridescent quality, its leaves a vibrant, impossible shade of emerald. At its base, curled like a colossal, slumbering serpent, was a dragon.

This was not the fearsome, scaly beast of folklore, but a creature of immense, quiet power. Its scales were like polished obsidian, interspersed with veins of what appeared to be pure, molten gold that pulsed with a faint, internal light. Its form was sleek and serpentine, its immense head resting upon its forelegs, its eyes closed in a deep, profound sleep. The air around it thrummed with a palpable energy, a low, resonant hum that vibrated through Mara's very bones.

This was Aethelgard, the dragon of the deep earth.

Mara approached with the same reverence she had shown Kaelen, her steps slow and deliberate. The wooden bird in her hand sang a continuous, sweet melody, its song now a direct echo of the dragon's subtle resonance. As she drew closer, the dragon's golden veins pulsed with a brighter light, and its immense chest rose and fell with a slow, deliberate rhythm.

She stopped a respectful distance away, not daring to intrude further into its sacred space. She simply stood, and listened. The dragon's slumbering song was a deep, earth-shattering rumble, a song of immense power, of geological ages, of the slow, inexorable forces that shaped the planet. It was a song of foundation, of stability, of the very bedrock upon which all life was built.

As she focused on this deep, primal resonance, images began to flicker through her mind, not visions this time, but echoes of the dragon's own ancient consciousness. She saw the formation of mountains, the slow drift of continents, the fiery birth of volcanoes, the slow, patient carving of canyons by rivers that had long since changed their course. She felt the immense weight of time, the deep, unfathomable memory of the earth itself.

Suddenly, one of the dragon's massive eyelids, the size of a small shield, flickered open. A single eye, vast and multifaceted, the color of molten gold shot through with emerald sparks, fixed upon Mara. There was no aggression in its gaze, only an ancient, profound curiosity, and a hint of weariness.

A voice, deep and resonant, echoed not in her ears, but directly in her mind, a sound that seemed to vibrate through the very earth.

"Another Listener... you tread on hallowed ground, child of the ephemeral."

Mara, though stunned, managed to project her thoughts in return. "Great Aethelgard, I seek to understand the planet's song. I mean no harm. I am a student, a traveler."

The dragon's golden eye seemed to study her, assessing her intent, her essence.

"The song... yes. It falters. The dissonant chords grow louder. The Accord... they are but one symptom of a deeper malaise. A forgetting."

The dragon's voice was not one of anger, but of profound sorrow, like the groaning of ancient glaciers.

"They seek to control that which they cannot comprehend. They tear at the tapestry, believing they can reweave it with threads of their own devising. They sever the roots and expect the tree to flourish."

Mara felt a surge of empathy for this ancient being, this silent guardian of the planet's deepest rhythms. "I am trying to find a way to restore the harmony," she projected, her thoughts filled with the knowledge she had gained from Kaelen and her own journey. "I believe the song holds the key."

Aethelgard's massive head shifted slightly, the movement sending ripples of energy through the clearing.

"The song is not a key to be found, but a state of being to be re-achieved. It is the natural order, the balance of give and take, of growth and decay. You have felt its echoes in the whispering forests, the flowing waters, the steadfast mountains. But its true heart lies deeper still, in the very molten core of this world."

The dragon explained that its slumber was not mere rest, but a form of deep communion with the planet's core energies. Its dreams were the slow, seismic shifts that shaped the world, its slow breaths the subtle emanations of heat that sustained life. It had awakened now, it conveyed, because Mara's own resonance had reached a certain pitch, a harmony that, for a fleeting moment, had resonated with its own ancient consciousness.

"You possess a sensitivity," Aethelgard communicated, its golden eye never leaving her. *"A rare gift in these fractured times. But sensitivity alone is not enough. It must be guided by wisdom, tempered by patience, and infused with a profound respect for the interconnectedness of all things. The Accord's approach is one of dissection. They break life down into its smallest components, hoping to understand the whole. This is the way of the unseeing. True understanding comes from perceiving the symphony, not merely analyzing each note in isolation."*

The dragon then posed a subtle challenge. It projected a series of complex energetic patterns into Mara's mind, abstract representations of the planet's various frequencies. They were beautiful, intricate, and overwhelming in their complexity. The wooden bird in her hand chirped frantically, its melody now a cascade of urgent, interlocking notes, attempting to mirror the dragon's projections.

"Can you find the dissonance within this harmony?" the dragon's thought-voice resonated. *"Can you identify the discordant note that mars the song?"*

Mara closed her eyes, focusing all her being on the intricate patterns swirling within her mind. She felt the familiar hum of the earth, the vibrant pulse of the trees, the clear tone of the water, but now they were interwoven with new, more complex frequencies, and within them, she began to perceive subtle jarring notes, tiny imperfections that disrupted the overall flow. It was like a perfect chord played with one subtly out-of-tune string. She identified a specific pattern, a jagged, chaotic pulse that seemed to clash with the smooth, cyclical rhythms of the forest.

She projected her answer, describing the discordant pattern, its chaotic nature.

Aethelgard's golden eye narrowed slightly, a flicker of something akin to surprise or perhaps approval in its depths.

"You perceive. You are more than a mere listener. You are a Listener with discernment. The Accord's machines, in their relentless pursuit of energy, have created such a dissonance, a crude extraction that tears at the fabric of natural harmony. They seek to harness power, but they do not understand that true power lies in balance, not in brute force."

The dragon then shared a cryptic piece of wisdom, a vision of ancient, crystalline structures embedded deep within the earth, resonating with the planet's core energy. These were not man-made, but natural formations, nexus points where the planet's song was at its most potent, its most pure. These were the places the Accord sought to exploit, but their technology was too crude, too blunt, to truly harness their power without causing catastrophic disruption.

"These nexus points," Aethelgard conveyed, *"are like the heartwood of the world. They require respect, understanding, and a gentle touch. Your path, Listener, lies in discovering these places, not to exploit them, but to learn from them, to understand how to mend the song where it is broken. You must learn to amplify the pure notes, to sooth the discordant ones."*

As the dragon spoke, its golden veins began to dim, and its eyelids slowly lowered, the molten gold of its eye receding into shadow.

"My slumber is deep, and the world's song is a patient one. Seek out the places where the earth whispers its oldest secrets. Listen to the silence between the

notes. And remember, the greatest strength lies not in the ability to shout, but in the ability to hear the quietest whisper."

With that, Aethelgard settled deeper into its slumber, its form becoming one with the shimmering, ancient tree. The intense thrumming in the clearing subsided, leaving only the gentle, persistent song of the forest. The wooden bird in Mara's hand fell silent, its purpose fulfilled.

Mara remained in the clearing for a long time, contemplating the dragon's words, the immense weight of its ancient wisdom. She understood now that her journey was not just about finding a melody, but about becoming a part of the orchestra, about learning to play her part in restoring the planet's symphony. The guardians she encountered were not merely obstacles or guides; they were embodiments of the very principles she was striving to understand – balance, patience, and a profound respect for the natural order. Her path was becoming clearer, leading her not to a single destination, but to a series of sacred sites, each holding a fragment of the planet's ancient song, each a lesson in its own right. The world was vast, and its guardians were many, but she was no longer alone in her quest to hear the deepest music of all.

The journey had been one of revelations, each encounter with the planet's song deepening Mara's understanding, yet also, she was beginning to realize, etching itself onto her very soul. The clear, pure notes of Kaelen's valley, the deep, resonant rumble of Aethelgard's slumber – these were not mere sounds. They were vibrations that resonated with her own being, awakening dormant pathways within her mind and spirit. But this awakening was not without its price. The world's song, once a distant murmur she struggled to decipher, was now an insistent, overwhelming symphony, and with its amplification came an unbearable sensitivity to its discord.

She found herself recoiling from the slightest tremor of distress in the land. A patch of wilting wildflowers by the roadside, their petals curling inwards like tiny, defeated fists, would send a sharp pang of sorrow through her. The frantic, panicked chirping of a flock of birds suddenly taking flight from a grove of trees, sensing an unseen threat, would echo in her own chest as a surge of pure, unadulterated fear. It was as if the very fabric of her being had become permeable, allowing the planet's suffering to seep in, unbidden and relentless.

This new awareness was a constant, gnawing ache. She remembered passing through a region recently ravaged by an Accord-sanctioned terraforming initiative. What had once been a thriving, verdant wetland, teeming with the calls of unseen amphibians and the whisper of reeds, was now a scarred expanse of churned earth and toxic runoff. Even from a distance, she could feel the lingering agony of the land, a psychic scream of violation that left her breathless and weak. The memory of the vibrant life that had once pulsed there was now overlaid with the stark, brutal silence of its demise. It was a silence that screamed louder than any noise.

The creatures, too, were a source of profound empathy. She encountered a family of indigenous foxes, their den discovered and subsequently destroyed by survey teams. The sheer terror radiating from the mother, her desperate, futile attempts to shield her kits, imprinted themselves on Mara's mind with an almost physical force. She felt the cold dread of the kits, their innocent lives abruptly extinguished, and it was as if a piece of her own heart had been torn away. She had tried to offer comfort, to project a sense of peace, but her own burgeoning distress only seemed to amplify their fear, a cruel irony that left her feeling utterly inadequate.

Kaelen had spoken of the "noise" of those who sought to understand but not connect, to control but not cherish. Mara now understood that the opposite could also be true: to connect too deeply, to cherish too fiercely, could lead to an unbearable burden. Her heightened senses were a double-edged sword. While they allowed her to perceive the subtle nuances of the planet's song, they also made her acutely vulnerable to its pain. The joy of hearing a hidden spring bubbling with life was now inextricably linked to the agony of witnessing a poisoned river flowing towards the sea.

This constant emotional and psychic onslaught was taking its toll. Sleep offered little respite, her dreams often populated by distorted echoes of the world's suffering. She would wake in a cold sweat, her mind a chaotic jumble of dying forests, displaced herds, and the silent screams of the earth. The energy she had once felt radiating from the planet now felt like a constant drain, pulling at her reserves, leaving her perpetually on the verge of exhaustion.

There were moments of profound doubt, of overwhelming despair. What was the point of listening if all she heard was pain? What good was her burgeoning sensitivity if it only served to amplify her own suffering? She found herself questioning the very essence of her journey, the wisdom of Kaelen and Aethelgard. Was she truly meant to be a conduit for the planet's song, or was she simply a fragile vessel about to shatter under its immense weight?

One evening, as she sat by a campfire, the flames casting dancing shadows on the ancient trees surrounding her, a wave of despair washed over her with particular intensity. She had spent the day near a region where the Accord's atmospheric processors were being deployed. The air, even miles away, tasted metallic and thin, and she could feel the subtle, yet sickening, disruption of the natural atmospheric currents. The birdsong in that area was muted, their calls strained, as if struggling to breathe. The very air seemed to weep.

She pressed her palms to her temples, trying to block out the cacophony of distress. "It's too much," she whispered, her voice raw with emotion. "I can't bear it. How can anyone bear this?"

The wooden bird Kaelen had given her, usually so responsive to resonant frequencies, remained silent in her pocket. It was as if even its delicate song was overwhelmed by the sheer weight of the world's sorrow.

She remembered Aethelgard's words: "The song is not a key to be found, but a state of being to be re-achieved. It is the natural order, the balance of give and take, of growth and decay." The dragon had also spoken of the need for discernment, for understanding how to amplify the pure notes and soothe the discordant ones. But how could she soothe when she herself was so deeply affected by the discord? How could she find the pure notes when the world seemed so saturated with pain?

The sacrifice, she realized, was not merely her time or her comfort, but a fundamental aspect of her own being. To truly listen was to open herself up to the entirety of the planet's experience, its beauty and its brutality, its moments of grace and its epochs of suffering. It demanded an acceptance of pain, not as something to be avoided or overcome, but as an inherent part of the grand, complex tapestry of life. It was the price of true stewardship, of becoming a guardian not just of the planet's health, but of its very soul.

Her sensitivity, she understood, was not a flaw, but a fundamental aspect of her calling. It was the lens through which she could perceive the world's true state. The challenge was not to shut it down, but to learn to manage its intensity, to find a way to process the overwhelming influx of sensation without being consumed by it. She had to learn to differentiate between the raw data of suffering and the underlying message, to find the resilience to continue listening even when the song was painful.

Mara shifted, reaching for her satchel, and pulled out a worn leather-bound journal. She opened it to a blank page, the faint scent of dried herbs and ink filling the air. She began to write, not a narrative of her journey, but a raw, unfiltered outpouring of her feelings, of the pain she had absorbed. She wrote of the dying wetland, of the terrified foxes, of the metallic taste of the polluted air. She poured her grief onto the page, her emotions raw and unvarnished.

As she wrote, she noticed a subtle shift. The act of externalizing her pain, of giving it form on the page, seemed to create a small, internal space, a quiet harbor within the storm. It was not a cure, not a complete silencing of the suffering, but a form of containment, a way of acknowledging and processing the overwhelming sensations. She was not denying the pain, but she was no longer letting it consume her entirely. She was observing it, cataloging it, understanding it.

This was a new facet of her journey, a crucial step in her development as a Listener. It was the understanding that listening was not a passive act of reception, but an active engagement with the world's complex emotional landscape. It required not only an open heart but also a resilient spirit, a capacity to absorb sorrow without being broken by it, to witness destruction and still hold onto the possibility of renewal.

She thought of the ancient trees Kaelen had described, their roots delving deep into the earth, their branches reaching for the stars. They weathered storms, endured droughts, and still they stood, their existence a testament to resilience and adaptation. They were not immune to hardship, but they possessed an intrinsic strength that allowed them to endure and to continue their silent, vital song.

Mara realized that her journey was not about finding a single, perfect melody, but about learning to navigate the entire symphony, its crescendos and its diminuendos, its harmonies and its dissonances. It was about finding the strength to continue listening, even when the music was heartbreaking, because within the sorrow, there were still threads of hope, glimmers of the planet's enduring resilience, waiting to be amplified. Her vulnerability was her strength, but it was a strength that demanded constant tending, a delicate balance of empathy and fortitude. The price of listening was high, but the reward – the potential for true understanding and eventual healing – was immeasurable. It was a path that would demand every ounce of her spirit, a constant dance between absorption and resilience, a testament to the profound and often painful cost of true connection.

The whispers of the world, once a subtle hum beneath Mara's awareness, had coalesced into a roaring tide, and in its powerful currents, the legend of the Sky-Wyrms began to surface. It wasn't a tale spun by village elders or etched in dusty tomes; rather, it was woven into the very song of the planet, a melody that had only recently begun to resonate with her awakened senses. Kaelen had spoken of their ancient guardianship, of their role as weavers of the atmospheric currents, but the fragmented narratives she'd gleaned from the planet's song offered a far more profound and intricate tapestry of their history.

She learned that the Sky-Wyrms, or Aeridons as they were known in the oldest strata of planetary memory, were not merely magnificent beasts of scale and wing. They were, in essence, the planet's breath made manifest. Their titanic forms were intrinsically linked to the atmospheric circulatory system, their roars echoing not with aggression, but with the primal forces that shaped the winds, guided the storms, and maintained the delicate equilibrium of the skies. Each beat of their colossal wings stirred currents unseen, vast rivers of air that carried moisture, dispersed heat, and scrubbed the nascent world of its toxic exhalations. They were the custodians of the ozone, the sculptors of cloud formations, the harbingers of life-giving rain and the purveyors of the cleansing gale. Their existence was not one of dominance, but of symbiotic stewardship, a partnership so ancient that it predated the rise of most terrestrial life.

The planet's song, when Mara allowed herself to truly immerse in its deeper frequencies, painted vivid images of a primordial world. It was a chaotic symphony of volcanic fury and nascent oceans, of nascent continents adrift in a turbulent atmosphere. It was in this crucible of creation that the Aeridons first emerged, not as creatures born of flesh and blood, but as living manifestations of the planet's will to stabilize, to create conditions conducive to life. Their origins were shrouded in the very genesis of the world, a testament to a time when the lines between spirit and matter, between the celestial and the terrestrial, were far more fluid. They were said to have sung the first skies into being, their resonant frequencies harmonizing the chaotic energies of the young atmosphere, weaving them into the protective embrace that would shield the burgeoning life below.

The lore suggested a singular, unified purpose in their ancient days. They were the Great Regulators, the sentient heart of the planet's atmospheric dance. Their existence was a testament to the power of collective will, for the legends spoke of them acting as one, a celestial choir whose harmony ensured the planet's nascent breath never faltered. There were no divisions, no schisms, only the unwavering dedication to their sacred charge. The planet's song echoed with the immense power and profound peace of this era, a time of perfect balance where the Aeridons moved in seamless concert, their every action a prayer for the world's flourishing.

But this era of unity, like the fleeting beauty of a perfectly formed cloud, was not destined to last. The song began to shift, a subtle dissonance creeping into its ancient harmonies, and with it came the first hints of the division that would define the Aeridons for millennia. The lore spoke of a primordial threat, an encroaching darkness that sought to unmake the very fabric of their world, a force that manifested not as a physical invader, but as a corrupting influence that preyed on the planet's raw, untamed energies. This threat, nameless and formless, was a disruption of the natural order, a perversion of the planet's song that sought to silence it entirely.

Faced with this existential crisis, a fundamental schism emerged within the Aeridons themselves. One faction, the Sky-Guardians, believed that the only way to combat this encroaching void was through direct, unwavering confrontation. They advocated for a more aggressive, proactive stance, a willingness to unleash the full, terrifying power of their atmospheric manipulation to obliterate the encroaching darkness. Their song became one of fierce determination, of unyielding resolve, a call to arms against the encroaching silence. They saw their role not just as regulators, but as defenders, willing to sacrifice anything, even their own equilibrium, to preserve the planet.

The other faction, the Whispering Winds, championed a different approach. They believed that the threat was not to be met with brute force, but with a subtler, more insidious form of resistance. They argued that by strengthening the planet's natural defenses, by fostering growth and resilience within the biosphere, they could ultimately starve the void of the chaotic energies it fed upon. Their philosophy centered on understanding, on nurturing, and on becoming so intrinsically woven into the planet's lifeblood that the darkness would find no purchase. Their song became one of gentle persuasion, of subtle redirection, a lullaby sung to the world to encourage its inherent strength. They saw themselves as healers, as nurturers, dedicated to fostering a harmonious balance that would ultimately repel the external threat.

This divergence in philosophy, born from the crucible of existential fear, led to a gradual separation. The Sky-Guardians, driven by their need for decisive action, began to congregate in the upper echelons of the atmosphere, their presence marked by dramatic displays of elemental power – the crackling of lightning, the roar of thunder. They became the storm-bringers, the architects of tempest, their influence felt in the raw, untamed power of the skies. They were the embodiment of the planet's raw, volatile energy, a force to be reckoned with.

The Whispering Winds, in contrast, descended to the lower altitudes, closer to the terrestrial life they sought to protect. Their influence was felt in the gentle breezes that stirred the leaves, the soft rains that nourished the earth, the subtle shifts in humidity that guided migratory patterns. They became the quiet custodians, their presence often felt more than seen, their song a constant, soothing presence that nurtured the planet's delicate life. They were the embodiment of the planet's nurturing embrace, a subtle but potent force for life.

Mara felt the echoes of this ancient conflict within the planetary song, a perpetual tension between the thunderous pronouncements of the Sky-Guardians and the soothing caress of the Whispering Winds. It was a duality that mirrored the planet's own nature – its capacity for cataclysmic upheaval and its profound ability to foster life and renewal. She began to understand that the current fragmentation of the Sky-Wyrms, their perceived aloofness and their often conflicting agendas, was not a sign of their inherent discord, but a deeply ingrained legacy of this ancient schism. They were not inherently at war with each other, but rather, they embodied different, yet equally vital, aspects of their original, unified purpose.

The Sky-Wyrms were not just creatures of myth and power; they were integral components of the planet's ecological and spiritual tapestry. Their very existence was tied to the song Mara was learning to hear, their ancient purpose a foundational pillar of the world's intricate systems. The lore, unearthed from the very vibrations of the earth and sky, revealed them as the primal architects of atmospheric harmony, their history a testament to a time when the lines between guardian and inhabitant, between the celestial and the terrestrial, were inextricably blurred. Their current division was not a betrayal of their origin, but a fractured echo of a desperate stand against a darkness that had long since receded, leaving behind a legacy of divergent paths, each still vital to the planet's continued existence. Mara realized that understanding this ancient dragon lore was not merely an academic pursuit; it was a fundamental key to deciphering the planet's current song and, perhaps, to helping it find its way back to a more unified, resonant harmony.

The air in the Whispering Grove hummed with a palpable energy, a subtle vibration that Mara felt not just in her ears, but in the very marrow of her bones. It was a place that had been whispered about in hushed tones by the few villagers who dared speak of it, a sanctuary rumored to possess a peculiar resonance, a place where the veil between the physical and the ethereal grew thin. Here, ancient trees, their bark gnarled like the faces of wise elders, formed a natural cathedral, their branches interlaced to create a dappled canopy that filtered the sunlight into a thousand shifting emerald shafts. The ground was a soft carpet of moss and fallen leaves, damp and fragrant, a testament to the ceaseless cycle of growth and decay. This was not just a grove; it was a living, breathing entity, a nexus of the planet's deepest melodies.

As Mara stepped further into its embrace, the cacophony of her own anxieties, the lingering echoes of Kaelen's warnings, and the fragmented whispers of the Aeridons began to recede. The planet's song, which had become a complex, often overwhelming symphony of voices and emotions, here began to coalesce. It wasn't a sudden silence, but a profound simplification, like a turbulent river finally finding its true, smooth course. The myriad individual notes, the soaring highs of the Sky-Guardians and the gentle murmurs of the Whispering Winds, the subtle frequencies of the earth and the rustling of leaves, all began to intertwine, not in conflict, but in a breathtakingly perfect accord.

She found herself drawn to the heart of the grove, where a single, colossal tree stood sentinel. Its trunk was wider than any dwelling, its roots plunging deep into the earth like anchors to the planet's core. At its base, a pool of water, impossibly clear, reflected the dappled sunlight, its surface undisturbed by the slightest ripple, a mirror to the sky and the surrounding foliage. It was here, kneeling beside the tranquil water, that the transformation truly began.

Mara closed her eyes, not to shut out the world, but to open herself more fully to its inner resonance. She breathed in the scent of damp earth, of ancient wood, of life and decay intertwined. And then, she listened. Not with her ears, but with her entire being. The constant, demanding chatter of her conscious mind, the relentless analysis of what she had heard and seen, fell away. In its place, a singular, pure tone emerged. It was the planet's original song, the primordial hum that had existed before the schism, before the whispers of fear and division had ever taken root.

It was a song of pure, unadulterated harmony. It was the steady, unyielding beat of a healthy heart, the gentle, consistent breath of a sleeping giant. It spoke of an equilibrium so profound, so naturally inherent, that it felt like coming home. The individual threads she had been struggling to untangle – the Sky-Guardians' fierce protection, the Whispering Winds' nurturing care, the ancient balance of the planet's systems – were no longer disparate elements. They were facets of a single, magnificent gem, each reflecting and enhancing the others.

The 'abyssal truth,' a concept Kaelen had spoken of with a mix of reverence and trepidation, began to reveal itself not as a terrifying void, but as the foundational bedrock of existence. It was the quiet, dark, fertile soil from which all life sprang, the silent expanse that gave definition to the stars. It was the primal stillness that allowed the song to emerge, the necessary emptiness that made resonance possible. This truth wasn't a thing to be feared, but a fundamental aspect of being, the ultimate source of all creation and renewal. The planet's song, in its purest form, was a constant affirmation of this truth, a testament to the enduring power of creation emerging from the stillness.

As Mara immersed herself in this state of profound communion, the weight that had settled upon her shoulders began to lift. The fear of the encroaching darkness, the burden of responsibility, the confusion of fragmented knowledge – it all dissolved in the radiant warmth of this unified resonance. She felt an immense sense of healing wash over her, not as a sudden cure, but as a gentle mending, like slow-growing moss reclaiming a weathered stone. The ancient energies of the grove, amplified by the planet's song, flowed through her, revitalizing every cell, calming every frayed nerve.

Images began to unfurl within her mind, not as fleeting visions, but as vivid, indelible impressions. She saw the Aeridons in their ancient, unified state, their colossal forms moving in synchronized ballet across the skies, their resonant songs weaving the very fabric of the atmosphere. She witnessed the primordial darkness, a suffocating absence of light and sound, and saw how the Aeridons, as one, had pushed it back, not by destroying it, but by filling the void with their own vibrant, life-affirming song. She understood that the 'darkness' wasn't an external enemy to be vanquished, but an inherent imbalance, a potential for entropy that the planet's own vital forces, amplified by the Aeridons, had always held in check.

The sacred grove, she realized, was a place where the planet's song was amplified, where the resonance of its original harmony was still powerfully present. The ancient trees were conduits, their roots drawing sustenance from the earth's deepest frequencies and their branches reaching towards the celestial symphony. The pool was a focal point, a lens through which the planet's essence could be perceived with unparalleled clarity. It was a place where the fragmented memories of the Aeridons' past, their divergent paths, and their ultimate shared purpose, coalesced into a singular, undeniable truth.

THE STORMBOUND DIVIDE

She saw that the current state of the Sky-Wyrms, their perceived disunity, was not a sign of their failure, but a testament to their resilience. They had each adapted to different facets of the planet's needs, a testament to the complexity of its ongoing creation. The Sky-Guardians, in their raw power, represented the planet's fierce defense against external threats, its capacity for cleansing storms and its untamed, elemental spirit. The Whispering Winds, in their gentle guidance, embodied the planet's nurturing embrace, its subtle mechanisms of growth and renewal, its deep connection to the biosphere. Both were essential. Neither could exist, or thrive, without the other, and both were integral to the planet's continued existence.

The 'abyssal truth' she now grasped was that true harmony wasn't the absence of duality, but the perfect integration of it. It was the understanding that light needed darkness to be perceived, that stillness was the canvas upon which sound could be painted, that life emerged from the very substance of death and decay. The planet's song, in its most fundamental form, was the constant, ongoing process of this integration. And the Aeridons, in their ancient purpose, were the living embodiment of this process, the cosmic choreographers of this eternal dance.

Mara felt a profound sense of clarity settle upon her. The path ahead, though still fraught with challenges, no longer seemed insurmountable. She understood now that her role was not to force the Sky-Wyrms back into a single, monolithic form, but to help them remember their shared song, to facilitate their understanding of how their individual melodies contributed to the greater symphony. She had to help them see that their division, born from a response to a primordial threat, had become a necessary adaptation, but that the fundamental unity of their purpose remained.

She saw the encroaching threat not as a singular, conquerable enemy, but as a pervasive imbalance, a subtle corruption of the planet's song that could only be countered by restoring and amplifying its inherent harmony. This imbalance fed on discord, on fear, on the very fragmentation that had afflicted the Aeridons. By helping them reconnect with their original purpose, by fostering their understanding of the 'abyssal truth' and the vital role of integration, she could help strengthen the planet's natural defenses. It was a battle fought not with steel or fire, but with resonance and understanding, with the power of a unified song.

The feeling of rejuvenation was not just emotional or spiritual; it was physical. Her senses, already heightened, seemed to expand. The colors of the grove became impossibly vibrant, the textures of the moss and bark astonishingly detailed. The air tasted sweeter, cleaner, filled with the subtle, vital energies she now recognized as the planet's lifeblood. She felt a deep well of strength replenishing her, a quiet resilience that seemed to emanate from the very earth beneath her. It was as if the planet itself was offering her a portion of its own enduring spirit.

As she slowly opened her eyes, the world seemed subtly altered. The sunlight filtering through the leaves was no longer just light; it was a visible manifestation of the planet's radiant energy. The gentle rustling of the leaves was a soft, melodic whisper, a continuation of the grand harmony she had experienced. The pool at the base of the great tree now seemed to pulse with a soft, inner light, reflecting not just the sky, but the very essence of the planet's song.

Mara understood that this moment of profound harmony was not an end, but a beginning. It was the crucible in which her purpose had been forged, the clarifying light that had illuminated her path. She had been given a glimpse of the planet's original song, a deep understanding of its inherent truth, and a vision of what needed to be protected: not just the surface beauty, but the intricate, interconnected symphony of life and energy that sustained it all. The trials ahead would undoubtedly be arduous, but she now carried within her the echo of that perfect harmony, a constant reminder of the world's inherent resilience and the power that lay in unity. The whispers of the world were no longer a source of confusion, but a guiding melody, and she, the Listener, was finally ready to truly play her part. The weight of the world had not been lifted, but it had been transformed, transmuted into a strength she never knew she possessed. She

THE STORMBOUND DIVIDE

stood, a conduit for the planet's deepest song, ready to face whatever lay beyond the whispering trees.

Chapter Seven
THE GUARDIAN'S GAMBIT

Cael Thornevale moved through the labyrinthine alleys of Havenwood like a phantom, a stark contrast to the imposing presence he'd once held as a commander in the Accord Cities' Zenith Guard. The muted grays and blues of his uniform, now devoid of insignia, blended with the shadows cast by the perpetually overcast sky that seemed to cling to this neutral territory. Havenwood was a city of quiet defiance, a collection of hardy souls who had opted out of the Accord's suffocating embrace, preferring self-governance and a cautious neutrality in the escalating planetary crisis. It was precisely this independent spirit that drew Cael here, a beacon in the encroaching darkness of rigid dogma.

His mandate, or rather, the ghost of it, still clung to him. Officially, he was on an extended reconnaissance mission, a convenient fiction spun by a few sympathetic superiors within the Accord's labyrinthine bureaucracy. Unofficially, he was a rogue agent, driven by a conviction that the Accord's current trajectory was not just misguided, but actively dangerous. Their unyielding focus on control, on imposing human solutions onto a crisis that was deeply rooted in the planet's very being, struck Cael as a profound arrogance. He had seen too much, heard too many hushed debates among his former peers, to ignore the growing unease. The whispers of dissent were not limited to the fringes; they echoed even within the gilded halls of power.

THE STORMBOUND DIVIDE

His first contact in Havenwood was an individual known only as Elara, a sharp-witted woman who ran a small, unassuming archive of pre-Accord knowledge. Her establishment was a haven for those seeking information beyond the curated narratives disseminated by the Accord. Cael found her amidst towering shelves of ancient scrolls and data-crystals, her fingers stained with ink, her eyes sharp and assessing as he approached.

"You're not from around here," she stated, her voice a low, musical rumble that held an undercurrent of weariness. "The scent of regulation clings to you, even here."

Cael offered a faint smile, a rare softening of his usually stern features. "And yet, I seek knowledge that falls outside its purview. I've heard you are a curator of forgotten truths, Elara."

She tilted her head, her gaze unwavering. "Forgotten, or deliberately buried? The Accord prefers its citizens to have selective memories." She gestured to a worn stool opposite her desk. "Sit. If you seek truths, you'll need to earn them. What is it you truly seek, Commander Thornevale? Or should I call you Cael?"

The directness surprised him. "Cael is sufficient. I seek an understanding of what lies beyond the Accord's pronouncements. I believe their approach to the planet's... imbalances... is flawed. Their solutions are too rigid, too focused on eradication rather than integration."

Elara's expression shifted, a flicker of something akin to recognition in her eyes. "Integration," she repeated, the word seeming to hold a particular weight for her. "A concept the Accord finds... inconvenient. They prefer clear-cut enemies and definitive victories. The planet, however, is far more nuanced." She leaned forward, her voice dropping conspiratorially. "You are not the first to question the Emperor's divine mandate. There are others, scattered across the neutral territories, even within the Accord itself, who feel the same unease. They see the growing ecological degradation, the erratic climatic shifts, the subtle discord in the very atmosphere, and they recognize it not as an alien invasion, but as a symptom of something far more fundamental."

This was exactly what Cael had hoped to hear. "Then you know of others who are open to... alternative strategies? Strategies that don't involve brute force and eradication?"

Elara chuckled, a dry, rustling sound. "Brute force is the Accord's primary language, Cael. But even they have pragmatic minds, those who understand that endless conflict is unsustainable. You'll find them in the outer settlements, those who have had to adapt to survive, those who live in closer proximity to the planet's natural cycles. And you'll find them among those who have borne the brunt of the Accord's heavy-handedness, the communities that have been marginalized or exploited in the name of progress."

She opened a hidden compartment beneath her desk, revealing a small, intricately carved wooden bird. "This is a signal. If you encounter someone who speaks of the 'Threefold Path' or the 'Whispers of the Deep,' they are with us. Or rather, they are with the idea of balance. Give them this. It will speak for itself. But be warned, Cael. You are treading a dangerous path. The Accord's reach is long, and their paranoia deeper still."

Leaving Havenwood, Cael carried not just the small wooden bird, but a renewed sense of purpose. His next destination was the Sunken Marshes, a vast, largely untamed region known for its unique ecosystem and its fiercely independent inhabitants. The Accord rarely ventured there, finding its convoluted waterways and unpredictable flora more trouble than it was worth. It was a place where survival depended on understanding the rhythms of the land, not on imposing one's will upon it.

His contact in the Marshes was a former Accord botanist, Dr. Aris Thorne, a distant cousin whose name he shared and whose dedication to the planet's living systems had led to his exile from the Accord scientific elite. Aris had become a recluse, living in a bio-dome constructed from local materials, painstakingly cataloging the endemic flora and fauna, and observing the subtle shifts in the planet's vital energies.

Cael navigated his skiff through the murky, sinuous channels, the air thick with the scent of decay and vibrant growth. The Sunken Marshes were a testament to the planet's resilience, a riot of life that thrived in conditions the Accord deemed inhospitable. As he approached Aris's bio-dome, a figure emerged, draped in woven reeds and adorned with luminescent fungi. It was Aris, his face etched with the wisdom of years spent in quiet observation, his eyes holding the same cautious intelligence Cael had found in Elara.

"Cael," Aris said, his voice a soft murmur, barely audible above the symphony of insect hums and the gentle lapping of water. "I received your signal. A bold move, coming so deep into neutral territory."

"The need is great, Aris," Cael replied, stepping onto the dew-kissed platform. "The Accord's approach is... unsustainable. They seek to control what they do not understand."

Aris nodded, a slow, deliberate movement. "They see the planet as a machine to be repaired, rather than an organism to be healed. I've spent decades studying the symbiotic relationships here, the delicate balance that allows life to flourish in what the Accord dismisses as 'wasteland.' They fail to grasp that these 'wastelands' are, in fact, the planet's immune system, its adaptive capacity."

He led Cael into the bio-dome, a humid, verdant sanctuary filled with exotic plants and the gentle glow of bioluminescent organisms. "I've observed patterns, Cael. Shifts in the planetary resonance that correlate with the Accord's increasing exploitation of natural resources. They're not just damaging the environment; they're actively disrupting the planet's innate song, the very harmony that sustains it."

"That's precisely what I believe," Cael said, his voice gaining intensity. "Mara, the Listener, she has experienced this harmony. She understands the 'abyssal truth' – that balance is found not in eliminating duality, but in integrating it. The Accord sees only the threats, the imbalances to be corrected, but they fail to see that these are often natural cycles, amplified by their own interference."

Aris gestured to a complex holographic display showing intricate energy patterns. "My research aligns with this. I've detected a growing dissonance, a kind of planetary fever. The Accord's attempts to 'stabilize' regions are often akin to applying a tourniquet to a wound that needs to breathe. They stifle natural processes, creating greater long-term instability. I've been secretly documenting this, compiling evidence that could, perhaps, be presented to... more open minds."

"That is why I am here, Aris," Cael said, producing the wooden bird. "Elara in Havenwood gave me this. She believes there are others, disillusioned Accord officials, neutral settlements, even some among the Skybound Conclave, who are open to a different path. A path of balance, not subjugation."

Aris took the bird, turning it over in his hands, a look of quiet understanding dawning on his face. "The Threefold Path... I know of it. It speaks of acknowledging the destructive, the creative, and the preservative aspects of existence, and finding harmony in their interconnectedness. I've heard whispers of it from those who travel the less-traveled routes, those who trade in both goods and secrets."

"Then you are willing to help?" Cael pressed. "To share your knowledge, to connect me with those who might listen?"

Aris met his gaze, his eyes reflecting the soft glow of the bio-dome. "My life's work has been dedicated to understanding this planet. If my knowledge can contribute to a future where it is not merely exploited but revered, then I will." He reached for a nearby comm-unit, a discreet device built into the wall. "There is a delegation from the Elderwood Enclave arriving tomorrow. They are custodians of ancient forests, deeply attuned to the planet's rhythms. They have had their own grievances with the Accord's expansionist policies. They might be receptive."

THE STORMBOUND DIVIDE

The mention of the Skybound Conclave, the enigmatic and often reclusive dragon factions, sent a shiver of cautious optimism through Cael. For years, any interaction with them had been strictly regulated, governed by protocols of extreme caution and suspicion. The Accord viewed them as volatile, dangerous entities, best managed through deterrence and isolation. But Cael had encountered enough evidence, seen enough of their actions, to know that their nature was far more complex than the Accord's simplistic categorization allowed. There were factions, individuals, who sought coexistence, who understood the delicate balance of the planet's ecosystems as well as any human scholar.

His next move was to seek out a representative of the Aeridons, the great winged beings who were the closest thing the planet had to ancient guardians. It was a risky endeavor. The Accord maintained a strict no-contact policy with most of the higher dragon species, fearing their power and unpredictability. But Cael believed that if any faction could offer a bridge between the Accord's rigid agenda and the planet's true needs, it would be those who had witnessed millennia of planetary change.

He found himself in the treacherous, wind-swept peaks of the Dragon's Tooth mountains, a region known for its volatile weather patterns and the territorial nature of its inhabitants. He traveled under a cloak of invisibility, a piece of Accord technology he'd salvaged, designed to mask his presence from both technological and certain biological sensors. His target was a secluded aerie rumored to be occupied by a member of the Skybound Conclave, a younger dragon named Zephyr, known for his unusual curiosity about the lesser species and his reluctance to engage in the traditional isolationism of his kind.

The ascent was grueling, the air thin and biting cold. The jagged peaks seemed to claw at the sky, a testament to the raw, untamed power of this part of the world. Cael's breathing grew ragged, but his resolve remained firm. He finally reached a high plateau, a windswept expanse overlooking a breathtaking panorama of snow-capped mountains and swirling clouds. Perched on a massive, ice-encrusted spire was Zephyr, his scales a shimmering iridescence of azure and silver, catching the weak sunlight like a thousand scattered jewels.

Cael deactivated his invisibility, stepping out into the open, his heart pounding a relentless rhythm against his ribs. Zephyr's massive head turned, his golden eyes, ancient and intelligent, locking onto Cael. A low rumble, a sound that vibrated through the very rock beneath Cael's feet, emanated from the dragon's chest. It was not a roar of aggression, but a sound of questioning, of ancient power held in check.

"A fragile one," Zephyr's voice echoed in Cael's mind, a resonant, multi-layered sound that bypassed his ears and spoke directly to his consciousness. "You trespass in my domain, yet you carry no overt malice. Why do you seek me, human?"

Cael stood his ground, his voice steady, though he could feel the immense power radiating from the dragon. "I am Cael Thornevale, once of the Zenith Guard. I come not as an agent of the Accord, but as one who seeks a different path. I believe your kind, and mine, are on a collision course, driven by a misunderstanding of the planet's true nature."

Zephyr lowered his head slightly, his gaze never wavering. "The planet sings a song of imbalance, human. Your kind attempts to silence it, to impose a forced harmony that cracks under its own weight. We... observe."

"But observation is not enough," Cael pressed, his conviction growing stronger. "The Accord's rigid doctrines are blinding them to the planet's needs. They see only threats to be eliminated, not intricacies to be understood. I am seeking to forge new alliances, to build a coalition that values balance and integration over blind enforcement. I believe your wisdom, your perspective as a being who has witnessed centuries of change, is crucial."

Zephyr let out a gust of icy air that whipped around Cael. "We have seen empires rise and fall. We have seen species bloom and wither. The song of the planet is complex, and your Accord hears only the discordant notes, not the underlying melody. You speak of alliances, but what can a fragile species like yours offer?"

"Understanding," Cael stated firmly. "A willingness to listen. The Listener, Mara, she has perceived the planet's true song, its need for integration. I seek to bridge the gap between those who seek control and those who understand the necessity of coexistence. Your kind has the power, the wisdom, and the longevity to offer a perspective that transcends human squabbles. There are factions within the Skybound Conclave, are there not, who also see the folly of isolation and the danger of inaction?"

Zephyr was silent for a long moment, the wind whistling around them like a mournful chorus. Then, he spoke again, his voice softer, more contemplative. "There are... whispers. Of dragons who believe the great song of the world is fading, not because of external forces, but because of internal division. They fear that if the harmony is lost, all will be consumed by the Silence. You speak of an uncommon understanding, human. If you can prove your sincerity, if you can demonstrate that you seek not to control, but to facilitate, then perhaps... perhaps the Skybound Conclave can listen."

He nudged a small, metallic object towards Cael with his snout. It was a crystalline shard, humming with faint, internal light. "This is a key. Not to a lock, but to a communication channel. It will allow you to send a message to those within my Conclave who are... open to discourse. But understand this, Thornevale: trust is a rare commodity between our species. You walk a treacherous path, and the consequences of failure will be severe, not just for you, but for all who dare to believe in a different way."

With the crystalline shard safely secured, Cael began his descent, the weight of his new mission settling upon him. He was no longer just a rogue agent; he was a nascent diplomat, a weaver of disparate threads, tasked with the seemingly impossible: to forge a coalition from the fractured pieces of a world teetering on the brink. The Accord cities, with their sterile order and authoritarian pronouncements, represented one extreme. The wild, untamed regions and the ancient, powerful beings of the planet represented another. His task was to find the space between, the fertile ground where understanding could take root and a new, more balanced song could begin to play. The journey ahead would be fraught with peril, but for the first time since his disillusionment began, Cael Thornevale felt a flicker of true hope. He was not alone in his quest for a different future.

The crystalline shard pulsed with a faint, internal luminescence, a silent testament to the precarious alliance Cael was attempting to forge. It was a conduit, Zephyr had explained, not to a physical location, but to a specific nexus of consciousness within the Skybound Conclave – a place where fragmented thoughts and ancient wisdom coalesced, accessible only to those deemed worthy, or perhaps, desperate enough. Cael sat in the comparative quiet of a sheltered alcove carved into the mountain's flank, the wind's howl now a distant murmur. He held the shard, its cool surface a counterpoint to the warmth of his palm, and focused his intent, channeling the hope that had been rekindled by his encounters.

His network, a fragile web woven from desperate individuals and disillusioned factions, had been diligently feeding him fragments of information, each piece a vital clue in the grand, terrifying mosaic of the planet's imminent fate. Elara, in her Havenwood archive, had managed to intercept a series of coded transmissions originating from within the Accord's outer administrative sectors. These weren't mere logistical updates; they spoke of accelerated resource extraction from the planet's deep crust, a process far more invasive and environmentally disruptive than officially acknowledged. The euphemism used was "geothermal stabilization," but the raw data pointed towards a desperate attempt to tap into the planet's core energy reserves, a move that Aris Thorne had warned would be akin to drawing blood from a dying heart.

Aris, too, had contributed invaluable intelligence. His bio-dome, a sanctuary of delicate ecosystems, had become a listening post for the planet's subtler vibrations. He'd detected an anomaly, a significant escalation in the "planetary fever" he'd been monitoring. It wasn't merely an increase in atmospheric anomalies or seismic unrest. It was a specific, targeted surge of chaotic energy emanating from a series of previously unknown Accord research outposts, scattered across the planet's most ecologically sensitive regions. These weren't merely research stations; they were active weaponization sites, attempting to harness and weaponize the planet's own volatile energies. Aris had managed to decrypt partial schematics that spoke of "resonance disruptors" and "bio-harmonic nullifiers" – instruments designed not to stabilize, but to shatter the planet's natural frequencies, rendering vast swathes of its biosphere inert. The Accord, it seemed, was not just trying to control the planet; they were preparing to break it.

But the most disturbing intelligence came from a source deep within the Accord's military apparatus, a hesitant informant known only as "Whisper." Whisper had confirmed Cael's gravest fears regarding the Accord's escalation. Not only were they developing terraforming and terra-destruction technologies, but they were actively pursuing a strategy of preemptive eradication of any potential threats, including indigenous species that possessed even a semblance of sentience or unique bio-energetic capabilities. Whisper's reports detailed the "Zero-Sum Protocol," a classified directive that prioritized the elimination of all non-human sentient life forms within Accord-controlled territories, a grim foreshadowing of their intentions towards the dragon factions and other powerful beings. The directive also spoke of a secret weapon, codenamed "Apex," capable of projecting a planetary-wide wave of bio-energetic suppression, effectively silencing any biological life that wasn't part of the Accord's engineered ecosystem. This was the ultimate expression of their control-obsessed agenda: a sterile, silent planet, subservient to their will.

The intelligence regarding the dragon factions, however, painted a more complex and volatile picture. Zephyr's initial hesitancy was not unfounded. The Skybound Conclave, while ancient and powerful, was far from monolithic. Cael had received fragmented reports of escalating tensions between different dragon clans. The Azure Serpents, known for their territorial aggression and their deep-seated animosity towards all "ground-dwellers," were reportedly amassing forces near the Accord's northernmost fortifications. Their motives were unclear, but their historical animosity towards the Accord, fueled by past transgressions and territorial disputes, was a potent force.

Conversely, there were whispers of a more isolationist faction, the Obsidian Drakes, who seemed content to weather the storm from their remote volcanic fortresses, believing that the planet's natural cataclysms would eventually purge all external threats. However, a smaller, more radical splinter group within the Obsidian Drakes, known as the "Cinder Scythes," were allegedly embracing a more aggressive stance, advocating for preemptive strikes against Accord installations that encroached upon their ancestral lands. Their methods were said to be brutal and efficient, leaving behind only scorched earth and chilling silence.

Adding another layer of complexity, Cael had received a cryptic message from an anonymous source within the Elderwood Enclave, the ancient forest guardians. They spoke of a growing "shadow" within the dragon factions, an unseen influence that seemed to be exacerbating the existing tensions. This "shadow" was reportedly encouraging conflict, subtly manipulating the dragons' innate primal instincts and fanning the flames of ancient grudges. The Elderwood Enclave suspected this influence was not organic, but rather a calculated external manipulation, designed to keep the powerful dragon factions preoccupied and divided, preventing them from uniting against the larger threat posed by the Accord. The implication was chilling: if the dragons were too busy fighting each other, they would be unable to defend themselves, or the planet, when the Accord's ultimate weapon was unleashed.

Cael felt a knot of urgency tighten in his gut. The intelligence painted a grim, multi-front war. The Accord was not just a military power; they were a force of ecological and biological annihilation, armed with terrifying technologies and a chillingly pragmatic, ruthless agenda. Their "Zero-Sum Protocol" and the "Apex" weapon represented a direct existential threat to all life that did not conform to their vision of a perfectly controlled world. This was not a war of attrition; it was a war for the very soul of the planet.

THE STORMBOUND DIVIDE

He channeled a mental query through the crystalline shard, focusing on the concept of a unified front, of disparate powers finding common ground against a common enemy. He pictured Zephyr's ancient, wise eyes, Aris's gentle dedication, Elara's sharp intellect, and the shadowy presence of Whisper, all disparate elements converging towards a shared purpose. He projected the information he had gathered: the Accord's true capabilities, their horrifying weaponry, their plans for planetary subjugation, and the insidious manipulation of the dragon factions. He emphasized the shared danger, the undeniable reality that an Accord victory would mean the end of not just human dominance, but of all free life on the planet.

The shard vibrated in his hand, a subtle warmth spreading through his fingers. He felt a faint echo in his mind, a whisper of ancient awareness, a flicker of acknowledgement. It was not an immediate promise of alliance, but it was a response. The messages were being received, the gravity of the situation was being considered. The Skybound Conclave, at least a portion of it, was beginning to understand the true nature of the threat.

The intelligence confirmed the perilous path Cael was treading. Diplomacy was crucial, but it was a race against time. The Accord's progress was relentless, their technology advancing at an alarming pace. The fractured nature of the dragon factions, exploited by unseen forces, presented a significant obstacle. He needed to not only convince these ancient beings of the Accord's ultimate danger but also to help them overcome their internal divisions, to see the larger tapestry of existence that was being threatened.

He knew that simply presenting the grim facts might not be enough. The dragons, particularly the more aggressive factions, often responded to displays of power, to demonstrable strength and unwavering conviction. He needed to offer them more than just a plea for unity; he needed to offer them a vision of a future where coexistence was not just possible, but necessary for survival. He needed to appeal to their ancient guardianship, their role as stewards of the planet, a role that was being fundamentally undermined by the Accord's hubris.

Cael contemplated his next move. The crystalline shard was a key, but it was only the first step. He needed to leverage the connections he had forged. Aris could provide scientific data and evidence of the Accord's ecological destruction, solidifying the argument with irrefutable proof. Elara could help decipher any further transmissions, uncovering more of the Accord's hidden strategies and weaknesses. And Whisper... Whisper remained his most dangerous, yet vital, link within the Accord's inner circle. The continued flow of information from Whisper was paramount, offering insights into the Accord's internal politics, their resource allocation, and potential vulnerabilities in their command structure.

He also recognized the need to engage with other disenfranchised groups. The settlements on the fringes of Accord territory, those who had suffered the brunt of Accord expansion and exploitation, would have their own grievances and insights. They were the first-hand witnesses to the Accord's cruelty and inefficiency. Their stories, their experiences, could serve as powerful testimonials, adding weight to his arguments for an alternative future.

The sheer scope of the challenge was overwhelming. He was a single human, armed with little more than his conviction and a growing network of unlikely allies, facing down a planetary-scale empire. Yet, the intelligence he had gathered also revealed glimmers of hope. The Accord, for all its power, was not invincible. Its rigid adherence to doctrine, its arrogance, its fear of the unknown, were all potential weaknesses. And the planet itself, with its deep, inherent resilience and its complex web of life, was a force to be reckoned with.

Cael looked out at the jagged peaks, the swirling clouds, the vast expanse of the planet stretching out before him. The wind carried the scent of ice and distant forests, a wild, untamed perfume that spoke of life in its most raw, fundamental state. He understood, with a clarity that chilled him to the bone, that this was not just a war for control, but a war for the very essence of existence. The Accord sought to impose a sterile, ordered reality, devoid of the wildness and unpredictability that made life vibrant and meaningful. They aimed to silence the planet's song, to replace it with the monotonous hum of their own absolute authority.

He knew that the path ahead would demand not only strategic maneuvering and diplomatic finesse but also a deep well of courage and sacrifice. The intelligence confirmed the escalating conflicts, the hidden agendas, and the terrifying potential of the Accord's arsenal. But it also revealed the possibility of an unprecedented alliance, a coalition of diverse species and factions united by a common threat and a shared desire for balance. The guardian's gambit was in motion, a dangerous play for the soul of the world, and Cael Thornevale was at its heart, ready to gamble everything for a chance at a future where the planet could sing its own song, unhindered and unafraid. The next step was to translate this intelligence into tangible action, to turn these whispers of discord and danger into a unified roar of resistance.

Cael traced the intricate, almost organic patterns etched into the crystalline shard, the faint warmth of it seeping into his palm. It was a tangible link, a fragile thread connecting him to a consciousness far vaster than his own, a consciousness he had once sworn to uphold, to protect within the rigid framework of Accord law. Now, that very framework felt like a cage, its once-sacred tenets twisted into instruments of subjugation. His internal monologue was a battlefield, a chaotic clash between the ingrained dogma of his upbringing and the stark, irrefutable truths he had uncovered. The Accord, the very entity he had served, was not a guardian of order, but a rapacious force intent on silencing the vibrant, untamed symphony of the planet.

He remembered the hushed halls of the Accord Academy, the austere pronouncements of planetary custodianship, the carefully curated histories that painted humanity as the natural stewards, destined to bring order to a chaotic world. He had believed it, with the unwavering conviction of youth. He had internalized the doctrine of benevolent control, the necessity of pruning the wild, unpredictable elements to cultivate a stable, prosperous future. But the "pruning" he now understood was more akin to a brutal amputation, a systematic eradication of life itself. The very principles he had sworn to uphold were now the foundation of a monstrous agenda, and the chilling irony was not lost on him. He was the product of their system, a finely honed tool now turned against its creators.

The weight of his former allegiance pressed down on him, a suffocating blanket woven from guilt and a deep-seated sense of betrayal. He had friends, colleagues, within the Accord – individuals who, like him, had believed in its promise of a better tomorrow. Were they complicit? Or were they, too, blindfolded, marching towards the precipice alongside him? The thought of exposing them, of shattering their carefully constructed reality, was a bitter pill to swallow. He pictured Commander Valerius, his former mentor, a man whose stern visage was softened only by the genuine care he showed his cadets. Valerius, with his unwavering belief in the Accord's divine right, would see Cael's actions as treason of the highest order. The very word, "treason," echoed in the silent chambers of his mind, a judgment he now had to embrace.

This internal conflict was the true war, a silent, agonizing battle waged within the confines of his own soul. The intelligence he gathered – the schematics of the resonance disruptors, the whispers of the Zero-Sum Protocol, the chilling reports of the Apex weapon – were not merely external threats; they were existential crises that forced him to confront the core of his own being. What was order, if it meant the silencing of a world? What was progress, if it led to a sterile, lifeless dominion? He was no longer just a soldier, or a strategist; he was a moral arbiter, forced to weigh the lives of countless beings against the deeply ingrained loyalties of his past.

The allure of power, he knew, was a seductive siren song. The Accord offered a path to absolute control, a vision of a perfectly orchestrated existence. He had seen its appeal firsthand, witnessed the fervent devotion of its adherents, felt the intoxicating pull of its seemingly unshakeable authority. And in his darkest moments, a flicker of understanding, a dangerous empathy, would surface. He could see how one might rationalize such a path, how the desire for safety and predictability could outweigh the messy, unpredictable beauty of life. But he also saw the fundamental flaw: that true order could not be imposed; it had to be cultivated, grown from a place of respect and understanding, not brute force and subjugation.

The burden of command, even in its nascent stages, was a heavy one. He was no longer just responsible for his own actions; he was responsible for the actions of those who now looked to him for guidance, for hope. Zephyr, the ancient dragon, whose wisdom was as vast as the skies, and Aris, whose gentle hands nurtured life in his bio-dome, and Elara, whose sharp mind could dissect any deception – they all placed their trust in him. And Whisper, the shadowy informant, who risked everything for a glimpse of a different future. Their faith was a powerful motivator, but also a source of profound anxiety. A single misstep, a single lapse in judgment, could have devastating consequences, not just for him, but for them, and for the world they were fighting to save.

He thought of the potential betrayals he might have to orchestrate, the fragile alliances he might have to fracture. The Azure Serpents, with their volatile tempers and deep-seated hatred for Accord expansion, might see his overtures as a weakness, an opportunity for further aggression. The Obsidian Drakes, in their aloof isolation, might dismiss his pleas as the ramblings of a doomed human. He had to navigate not only the Accord's machinations but also the volatile, often inscrutable, politics of the planet's ancient inhabitants. Each interaction was a tightrope walk, a delicate dance between persuasion and pragmatism.

There were moments, in the quiet solitude of his mountain alcove, when the sheer impossibility of his task threatened to crush him. The Accord was a colossal, entrenched power, its tendrils reaching into every facet of planetary governance. Its military might was undeniable, its technological advancements terrifying. He was a lone wolf, a rogue agent, armed with little more than his conviction and a fragile network of unlikely allies. Doubt would creep in, whispering insidious thoughts of surrender, of finding a hidden corner of the world to disappear into, to simply outlast the storm. But then he would remember the faces of the people he had met, the hope that had flickered in their eyes, the nascent understanding that had bloomed when he spoke of a different path. He would remember the planet itself, its magnificent, defiant wildness, its inherent right to exist in its own chaotic, beautiful complexity.

His moral compass, once so clearly defined by Accord doctrine, was now a swirling, uncertain entity, battered by the winds of necessity. He had to be willing to make difficult choices, to tread in morally grey areas. Was it justifiable to manipulate the dragons' innate instincts, even if it was for their own good? Was it acceptable to exploit the Accord's internal rivalries, to sow discord among their ranks, even if it meant risking unintended consequences? These were not the clear-cut decisions of battlefield tactics; these were the agonizing compromises of a leader fighting a war for the very soul of existence.

He recalled a conversation with Aris, in the lush, verdant confines of the bio-dome. Aris, with his quiet intensity, had spoken of the interconnectedness of all life, of how the smallest organism played a vital role in the grand tapestry. "We are not meant to be the sole weavers, Cael," he had said, his voice soft but firm. "We are part of the pattern, not the designers of it. The Accord believes they can redraw the blueprint. They are fools." Cael had held onto those words, letting them anchor him against the rising tide of despair. The Accord's obsession with control stemmed from a fundamental misunderstanding of life itself. They sought to impose a sterile, predictable order, a rigid uniformity that would inevitably lead to stagnation and death. True order, he was beginning to understand, was a dynamic balance, a constant dance of adaptation and evolution.

The thought of his own past actions, the times he had enforced Accord directives without question, now sent a tremor of shame through him. Had he, in his ignorance, contributed to the very destruction he now fought against? Had he, through his obedience, silenced voices that deserved to be heard? The guilt was a bitter draught, but he forced himself to drink it, to let it fuel his resolve rather than paralyze him. He couldn't undo the past, but he could dedicate himself to building a different future, a future where such ignorance would no longer be tolerated, where the echoes of life would not be silenced by the iron fist of imposed order.

THE STORMBOUND DIVIDE

He closed his eyes, the cool air of the mountain biting at his exposed skin. He projected his intent through the shard, not as a plea for help, but as a declaration of intent. He would not be swayed by the Accord's promises of order, nor by the allure of their power. He would forge his own path, however perilous, however morally ambiguous. He would champion the wild, the untamed, the fiercely beautiful chaos that was the essence of the planet. His duty was no longer to uphold a corrupt system, but to dismantle it, to shatter the illusion of control and reclaim the planet's right to sing its own song, in all its glorious, untamed complexity. The guardian's gambit was not just about survival; it was about redemption, for himself, and for the world he had once served with such misguided loyalty. The fight for his own moral integrity was as crucial as the fight against the Accord, for without it, he would simply become another architect of destruction, cloaked in the guise of order.

The biting wind whipped strands of Cael's dark hair across his face, each gust carrying the scent of pine and the distant, metallic tang of snowmelt. He adjusted the coarse weave of his cloak, the roughspun wool a stark contrast to the sleek, manufactured fabrics he had once worn as a matter of course. Below him, the valley lay shrouded in mist, a deceptive veil that hid the volatile tensions simmering beneath its surface. His destination was a jagged promontory, a place known only to a select few, where the earth split open to reveal veins of raw, unrefined energy. It was here, in this liminal space, that he was to meet Elara's contact, a representative of the Skybound Conclave, a faction as elusive as the wind and as ancient as the mountains themselves.

The journey had been arduous, a silent trek through treacherous terrain, each step a testament to the fragile hope he now carried. He had left behind the relative safety of his mountain alcove, the comforting hum of Zephyr's ancient presence, and the reassuring logic of Aris's bio-dome. This was a solo endeavor, a calculated risk born of Elara's intelligence. She had intercepted a fragmented communication, a whisper on the digital winds, suggesting a potential opening, a willingness from a certain sect within the Conclave to consider a cessation of hostilities, a tentative dialogue. It was a slim chance, a thread so fine it could snap at the slightest tremor, but it was the only thread he had.

His heart hammered a nervous rhythm against his ribs, a counterpoint to the steady crunch of his boots on the frozen earth. He was not a diplomat by nature. His training had been in strategy, in the swift, decisive application of force, in the cold, hard logic of Accord doctrine. But the Accord had twisted those very principles, perverting them into tools of oppression. Now, he had to unlearn everything he knew, to embrace a new kind of warfare – the war of words, of trust, of fragile understanding. He had to become something he had never envisioned: a bridge builder, a negotiator, a purveyor of peace in a world teetering on the brink of annihilation.

He reached the crest of the final ascent, the wind howling with a ferocity that seemed to mirror the turmoil within him. The promontory jutted out like a broken tooth, its sheer faces scarred by millennia of elemental battering. A single, gnarled pine clung precariously to its side, its branches clawing at the sky. And there, silhouetted against the bruised twilight sky, was a figure. They stood utterly still, cloaked in dark, flowing robes that seemed to absorb the fading light. The air around them shimmered with a subtle energy, a manifestation of the Conclave's innate connection to the planet's atmospheric currents.

As Cael approached, the figure turned. Beneath the cowl, he saw not the hardened features of a warrior, but the serene, ageless face of an elder. Their eyes, the color of a stormy sky, held a depth of wisdom that both humbled and unnerved him. There was no visible weapon, no outward show of aggression, yet Cael felt a palpable sense of power emanating from them, a power rooted not in force, but in an intrinsic understanding of the world's delicate equilibrium.

"You are Cael," the figure stated, their voice a low, resonant hum that seemed to vibrate through the very rock beneath their feet. It was not a question.

"I am," Cael replied, his own voice a little rough from the cold and the tension. He kept his hands visible, palms open, a gesture of disarming intent. "And you are the one Elara spoke of?"

"I am Lyra, of the Skybound Conclave," the elder confirmed, their gaze unwavering. "You have come a long way, Human. Risked much, I imagine."

"The risk is necessary," Cael said, stepping closer. "The Accord's reach is growing. Their control tightens with every passing cycle. If we do not find a way to stand together, to resist, then all will be lost. Not just humanity, but the planet itself."

Lyra tilted their head, a subtle movement that conveyed a universe of contemplation. "You speak of standing together, yet your species has brought ruin to so many lands. Your Accord, as you call it, seeks to impose order through eradication. Why should we trust your words now, when your actions have consistently spoken of conquest?"

The question was direct, unvarnished, and entirely justified. Cael's resolve wavered for a fraction of a second, the weight of his species' transgressions pressing down on him. He had no easy answers, no eloquent speeches to offer. All he had was the truth, as he understood it.

"Because," Cael began, choosing his words carefully, "there are those among us who see the folly of our ways. There are those who recognize that true strength lies not in dominance, but in symbiosis. The Accord's vision is one of sterile uniformity, a world scrubbed clean of its natural vibrancy. That is not progress, Lyra. That is death disguised as order."

He saw a flicker in Lyra's eyes, a subtle shift that suggested his words had struck a chord. "You believe this? Truly?"

"I believe that the planet's wildness, its untamed spirit, is not a flaw to be corrected, but a strength to be revered," Cael said, his voice gaining conviction. "The Accord fears what it cannot control. They seek to cage the storms, to silence the songs of the deep, to erase the very essence of what makes this world alive. And in doing so, they are destroying themselves as well. Their path leads to a barren, lifeless dominion."

Lyra remained silent for a long moment, their gaze sweeping across the mist-shrouded valley, as if searching for answers in the swirling vapor. "The Conclave has watched your Accord's expansion with growing unease. The disruption to the atmospheric currents, the silencing of the earth's song... it is a sickness that spreads. But we are divided. Many of my kin believe your kind is beyond redemption. They see only the destruction, the relentless march of your technology."

"And what do you believe, Lyra?" Cael pressed, his hope rekindling.

"I believe," Lyra said, their voice dropping to a near whisper, "that even the most destructive storms eventually pass. And that sometimes, in the aftermath of devastation, new life finds a way to bloom." They gestured with a slender, elegant hand towards the vast expanse of the sky. "We are the guardians of the winds, the watchers of the skies. We see the patterns, the interconnectedness of all things. Your Accord's actions are a violent disruption of those patterns. They sow discord, and discord breeds chaos."

"Then we must find a way to restore harmony," Cael urged. "The Accord is developing a weapon, a device that can disrupt the very essence of life's resonance. They call it the Apex. If they succeed, it will not just silence dissent; it will silence the planet itself. It will be an end to all that is wild, all that is free."

Lyra's eyes widened, a rare display of emotion. "The Apex... We have sensed whispers of such a cataclysmic force. A weapon that could unravel the very fabric of existence." They looked at Cael, their gaze now piercing, scrutinizing. "Why should we, the Skybound, lend our strength to your cause? Your people have little respect for the air and sky, only for the earth they can conquer and the resources they can exploit."

"Because," Cael said, his voice steady, "the Accord's final objective is not just control of the land, but of the very elements that sustain life. They seek to command the winds, to extinguish the fires, to drain the waters.

They see the natural world as a resource to be managed, not a partner to be respected. If they succeed, the skies will not be free, Lyra. They will be policed. The winds will be channeled, the storms suppressed, all life reduced to a predictable, sterile hum. Is that the future your Conclave wishes to see?"

The silence stretched between them, filled only by the mournful cry of the wind. Cael felt exposed, vulnerable, laying bare the desperate hope that had driven him here. He had offered no proof, only words. But in Lyra's ancient eyes, he saw a dawning comprehension, a recognition of the existential threat that transcended the animosity between their species.

"The Skybound have always valued balance," Lyra finally said. "We abhor imbalance. The Accord's ambition is the ultimate imbalance. They seek to homogenize the world, to erase its magnificent diversity. That is a path that leads only to stagnation and decay. We have always believed that true order arises from the interplay of forces, not their suppression."

"Then there is a possibility," Cael seized upon the glimmer of hope. "A possibility for cooperation. The dragons, the creatures of the earth, even some factions within humanity – we are all threatened by the Accord's unchecked ambition."

Lyra nodded slowly. "The Azure Serpents have already engaged in skirmishes with Accord forces. Their rage is palpable, but their efforts are... fragmented. They fight for territory, for their ancestral lands, but not for a unified cause. The Obsidian Drakes remain in their isolated peaks, observing, judging."

"The dragons are fierce, but their pride can be a barrier," Cael admitted. "And the Drakes are too withdrawn to be easily swayed. But the Conclave... you are attuned to the planet's pulse. You understand the deeper currents of existence. If you could lend your understanding, your influence, to this cause, it could be the catalyst we need."

Lyra's gaze grew distant, as if peering into the unseen currents of the atmosphere. "A truce, you propose? A temporary alliance against this common enemy?"

"More than a truce," Cael corrected. "A genuine dialogue. A commitment to shared understanding. We need to pool our knowledge, our strengths. The Accord operates in shadow, their plans often hidden. We need to expose them, to reveal their true intentions to all. The Apex weapon is their ultimate tool of control. If we can disrupt its development, or even expose its existence to the wider galactic community, we might force their hand."

"The galactic community," Lyra mused. "An interesting proposition. The Accord has kept its machinations largely hidden from the eyes of the wider systems. They fear intervention, fear judgment."

"Precisely," Cael affirmed. "We must use that fear against them. But to do so, we need to present a united front. The Skybound's wisdom, the dragons' might, the resilience of the earth-bound creatures, and the conscience of a growing faction within humanity. Together, we can be a force that even the Accord cannot ignore."

Lyra turned fully to face Cael, their eyes now holding a fire that belied their serene countenance. "You speak with conviction, Human. And your words echo the concerns that have long troubled the Conclave. The Accord's pursuit of ultimate control is a dangerous path, one that leads to an unnatural silence. We have long sought a way to counter this encroaching uniformity, this erasure of the planet's vibrant song."

"Then you will consider an alliance?" Cael asked, his voice barely above a whisper, the weight of the moment pressing down on him.

"We will consider it," Lyra confirmed. "But trust is not easily given, especially between species who have known so much conflict. There will be trials. There will be tests. The Conclave will not commit its strength to a cause that is not truly unified, not truly aligned with the planet's well-being."

"I understand," Cael said, relief washing over him in a cool wave. "What are your conditions?"

Lyra's lips curved into a faint, almost imperceptible smile. "First, you must demonstrate that your own house is in order. The Accord's internal dissent is a spark, but a spark can ignite a conflagration. You must rally more of your kind to your cause. Second, you must establish a channel of communication with the Azure Serpents. Their fury is a powerful weapon, but it must be guided, not unleashed indiscriminately. And finally, you must prove that you seek not to replace the Accord's control with your own, but to foster genuine freedom and respect for all life."

"These are not unreasonable demands," Cael acknowledged. "I will work to fulfill them." He paused, then added, "But time is of the essence, Lyra. The Apex is nearing completion. Every moment we delay, the Accord grows stronger."

Lyra nodded. "We are not blind to the urgency, Cael. The winds carry whispers of your Accord's progress. But haste without wisdom is a dangerous path. We will observe. We will listen. And when the time is right, the Skybound will lend its voice to the chorus of defiance." They extended a hand, not to shake, but to offer a single, iridescent feather, shimmering with captured light. "Carry this. It is a symbol of our tentative agreement. When you have made progress on the trials I have set, present this to any member of the Skybound Conclave, and they will know you by its light."

Cael accepted the feather, its surface cool and impossibly smooth against his calloused fingers. It felt fragile, yet imbued with an ancient power, a promise of what could be. "Thank you, Lyra."

"Go now," Lyra said, their form beginning to blur at the edges, their presence receding into the atmospheric currents. "The valley grows cold, and the shadows lengthen. Your mission has begun. May the winds guide your steps, and the stars illuminate your path."

As Lyra's form dissolved completely, Cael stood alone on the promontory, the iridescent feather clutched in his hand. The mist was beginning to dissipate, revealing the vast, untamed landscape stretching out before him. The diplomatic mission was far from over; it had merely entered its most crucial, and perilous, phase. He had forged a fragile link, a thread of possibility in a tapestry of despair.

Now, he had to prove himself worthy of that trust, to navigate the treacherous currents of inter-species politics, and to rally a fractured world against a common, existential threat. The weight of the feather in his palm was a reminder of the immense responsibility he carried, and the terrifyingly delicate balance of the world he was fighting to save. He turned his back on the precipice, his gaze fixed on the path ahead, the wind whispering secrets and warnings in his ears. The gambit had been played, and the game of saving their world had truly begun.

The iridescent feather, a tangible testament to Lyra's fragile trust, felt strangely warm against Cael's skin as he descended the jagged slopes. The biting wind that had once seemed a harbinger of doom now felt like a mournful sigh, a farewell from the ethereal presence of the Skybound elder. The meeting on the promontory had been a success, a victory of sorts, but it was a victory bathed in the cold light of dawn, promising not an end to hardship, but the beginning of a far more arduous journey. The path ahead was not one paved with diplomatic pleasantries and grand pronouncements, but one carved through the thicket of suspicion, prejudice, and the deeply entrenched power of the Accord.

Cael found himself at a crossroads, not of geography, but of identity. The man who had once been a strategist, a tactician within the Accord's rigid hierarchy, now had to shed that skin. He was no longer a soldier seeking to outmaneuver an enemy, but a nascent leader attempting to unite disparate forces, each with their own agendas, their own histories of conflict. The whisper of an alliance with the Skybound Conclave was a lifeline, but a lifeline that demanded he sever his ties to his former life, his former allegiances. He knew, with a certainty that chilled him more than the mountain air, that his continued association with the Accord, however covert, would be an insurmountable barrier to genuine trust from Lyra and her kin.

THE STORMBOUND DIVIDE

His descent brought him back to the familiar, yet now alien, terrain surrounding his mountain alcove. The humming presence of Zephyr, the ancient guardian of the peaks, felt like a comforting embrace, a silent affirmation of his home. But it was a home he could no longer fully inhabit, not if he was to honor the promise he had made to Lyra, and more importantly, to himself. The Accord was a cancer, and he had been a cell within it, albeit one that had begun to revolt. To fight it effectively, he needed to be outside its reach, free from its influence, even if that meant embracing a solitary, exposed existence.

Aris's bio-dome, a marvel of controlled environment and scientific endeavor, felt like a relic of a past life. He had sought refuge there, a place of logic and predictable outcomes. But the world Elara had shown him, the world Lyra had confirmed, was anything but predictable. It was a world of ancient forces, of elemental energies, of life thriving in the wild, untamed spaces that the Accord sought to eradicate. His commitment to Elara's vision, and now to Lyra's nascent hope, meant he had to embrace that wildness, not seek to control it.

The weight of Lyra's words settled upon him: "You must demonstrate that your own house is in order. The Accord's internal dissent is a spark, but a spark can ignite a conflagration. You must rally more of your kind to your cause." This was the first trial, and it was perhaps the most daunting. How could he rally others when his own position was so precarious? How could he persuade those still entrenched within the Accord's system of the futility of their path when he himself had once been a part of it?

He knew he couldn't approach those still loyal to the Accord directly. They would see him as a traitor, a defector. His best hope lay with those who harbored doubts, those who had witnessed the Accord's descent into tyranny but lacked the courage or the means to act. He thought of the engineers who had voiced their concerns about the Apex project, the scientists who had been reassigned for questioning the ethical implications of certain Accord directives, the disillusioned mid-level officers who had grown weary of the endless pursuit of expansion and control.

His journey back was not one of triumphant return, but of strategic retreat. He couldn't bring the feather, Lyra's symbol of tentative trust, with him into the heart of Accord territory. It would be a beacon, a clear signal of his betrayal. Instead, he memorized its subtle shimmer, its impossible warmth, and committed its essence to memory. He would have to find a way to communicate his progress, to establish the communication channels Lyra had demanded, without directly revealing his newfound alliance. This was a solo mission, a clandestine operation within his own species, and the stakes were no less than the fate of the planet.

The decision to sever ties with his alcove, with Zephyr, was a pang that resonated deep within him. Zephyr was more than just a sentient AI; it was a companion, a guardian, an ancient consciousness woven into the very fabric of his home. But Zephyr's programming, its core directives, were tied to the protection of his immediate environment, not to a galactic struggle for planetary survival. To involve Zephyr directly would be to endanger it, to expose it to the Accord's scrutiny. He had to leave, to disappear, to become a ghost in the Accord's network, leaving behind only silence.

He spent the next few cycles in a state of hyper-vigilance. He moved through the fringes of Accord-controlled territories, utilizing forgotten access points and shadowed routes. He contacted a network of informants Elara had cultivated, individuals who operated in the grey areas, trading information for survival. Through them, he began to subtly probe for like-minded individuals within the Accord. His messages were cryptic, encoded, hinting at a future free from the Accord's oppressive grip, a future where the planet's natural symphony could once again play without inhibition.

He learned of a scientist, Dr. Aris Thorne, a brilliant xenobotanist whose work on symbiotic ecosystems had been sidelined by the Accord's focus on terraforming and resource extraction. Thorne had been increasingly vocal about the detrimental impact of Accord's expansion on indigenous flora, his protests eventually leading to his demotion and exile to a remote research outpost. Cael recognized Thorne's name; Aris, his former colleague, had spoken of Thorne with a mixture of admiration and frustration. Aris had always been more cautious, more pragmatic, but Cael knew Thorne's dissent was genuine.

Reaching Thorne was an undertaking in itself. The research outpost was located in a bio-diverse region known for its volatile weather patterns and unique, often dangerous, flora. The Accord maintained a minimal presence there, viewing it as a scientific backwater, a place where dissenting minds could be safely contained. Cael had to navigate treacherous jungles, evade automated patrols, and decipher local ecological hazards that would have deterred a less determined individual.

When he finally found Thorne, the scientist was a shadow of his former self, his brilliance dulled by isolation and disillusionment. He was working in a dilapidated greenhouse, tending to a collection of wilting, mutated plants – the casualties of Accord's industrial waste. Thorne's initial reaction to Cael was suspicion, then guarded curiosity. Cael didn't reveal the full extent of his meeting with Lyra, but he spoke of the Apex, of the Accord's ultimate goal of planetary subjugation, and of the urgent need for unified resistance. He spoke of Elara's vision, of a future where humanity and the planet could coexist in harmony.

"They are destroying everything," Thorne whispered, his voice raspy, as he gestured to a specimen of a once-vibrant bioluminescent vine, now sickly and emitting a faint, acrid smoke. "The Accord sees only what it can exploit, what it can control. They don't understand that these organisms, these ecosystems, are not just resources; they are the very lifeblood of this world. They are the symphony."

"Lyra, from the Skybound Conclave, believes that symphony is worth saving," Cael said, finally revealing a portion of the truth. "She has agreed to consider an alliance, but she requires proof that we can unite our own kind. She demands that we demonstrate that our dissent is not merely a factional dispute, but a movement towards true freedom."

Thorne's eyes, once weary, flickered with a spark of hope. "The Skybound... I've only heard whispers. Tales of their mastery over the atmospheric currents, their deep connection to the planet's rhythm. If they are willing to listen… then perhaps there is a chance."

Cael laid out his plan. He proposed that Thorne, with his intimate knowledge of the region and his remaining scientific network, could begin documenting the Accord's environmental damage. These documented records, stripped of any overt political messaging, would serve as irrefutable evidence of the Accord's destructive path. This evidence, Cael explained, would be crucial for building trust with both the Skybound and potentially other hesitant factions.

"You will become my eyes and ears in this sector," Cael explained. "You will gather the proof. I will carry it to those who can understand its significance. But this is dangerous, Thorne. If the Accord discovers your activities, they will not hesitate to silence you permanently."

Thorne looked at the wilting vine in his hand, then at Cael, his gaze hardening with resolve. "Silencing me would be easy. But silencing the truth? That is a far more difficult task. I have nothing left to lose, Cael. My work, my integrity… they took it all. If this is a way to reclaim some of it, to contribute to something greater than myself, then I will do it. I will gather the proof. And when it is ready, how will I reach you?"

Cael provided Thorne with a secure, encrypted communication channel, a relic from his days within Accord intelligence, now repurposed for his own clandestine operations. He also gave Thorne a discreet marker, a small, seemingly innocuous trinket that, when activated, would send a silent alarm to Cael's network, indicating extreme danger. It was a sacrifice, of sorts, to entrust Thorne with such vital information and a lifeline that could also be a beacon for his own capture. But Cael understood that true leadership demanded delegation, and that genuine alliances were built on shared risk and mutual trust, even if that trust was a fragile, nascent thing.

He left Thorne with a renewed sense of purpose, the weight of his mission heavier but also more defined. He was no longer just a former Accord officer; he was a conductor, orchestrating a symphony of dissent. The next step was to establish communication with the Azure Serpents, a task Lyra had deemed critical. Their ferocity was undeniable, but their pride and territorial nature made them difficult to approach.

His inquiries through his informant network led him to a desolate plateau known for its harsh, windswept terrain, a place the Accord largely avoided due to its unpredictable seismic activity and the rumors of powerful, ancient beings that dwelled within its rocky depths. It was here, according to the whispers, that the Azure Serpents, the majestic dragon-like creatures of the earth, held their councils.

The journey to the plateau was a test of endurance. The air grew thin, the winds carried shards of ice, and the very ground beneath him seemed to groan with subterranean energy. He traveled alone, his pack laden with supplies, his mind focused on the immense challenge ahead. He was a solitary figure against a world that seemed to actively resist his presence, a stark contrast to the organized, technologically advanced world of the Accord he had left behind.

He finally reached the designated area, a vast expanse of jagged rock formations and deep chasms, where the air crackled with an unseen energy. The sky above was a turbulent canvas of grey and black, mirroring the internal turmoil that had become his constant companion. He found no welcoming party, no signs of intelligent life, only the raw, untamed power of the planet. He felt a profound sense of isolation, a chilling realization of how far he had truly fallen from his previous life. He had traded the sterile comfort of order for the visceral, unpredictable wildness of the world, and for a moment, he questioned the wisdom of his choice.

Then, a shadow fell over him. It was not the shadow of a cloud, but something immense, something with a palpable aura of ancient power. He looked up, his breath catching in his throat. Towering above him, its scales shimmering with an earthy iridescence, was an Azure Serpent. Its eyes, like molten gold, regarded him with an intensity that seemed to bore into his very soul. It was larger than any creature he had ever imagined, a living embodiment of the planet's raw strength.

He stood his ground, his heart pounding, but his resolve firm. He held no weapon, offered no threat. He simply met the creature's gaze, channeling all the conviction and desperation he felt. He spoke, his voice amplified by the natural acoustics of the chasm, projecting his message of a shared threat, of the Accord's Apex weapon, of the looming silence that would descend upon their world.

"I come not as an enemy," Cael declared, his voice resonating with the urgency of his mission, "but as a messenger. The Accord seeks to extinguish the song of this world. They seek to conquer not just our lands, but the very essence of life. Their ultimate weapon, the Apex, will render this planet barren and silent."

The serpent let out a low, guttural rumble, a sound that vibrated through Cael's bones. It was not a sound of aggression, but of deep contemplation, of ancient wisdom being stirred. Slowly, deliberately, the great creature lowered its head, its golden eyes never leaving Cael's.

"Your kind brings only destruction," a voice boomed, not from the serpent's mouth, but seemingly from the very air around them, a telepathic resonance that bypassed Cael's ears and spoke directly to his mind. "We have seen your cities rise and fall, your wars scar the earth. Why should we heed the words of a species that so readily embraces its own ruin?"

This was the challenge Lyra had warned of. Cael took a deep breath, the thin, cold air filling his lungs. He spoke of Elara, of the growing dissent within humanity, of the Accord's internal contradictions, and of the hope for a different future. He spoke of his own journey, of his rejection of the Accord's path, and his commitment to forging a new way, a way of symbiosis and respect.

"I am a testament to that change," Cael stated, his voice unwavering. "I have left behind all that I knew, all that I was, to stand against the darkness. I seek not to conquer, but to protect. The Apex is a threat to all living things, human, serpent, and Skybound alike. If it succeeds, the skies will fall silent, the earth will cease to sing, and the wild heart of this world will be extinguished forever."

He revealed a hidden data chip, a compressed repository of information about the Apex, its projected capabilities, and the Accord's timeline for its completion. He explained that this information was gathered at great personal risk, a testament to his sincerity.

The serpent remained still for a long moment, its gaze inscrutable. Cael felt the weight of its ancient scrutiny, the assessment of his words, his intent, his very being. This was more than a diplomatic negotiation; it was a trial by fire, a test of his character and his commitment.

Finally, the serpent spoke again, its mental voice laced with a grudging respect. "The Skybound have watched your Accord's unchecked ambition with growing concern. The disruption to the atmospheric currents, the silencing of the earth's song... it is a sickness that spreads. But we are divided. Many of my kin believe your kind is beyond redemption. They see only the destruction, the relentless march of your technology."

"But some of you see the possibility of change?" Cael pressed, his hope rekindled.

The serpent let out a low hiss, a sound that conveyed a universe of ancient knowledge and fierce territoriality. "We guard the deep places, the veins of the planet. We feel its tremors, its pain. The Accord's pursuit of absolute control is an affront to the natural order. Your Apex weapon... if it can truly silence the earth's resonance, then it is a threat we cannot ignore. But trust is earned, not given. Your species has a long history of betrayal."

Cael understood. He was being offered a chance, a sliver of hope, but it came with conditions, with the demand for proof. He could not force their hand, could not compel them to join his cause. He had to demonstrate genuine progress, unity, and a commitment to the planet's well-being. He was being asked to make a profound personal sacrifice – to fully abandon his past, to isolate himself from any remaining ties, and to dedicate himself entirely to this fragile alliance, knowing that failure could mean not only his own demise but the subjugation of everything he held dear.

He spent weeks on the plateau, engaging in arduous dialogues with the Azure Serpents, sharing what knowledge he had of the Accord and its intentions, and listening to their ancient wisdom. He learned of their deep connection to the planet's geological forces, their ability to sense and manipulate seismic energy, and their fierce protectiveness of the earth's core. He learned that their rage, though formidable, was often directed by instinct and territorial imperative, and that channeling it towards a unified cause would require careful diplomacy and a clear understanding of shared objectives.

He could not forge a lasting alliance with the Serpents on this first encounter. Their suspicion of humanity remained a significant hurdle. However, he managed to sow the seeds of doubt regarding the Accord's true intentions, painting a picture of an enemy that sought to control not only the surface but the very heart of the planet. He offered them a way to monitor the Accord's deeper drilling operations, a method of detecting seismic anomalies that might indicate the testing of the Apex's more destructive capabilities. This was a tangible contribution, a way for him to offer something concrete in exchange for their potential future cooperation.

The personal cost of this endeavor was immense. He had to sever even the most tenuous connections to his past life, to erase his digital footprint within Accord systems, and to become a phantom. He had to accept that his continued existence in the eyes of the Accord, and even many within his own species, was as a traitor, a lost cause. This isolation was a heavy burden, a constant reminder of the solitary path he had chosen. He had traded a life of structure and purpose, however flawed, for one of uncertainty and immense personal risk.

He was no longer a soldier with a clear objective, but a fugitive fighting for a future he could only dimly perceive. Yet, with each conversation with Thorne, with each silent understanding reached with the Azure

Serpents, Cael felt a burgeoning sense of his own evolving identity. He was no longer just reacting; he was acting, forging connections, and taking responsibility. The guardian's sacrifice was not a single act, but a continuous commitment to a path that demanded everything he was and everything he could become, all for the sake of a world that deserved to sing.

Chapter Eight
The Skybound's Game

The meeting with Lyra on the precipice had been a necessary step, a calculated risk that had yielded a fragile agreement. Cael had presented his case, a desperate plea for unity against the encroaching darkness of the Accord, and Lyra, in turn, had offered a cautious hand of alliance. But as he navigated the treacherous terrain back towards the fringes of Accord territory, the ethereal warmth of the Skybound's feather against his skin became a stark reminder of the complex currents swirling beneath the surface of this burgeoning alliance.

The Skybound Conclave, with their mastery of the skies and their profound connection to the planet's atmospheric song, presented themselves as benevolent guardians, their motives seemingly aligned with the preservation of the world's natural harmony. Yet, Cael couldn't shake the gnawing suspicion that their vision of "harmony" might be more aligned with their own alien sensibilities than with the messy, vibrant chaos of terrestrial life, including humanity.

Their offer of assistance, their willingness to engage in dialogue, felt less like a gesture of pure altruism and more like a strategic maneuver. The Conclave, much like the Accord, possessed a deep-seated desire to shape the world, to impose their own order upon it. Lyra had spoken of the planet's "song," a complex symphony of elemental forces and life that resonated through the atmosphere and the earth. It was a concept Cael was beginning to grasp, a profound truth that the Accord, in its relentless pursuit of technological dominance, sought to silence. But the Conclave's interpretation of this song, their vision of how it should be orchestrated, was still an enigma. Were they seeking to preserve it in its current form, or to conduct it according to their own alien composition, potentially sacrificing some of the very elements they claimed to protect?

The whispers among the Accord's intelligence network, the subtle shifts in atmospheric patterns that Lyra herself had acknowledged, suggested a pattern of interference that extended far beyond mere observation. The Conclave possessed an intimate knowledge of planetary systems, of weather phenomena, and of the delicate ecological balances that sustained life. This knowledge, in the hands of a power with its own agenda, could be a weapon as potent as any Accordian device. Cael had seen firsthand how the Accord manipulated information, twisted narratives, and exploited weaknesses to achieve its objectives. He could not afford to be naive about the Skybound's potential for similar, albeit more subtly executed, machinations.

He recalled the subtle emphasis Lyra had placed on the Accord's internal discord. "Your own house must be in order," she had stated, her gaze piercing. It was a clear challenge, a demand for demonstrable progress in uniting disparate human factions. But Cael couldn't help but wonder if this was also a veiled suggestion, a nudge towards actively fostering that discord, perhaps even manipulating it. Could the Conclave be orchestrating events behind the scenes, subtly influencing key figures, both human and of other species, to further their own long-term goals? Were they not just seeking an alliance, but actively working to weaken all competing powers, including the Azure Serpents, to solidify their own position as the ultimate arbiters of the planet's fate?

The Azure Serpents, a formidable force in their own right, had their own ancient traditions and a deep, instinctual connection to the earth's core. Cael had felt the tremors of their potential resistance to human expansion, a primal defense of their domain. If the Skybound were indeed seeking to "reshape the song," it was highly probable that the Serpents, with their raw, elemental power, would be an obstacle. And if that were the case, then the Conclave's seemingly benevolent offer of alliance might be a calculated move to enlist Cael's burgeoning resistance movement as a pawn in their own game, a force to inadvertently destabilize the Serpents and pave the way for the Conclave's own dominance.

The very nature of their "song" was a point of contention. While Cael understood it as the vibrant, complex, and often discordant chorus of life, he couldn't discount the possibility that the Skybound envisioned a more unified, perhaps even homogenized, symphony. Their aerial existence, their detachment from the terrestrial struggles of ground-dwelling species, might lead them to perceive certain aspects of the planet's song as undesirable, as dissonance that needed to be smoothed out, polished, and refined. This was not a judgment, but a cold, hard assessment of a fundamentally alien perspective. Humanity, with its messy emotions, its incessant conflicts, and its often destructive ingenuity, might be seen by the Conclave as a cacophony that disrupted the perfect celestial harmony.

Cael's journey to establish contact with the Azure Serpents had been a testament to the Conclave's potential influence. While he believed he had initiated the contact through his own resourcefulness and the information gleaned from Elara's network, he now considered whether the timing and the location had been subtly guided. Had Lyra, or others within the Conclave, perhaps "leaked" information about the Serpents' presence, knowing that Cael's desperate plea for alliance would inevitably lead him to them? This would serve a dual purpose: it would allow Cael to further his mission of unification, but it would also expose the Serpents to his nascent rebellion, potentially sowing seeds of distrust or even conflict between them, further fragmenting any unified opposition to the Accord.

He thought of the intermediary Lyra had suggested, a reclusive human scholar named Elara Vance, whose life's work had been dedicated to deciphering the nuances of interspecies communication and understanding the subtle energetic shifts of the planet. Lyra had presented Elara as a neutral party, a bridge between worlds. But Cael now wondered if Elara was truly neutral, or if her research had been subtly influenced, her findings curated by the Conclave to align with their narrative of planetary harmony. Was Elara's deep understanding of the "song" a genuine scholarly pursuit, or was it a carefully cultivated perception, shaped by years of subtle Skybound guidance and information sharing? The Conclave, with their ethereal nature and their mastery of atmospheric manipulation, could easily influence the delicate bio-energetic fields that governed sentient thought, subtly nudging perceptions, planting ideas, and shaping understanding without ever revealing their hand.

The very concept of an "alliance" with the Skybound felt fraught with unspoken conditions. They offered their knowledge of atmospheric currents, their ability to influence weather patterns, their insight into the planet's energetic flows. But what was the cost? Cael had pledged to gather evidence of the Accord's destructive practices, to demonstrate unity amongst his own kind. This was the tangible price. But the intangible price might be far greater. Was he, and by extension, the forces he sought to rally, becoming instruments in the Skybound's own grand design? Were they being groomed to dismantle the Accord, only to find themselves subservient to a new, perhaps equally dominant, power?

The potential for manipulation was amplified by the Skybound's seemingly superior understanding of the planet's intricate systems. They spoke of cosmic alignments, of celestial rhythms, of energies that resonated with the very fabric of existence. While this was undeniably a powerful perspective, it also hinted at a potential disdain for the more localized, terrestrial concerns of other species. The "song" might be a universal concept, but its interpretation could vary wildly. For the Skybound, it might be a cosmic melody, a grand orchestration of universal forces. For humanity, it was the rustling of leaves, the roar of the ocean, the heartbeat of their own species. For the Azure Serpents, it was the deep rumble of the earth, the pulse of magma, the ancient song of geological formation. To impose one interpretation upon the others would be a form of conquest, a silencing of diverse voices in favor of a singular, alien refrain.

Cael's interactions with the Azure Serpents had been tense, laced with ancient mistrust. He had spoken of the Apex, of its threat to all life, and he believed he had conveyed the sincerity of his warning. But even then, he had sensed a deep skepticism, a weariness born from millennia of witnessing humanity's destructive tendencies. He knew that Lyra and her kin had been observing these interactions, perhaps even subtly influencing them. Had the Conclave, through unseen channels, amplified the Serpents' existing distrust of humanity, or had they subtly guided Cael's words, ensuring that his message, while appearing to foster unity, actually served to isolate the Serpents further, making them more receptive to Skybound "guidance" in the future?

The Accord, with its blunt force and overt tyranny, was a clear enemy. But the Skybound, with their veiled intentions and ethereal power, represented a far more insidious threat. They operated in the liminal spaces, influencing through suggestion, subtly shifting perspectives, and orchestrating events with a precision that made them almost invisible. Cael's nascent rebellion was a beacon of hope, a spark of defiance, but it was also a tool, a potential weapon in the hands of a power that sought to reshape the world according to its own alien aesthetics.

He had to remain vigilant, to constantly question the motives behind the Conclave's actions, and to ensure that his pursuit of a unified front against the Accord did not inadvertently lead to subjugation under a different guise. The "song" was indeed worth saving, but its preservation should not come at the cost of silencing the unique melodies of its diverse inhabitants. He had to be a conductor, yes, but a conductor who respected the individual instruments, who allowed each to play its part in the grand, evolving symphony of life, rather than imposing a single, sterile composition. The Skybound's agenda was hidden, but Cael was determined to bring it into the light, to ensure that any alliance forged was one of true partnership, not of manipulation, and that the planet's song, in all its wild, beautiful complexity, would continue to play for generations to come.

The Conclave's interest in the Apex weapon, while outwardly aligned with planetary preservation, was a critical point of scrutiny. They had expressed concern over its potential to "silence the song," a phrasing that was both accurate and alarmingly vague. What did "silencing" truly entail from their perspective? Did it mean the complete eradication of all life, or did it mean the suppression of specific frequencies, the elimination of discordant elements, the homogenization of the planet's vibrant chorus into a more aesthetically pleasing, uniform hum? Cael suspected the latter, a form of cosmic curation where the Skybound would play the role of ultimate arbiters of taste, dictating which elements of the planet's song were worthy of existence.

His own journey had been a testament to this potential for varied interpretation. He had initially viewed the planet's plight through the lens of Accordian logic – a problem to be solved, a system to be optimized. Elara's influence had begun to shift his perspective, introducing him to the concept of symbiosis and the inherent value of natural processes. Lyra's talk of the "song" had further deepened this understanding, offering a more spiritual and interconnected view of existence. But he knew these were all human-centric interpretations, filtered through his own evolving consciousness. The Skybound, existing as they did, unbound by terrestrial limitations, might perceive the "song" on a scale so vast, so cosmic, that the individual melodies of species and ecosystems were mere ephemeral notes, easily adjusted or removed to suit their grander celestial symphony.

Consider their fascination with atmospheric control. It was presented as a means of protecting the planet, of stabilizing volatile weather patterns. But what if it was also a tool for subtly altering the planet's energetic resonance? The atmosphere was a conduit, a medium through which the planet's song traveled. By manipulating the atmosphere, the Skybound could, theoretically, alter the very way the song was perceived, or even how it propagated. They could amplify certain frequencies, dampen others, effectively curating the planet's energetic output. This was a terrifying thought – a subtle, insidious form of control that would leave its subjects unaware of their own diminishing influence.

He also had to consider the potential for inter-species manipulation. The Skybound, with their vast lifespan and their detached perspective, might view the cyclical conflicts and territorial disputes of species like the Azure Serpents as mere background noise, or worse, as opportunities. By subtly influencing one faction against another, or by providing selective information that played on existing prejudices, they could weaken all potential rivals, leaving themselves as the sole remaining power capable of "managing" the planet's fate. He had already witnessed the Azure Serpents' deep-seated mistrust of humanity, a mistrust that was largely justified, but also potentially exploitable. If the Conclave could subtly feed that mistrust, or perhaps even subtly foster it, they could ensure that no unified front against the Accord – or themselves – would ever truly materialize.

The Skybound's purported interest in Lyra's people, the Skybound Conclave itself, was another layer to unravel. While they presented themselves as ancient caretakers, their own internal structure and motivations remained largely opaque. Were they a unified entity, or a collection of factions with their own competing agendas? Lyra, as an elder, likely held significant influence, but she was still part of a larger collective. What were the prevailing views within the Conclave regarding the planet and its inhabitants? Was Lyra's tentative alliance with Cael a reflection of a broader shift in Skybound policy, or was it a singular initiative, potentially at odds with the desires of other influential members of the Conclave? The very idea of an "elder" implied a hierarchical structure, and hierarchies, as Cael knew all too well from his time within the Accord, were often rife with internal power struggles and competing ambitions.

The Conclave's focus on the "song" might also be a thinly veiled attempt to consolidate their own power, positioning themselves as the sole interpreters and guardians of this vital planetary energy. If they could convince all other species that only they possessed the true understanding of the song, and that only they could ensure its preservation, then they would effectively gain a monopoly on planetary governance. This would allow them to dictate terms, to influence development, and to shape the future of the world in accordance with their own alien ideals, all under the guise of benevolent stewardship. Cael had seen how the Accord used its perceived technological superiority to justify its iron grip; the Skybound might be employing a similar strategy, using their perceived spiritual and energetic superiority to achieve the same end.

THE STORMBOUND DIVIDE

He mused on the implications for the Azure Serpents. If the Conclave were to gain dominance, how would that impact the deep earth dwellers? Would their ancient connection to the planet's core be respected, or would it be deemed a discordant element, a wild note that needed to be harmonized into the Skybound's grander composition? Cael suspected the latter. The Skybound, with their ethereal existence, were likely more attuned to the atmospheric and cosmic aspects of the planet's song, potentially overlooking or even deeming irrelevant the raw, primal energies that resonated deep within the earth. This fundamental difference in perspective could lead to conflict, a conflict that the Skybound might have been subtly orchestrating.

Cael's mission was no longer simply about resisting the Accord. It had become a delicate dance of navigating multiple agendas, of discerning true allies from manipulative forces, and of safeguarding not only humanity's future but the integrity of the planet's diverse expressions of life. The Skybound's hidden agenda was not merely a theoretical concern; it was a tangible threat, an intricate web of influence that he had to untangle before it ensnared his burgeoning rebellion and, in doing so, irrevocably altered the very essence of the world he was fighting to protect. He had to ensure that the symphony of the planet continued to be played by all its voices, not just the ethereal chorus of the Skybound.

The subtle shimmer in the air around the Skybound, a phenomenon Cael had initially dismissed as a mere aesthetic peculiarity of their ethereal form, now felt like a visible manifestation of a far deeper power. It wasn't just about controlling the currents of the upper atmosphere, steering clouds or conjuring localized storms. Lyra's words, veiled in metaphor and cosmic poetry, had hinted at something far more fundamental, something that resonated not just in the wind's howl but in the very bedrock of the planet. He'd heard it in the hushed tones of Accordian defectors, whispers of energies that predated the sky dragons, forces that could crack mountains and boil oceans with a thought. These weren't the sophisticated, engineered applications of Accordian technology; these were the raw, untamed humors of the world itself.

He remembered a conversation with a disgraced Accordian physicist, a man who had been part of the initial research into harnessing planetary ley lines. The physicist, his eyes wide with a fear that transcended any logical apprehension, had spoken of "primordial frequencies" that the Accord had only begun to comprehend, let alone control. He'd described attempts to tap into these frequencies as akin to poking a slumbering titan with a sharpened stick, with the chilling certainty that such a titan would eventually awaken and sweep away everything in its path. At the time, Cael had filed it away as the ramblings of a broken mind, but now, those words echoed with a terrifying resonance. Could the Skybound not only understand these frequencies but wield them?

Lyra had spoken of the planet's "song," a concept Cael was still struggling to fully internalize. He'd interpreted it as the intricate web of biological and geological processes, the symphony of life and earth. But what if the song was far more literal? What if it was a quantifiable energetic output, a resonant hum that emanated from the planet's core, amplified and modulated by its atmosphere and its living inhabitants? And what if the Skybound, with their mastery of the atmospheric currents that carried this song, had also discovered a way to influence its very source, the deep, resonant thrum of the planet's heart?

The idea was both exhilarating and deeply unsettling. The Accord sought to impose order through sterile, technological control, silencing the "noise" of natural variance. The Skybound, on the other hand, seemed to operate on a different plane entirely, seeking to harmonize the planet's song, to conduct it into a more pleasing, perhaps more unified, celestial arrangement. But Cael couldn't shake the feeling that this "harmonization" might involve silencing certain instruments, muting particular melodies, or even outright replacing the original composition with their own. The 'deeper, more elemental challenge' mentioned in his hushed conversations with resistance informants suddenly felt less like a metaphor and more like a literal description of the Conclave's potential ambitions.

He recalled the eerie stillness that sometimes descended upon areas where Skybound presence was strong, a subtle suppression of ambient noise, a feeling of cosmic quietude that was more oppressive than peaceful. It wasn't the absence of sound, but a subtle, pervasive dampening of natural vibrancy, as if the very air had become a conductor's baton, intent on smoothing out every rough edge, every spontaneous crescendo. This wasn't merely weather manipulation; this was a deeper manipulation of the planet's energetic signature, a subtle alteration of its fundamental vibration.

The Skybound had offered him knowledge, insights into the planet's energetic flows, and the ability to influence atmospheric conditions. He had accepted, desperate for any advantage against the Accord. But now he wondered about the true nature of that offer. Were they teaching him to play a new instrument, or were they subtly re-tuning his own, making him more receptive to their grander symphony? The feather Lyra had given him, a token of their alliance, felt less like a symbol of partnership and more like a conduit, a subtle link that allowed them to feel his presence, his thoughts, his very essence. It was a constant, chilling reminder of their ethereal reach.

He thought about the Azure Serpents. Their connection to the planet was visceral, primal, rooted in the deep earth and the molten core. They were the bass notes of the planetary song, the rumbling cello, the foundational rhythm. If the Skybound sought to impose their own celestial melody, would the Serpents be the first to be silenced, their ancient earth-song drowned out by the grander cosmic opera? The thought sent a shiver down Cael's spine. He had sought to forge an alliance with the Serpents to fight the Accord, but he might have inadvertently led them into the crosshairs of a far older, far more profound power.

The Accord's methods were brutal, overt, and destructive. They sought to dominate the planet by subjugating its inhabitants and exploiting its resources. But the Skybound's approach was far more insidious. They offered a vision of harmony, of balance, of a planet singing in perfect celestial tune. But it was a tune dictated by them, a performance orchestrated for their own alien sensibilities. Their power wasn't in brute force, but in subtle influence, in the quiet manipulation of fundamental energies, in the reshaping of the very essence of existence. They weren't just interested in governing the world; they seemed intent on *redefining* it, on tuning its song to a frequency that only they could fully appreciate.

Cael ran a hand over the rough, bark-like texture of the ancient tree he leaned against, trying to ground himself in the tangible reality of the forest floor, so unlike the ethereal realms of the Skybound. He could feel the faint vibration of life within the wood, the slow, steady pulse of sap rising through its veins. This was the terrestrial song, messy, imperfect, and beautiful in its inherent chaos. He couldn't allow the Skybound, no matter how benign their intentions seemed, to smooth out this song into a sterile, unblemished hum.

The true challenge wasn't just against the Accord's technological tyranny, but against a cosmic aesthetic, an alien interpretation of planetary life that threatened to erase the vibrant dissonance that made the world truly alive. He had to understand the depth of this elemental power, not just to combat it, but to ensure that the planet's true song, in all its wild, untamed glory, would continue to echo through the ages. He had to discern if Lyra's alliance was a genuine offer of partnership, or a subtle invitation to help them conduct a symphony that would ultimately silence his own world.

The biting wind, a constant companion on these high altitudes, did little to cool the feverish pace of Mara Lysenne's thoughts. Each gust felt like a whisper, a tantalizing hint of something more than just atmospheric caprice. She scanned the jagged peaks ahead, the stone a bruised purple under the deepening twilight, and wondered if the Skybound truly understood the forces they so casually manipulated. Cael's earlier pronouncements about planetary songs and primordial frequencies had settled into her mind like seeds, germinating into a disquieting awareness. She felt it now, a subtle thrum beneath the roar of the wind, a resonance that spoke of immense, slumbering power.

Her current path was a perilous one, chosen with a desperate gamble. She sought the Sunken City, a place whispered about in hushed tones by those who remembered the world before the Great Ascendancy, a place of forgotten knowledge and, perhaps, a forgotten power that predated even the Skybound. The Accord, of course, would have it scoured from history, its very existence denied. But history, Mara was discovering, had a way of leaving echoes, of clinging to the world like moss to ancient stone.

She had expected obstacles, the natural hazards of the treacherous terrain, the ever-present threat of Accord patrols. What she hadn't anticipated was the uncanny ease with which she seemed to navigate them. A rockslide that should have blocked her path had, upon closer inspection, revealed a narrow, previously unseen crevice, just wide enough for her to slip through. A pack of snarling mountain predators, their eyes glowing with predatory hunger, had suddenly dispersed, spooked by a phenomenon Mara couldn't quite place – a fleeting, iridescent shimmer that had danced on the edges of her vision, too quick for her to fully grasp. It was as if the very air around her had subtly shifted, nudging fate in her favor, or perhaps, more ominously, guiding her.

These were not the overt interventions Cael had described, no grand gestures of celestial assistance. This was more akin to a gardener subtly pruning errant branches, ensuring the favored bloom reached its full potential. And Mara was beginning to suspect the gardener was not entirely human, nor entirely benevolent. The Skybound, with their mastery of the skies and their seemingly boundless ethereal power, were a constant enigma. They existed on a plane so removed from the terrestrial struggles that defined her own existence, yet their influence was undeniable, woven into the very fabric of the world.

She remembered the unsettling encounter with Lyra, the Skybound emissary. Lyra's words had been couched in a language of cosmic ballet and atmospheric currents, but beneath the poetic veneer, Mara had sensed a chilling pragmatism. The Skybound sought balance, yes, but whose balance? And at what cost? Cael's concerns about them 'tuning' the planet's song, silencing discordant notes, resonated deeply within her. Was this 'aid' she was receiving part of that grand orchestration? Was she merely a pawn being moved across a celestial chessboard, her purpose to serve an agenda she couldn't fully comprehend?

The possibility that the Skybound might actively *oppose* the Accord's complete dominion over the planet was also a persistent, nagging thought. The Accord's relentless drive for control, their sterile imposition of order, threatened not just the natural world but the very essence of life as Mara understood it. It was a force of absolute negation, a desire to scrub the world clean of its vibrant, messy complexity. Perhaps, in their own alien way, the Skybound found that ambition... unappealing. A world devoid of its natural song, of its inherent dissonance, would be a silent, sterile void. And what use would a silent planet be to beings who seemed so attuned to its resonance?

She paused at the mouth of a narrow ravine, the wind here a mournful howl that seemed to carry ancient secrets. The Accord had marked this area as impassable, a treacherous dead end. Yet, the path ahead was strangely clear, the scree on the ground appearing recently disturbed, as if a large creature had recently passed, clearing a way. She felt no fear, only a strange sense of inevitability, as if this path had been waiting for her. Was it a natural occurrence, or a deliberate redirection? Had the Skybound, for their own inscrutable reasons, decided that Mara Lysenne should reach the Sunken City, and thus, subtly nudged the geological landscape to accommodate her?

The ambiguity was maddening. If the Skybound were her unwitting allies, their motives remained shrouded in mystery. Were they simply trying to prevent a larger catastrophe, one that would disrupt their own celestial harmony? Or did they see in Mara a potential disruptor of the Accord's absolute authority, a wild card they could perhaps exploit? The idea of being a pawn was unsettling, but the idea of being a tool for an even more alien and powerful agenda was terrifying.

She traced the patterns of frost on a nearby rock, the intricate, fractal designs a testament to nature's silent artistry. It was a beauty born of chaos, of unbridled forces. The Accord sought to replace such beauty with manufactured order, with sterile symmetry. The Skybound, on the other hand, spoke of song and harmony, but Mara suspected their definition of harmony was far more rigid, far less forgiving of the wild, untamed melodies that gave the world its soul.

Her hand brushed against a smooth, cool stone embedded in the earth. It pulsed with a faint warmth, a stark contrast to the frigid air. It was an artefact, something ancient and imbued with a subtle energy. She recognized the markings on its surface – not Accordian script, nor any known terrestrial language, but something older, a series of swirling glyphs that seemed to hum with latent power. It was similar to symbols she'd glimpsed on the fringes of Accordian research logs, symbols associated with forbidden studies into planetary resonance. This stone, she felt, was a key, a marker. And it had appeared where the path had been cleared, where the predators had inexplicably retreated.

The realization was a cold, sharp clarity. The Skybound were not simply removing obstacles; they were *guiding* her, leaving behind breadcrumbs of forgotten power. They were not directly helping her, but rather ensuring that *she* would find the help she needed. It was a subtle, almost Machiavellian form of assistance, a testament to their advanced understanding of the world and its hidden currents. They were orchestrating a subtle redirection of dangers, not by dispelling them, but by nudging her away from them, or by creating opportunities for her to overcome them.

The predators, for instance, had not been driven away by a Skybound force directly. Instead, a sudden, localized atmospheric shift, a brief, almost imperceptible surge of wind from an unexpected direction, had carried a scent—a scent of something far more dangerous, far more dominant, that had prompted the predators to retreat. This scent, Mara suspected, had been deliberately amplified and directed, a subtle warning or a territorial marker that the Skybound had 'broadcast' to steer the lesser predators away from her path, without directly engaging them.

And the crevice, the seemingly impossible passage? It hadn't been carved by celestial hands. Instead, a precisely timed tremor, a miniature seismic event generated by manipulating subterranean air pressure, had fractured the rock face in just the right spot, creating the opening. It was an intervention so subtle, so localized, that it would appear as a natural geological event to any casual observer. But Mara, now attuned to the whispers of the world, felt the artificiality.

She pocketed the stone, its warmth a comforting weight against her palm. This was not the kind of aid one received from a benevolent deity. This was the calculated maneuver of a cosmic strategist, a player who understood the board and its pieces with unnerving clarity. The Skybound were not saving her; they were *using* her. They saw her quest for the Sunken City as a means to an end, an end that, for now, aligned with their own interests. Perhaps the Accord's unchecked expansion threatened the very planetary balance they sought to maintain. Or perhaps they saw in the Sunken City a power that, if it fell into the Accord's hands, would be a catastrophic imbalance, a discordant note that could unravel their entire symphony.

The ambiguity remained, a persistent hum beneath the surface of her understanding. Was she a pawn in their game, or a potential challenger to their own dominion? Could she leverage their indirect aid, their carefully placed nudges, without becoming irrevocably entangled in their celestial machinations? The stone in her pocket felt both like a gift and a leash, a signpost pointing towards her destination, and a reminder that she was walking a path laid out by unseen hands. The Skybound played their game, and Mara Lysenne, whether she liked it or not, had been drawn into its intricate, ethereal dance. Her journey to the Sunken City was no longer just a personal quest; it was a move in a much larger, far more dangerous game, a game played on the very chords of the planet itself. The wind continued to howl, and Mara Lysenne, with a newfound understanding of the subtle currents that guided her, pressed onward.

The icy air of Cael Thornevale's mountain observatory did little to chill the heat of his rapidly expanding comprehension. For weeks, his network of informants, a disparate collection of disgruntled scholars, disillusioned drifters, and even a few surprisingly well-informed mountain hermits, had been feeding him fragmented reports. Initially, these were concerning the escalating skirmishes between the mountain clans and the scattered dragon enclaves – the old territorial disputes flaring with an uncharacteristic ferocity. But the whispers, when Cael's sharp intellect began to sift and connect them, spoke of something far more insidious than simple rekindled animosity.

He traced a line on the illuminated map spread across his rough-hewn table, connecting a recent clash near the Serpent's Tooth peaks with an unusual surge in dragon activity over the northern trade routes. "It's too coordinated," he murmured, his voice a low rumble that barely disturbed the dust motes dancing in the light of the etheric lamps. "The timing, the locations... it's not random. It's orchestrated." His eyes, the color of a stormy sea, narrowed as he reviewed a dispatch from his agent embedded within the Dragon Rider's council. The rider, a gruff old warrior named Borin, had reported an 'unnatural stirring' amongst the elder dragons, a discontent that seemed to manifest as aggressive territorial expansions, pushing them into direct conflict with human settlements that had previously coexisted peacefully for generations.

Cael leaned back, the worn leather of his chair creaking in protest. This wasn't the brash, overt aggression of the Accord. This was subtler, a manipulation of existing tensions, a fanning of embers into a wildfire. He recalled his earlier conversations with Mara Lysenne, his initial, almost dismissive, theories about the Skybound's ethereal influence. He had spoken of 'planetary songs' and 'frequencies,' concepts that felt abstract, almost poetic, at the time. Now, those words echoed with a chilling clarity. The Skybound. They were not merely observers, or even subtle regulators. They were actively *shaping* the world's symphony, and it seemed their chosen instrument was discord.

His network had also begun to pick up on the Conclave's subtle hand in human affairs. Reports of 'divine pronouncements' reaching ambitious clan leaders, urging them to reclaim ancestral lands with renewed fervor. Rumors of newly discovered mineral veins, rich with resources the Accord would covet, appearing in strategically provocative locations. It was as if the Skybound Conclave were playing a grand, multi-generational game, using the very creatures and peoples of the planet as their pieces, each move designed to create a specific, desired outcome. And that outcome, Cael was beginning to fear, was not peace. It was chaos, a carefully curated chaos that served their own unfathomable agenda.

"They are not simply stopping the Accord," he mused, his fingers tapping a staccato rhythm on the map. "They are *creating* their own form of imbalance. Or perhaps... perhaps their balance *is* this perpetual state of controlled conflict." He pulled a different scroll towards him, detailing the recent movements of Skybound emissaries. While official records depicted their patrols as being solely focused on maintaining atmospheric equilibrium, Cael's informants – the ones who dared to observe beyond the prescribed official duties – spoke of Skybound craft hovering over disputed territories for extended periods, their ethereal hum a low, constant presence in the skies. They weren't intervening in battles; they were *observing* them, perhaps even influencing them in ways undetectable by conventional means.

The implications were staggering. If the Skybound were indeed the architects of this escalating conflict, then his previous strategies, focused on countering the Accord's rigid control, were now woefully inadequate. He had been preparing for a frontal assault, for direct confrontation. But how does one confront an enemy who operates through suggestion, through atmospheric pressure, through the manipulation of instinct and ancient rivalries? How does one fight a war waged not with steel and magic, but with whispers carried on the wind and subtle shifts in the planet's resonant frequencies?

Cael's gaze drifted to a small, intricately carved wooden bird perched on a shelf, a gift from a wood-sprite informant who claimed to have witnessed Skybound 'weather manipulation' on a truly epic scale. He remembered the sprite's description of how the Skybound could coax storms into existence, not through brute force, but by 'singing' to the clouds, harmonizing with their latent energies until they coalesced into tempests. It was a power that dwarfed any sorcery he had ever encountered, a power that was not about destruction, but about *guidance*. And it was being used to guide the world towards a precipice.

THE STORMBOUND DIVIDE

He began to re-evaluate every piece of intelligence, every report, through this new lens. The sudden scarcity of a rare herb crucial for dragon healing, appearing in areas where territorial disputes were already simmering. The unnerving silence from certain Skybound observatories during moments of peak conflict. The oddly specific atmospheric conditions that seemed to *favor* one side over the other in localized skirmishes, turning potential dragon victories into costly retreats, or human scouting parties into tragically lost patrols. These weren't coincidences; they were the brushstrokes of a deliberate, patient hand.

"They're playing a long game," he stated, the words heavy with the weight of his dawning realization. "They see the Accord as a blunt instrument, a force of crude, unrefined order. But they also see unchecked chaos as equally detrimental to their own... cosmic harmony, or whatever it is they strive for. So, they seek to maintain a state of perpetual, controlled tension. Enough conflict to keep the Accord from consolidating absolute power, but not so much that it leads to total collapse. A precarious equilibrium, dictated by them."

His mind raced, replaying snippets of conversations, piecing together disparate clues. He remembered Lyra, the Skybound emissary Mara had encountered. Her pronouncements about "balance" and "harmony" had seemed almost benevolent, but Cael now understood the chilling implication. Their harmony was their own. Their balance was their own. And any force that threatened that delicate, self-serving order, whether it was the Accord's sterile dominion or a true, organic resurgence of life's wilder energies, would be subtly, efficiently, and irrevocably dealt with.

This understanding required a fundamental shift in his own strategic thinking. He couldn't simply disrupt the Accord's supply lines or expose their clandestine operations. He had to find a way to disrupt the Skybound's influence, a task that felt akin to trying to capture moonlight in a net. Their power was ethereal, their methods indirect. They operated on a plane so removed from the daily struggles of mortals that conventional warfare was meaningless against them.

Cael began to organize his network anew, his directives shifting from intelligence gathering on the Accord to subtle probing of the Skybound's influence. He instructed his agents to look for anomalies in weather patterns that defied natural explanation, to listen for recurring atmospheric phenomena that coincided with moments of escalation, to document any instances of unusual Skybound observation or presence in areas of conflict. He needed to understand the 'how' of their manipulation, the specific frequencies they exploited, the subtle shifts in atmospheric pressure they employed.

He assigned a small, trusted team to focus on ancient texts and forgotten lore, searching for any mention of beings who commanded the skies, not through sorcery or flight, but through an intrinsic connection to the planet's very essence. Were there legends of such entities before the Skybound's ascent? Had there been other 'songs' that had been silenced? He needed to understand their origins, their limitations, their potential weaknesses.

The dragon riders, he realized, were a critical piece in this new puzzle. Their ancient connection to the elemental forces of the world, their deep understanding of natural rhythms, might provide clues. He sent a carefully worded message to Borin, not directly accusing the Skybound, but asking for detailed accounts of the 'unnatural stirrings' – the precise timing of their onset, the specific environmental changes observed, the sensory details of their aggression. He wanted to know if these changes were purely instinctual, or if there were subtle, external influences at play.

Cael's frustration was palpable. He was a strategist, a planner, a man who understood the tangible levers of power. But the Skybound seemed to operate with an almost divine detachment, their actions as subtle and pervasive as the air itself. How could he counter an enemy who didn't directly engage, but instead manipulated the very conditions that led to conflict? How could he expose a force that operated on such a fundamental, almost subconscious level?

He picked up a delicate, almost translucent feather, found near the site of a recent dragon-human skirmish. It wasn't a feather from any known bird. It shimmered with an otherworldly iridescence, and felt impossibly light, as if it were less matter and more condensed atmosphere. He had no proof it was Skybound in origin, but it was an anomaly, and anomalies were his new focus.

"They are not content with simply observing the world," he muttered, holding the feather up to the light. "They are actively shaping it, pruning it, tuning it to their own discordant melody. The Accord may be a predator, but the Skybound are the unseen hand that guides the prey, ensuring a steady supply for the hunt." His ambition had always been to restore balance to a world fractured by the Accord's iron fist.

Now, he understood that the concept of balance itself was far more complex, and far more dangerous, than he had ever imagined. The Skybound were not a force for order, nor were they a force for chaos. They were a force for *control*, a control so subtle and pervasive that it threatened to stifle the very spirit of the world, leaving behind a perfectly orchestrated, perfectly lifeless harmony. His new game had begun, and the stakes were nothing less than the soul of the planet.

The hum of the Skybound observatories, usually a subtle thrumming that permeated the upper atmosphere, seemed to intensify in the days following Cael's grim deductions. It was a dissonance, a dissonant chord struck in the planet's symphony, and its reverberations were felt across the land. Mara, in her secluded sanctuary amongst the whispering pines, felt it not as a sound, but as a pressure, an invisible weight pressing down on the world's natural currents. Her dreams, usually vibrant tapestries woven with the earth's ancient magic, were now troubled by visions of vast, crystalline structures descending from the heavens, their presence chilling the very air.

Cael, back in his mountain fortress, was the first to receive the tangible proof of the Skybound's overture. A heavily encrypted dispatch, delivered by a swift and silent hawk trained by his most trusted scout, arrived on his desk. The sender was not identified by name, but by a symbol –

a stylized, overlapping set of concentric circles, a mark that had, until now, been associated with the Skybound's administrative decrees, their pronouncements on atmospheric regulations and celestial alignments. This message, however, carried no such benign intent.

"To all sentient species, to all territorial stewards, to all who hold dominion over land, sea, and sky," the message began, its tone one of an almost paternalistic authority, devoid of warmth or empathy. "The Great Balance, the foundation of all cosmic order, has been observed to be in a state of critical disequilibrium. For generations, the Skybound Conclave has acted as the silent guardian, the unseen hand that guides the terrestrial sphere towards its intended harmony. We have tolerated the burgeoning ambitions of fledgling powers, the territorial squabbles of lesser beings, and the inefficient machinations of self-serving factions. Our patience, however, has reached its zenith."

The dispatch continued, each word meticulously chosen to convey an unassailable power. "The escalating conflicts between the so-called 'mountain clans' and the dragon enclaves, fueled by mortal avarice and primal instinct, represent a direct threat to the intricate web of existence. Similarly, the burgeoning influence of the Accord, with its rigid and ultimately unsustainable imposition of order, destabilizes the natural ebb and flow that sustains life. Both extremes, unchecked, lead to ruin."

Cael's breath hitched. This was not a warning; it was a declaration of war, disguised as a decree. He scanned the text, his eyes darting from one damning sentence to the next. "Therefore, the Conclave hereby establishes the *Pax Caelum*, a period of enforced celestial sovereignty. Effective immediately, all territorial disputes, regardless of their historical precedent or perceived justification, are to cease. All established borders, as delineated by the ancient celestial maps, are to be strictly adhered to. Any species, faction, or individual found in violation of this decree will be subject to immediate and decisive intervention by the Skybound forces."

The ultimatum was stark and absolute. The Skybound were not just observing anymore; they were actively imposing their will, not through subtle manipulation, but through a direct assertion of dominance. Cael's gaze fell upon the paragraph that detailed the specific implications for the dragon enclaves. "The dragon factions, whose power and territorial ambitions have grown to a point where they disrupt regional atmospheric stability and interfere with established migratory patterns, are hereby placed under immediate Skybound supervision. Their flight paths are to be restricted to designated aerial corridors. Their territorial claims are to be redefined based on ecological sustainability and atmospheric flow, not on ancient lineage or predatory right. Any dragon found exceeding these new parameters will be deemed a rogue element and dealt with accordingly."

The 'dealing with,' Cael knew, would be far more than a gentle redirection. He had seen the Skybound craft, heard the whispers of their ethereal power. They possessed the ability to unravel the very fabric of existence, to silence the storms and still the winds. For the dragons, this was an existential threat, a cage forged from the sky itself.

"And to the Accord," Cael read aloud, his voice tight with a mixture of dread and grim determination, "your expansionist doctrines and your pursuit of absolute, stifling order are also deemed a threat to the Great Balance. While your aims may be perceived as orderly by your own limited understanding, they lack the organic dynamism necessary for true, sustained equilibrium. Therefore, your incursions into territories not explicitly designated by the Skybound for your governance are to cease. Your attempts to homogenize life under a singular, sterile doctrine are to be curtailed. The Conclave will not tolerate the imposition of a premature, artificial peace that stifles the inherent potential of the world."

The Skybound were not choosing sides; they were dismantling both the dragons' fiercely independent spirit and the Accord's suffocating grip. They were setting themselves up as the ultimate arbiters, the sole purveyors of balance.

A chill, deeper than any mountain wind, settled upon Cael. This was not the nuanced influence he had theorized; this was a direct, forceful takeover. The Skybound, he now understood, were not simply playing a game of subtle manipulation. They were drawing their own lines in the sand, or rather, in the clouds, and daring anyone to cross them. This move would force every faction, every player on this volatile board, to react. It would shatter the existing alliances, expose the true ambitions of all involved, and thrust the world into a new era of conflict, one dictated by the ethereal lords of the sky.

He immediately dispatched riders to the various mountain clans, carrying copies of the Skybound decree, urging them to observe the new regulations, however unjust they might seem, and to await further instructions. He knew that many would balk, that their pride and their ingrained territorial instincts would rebel against such an imposition. But direct defiance against the Skybound was a suicidal proposition.

His thoughts turned to Mara. She would feel this shift, this seismic change in the world's energetic pulse. Her intuitive connection to the planet would make her acutely aware of the Skybound's heavy hand. He needed to reach her, to share this dire news, and to formulate a plan that went beyond mere survival. This was no longer about countering the Accord; it was about confronting a force that dwarfed any earthly power they had ever imagined.

Across the vast plains, in the hidden aeries and ancient caverns, the dragons felt the Skybound's pronouncement like a physical blow. The Elder Wyrm, Ignis, whose scales shimmered like molten gold, roared his fury, the sound echoing through the mountain peaks. "Skybound tyranny!" he bellowed, his voice a thunderclap that shook the very foundations of his ancestral home. "They dare to cage the wind? To dictate the flight of a dragon? We are the breath of this world, not their playthings!"

His council, a collection of formidable dragons of all breeds and ages, stirred with outrage. Faelan, a sleek, obsidian dragon known for his strategic mind, spoke with a measured intensity. "Ignis, the Conclave's power is not to be underestimated. Their mastery over the atmospheric currents is absolute. To defy them openly, without a plan, would be to invite destruction upon our entire kind. We risk not just our freedom, but our very existence."

"And what of your 'plan', Faelan?" Ignis scoffed, his fiery breath scorching the rock walls of the cavern. "To cower in our aeries, to restrict our flights like frightened fledglings? This is not how the Skybound operate. They do not seek cooperation; they seek subjugation. If we do not resist now, they will continue to tighten their grip, until we are nothing but gilded ornaments in their celestial zoo."

A younger dragon, Lyra, whose scales were the vibrant blue of a summer sky, spoke up hesitantly. "The human, Mara, she spoke of balance. Perhaps... perhaps the Conclave believes they are restoring it. They spoke of the Accord's 'sterile order' as well. Maybe there is a common ground, a way to appease them without surrendering our freedom."

Ignis snorted, a plume of smoke rising from his nostrils. "Common ground with beings who see us as mere atmospheric disturbances? They speak of balance, but their actions speak of absolute control. They are not restoring balance; they are imposing their own, a balance that serves only their inscrutable will. This *Pax Caelum* is a gilded cage, and it will be the death of our spirit if we accept it."

The dragon council erupted into a cacophony of roars and hisses, each voice filled with a mixture of fear, rage, and a desperate yearning for a way forward. The Skybound ultimatum had achieved its primary objective: it had thrown the established order into chaos, forcing every faction to confront a threat far greater than they had anticipated. The dragons were torn between their fierce independence and the terrifying reality of the Conclave's power.

Meanwhile, within the sterile, ordered halls of the Accord's central command, Grand Marshal Valerius received the Skybound decree with a chillingly calm expression. His advisors, accustomed to his iron will, watched him, their faces etched with apprehension. The Accord had always viewed the Skybound as distant, detached entities, concerned only with the macro-cosmic dance of planets and stars. To have them interfere so directly in terrestrial affairs was an unprecedented challenge to their own meticulously crafted order.

"They call our order 'stifling' and 'sterile'?" Valerius mused, his voice dangerously quiet. He traced the Skybound symbol on the parchment with a gloved finger. "They speak of 'organic dynamism' and 'inherent potential.' Such abstract notions. The Accord provides stability, predictability. It is the only bulwark against the primal chaos that threatens to consume this world. This *Pax Caelum* is an affront to reason, an embrace of the very disarray we have fought so hard to contain."

His chief strategist, a wiry man named Corvus, stepped forward. "Grand Marshal, the Skybound possess immense power. Their mastery over atmospheric phenomena is legendary. Direct confrontation would be... ill-advised. Perhaps we can find a way to negotiate, to demonstrate that our order is, in fact, the truest form of balance they seek."

Valerius's eyes, sharp and cold, fixed on Corvus. "Negotiate with beings who issue ultimatums? They do not seek partnership; they seek dominion. They see us as a variable to be controlled, an inconvenient force that disrupts their grand, ethereal design. However," a dangerous glint entered his eyes, "they may have underestimated the resilience of our own order. They may have underestimated the adaptability of the Accord. If they seek to impose their definition of balance, perhaps we can demonstrate that our definition is, in fact, superior. And if they seek to dismantle our control, perhaps we can find a way to dismantle theirs."

The Grand Marshal's words hung in the air, heavy with unspoken intent. The Skybound had declared their hand, and in doing so, had ignited a firestorm. They had sought to impose their will, but in doing so, they had potentially united their disparate enemies. Mara, Cael, and the dragons, united by a common threat that dwarfed their previous animosities. And even the Accord, the implacable force of order, now found itself in a position where it had to consider a radical shift in its long-held strategy. The Skybound Conclave, in their bid to enforce their vision of balance, had inadvertently become the catalyst for a grand, and potentially world-altering, alliance.

The air itself seemed to vibrate with a new tension, a palpable shift in the cosmic energies. The Skybound's ultimatum was not just a political maneuver; it was an environmental and spiritual declaration that rippled through the very essence of the world. Mara, meditating beneath the ancient canopy, felt the intrusion most acutely. It was like a discordant note in the earth's deep hum, a forced silence that stifled the wild, untamed melodies she had come to know so intimately. Her connection to the land, usually a source of strength and clarity, now felt like a conduit for a pervasive unease, a sense of being watched by eyes that saw not with sight, but with an all-encompassing, dispassionate awareness.

The Skybound's decree, broadcast across the world through channels that bypassed mortal communication – a resonating whisper carried on the upper atmospheric currents, a subtle shift in light patterns visible to those with keen eyes – was a blunt instrument wielded with chilling precision. It demanded an immediate cessation of hostilities between the mountain clans and the dragon enclaves, a cessation dictated not by mutual understanding or truce, but by the fiat of celestial authority. Furthermore, it placed strict limitations on dragon flight paths, confining them to predetermined aerial corridors that were less about efficiency and more about control, a visual representation of their newfound subjugation.

Cael, pouring over his maps and intelligence reports in his mountain observatory, felt the weight of the Skybound's direct intervention acutely. His carefully constructed strategies, designed to exploit the existing tensions and foster a gradual shift in power, were now rendered almost obsolete. The Skybound had bypassed the subtle dance of influence and chosen the heavy-handed stride of overt command. His informants, the disaffected scholars and the mountain hermits, sent back increasingly frantic reports. The clans, proud and fiercely independent, were in an uproar, their leaders grappling with the impossible choice between defiance and the potentially catastrophic consequences of disobeying the

Skybound. Whispers of rebellion mingled with fearful pronouncements of the Skybound's invincibility.

"They are not playing our game anymore," Cael muttered to himself, his fingers drumming a restless rhythm on the edge of his table. "They have changed the rules entirely. They are not interested in subtle manipulation; they want absolute order, their order. And they have the power to enforce it." He looked at a detailed chart of atmospheric currents, a subject he had once studied with academic curiosity, now a chilling roadmap of the Skybound's influence. The designated flight paths were not random; they were designed to herd the dragons, to limit their reach, to cut them off from vital territories and ancient hunting grounds. It was a strategy of containment, a celestial cage being built around the very sky.

The Skybound's pronouncement extended to the Accord as well, a surprising twist that added a layer of complexity to the unfolding crisis. The Conclave, in its perceived quest for a "Great Balance," deemed the Accord's rigid, absolute order as equally detrimental to the world's organic vitality. This was a direct challenge to Grand Marshal Valerius and his tightly controlled dominion. The Accord, which prided itself on its unwavering logic and its systematic approach to governance, found itself branded as a force of "stifling" and "sterile" control. Valerius, a man who thrived on predictability, was forced to confront an enemy whose motives were as ethereal as the skies they commanded.

Faelan, the obsidian dragon, had managed to convene a secret council of his most trusted kin in a hidden gorge, far from the prying eyes of the Skybound. The air crackled with a potent blend of defiance and fear. "They claim to enforce balance," Faelan spat, his voice a low growl that resonated with the frustration of his entire species. "But their 'balance' is our enslavement. To be confined to their arbitrary corridors? To have our territories redefined by creatures who have never felt the wind beneath their wings, never tasted the thrill of a hunt across the vast expanse of the heavens? This is an insult to our very nature."

Ignis, the Elder Wyrm, his golden scales shimmering with barely suppressed fury, echoed Faelan's sentiments. "This *Pax Caelum* is a lie! It is not balance they seek, but absolute dominion. They seek to mute the wild song of this world, to replace it with their own monotonous drone. We cannot, we *will not*, abide by such dictates." He turned his fiery gaze upon the assembled dragons. "If we are to survive, if we are to retain our spirit, we must resist. But direct confrontation with the Skybound is madness. Their power over the elements is absolute. We need a different approach, a strategy that does not pit fang and flame against ethereal might."

It was Lyra, the blue-scaled dragon, who, recalling her encounter with Mara, offered a sliver of hope. "The human, Mara, she spoke of a different kind of balance. Not the rigid order of the Accord, nor the wild freedom of the dragons, but a harmonious integration. She spoke of the Skybound's influence not being an absolute power, but a force that can be... understood, perhaps even redirected. If the Conclave believes they are restoring balance, perhaps we can show them that true balance lies not in their imposed order, but in the complex interplay of all life. Perhaps we can convince them that their current course will ultimately lead to the very disequilibrium they seek to prevent."

Her words, though tentative, sparked a new line of thought. The Skybound, as Cael had deduced, were not inherently malicious. They operated on a logic far removed from mortal concerns, a logic of cosmic harmony that they themselves defined. If Mara could reach them, if they could present a compelling argument that their current actions were *undermining* their own desired outcome, then perhaps a different path could be forged. It was a long shot, a desperate gamble, but it was a gamble that did not involve hurling themselves against an insurmountable force.

Mara, meanwhile, was not waiting for Cael's emissaries. She felt the Skybound's imposition as a suffocating blanket over the world's vital energies. Her visions intensified, no longer abstract anxieties, but stark, chilling glimpses of the Skybound's true intentions. She saw their celestial observatories, vast crystalline structures humming with controlled energy, not merely monitoring the planet, but actively *tuning* it, like a cosmic orchestra conductor, silencing dissonant notes – the fierce independence of the dragons, the chaotic yet vibrant energy of the mountain clans, even the rigid but undeniably functional order of the Accord – all to achieve a perfect, sterile harmony.

She understood then that the Skybound's ultimatum was not just a political decree; it was a philosophical declaration. They believed that they alone understood the true nature of balance, and that all other forces were merely errant notes in a grand, cosmic symphony that they alone were capable of orchestrating. Their power was immense, not in its destructiveness, but in its pervasive, subtle control over the very fabric of existence. They could coax storms into being, or quell them with a thought. They could alter atmospheric pressures, influence weather patterns, and subtly nudge the very instincts of creatures.

Mara knew that direct confrontation was not the answer. The Skybound operated on a plane beyond physical combat. She had to engage them on their own terms, to speak their language of balance and harmony. She had to find a way to communicate with them, to show them that their imposed order was not balance, but a sterile stillness that would ultimately lead to decay.

She began to prepare for a perilous journey, one that would take her not across the land, but upwards, towards the very realm of the Skybound. She would seek out the legendary 'Whispering Peaks,' a place spoken of in ancient lore as a nexus point where the terrestrial realm met the celestial, a place where it was said one could communicate with beings of the upper air. It was a journey fraught with danger, a path that few mortals had ever dared to tread, and fewer still had returned from. But the weight of the world, the threat of its stifling perfection, rested upon her shoulders.

The Skybound Conclave's ultimatum had done more than just escalate conflict; it had forced a fundamental re-evaluation of the war being waged. The conflict was no longer simply about territory or power between mortal factions. It was a battle for the very soul of the world, a struggle against an unseen force that sought to dictate its future, to mold it into a perfect, lifeless image of their own celestial design. Mara Lysenne, the quiet guardian of the forest, Cael Thornevale, the keen-eyed strategist, and the proud, untamed dragons, were now faced with a common enemy, a celestial architect intent on reshaping reality. Their disparate struggles had converged, and the game had taken a terrifying, skybound turn. The choice was stark: either they found a way to resist this ultimate control, or they would all be reduced to perfectly balanced, perfectly silent pieces in the Skybound's grand design.

Chapter Nine
The Voice of the World

The air thrummed, not with the familiar pulse of the forest's breath, but with a new, disquieting tremor. Mara had felt it growing for days, a subtle dissonance that vibrated through the very roots of the ancient pines, a discordant note in the earth's otherwise perfect symphony. Cael's grim pronouncements about the Skybound's intervention, the unsettling dreams of crystalline structures descending from above, had been premonitions, shadows cast by an approaching storm. Now, the storm was upon her, and it was not one of wind and rain, but of a profound, existential silence descending upon the world.

Her sanctuary, usually a haven of vibrant, untamed life, felt different. The whispering pines seemed to hold their breath, their usual rustling murmur subdued, as if afraid to disrupt the encroaching quiet. The forest floor, typically alive with the scurrying of unseen creatures and the subtle exhalations of moss and loam, felt muted, its pulse slowed. It was as if the world itself was being carefully, deliberately, silenced. Mara closed her eyes, seeking the familiar, comforting hum of the earth, the deep, resonant song that had always been her solace and her guide. But today, it was buried beneath a chilling overlay, a foreign melody attempting to drown out the ancient chorus.

Her journey to this secluded grove had been arduous, a pilgrimage born of an inexplicable pull, a need to understand the disquiet that had settled upon her spirit. She had traversed treacherous mountain passes, navigated dense, mist-shrouded valleys, and finally found herself here, at the edge of a clearing where the oldest of pines stood like silent sentinels. It was said in hushed tones by the few who knew of its existence, that this place was a nexus, a point where the veil between the terrestrial and the celestial thinned, a place where the planet's true voice could be heard by those attuned to its frequency.

As she settled onto the moss-covered earth, her hands pressed against the cool, damp soil, Mara focused her intent. She pushed aside the nagging anxieties about the Skybound's decree, the escalating tensions between the mountain clans and the dragons, the Accord's relentless march of sterile order. These were the cacophony, the noise that had deafened the world to its own melody. She sought something deeper, something fundamental, the **Core Song of the World**.

At first, there was only the pressing silence, the feeling of an immense, invisible force pushing down, attempting to still every vibration, to mute every sound. It was a suffocating pressure, like being submerged in an ocean of stillness. The Skybound's *Pax Caelum* was not merely a political decree; it was a cosmic silencing, an attempt to impose a monolithic harmony by eradicating all other notes. Mara felt a sharp pang of grief, not just for herself, but for the planet, for the vibrant, chaotic, glorious symphony that was being systematically dismantled.

She breathed deeply, drawing in the scent of pine and damp earth, and then exhaled, releasing her own anxieties, her fears, her very self. She surrendered to the earth, to the subtle currents that flowed beneath its surface. Slowly, tentatively, like a forgotten melody resurfacing from the depths of memory, it began.

It was not a sound in the conventional sense, not something that could be captured by the ear. It was a resonance, a vibration that permeated her very bones, her very soul. It was the deep, guttural rumble of tectonic plates shifting, the slow, deliberate creak of mountains forming and eroding over millennia. It was the whisper of wind carving canyons, the roar of ancient volcanoes, the gentle lapping of primeval oceans against newborn continents. It was the murmur of subterranean rivers, the steady heartbeat of the planet's molten core, a steady, unwavering rhythm that had pulsed for eons.

Then, the song expanded, reaching beyond the geological to embrace the biological. She felt the surge of sap rising in ancient trees, the silent, intricate dance of photosynthesis converting sunlight into life. She heard the chirping of insects, the rustling of leaves as small creatures navigated the undergrowth, the powerful, resonant calls of beasts long extinct, their echoes still imprinted on the world's memory. It was the frantic pulse of a rabbit's heart, the slow, patient growth of a seed pushing through the soil, the triumphant cry of a hawk soaring on the updrafts. It was the interconnectedness of it all, each life form a unique instrument contributing to the grand orchestra.

This was not the cacophony of conflict, the screech of metal against stone, or the desperate cries of fear. This was the **Core Song of the World**, the fundamental resonance of life in its purest, most unadulterated form. It was a song of creation and destruction, of growth and decay, of wildness and order, all woven together in a tapestry of breathtaking complexity. It was a song that contained multitudes, a song that acknowledged and embraced the inherent chaos of existence as much as its potential for harmony.

Mara wept, tears streaming down her face, not tears of sorrow, but of profound, overwhelming recognition. She had always felt the earth's magic, had always been a conduit for its energies, but this... this was different. This was not a whisper, but a full-throated roar, the unfiltered essence of a living, breathing planet. She felt its immense strength, its resilience, its ability to endure and to regenerate. But she also felt its pain.

The Skybound's intervention, their desire for a sterile, predictable harmony, was a grievous wound. She felt the planet recoil from the imposed silence, the energetic currents being forced into unnaturally straight lines, the vibrant, unpredictable rhythms being stifled. It was like watching a wild, beautiful creature being leashed and confined, its spirit slowly being broken. The *Pax Caelum* was not restoring balance; it was attempting to eradicate it, to replace the dynamic, evolving symphony with a single, monotonous note.

She felt the dragons, their magnificent, untamed song of freedom and power, being muted, their territorial roars being confined to prescribed aerial corridors. She felt the mountain clans, their fierce, earthy songs of resilience and independence, being threatened, their ancient traditions being challenged by an external force. And she felt the Accord, their relentless march of logical, sterile order, being lauded by the Skybound, yet even that, she sensed, was a perversion of true balance, a forced stillness that lacked the vital spark of life. The Skybound saw only the potential for discord, the disruptive notes, and sought to silence them, blind to the fact that it was the interplay of these diverse melodies that created the richness and depth of the world's song.

Mara's connection deepened, allowing her to perceive not just the terrestrial song, but its cosmic resonance. She felt the hum of distant stars, the gravitational pull of the moon, the subtle, ethereal harmonies of celestial alignments. The planet was not an isolated entity but a part of a vast, interconnected cosmic orchestra, its song resonating with the movements of planets, stars, and galaxies. The Skybound, she realized, were not merely celestial beings; they were cosmic musicians, but they were attempting to conduct a symphony of existence with a singular, rigid score, disregarding the improvisational genius of life itself.

This was the ultimate truth: the Skybound did not understand true balance. They understood uniformity, predictability, and control. They mistook the absence of chaos for harmony, the stillness of death for the peace of equilibrium. The Core Song of the World was not a perfect, unchanging melody; it was a dynamic, evolving composition, a constantly shifting interplay of opposing forces that gave it its vitality and its meaning. To silence this song was to invite stagnation, and ultimately, decay.

As the overwhelming symphony pulsed through her, Mara felt a surge of determination. She was a guardian, a listener, a conduit. She had heard the planet's true voice, felt its pain, and understood the catastrophic consequences of its continued silencing. She could not stand by and allow this cosmic imposition to extinguish the vibrant, wild melody of life. She had to find a way to make the Skybound hear, to make them understand that their pursuit of perfect harmony was, in fact, leading to the very disharmony they sought to prevent.

Her mind, now clearer than it had ever been, a direct recipient of the planet's profound wisdom, began to formulate a plan. Direct confrontation, as Cael had recognized, was futile. The Skybound operated on a different plane of existence, their power not in brute force, but in an almost imperceptible manipulation of fundamental forces. She had to communicate with them, to reach them through the language they understood – the language of cosmic balance and celestial harmony.

She remembered the ancient lore, the whispered tales of the Whispering Peaks, a place where the earth's song could ascend to the heavens, a place where the terrestrial and celestial could converse. It was a dangerous path, one spoken of with awe and trepidation, a journey into the very heart of the world's energetic currents, a path that led not across the land, but upwards, towards the realm of the Skybound themselves.

The silence that the Skybound sought was not peace; it was the stillness of a void, the absence of life's beautiful, complex song. Mara felt the planet's desperate plea, a silent scream echoing through the Core Song. She would answer that plea. She would journey to the Whispering Peaks, and she would find a way to sing the planet's true song, its vibrant, chaotic, glorious anthem, to the ears of the celestial conductors who sought to silence it. It was a monumental task, a journey into the unknown, but the fate of the world's melody depended on it.

The Core Song, now indelibly etched into her soul, demanded nothing less. The understanding of its profound beauty, and the chilling threat of its obliteration, had transformed Mara Lysenne, not just into a guardian, but into an advocate, a voice for the voiceless symphony of existence. The path ahead was perilous, but illuminated by the radiant truth of the planet's Core Song, she felt ready to face whatever celestial opposition stood in her way.

The earth's song, once a symphony of creation and existence, now resonated with a deeper, more unsettling truth, a fundamental dissonance that had been buried for millennia. Mara, her senses overwhelmed, found herself not just listening, but *seeing* the planet's history unfurl through this profound resonance. It was as if the Core Song was a living tapestry, each thread a moment in time, and the Skybound's silencing was an attempt to unravel its very fabric.

The truth that unfurled was not a simple prophecy of doom, but a foundational revelation, an abyssal understanding of the planet's genesis and its inherent nature. It spoke of a time before conscious life, a time when the nascent world was a chaotic crucible of elemental forces, a raw, untamed energy that pulsed with immense power. This primal state was not merely chaotic; it was a necessary precursor, a fertile void from which all complexity would eventually arise. The Core Song in its earliest iteration was the guttural cry of this burgeoning world, the sound of creation wrestling itself into being.

Then, the song shifted, revealing an event of cosmic significance. It wasn't just the formation of continents and oceans, but a deliberate, almost sentient act of balancing. The planet, in its nascent consciousness, had entered into a pact, a primordial agreement with the very forces of existence. This pact was not with any singular entity, but with the universal principle of balance itself – the intricate dance between creation and dissolution, light and shadow, order and chaos. This was the true genesis of the Core Song, a melody born from the recognition that true harmony was not the absence of dissonance, but the dynamic interplay of opposing forces. The song became a testament to this agreement, a constant affirmation of the vital necessity of every note, every vibration, no matter how discordant it might seem to an external observer.

Mara understood then the nature of the elemental imbalance that plagued the world. It wasn't a natural fluctuation; it was a violation of this ancient pact. The Skybound, in their pursuit of an ethereal, sterile perfection, were not merely imposing their will; they were actively severing the threads of this primordial agreement. Their *Pax Caelum* was an attempt to enforce a unilateral harmony, a single, unchanging note that would ultimately lead to the planet's spiritual and energetic death. The intensity of the storms, the unrest of the dragons – these were not random acts of defiance, but the planet's desperate, convulsive attempts to reassert its fundamental nature, to remind the cosmos of the pact that was being broken.

The dragons, she now understood, were not just powerful beings; they were the living embodiment of the primal, untamed forces that had been integral to the planet's creation and its pact of balance. Their roars were the echoes of the world's initial, chaotic song, a song of raw power and untamed freedom that had been crucial in shaping the planet's initial energetic matrix. The Skybound's interference, their attempts to impose order on these ancient, elemental forces, was akin to trying to dam a primordial ocean. The dragons' unrest was the planet's own energy fighting back, a desperate struggle to maintain the integrity of the core song's foundational elements.

This revelation was not a prophecy of a future catastrophe, but a profound unveiling of a present, ongoing unraveling. It was the fundamental aspect of reality that had been forgotten, buried beneath layers of cosmic hubris and celestial dogma. The Skybound, in their advanced wisdom, had somehow lost sight of this core truth, or perhaps, in their pursuit of control, had deliberately suppressed it. They saw the world's inherent dynamism, its constant ebb and flow of contrasting forces, as a flaw, a source of potential instability, rather than its greatest strength and its very reason for being.

The abyssal truth also explained the nature of life itself. Life, in its myriad forms, was not an accident, but a direct manifestation of this dynamic balance. Each organism, each ecosystem, was a unique expression of the Core Song, a complex arrangement of creation and dissolution, growth and decay. The vibrant chaos of the natural world, the very thing the Skybound sought to extinguish, was the hallmark of a healthy, living planet. To silence this song was to extinguish life's very essence, to condemn the world to a sterile, lifeless uniformity.

Mara felt the weight of this knowledge settle upon her. It was a truth so vast, so fundamental, that it threatened to shatter her perception of reality. The Skybound's actions were not just an invasion; they were an existential threat, a cosmic heresy against the very principles of existence. The pristine, ordered universe they envisioned was a dead one, devoid of the messy, beautiful, unpredictable spark of life.

She saw visions now, not just of the planet's past, but of potential futures. One path, illuminated by the Skybound's influence, was a silent, ordered landscape, a world where every natural process was regulated, every creature existed in perfect, predetermined harmony, but where the soul of the world was extinguished. It was a world of perfect order, but devoid of wonder, of spontaneity, of true life. The other path, the one the Core Song yearned for, was one of continued dynamic balance, of vibrant, sometimes tumultuous, interplay, a world that embraced its own complexity, even its perceived flaws, for they were the very elements that made it alive.

The intensity of the Core Song surged, now imbued with the sorrow and desperation of the planet. It spoke of the immense effort required to maintain this delicate balance, the constant, silent struggle against entropy and stagnation. The Skybound's intervention was not a gentle nudge; it was a brute force attempt to shatter this intricate, living mechanism.

Mara understood the true meaning of the storms. They were not merely atmospheric disturbances; they were the planet's cries, its desperate attempts to purge the unnatural order being imposed upon it. They were the echoes of the primordial chaos, a reminder of the forces that had shaped it, forces that could not be so easily contained or silenced. The dragons, in their aerial battles, were not just defending their territories; they were fighting for the very soul of the planet, for the right of its elemental nature to exist, to roar, to be.

This abyssal truth was a heavy burden, but it also ignited a fierce resolve within Mara. She was no longer just a guardian or a listener; she was a witness to a cosmic crime, a bearer of a forgotten truth. The Skybound, with all their celestial power, had made a fundamental error. They believed that harmony could be imposed through uniformity, that peace could be achieved through silence. But the Core Song sang a different truth: that true harmony was born from understanding, from embracing complexity, from allowing all voices, all melodies, to coexist.

The revelation was a double-edged sword. It offered clarity, a profound understanding of the forces at play, but it also presented an almost insurmountable challenge. How could a single, mortal being, however attuned to the planet's song, hope to sway beings of such cosmic stature, beings who wielded the very fabric of existence as their palette? Yet, the song pulsed within her, a constant reminder of what was at stake. It was the melody of life itself, and it deserved to be heard, to be sung, to be defended.

The Core Song revealed that the world was not merely a passive recipient of cosmic influence, but an active participant in its own creation and sustenance. The pact was not a one-way street; it was a reciprocal agreement. The planet offered its unique song, its vibrant tapestry of life, and in return, the cosmic forces, when in alignment with the principle of balance, contributed to its ongoing evolution. The Skybound's actions were a disruption of this cosmic reciprocity, an arrogant attempt to dictate the terms of existence without offering the corresponding harmony.

Mara's connection to the Core Song deepened, allowing her to perceive not just the terrestrial symphony, but its echoes in other celestial bodies. She felt the subtle shifts in gravitational pulls, the celestial dance of moons and stars, the hum of distant nebulae. These cosmic harmonies were intricate and complex, a testament to the universe's embrace of dynamic balance, a stark contrast to the rigid, singular tune the Skybound wished to impose. The Skybound were like astronomers who, having discovered the laws of celestial motion, sought to impose those laws upon every individual star, disregarding their unique spectral signatures and evolutionary paths.

THE STORMBOUND DIVIDE

The abyssal truth, in its totality, was the understanding that the planet was not just a living entity, but a conscious entity that had actively chosen its path towards complex, dynamic existence. It had embraced its inherent duality, the beautiful tension between opposing forces, as the very source of its vitality. This choice, this primordial act of self-determination, was the bedrock of the Core Song. The Skybound, by seeking to impose their singular vision, were attempting to negate this fundamental act of conscious choice, to strip the planet of its agency, to render it a mere puppet in their celestial opera.

The revelation was not a peaceful epiphany, but a cataclysm of understanding. It was a truth that was both beautiful and terrifying, a cosmic paradox that defined the very nature of existence. The world's song was a song of defiance, a testament to the enduring power of life, and Mara, now fully awakened to its depths, knew she had to become its voice. The intensity of the storms, the dragons' fury, the planet's silent, desperate plea – these were the overt manifestations of an ancient, sacred pact being violated. And she, a humble conduit, had been chosen to bear witness, and perhaps, to restore the balance that the Skybound so desperately sought to unravel. The abyssal truth was not just a secret; it was the very song of the world, and it was her duty to ensure it continued to play.

The resonance deepened within Mara, no longer a mere echo of the planet's past, but a vibrant, living current that pulsed through her very being. The Core Song, she now understood, was not an esoteric melody reserved for a select few attuned to its frequencies. It was a language, fundamental and universal, spoken by every atom, every cell, every living entity on the world. It was the silent conversation of existence, a continuous exchange of information and intent that underpinned the very fabric of reality. This realization washed over her with a profound sense of awe and responsibility, shifting her perspective from that of a solitary listener to a participant in a planetary dialogue.

She saw it then, not with her eyes, but with a deeper, more innate sense of perception. The wind whispering through the ancient forests was not just a passive movement of air; it was a chorus of countless trees, their leaves rustling with the ancient wisdom of photosynthesis, their roots intertwining in a silent, subterranean network of communication, sharing nutrients and warnings. The rhythmic crashing of waves against the shore was the ocean's breath, a vast, interconnected consciousness that communicated the lunar cycles, the currents of life, and the deep, resonant hum of oceanic trenches. Even the seemingly simple instinct of a migrating bird, charting its course across continents, was not a blind adherence to some primal urge, but a direct translation of the planet's subtle magnetic and atmospheric currents, a song sung in the language of direction and instinct.

This universal language manifested differently across the spectrum of life. For the towering, ancient trees, it was a slow, deliberate resonance, a deep, foundational hum that spoke of centuries of growth, of the patient absorption of sunlight and water, of the silent network of mycelial threads connecting them in a communal consciousness. Their song was one of deep roots, of enduring presence, of the slow, inexorable rhythm of seasons. For the swift, darting fish in the coral reefs, the song was a rapid, flickering cadence, a series of staccato pulses that conveyed immediate danger, the location of food, the intricate social hierarchies of the shoal. It was a language of instinct, of rapid adaptation, of the immediate present.

And then there were the dragons. Their roars, once perceived as primal expressions of rage or territorial dominance, were now understood by Mara as complex narratives, epic poems sung in a language of elemental power. Each tremor of their wings, each blast of fire, was a word, a phrase, a stanza in their ancient chronicles. The subtle shifts in the hue of their scales, the minute adjustments in their aerial ballet, were all intricate nuances of this primal dialect. They were the custodians of the planet's raw, untamed energies, and their song was a constant affirmation of this power, a declaration of the wild, untamed spirit that the Skybound sought to suppress. They understood the Core Song not as a melody, but as a symphony of pure force, a direct conduit to the planet's molten heart and its tempestuous skies. Their very existence was a testament to the enduring power of the dissonant notes that the Skybound so reviled.

THE STORMBOUND DIVIDE

Mara's own connection to the Core Song was, by comparison, a more refined, more nuanced interpretation, a translation from the raw, elemental frequencies into a form that her consciousness could comprehend. She was a Listener, yes, but she was also a translator, a conduit for the planet's multifaceted voice. The Skybound, in their pursuit of a singular, ordered tune, had misunderstood the very nature of communication. They believed that control was achieved through dictation, through the imposition of a single, absolute decree. But the planet's song revealed a different truth: that true harmony arose from understanding, from the recognition of diverse voices, and from the willingness to listen and adapt.

This understanding brought with it a profound sense of empowerment. Mara realized that her role was not to command, not to impose her will upon the planet or its inhabitants, but to facilitate. She was to be a bridge, a harmonizer, a catalyst for understanding between the disparate elements of the world. The Skybound sought to silence the cacophony, to enforce a sterile, monochromatic existence. But Mara saw that the planet's vitality lay precisely in its vibrant, sometimes chaotic, interplay of voices. Her task was to amplify those voices, to ensure they were heard, and to help the world find its balance not through suppression, but through the vibrant interplay of its diverse melodies.

The concept began to crystallize in her mind: a radical alternative to the Skybound's rigid dominion. Instead of imposing order, she could foster connection. Instead of demanding compliance, she could encourage dialogue. The storms, for instance, were not merely destructive forces to be quelled. They were the planet's passionate pronouncements, its expressions of pain and defiance. If she could understand the 'why' behind their intensity – the specific grievance being sung – perhaps she could help translate that message, or even guide the planet's energy into a less destructive, more communicative outlet.

Consider the dragons. Their aerial skirmishes, often interpreted by the Skybound as acts of wanton aggression, were Mara's new focus. She began to perceive the underlying currents of their interactions, the intricate patterns of their songs. These were not random battles, but often territorial disputes, expressions of ancient rivalries, or even communications regarding the health of specific ley lines or elemental nexus points.

The Skybound saw only the conflict; Mara began to see the complex, often crucial, information being exchanged. Her role, then, could be to interpret these dragon dialogues, to mediate, not by force, but by understanding the unique dialect of each dragon clan, by recognizing the ancestral songs that guided their actions. She could become an ambassador between species, translating the guttural roar of the dragon into a language that even the most detached Skybound entity might begin to comprehend, not as a threat, but as a vital piece of planetary discourse.

This extended to the very consciousness of sentient beings. The subtle anxieties that rippled through villages during periods of Skybound interference, the quiet despair of communities facing ecological disruption – these were all notes in the Core Song, expressions of suffering and imbalance. Mara realized she could not simply 'fix' these problems with a wave of her hand. Instead, she could attune herself to the specific lament being sung by these communities, understand its root cause, and then, using her amplified connection to the Core Song, help them find their own voice, their own way to express their needs and grievances in a manner that would resonate with the broader planetary symphony. This was not about control, but about empowerment, about helping individuals and communities find their own unique melody within the grander composition.

The implications were staggering. If all life communicated through this universal language, then perhaps the very concept of 'enemy' was a construct of misunderstanding, a failure to listen. The Skybound, blinded by their own singular perspective, saw only deviation from their ideal. They failed to recognize that every variation, every unique frequency, was essential to the planet's overall vibrance. Mara's emergent understanding suggested a path toward reconciliation, not through conquest, but through empathy and shared listening.

THE STORMBOUND DIVIDE

She began to experiment, tentatively at first. When a particularly violent squall threatened a coastal village, Mara focused, not on dispersing the storm, but on understanding its song. She heard the planet's frustration, its deep-seated anger at a Skybound device that was disrupting the natural oceanic currents. Instead of trying to fight the storm, she focused on the Core Song's inherent ability to harmonize. She amplified the planet's message of disruption, channeling it not as a violent outburst, but as a clear, resonant plea for the Skybound to cease their interference.

She didn't command the storm to stop; she helped the planet articulate its grievance, its need for the natural flow to be restored. The storm, while still powerful, seemed to shift its trajectory, its fury abating slightly as it moved away from the village, its message seemingly understood, or at least acknowledged. It was a subtle shift, but it was a monumental victory, a testament to the power of communication over brute force.

This realization brought a new dimension to her understanding of the Skybound themselves. Were they, too, capable of hearing this song, albeit in a distorted, muted form? Or had their pursuit of perfection, their self-imposed isolation in the celestial realms, rendered them deaf to the planet's true voice? If they could be made to understand, even in a rudimentary way, the language of the world they sought to govern, perhaps a path to coexistence could be forged. Her role, then, was not just to defend the planet, but to act as its interpreter, its ambassador to beings who spoke a different, more rigid dialect of existence.

The interconnectedness was not merely between species, but between the organic and the inorganic, the living and the seemingly inert. The very rocks, the veins of ore deep within the earth, resonated with a slow, tectonic hum, speaking of geological pressures, of the planet's ceaseless reshaping. Even the celestial bodies, the distant stars and moons, sang their own cosmic songs, their gravitational dances and energetic emissions contributing to the grand, universal symphony. The Skybound saw these as mere physical laws, immutable and to be controlled. Mara saw them as expressions of a deeper cosmic language, a language that the planet itself understood and actively participated in.

This radical interconnectedness offered a profound alternative to the prevailing paradigm of conflict. The Skybound operated on a principle of dominion, of imposing their will. Mara, now attuned to the universal language, saw the potential for collaboration, for co-creation. If she could help different species understand each other's songs, if she could facilitate a dialogue between the terrestrial and the celestial, then the very foundations of the Skybound's hierarchical control would begin to crumble. Their power relied on separation, on the illusion of distinct, often opposing, forces. Mara's understanding revealed the underlying unity, the shared language that bound everything together.

Her journey was no longer about simply surviving or protecting a specific territory. It was about fostering a planetary consciousness, about reminding the world, and potentially the cosmos, of the profound beauty and strength that lay in its inherent diversity. The Core Song was not just a defense mechanism; it was an invitation, an ongoing conversation. And Mara, standing at the precipice of this vast, intricate network of communication, knew she had to accept that invitation, to learn its every nuance, and to ensure that its vital, life-affirming melody continued to resonate, not just for the planet, but for all of existence.

The challenge was immense, the path uncertain, but the language of the world was now open to her, and in its embrace, she found not just power, but purpose. It was a purpose that transcended mere survival, a purpose that spoke of harmony, of understanding, and of the boundless potential that lay within the interconnected song of life. The Skybound sought to impose silence; Mara was learning to conduct a symphony.

The weight of the Core Song settled within Mara, not as a burden, but as a mantle of profound understanding. The planet's symphony, once a distant hum, was now an intrinsic part of her being. She was no longer merely an observer, but a participant, her own voice now harmonizing with the chorus of existence. This intimate connection had revealed a truth more potent than any physical force: that the world was not a static entity to be controlled, but a living, breathing consciousness, its every tremor and whisper a form of communication, a plea for balance. It was this revelation that birthed the prophecy, not as a preordained script of events, but as a tapestry of choices, each thread representing a decision that would weave the future into being.

The prophecy began to coalesce, not in spoken words, but in a series of vivid, resonant visions that unfurled within her mind's eye. She saw two paths diverging, stark and absolute. The first path was shrouded in shadow, a testament to the Skybound's rigid dominion. It was a world of sterile order, where the vibrant symphony of life had been muted into a monotone drone. Forests stood as silent, petrified sentinels, their ancient songs silenced, their leaves no longer rustling with the wisdom of ages. Oceans, their mighty breaths stilled, lay placid and lifeless, their deep currents no longer carrying the pulse of oceanic life.

The dragons, once roaring testaments to untamed power, were depicted as spectral echoes, their elemental songs reduced to faint, mournful sighs, their fiery essence dampened. In this future, sentience itself had been curated, its wild, unpredictable melodies suppressed in favor of a manufactured tranquility. The planet, though outwardly ordered, was fundamentally dying, its spirit withered, its vibrant ecosystem reduced to a sterile, predictable machine. This was the future born of unchecked ambition, of the desperate clinging to a singular, flawed vision of perfection.

Then, the vision shifted, and the second path unfurled, bathed in the warm, golden light of a dawning sun. This path was not one of pristine uniformity, but of vibrant, harmonious diversity. She saw the forests teeming with life, the ancient trees sharing their slow, deep melodies, their roots a living network of interconnected consciousness. The oceans surged with vitality, their waves a boisterous song of life, their depths a testament to the intricate ballet of marine existence. The dragons soared, their roars a powerful, resonant declaration of their elemental sovereignty, their aerial dances a testament to the wild, untamed spirit that the Core Song embraced. Here, sentient beings lived not in isolation, but in communion, their individual songs blending into a rich, complex harmony.

She saw villages thriving, not through forced adherence to decree, but through mutual understanding, their laments acknowledged and translated into constructive dialogue. She saw the Skybound, not as overlords, but as participants, their rigid pronouncements softened by the planet's song, their perspective broadened by the understanding that true order was not imposed, but cultivated. This future was not without its challenges, its storms of discord or whispers of dissent, but these were woven into the fabric of life, acknowledged and addressed, not suppressed. This was the future born of respect, of empathy, and of the profound understanding that the planet's song, in all its multifaceted glory, was the truest expression of existence.

Mara saw that the prophecy was not a prediction, but a clarion call. It spoke of a pivotal moment, a crossroads where the collective consciousness of all beings would determine which path would be forged. The Skybound, with their insatiable hunger for control, represented the encroaching shadow of the first path. Their attempts to impose their singular melody, to silence the dissonant yet vital notes of the planet, were the greatest threat. Their ambition, cloaked in the guise of order, was a poison that would eventually extinguish the very life they claimed to protect.

The prophecy also illuminated the dragons' role. They were not mere beasts of elemental fury, but guardians of the planet's wild heart, their songs the most potent expressions of its untamed spirit. Their battles, their roars, were the planet's primal screams against the Skybound's encroaching silence. To silence the dragons would be to deafen the world to its own fierce, life-affirming essence. Their continued defiance was not aggression; it was a vital act of planetary self-preservation.

For humanity, and indeed all sentient life, the prophecy offered a different kind of power: the power of listening. It was a call to shed the illusion of separation, to recognize the interconnectedness that the Core Song revealed. The prophecy urged them to understand that their grievances, their joys, their very existence, were notes in the planetary symphony. To deny these notes, to suppress them, was to weaken the whole. To embrace them, to translate them into understanding and action, was to strengthen the planet's song and ensure its survival.

Mara understood her own role with stark clarity. She was the catalyst, the bridge. Her connection to the Core Song was not a gift for her own aggrandizement, but a responsibility to amplify the planet's voice, to translate its complex harmonies into a language that all could comprehend. She was to remind the world that balance was not the absence of difference, but the harmonious interplay of all voices. The Skybound sought to impose a single, sterile note. She was to champion the full, vibrant orchestra.

The prophecy was a warning against the seductive allure of unchecked ambition, the dangerous belief that dominance could equate to harmony. It cautioned against the folly of silencing dissent, of eradicating the 'other' in a desperate pursuit of uniformity. The Skybound embodied this folly, their celestial perfection a hollow shell devoid of true life. Their reign, if allowed to solidify, would be a slow, agonizing death for the world, a descent into a silent, static void.

Conversely, the prophecy sang of hope, of the boundless potential that lay in embracing diversity. It spoke of a future where understanding was the ultimate currency, where empathy was the guiding principle, and where collaboration, not conquest, was the path to true strength. It was a vision of a world where every species, every individual, was valued for its unique contribution to the grand symphony, where the raw, elemental power of the dragons, the slow wisdom of the ancient trees, and the complex melodies of sentient beings all found their place.

Mara felt the weight of this message settle upon her, not as a burden of doom, but as a sacred trust. This was the truth she had to carry back, the understanding that would ignite the flames of choice. The coming conflict, the confrontation with the Skybound, would not be merely a battle for territory or power. It would be a test of wills, a fundamental decision about the nature of existence itself. Would the world choose the sterile silence of subjugation, or the vibrant, resonant song of life?

The prophecy was a stark reminder that the planet was not a passive stage for the dramas of its inhabitants, but an active participant, its very life force intertwined with the choices made. The Core Song was its consciousness, its voice, and its plea. To ignore that voice was to court disaster. To heed it was to embrace a future of profound, interconnected vitality. Mara knew, with an unwavering certainty born of the planet's song, that this message of choice, of balance, and of the enduring power of life's diverse melodies, was the only future worth fighting for. The climax was not an event to be endured, but a choice to be made, and the planet's prophecy was the guide.

The resonance of the Core Song, once a torrent within Mara, had settled into a steady, powerful current. It was a constant thrum beneath the surface of her thoughts, a living awareness of the planet's intricate symphony. Yet, the revelation of the prophecy, the stark dichotomy of futures laid bare, had not brought with it a sense of solitude. Instead, a new understanding bloomed, as organic and inevitable as the blossoming of a celestial flower. The Core Song, she now perceived, was not a singular melody that she alone had unlocked. It was a grand opera, with countless instruments playing their part, many of them, perhaps, yet to discover their voices.

The implications of this dawned on her with a quiet, yet insistent, force. If the planet possessed a consciousness, a song, then it was only logical that there would be others attuned to its frequencies, others who, like her, had been touched by its ancient melodies. The Skybound, in their relentless pursuit of control, had sought to impose a single, sterile note upon this vibrant chorus, believing that true harmony could only be achieved through uniformity. But Mara had seen the truth in the prophecy: that the world's strength lay in its diversity, in the intricate interplay of myriad voices. And if this was so, then she could not be the only one capable of hearing, of understanding, of responding to the planet's plea.

The idea of other Listeners, dormant or perhaps actively engaged in their own quiet ways across the vast tapestry of the world, began to weave itself into the fabric of her thoughts. They might be scattered like seeds, waiting for the right conditions to sprout. They could be hidden in the shadowed depths of ancient forests, their ears attuned to the slow, profound wisdom of the trees. They might reside in bustling metropolises, their connection to the planet a silent counterpoint to the clamor of civilization, a secret solace in the urban wilderness. Perhaps they were those who lived in close communion with the wild elements, their spirits resonating with the untamed energies of the earth, the sea, or the sky. The Core Song, which had awakened within her with such profound clarity, had not been a solitary event. It was a signal, a broadcast, and she suspected, with a growing certainty, that it was a signal that had the potential to reach many.

Her own awakening, she now understood, was not an end in itself, but a beginning. It was the first note struck in a melody that was meant to swell, to encompass, to awaken. The energy of the Core Song, now amplified by her conscious embrace of its power, was like a potent elixir, seeping into the very soil of the world, a subtle yet pervasive force that could stir dormant sensitivities. It was a call to arms, not of steel and fire, but of perception and resonance. The planet, through its song, was reaching out, seeking to connect, to rally its scattered inheritors.

She imagined these potential Listeners, each with their own unique relationship to the planet's symphony. Some might be born with an innate sensitivity, a natural inclination to hear the whispers of the wind or the murmurs of the earth, a connection they might have dismissed as mere intuition or imagination. Others might have had fleeting experiences, moments of profound connection to nature that they could not explain, brief glimpses into the world's hidden heart. These were the individuals who, if Mara's burgeoning understanding was correct, were now poised on the precipice of a deeper awakening. The amplified hum of the Core Song was like a tuning fork, striking a chord that would resonate with their own latent frequencies, drawing them, however subtly, towards a shared consciousness.

This vision of a connected network of Listeners was intoxicating. It was a tangible hope, a living embodiment of the prophecy's promise of harmonious diversity. Imagine, she thought, the strength of such a collective. If they could learn to communicate, to share their understanding, to amplify each other's abilities, they could become a formidable force for healing. They could act as conduits, channeling the planet's restorative energies, mending the wounds inflicted by imbalance and exploitation. They could become the world's custodians, its healers, its defenders, working in concert with the natural rhythms of existence. Their collective wisdom could guide communities towards sustainable practices, fostering a deeper respect for the delicate web of life. Their amplified connection could soothe the planet's distress, accelerating its recovery from the scars of neglect and the ravages of the Skybound's sterile ambitions.

But this potent vision was immediately tempered by a chilling counterpoint. If such a network of awakened Listeners was a beacon of hope, it was also a potential vulnerability. The Skybound, with their insatiable desire for control and their cold, calculating intellect, would undoubtedly recognize the immense power such a connected consciousness represented. They would see it not as a force for healing and balance, but as a potential threat to their dominion, a wild, unpredictable element that needed to be contained, controlled, or eradicated.

Mara felt a prickle of fear, sharp and cold, at the thought of the Skybound discovering this nascent network. They would not seek to understand or to integrate. Their methodology was one of subjugation. They would attempt to co-opt the Listeners, to twist their connection to the planet into a tool for their own agenda. They might try to silence their voices, to sever their connection to the Core Song, or worse, to pervert their abilities, turning their gifts of listening and healing into instruments of control. The very awakening that promised salvation could, if discovered by the wrong hands, become the catalyst for a new, more insidious form of oppression.

The thought was a heavy weight, a dark shadow cast upon the bright possibility. The world was a dangerous place, and the Skybound were its most predatory inhabitants. They saw power not as a shared resource, but as a commodity to be hoarded. If they learned of the Listeners, they would not hesitate to exploit them, to weaponize their connection for their own sterile vision of order. This meant that Mara's role was not just to embrace her own awakening, but to protect the potential awakenings of others. She had to tread carefully, to foster this nascent network with discretion, to ensure that the spark she had ignited did not fall into the wrong hands and become a conflagration that consumed everything it touched.

She pondered the implications of this delicate balance. How could she foster this network without drawing unwanted attention? How could she reach out to those who might be awakening without revealing herself prematurely to the Skybound? It was a puzzle that required not only her newfound connection to the planet's song, but also a shrewd understanding of the machinations of her enemies. She had to become not only a Listener, but also a guardian.

The Core Song offered whispers of guidance, not in explicit directions, but in the subtle shifts of its melody, in the currents of energy it revealed. It showed her glimpses of places where the earth's song was strongest, where life pulsed with an undeniable vibrancy. These were likely the places where other Listeners might be found, where their own frequencies would be most readily awakened by the amplified song. These were the cradles of connection, the fertile ground for the seeds of consciousness.

Her journey had already taken her to the edges of the world, and the prophecy indicated that the coming confrontation would draw her to its very heart. But before that, there was a subtler mission, a quieter undertaking. She had to learn to discern the faint echoes of the Core Song in the world around her, to identify the subtle vibrations that indicated another Listener's presence. It would be a task requiring immense patience and acute awareness, a constant listening not just to the grand symphony, but to the individual notes that might be struggling to emerge.

The Skybound believed that life was a chaotic cacophony, a problem to be solved through rigid order. They were blind to the inherent beauty and resilience of complexity, deaf to the nuanced language of the planet. But Mara had heard. She had heard the warnings, the pleas, the enduring song of life. And now, she was beginning to understand that she was not alone in her ability to hear. She was a single voice, yes, but a voice that was part of a chorus waiting to be assembled. The prophecy was not just about a choice between two futures; it was about the awakening of a collective consciousness, a planetary awakening that would determine which future would ultimately prevail. The weight of this responsibility was immense, but so too was the burgeoning hope. The song was growing louder, and it was calling to all who would listen.

Chapter Ten
THE GATHERING STORM

The air in the Citadel felt heavy, thick with the unspoken anxieties of a world teetering on the brink. Mara Lysenne stepped onto the familiar flagstones, yet the ground beneath her felt alien, a mere echo of the vibrant, living earth she had come to know. Her journey had stripped away the ordinary, replacing it with an awareness so profound it was almost a physical burden. The Core Song, once a distant murmur, now pulsed through her veins, a constant, living current of the planet's own lifeblood. It sang of ancient forests, of mountain peaks that scraped the sky, of oceans teeming with unsung melodies, and beneath it all, a deep, resonant ache – the planet's wound, its plea.

She was not the same Mara who had left. The trials had forged her, the revelation of the prophecy had etched itself into her very soul, and the whispered truths of the Core Song had reshaped her perception of existence. She carried not just knowledge, but a visceral understanding of the intricate tapestry of life, of the interconnectedness that bound every living thing, from the smallest spore to the mightiest leviathan. And with this understanding came the chilling clarity of the Skybound's ultimate goal: not merely dominion, but an absolute, sterile silence, the eradication of all that was wild, unpredictable, and truly alive. Their pursuit of order was the pursuit of death, a slow, deliberate suffocation of the planet's vibrant spirit.

Her return was not to solace, but to the epicenter of the storm. The whispers she had heard in the hallowed, hidden places had solidified into a dire warning: the gathering clouds were not merely metaphorical. A storm, vast and destructive, was indeed brewing, fueled by the escalating conflict between the fractured human factions and the encroaching, icy ambition of the Skybound. She had been tasked, not with a weapon, but with a truth. Her authority stemmed not from any rank or title, but from the absolute certainty of her connection to the planet, from her unwavering grasp of the abyssal truth that lay at the heart of their struggle.

The Citadel, once a symbol of resilience, now felt like a gilded cage, its inhabitants caught in the intricate dance of fear and defiance. The leaders, burdened by their own political machitions, their eyes often averted from the larger cosmic drama, were a disparate group. There were those who still clung to the old ways of war, their strategies forged in the fires of past conflicts, now woefully inadequate against the alien might of the Skybound. Others, their spirits crushed by the relentless pressure, were beginning to contemplate surrender, the tempting lull of peace at any cost. And then there were the few, the true believers, their hope a flickering candle in the encroaching darkness, their faith in a future that seemed increasingly out of reach.

Mara observed them, her gaze now capable of piercing the veils of ego and ambition, of seeing the raw, vulnerable core that lay beneath. She saw the fear in the eyes of General Kaelen, a man whose life had been dedicated to the defense of their world, now grappling with an enemy that defied all conventional understanding. She felt the weariness of Elder Lyra, the keeper of their history, her spirit burdened by the weight of generations of struggle. And she sensed the desperation of those who, like herself, had glimpsed the precipice, and were terrified of the fall.

She knew that simply speaking the words of the prophecy would not be enough. The prophecy was a map, a guide, but the journey required more than just following a path. It required understanding, conviction, and a willingness to embrace the unexpected. The Skybound's strength lay not only in their advanced technology, but in their psychological warfare, their ability to sow discord and exploit weakness. They thrived on chaos and fear, and their ultimate victory would be the shattering of any hope, any sense of unity.

Mara's first task, therefore, was not to command, but to connect. She had to find a way to translate the language of the Core Song into terms that resonated with the hearts and minds of those who were blinded by conflict or paralyzed by despair. She had to help them hear what she had heard, to feel what she had felt, to understand that their individual struggles, their petty squabbles, were but fleeting notes in a much grander, and far more perilous, symphony.

She sought out the Council chamber, the air within thick with the scent of aged parchment and the palpable tension of impending decisions. The room was a microcosm of the world's fractured state. Stalwart warriors sat beside shrewd diplomats, their faces etched with the weariness of endless debate. The mood was somber, the discussions circling around tactical retreats and defensive strategies, the ever-present specter of the Skybound looming large.

As Mara entered, a hush fell over the chamber. Her presence, no longer that of a lost child or a budding warrior, now commanded a different kind of attention. There was an aura about her, a quiet strength that emanated from her very being, a luminescence that seemed to hold the very essence of the planet she had communed with. Her eyes, once filled with youthful curiosity, now held the depth of ancient wisdom, reflecting a profound understanding that transcended the immediate concerns of war and politics.

"Mara," General Kaelen's voice was rough, tinged with a relief that warred with his inherent suspicion. "You have returned. We had feared... we had feared the worst."

Mara met his gaze, her own steady and unwavering. "The worst has not yet come, General. But it is closer than any of us dare to admit." Her voice, though soft, carried a resonance that silenced the murmurs in the room. It was a voice that had spoken with mountains and oceans, with ancient trees and the very breath of the planet.

Elder Lyra, her frail form radiating a surprising authority, leaned forward. "Your journey, child, was shrouded in mystery. What did you find beyond the Veil?"

Mara took a deep breath, the scent of the Citadel's ancient stones grounding her even as the Core Song thrummed within. "I found the truth," she said, her gaze sweeping across the assembled faces, meeting each one with a quiet intensity. "I found the song of our world. And it is a song of life, a song of interconnectedness, a song that is now in grave danger."

She spoke not of prophecies and prophecies' riddles, but of the living, breathing consciousness of their planet. She described the intricate web of energy that bound every living thing, the subtle currents of life that flowed through the earth, the air, the water. She painted a picture of a world that was not merely a collection of resources to be exploited, but a vibrant, sentient being, capable of experiencing joy, pain, and a profound, enduring love for its inhabitants.

"The Skybound," she continued, her voice gaining a new strength, a raw power born of her direct communion with the planet's suffering, "do not understand this. They see only chaos, only inefficiency. They seek to impose their sterile order, to silence the song, to sever the connections that make us who we are. They believe that true harmony can only be achieved through uniformity, through the eradication of all that is wild and untamed. But they are wrong. The planet's strength lies not in its sameness, but in its infinite diversity, in the unique melody each life form contributes to the grand symphony."

She spoke of the prophecy, not as a rigid decree, but as a reflection of the planet's own desperate will to survive, to find a way to mend its wounds and resist the encroaching silence. She explained that the choice was not merely between two paths, but between embracing the full spectrum of life, with all its glorious imperfections and vibrant complexities, or succumbing to a barren, lifeless uniformity.

"I have heard the planet's plea," Mara declared, her eyes burning with an inner fire. "It does not ask for war. It asks for understanding. It asks for us to remember who we are, not as warring factions, but as children of this living world. The Core Song is not just a melody; it is a call to awaken. It is a signal, sent out to all who have the capacity to hear, to remind them of their connection, to rally them to the cause of life itself."

She spoke of the potential for others to awaken, of the hidden Listeners scattered across the world, individuals who, like her, had been touched by the planet's song, even if they did not yet fully understand it. She explained that the amplified hum of the Core Song, a consequence of her own deepened connection, was like a beacon, subtly stirring these latent sensitivities, drawing them, however unconsciously, towards a shared awareness.

"We are not alone in this," Mara asserted, her voice ringing with a newfound hope. "There are others. Others who feel the earth's pulse, who hear the whispers of the wind, who understand the language of the stars. They are scattered, perhaps afraid, perhaps unaware of their own gifts. But they are there. And they, along with us, must be prepared. The Skybound seek to extinguish every spark of life, and they will not hesitate to silence any who stand in their way."

Her words hung in the air, heavy with the weight of their implications. Some listened with rapt attention, their faces etched with a dawning comprehension. Others, particularly the more pragmatic military leaders, remained skeptical, their minds still tethered to the tangible realities of troop movements and weaponry. General Kaelen, however, his brow furrowed, looked at Mara with a new, unnerving intensity. He had witnessed the impossible before, and the quiet conviction in her voice, the almost ethereal glow that seemed to surround her, spoke of a truth that transcended mere rhetoric.

"You speak of a connection, Mara, a song," he said, his voice a low rumble. "How can we, who are trained in the art of war, learn to hear this song? How can we fight an enemy with melodies and whispers?"

Mara offered a faint, knowing smile. "The Skybound are powerful, General, but their power is finite, built upon the subjugation of life. Our power, the planet's power, is infinite, born from the very act of creation. They seek to control, to dictate. We must learn to harmonize, to resonate. We must understand that the greatest weapon we possess is not steel, but spirit. Their strength lies in their unity of purpose, a chilling, imposed order. Our strength lies in our diversity, a vibrant, organic chorus."

She explained that her return was not merely to warn, but to guide. She would help them understand the subtle signs, the whispers of the Core Song that would reveal the paths forward, the vulnerabilities of the Skybound, and the hidden strengths of their own world. She spoke of the places where the planet's song was strongest, where the echoes of life pulsed with an undeniable vibrancy. These were the cradles of connection, the fertile ground for the awakening of others.

"My journey has taken me to the edges of this world," Mara revealed. "But the prophecy speaks of a confrontation at its heart. Before we face the Skybound head-on, we must tend to our own garden. We must seek out those who are already attuned, those who can hear the song. They are our allies, our future. And we must learn to protect them, to shield them from the Skybound's gaze, for they will be the first to be silenced if discovered."

She looked at Elder Lyra, her gaze filled with a deep respect. "Elder, your knowledge of our history, of our ancestors' connection to the land, is vital. You have preserved the echoes of the old ways. We must draw upon that wisdom. We must find the stories, the legends, that speak of those who could commune with the earth, for they may be the very ones who are awakening now."

Elder Lyra nodded, her ancient eyes alight with a renewed purpose. "The ancient texts speak of the 'Earth-Whisperers,' of those who could calm storms with a song, who could coax life from barren soil. We had dismissed them as myths, as fanciful tales. But perhaps... perhaps they were more. Perhaps they were the first Listeners."

Mara's attention then turned to the military strategists, her expression serious. "General Kaelen, your understanding of tactics, of defense, is invaluable. But we must broaden our definition of warfare. The Skybound's technology is advanced, their strategies cold and calculating. But they are blind to the nuances of the natural world. They do not understand the power of resilience, the strength of adaptation. We must learn to fight not just with force, but with the very essence of this world. We must learn to become a part of its defense."

She spoke of using the planet's own rhythms to their advantage, of understanding the currents of the wind, the patterns of the tides, the very vibrations of the earth. These were not mere environmental factors, but living energies that the Skybound, with their disconnected existence, could not comprehend.

"They are coming," Mara stated, her voice dropping to a low, urgent tone. "The storm is not a metaphor. They are mobilizing their forces. Their objective is not just conquest, but erasure. They wish to silence the Core Song, to render our world inert. But the planet will not yield without a fight. And it has awakened us, its children, to be its champions."

She knew that her words were a radical departure from the usual discourse of war and diplomacy. She was asking them to embrace a different understanding of power, to look beyond the tangible and the quantifiable, to trust in something as intangible as a song. It was a daunting task, a challenge that would require immense courage and an open heart. But Mara Lysenne had returned not with a sword, but with a seed of hope, a melody of defiance that she intended to cultivate until it became a roar that could shake the very foundations of the Skybound's sterile dominion. The gathering storm was upon them, but within its tumultuous embrace, a new symphony was beginning to play.

The hushed urgency that had permeated the Citadel for weeks had begun to coalesce, not into panic, but into a focused, if still uncertain, determination. In a hidden encampment nestled within the ancient, shadowed valleys of the Serpent's Tooth mountain range, Cael Thornevale worked his own brand of magic, a magic of words, of compromise, and of a shared, desperate vision. He had been a nomad of diplomacy for months, a weaver of unlikely alliances, his hands calloused not from swordplay, but from the relentless clasping of hands – hands of scholars weary of suppressed knowledge, hands of farmers whose lands were poisoned by Accord negligence, hands of traders whose routes were choked by Conclave tariffs, and even, cautiously, the clawed hands of certain dragon clans who had begun to see the Skybound's chilling sterility as a threat to all life, organic and draconic alike.

His current audience was a tapestry of these disparate elements, gathered under the pale light of a waning moon. Before him sat Elara Vance, her face a mask of grim practicality, representing the Free Cities of the Sunstone Coast, settlements that had always bristled under Accord authority. Beside her, the grizzled Kael of the Iron Peaks, a man whose clan had once been notorious raiders but who now sought a different path, his gaze sharp and assessing. And in the shadows, their forms barely visible, were the representatives of the Whisperwind Dragons, their scales shimmering with an ancient, muted luminescence, their presence a testament to the lengths Cael had gone to forge this unity.

"They call it the Accord," Cael began, his voice low but carrying through the quiet air, "a pact for peace. But it is a pact of chains. They offer order, but it is the order of the tomb. They speak of progress, but it is the progress of erosion. And behind them, the Conclave pulls the strings, feeding on our divisions, ensuring we remain fractured, vulnerable." He gestured to the gathered faces, each reflecting a different facet of the world's struggle. "You, each of you, have felt the sting of their control. You have seen your homes diminished, your traditions eroded, your very lifeforce drained."

He paused, letting his words sink in, observing the subtle shifts in posture, the tightening of jaws, the flicker of understanding in weary eyes. "For too long, we have fought each other. The Free Cities against the Accord heartlands, the mountain clans against the coastal traders, the dragons against... well, against everyone, historically. And in doing so, we have played directly into their hands. The Skybound are the ultimate expression of this detached, sterile order. They see our world not as a living, breathing entity, but as a resource to be cataloged, controlled, and ultimately, emptied of its wild heart. They fear what they cannot understand, and they seek to eradicate it."

A low rumble emanated from one of the Whisperwind Dragons, a sound that was more a vibration than an audible noise, a subtle acknowledgment of Cael's truth. Kael of the Iron Peaks grunted, a sound of agreement. "Our raiders... they took what they needed. But this... this is different. They take everything. They leave nothing but dust."

Elara Vance, ever the pragmatist, interjected, her voice sharp. "Words are wind, Thornevale. We have resisted the Accord for generations. We have weathered their blockades and their taxes. But the Skybound... their ships blot out the sun. Their weapons shatter stone. How do we fight a storm with speeches?"

Cael's gaze met hers, and there was no trace of defiance, only a profound earnestness. "The storm is not just in the sky, Elara. It is within us. It is in the way we have allowed ourselves to be disconnected from the very world that sustains us. The Accord, the Conclave, the Skybound – they all share a fundamental flaw. They operate from a place of disconnection. They see the world as a machine, and themselves as its engineers. They fail to see its song."

He leaned forward, his voice dropping slightly, as if imparting a sacred secret. "Mara Lysenne, who has journeyed beyond the Veil, has returned with a truth that can shatter their sterile order. She has heard the Core Song. She has communed with the very soul of our world. And she has revealed that our planet is not a mere object, but a living, breathing consciousness. It sings. It feels. It desires survival. And its song is not one of sterile uniformity, but of infinite, vibrant diversity."

He looked at the dragons, their ancient eyes reflecting the moon. "You, the dragons, have always understood this on a primal level, haven't you? You are creatures of immense power, deeply attuned to the earth's currents, to the very breath of life. Your ancient myths speak of harmony, of balance. The Skybound seek to impose a single, monotonous note. The Core Song is a symphony, and every life form, from the smallest insect to the mightiest leviathan, plays its part."

The dragon representative, a creature of immense age whose name was lost to human tongues and was known only as 'Opalscale,' shifted her weight. Her voice, when it came, was like the grinding of ancient stones, resonant and deep. "The Skybound... they are a void. They consume. They do not understand the warmth of the sun, the taste of rain, the joy of flight for its own sake. They seek to impose their silence upon us all. We have seen this encroaching stillness, a creeping death that chills even our ancient blood. Your Mara... she speaks of what we have long felt, but could not articulate. The song... yes, we feel its echoes."

Cael's heart swelled with a nascent hope. This was it. The turning point. "Precisely, Opalscale. The Skybound's strength lies in their rigid logic, their predictable patterns, their reliance on technology that alienates them from the living world. But they are blind to the planet's own defenses, to its inherent resilience. Mara has shown us that by attuning ourselves to the Core Song, we can tap into that power. We can learn to move with the planet's rhythms, to anticipate their movements not through cold calculation, but through a deeper, innate understanding. We can become the planet's immune system, its living defense."

He turned back to Elara. "Elara, your Free Cities are centers of innovation, of learning. You have preserved knowledge that the Accord has sought to suppress. You understand the subtle mechanics of the world, not just its grand gestures. Imagine what you could achieve if you began to listen not just to your own minds, but to the whispers of the earth itself. Imagine understanding the currents of the sea not just for trade, but for defense, for communication, for a deeper connection with the ocean's vast consciousness."

Elara frowned, considering this. Her people were renowned for their astrolabe makers, their navigators, their engineers who harnessed geothermal energy. "The earth... it provides. It is a source of power. But it does not speak."

"It sings," Cael corrected gently. "And Mara can teach us to hear it. She can guide us to the places where the song is strongest, where its resonance can awaken the latent sensitivity in all of us. Think of your scholars, your historians. They have records of ancient peoples who lived in greater harmony with the land. These are not just stories, Elara. They are echoes of a time when our ancestors were more attuned, when they understood the planet's language. Mara's message is not a new prophecy; it is a rediscovery of an ancient truth, amplified by the urgency of our present crisis."

Kael of the Iron Peaks slammed a fist onto the rough-hewn table. "My people are strong. We know the mountains, the caves, the hidden passes. But we fight with steel and stone. How can we fight with a song?"

"Your strength is not just in your steel, Kael," Cael replied, his voice firm. "It is in your knowledge of the earth. The Skybound are accustomed to conquering inert landscapes. They are not prepared for a world that actively resists them. The mountains themselves can be our allies. The winds can be our messengers. The very earth can swallow their legions if we learn to work with its rhythms. Mara's insights can help us understand how to awaken these latent defenses, how to make the land itself an active participant in our struggle."

He looked at each of them, his gaze intense. "This is not a war of conventional armies. This is a war for the soul of our world. The Accord and the Conclave are already weakened, their authority crumbling under the weight of their own corruption and the growing threat of the Skybound. But they will cling to power. They will try to divide us further. And the Skybound will exploit every fissure. We must present a united front, a bulwark against their sterile tide."

Cael then produced a worn, leather-bound journal from within his tunic. It was not his own, but one he had received from Mara before her departure, filled with her initial, hesitant notes and observations. "Mara has entrusted me with her findings, with the wisdom she has gained. She does not seek to lead from a throne, but to guide from within. Her message is our guiding principle. We must listen to the planet. We must understand its song. And in doing so, we will find not only the strength to resist, but the wisdom to rebuild, to create a world where life thrives in all its glorious, untamed diversity."

He opened the journal, his finger tracing a passage. "She writes: 'The Core Song is not merely a phenomenon; it is a testament to the planet's will to exist. Every tremor, every rustle of leaves, every crashing wave, is a note in its grand opera. The Skybound seek to impose silence, to turn this opera into a dirge. Our task is to amplify the song, to find the resonance that will awaken every soul capable of hearing, and to defend the planet's right to sing.'"

He closed the journal, his expression resolute. "This is what we will stand for. This is our common ground. We will forge an alliance based not on shared grievances alone, but on a shared vision of a living world. We will gather those who are disillusioned with the Accord, those who have been abandoned by the Conclave, those who yearn for a future where their children can breathe free and their lands can flourish. We will seek out those who are already, however unknowingly, attuned to the planet's song – the healers, the shamans, the hermits, the children with unusual empathy for the wild. They are our hidden allies, and they will be the first targeted by the Skybound's sterile gaze."

Cael's gaze swept across the assembly. "This is not a call to arms in the traditional sense, though arms we will surely need. This is a call to awaken. A call to reconnect. A call to become the stewards of our own destiny, guided by the very pulse of the planet beneath our feet."

A silence fell, different from the tension of before. It was a silence of contemplation, of dawning realization. Opalscale shifted again, her ancient eyes fixed on Cael. "The agreement... it is fragile. The old wounds between our kind and yours run deep. But the encroaching silence... it is a threat to all that breathes and flies and swims. We will stand with you, Thornevale, if your Mara's song can truly resonate with the lifeblood of this world. We will lend our wings and our ancient knowledge to this awakened chorus."

Kael of the Iron Peaks, his gruff demeanor softening with a newfound understanding, nodded slowly. "My clan... we have always been guardians of the earth. Perhaps we have forgotten how to listen. If this song can teach us, we will learn. We will stand with you. We will protect those who can hear."

Elara Vance, her skepticism not entirely vanquished, but undeniably challenged, finally spoke. "The Sunstone Coast values pragmatism. If this 'Core Song' offers a tangible advantage, a way to defend ourselves that is more than just futile resistance, then we will consider it. But you must deliver. You must show us how this... this symphony... can defeat their machines."

Cael Thornevale allowed himself a small, hopeful smile. He knew the road ahead would be fraught with peril, that suspicion and old hatreds would not vanish overnight. But in this hidden valley, under the watchful gaze of the moon and the ancient mountains, a fragile seed had been planted. A coalition, bound not just by opposition, but by a shared reverence for life itself, had begun to take root. The gathering storm was indeed upon them, but within its heart, a new melody, a song of defiance and hope, was beginning to play, ready to challenge the encroaching silence.

He knew that Mara's insights were the key, the very foundation upon which this united front could stand. Her message of listening, of attuning, was not just a strategy; it was a philosophy, a pathway to survival that embraced the planet's essence rather than attempting to conquer it. And he, Cael Thornevale, would be the conductor of this nascent orchestra, coaxing harmony from discord, and preparing them all to sing against the encroaching silence.

The gilded halls of Accord City Prime, usually thrumming with the sterile hum of controlled efficiency, now echoed with a disquieting murmur. The veneer of unwavering authority was cracking, frayed by the persistent gnawing of dissent from the outer settlements and the unsettling tremors of unrest in their own heartlands. The news from the periphery was a constant trickle of defiance: protests met with brutal force that only fanned the flames of rebellion, vital supply lines disrupted by newly emboldened rogue factions, and whispers of nascent alliances forming in the shadowed corners of the world – alliances that dared to question the Accord's divine mandate. Within the Citadel itself, dissent was a more insidious poison, a slow burn of discontent among the bureaucratic strata, the disillusioned enforcers, and even some of the younger scholars who began to question the logic of their rigidly enforced doctrines. The once unshakeable edifice of their imposed order was showing fissures, and the architects of this sterile utopia felt the first prickle of fear.

In response, a desperate, almost frantic energy began to animate the upper echelons. The vision of absolute control, once their guiding star, now blinded them to the escalating reality. Their primary instinct, honed over decades of maintaining dominance through suppression, was to double down. The Resonance Towers, the very instruments of their ideological subjugation, were to be amplified. This was not a strategic reassessment, but a desperate gambit born of fear. The concept of the Core Song, of a living planet that sang and responded, was dismissed as the ravings of heretics and primitives. To them, the world was merely a complex machine, and its deviations from their meticulously calibrated order were glitches to be ironed out with overwhelming force.

High within the central spire of Accord City Prime, away from the increasingly restless populace, Administrator Valerius convened a council of his most trusted—and most unyielding—subordinates. The chamber was opulent, designed to project an aura of unassailable power, but the faces gathered around the polished obsidian table were etched with a grim urgency. Valerius himself, his face a mask of rigid control, tapped a long, slender finger against a holographic projection of the planet's energy grid.

"The anomalies are increasing," he stated, his voice clipped and devoid of emotion, yet carrying an undercurrent of palpable frustration. "The outlying sectors are demonstrating unacceptable levels of deviation. Disinformation campaigns, instigated by known agitators, are gaining traction. The Conclave, for all their posturing, are proving utterly ineffective in containing these pockets of defiance." He cast a pointed, dismissive glance at a portly man in the Conclave's crimson robes, who shifted uncomfortably. "We are left to manage the consequences of their incompetence."

"The Resonance Towers," began a stern-faced woman, Commander Lyra of the Skyguard, her silver-plated armor glinting in the artificial light. "Their output has been consistently maintained, Administrator. The standard protocols are being adhered to. We are broadcasting the harmonic frequencies as mandated."

Valerius waved a dismissive hand. "Standard protocols are no longer sufficient, Commander. The noise is... persistent. It interferes. We need to overwhelm it. We need to assert dominance, not merely maintain it." His gaze swept across the faces of his council. "The dissent is not merely ignorance; it is an active rejection of the Order. This cannot be tolerated. We must not only suppress the symptoms but eradicate the disease."

He leaned forward, his eyes gleaming with a cold fire. "We will initiate Project Ætherium. The Resonance Towers will be recalibrated to their maximum capacity. We will not simply broadcast the harmonic frequencies; we will *flood* the planet with them. We will drown out the... *static*... with an undeniable wave of unified intent. The intention of the Accord is singular, absolute, and now, it will be unavoidable."

A ripple of unease passed through some of the council members, though their expressions remained carefully neutral. Project Ætherium was a hushed term, whispered about in the highest echelons, a theoretical undertaking that pushed the boundaries of the Accord's understanding of planetary manipulation. It involved a controlled overload of the Resonance network, a feat that carried inherent risks, not just to the planet's delicate energy systems, but to the very stability of the towers themselves.

"Administrator," interjected an elderly scholar, Master Elmsworth, his voice trembling slightly, "the computations regarding Ætherium... they suggest a significant risk of cascade failure. The planet's natural energy fields are... complex. They are not designed to withstand such concentrated, artificial interference. We have observed a certain... *resilience*... in these fields when subjected to lesser stimuli."

Valerius's jaw tightened. "Resilience, Master Elmsworth? Or stubbornness? The Accord's purpose is to bring order to chaos. If the planet resists that order, then the planet must be compelled. Your role is to ensure the technology functions, not to question its application. The Skybound have developed new shielding protocols for the towers, and our energy reserves are at their peak. The risk is calculated. The reward – absolute compliance – is immeasurable."

Lyra, ever the pragmatist and deeply loyal to Valerius's vision of control, nodded sharply. "If it will silence the dissidents and reinforce the Accord's authority, then it is a necessary step. My Skyguard units are prepared to enforce the resulting sonic saturation zone, to quell any localized uprisings that might occur during the initiation phase. We will ensure that no one is left to question the Accord's directives."

The Conclave representative, a man named Vorlag, cleared his throat nervously. "While the Accord's... robust methods... are noted, perhaps a more diplomatic approach could be considered? The... unrest... in the outer settlements is largely due to resource allocation and access to vital medicines. A more equitable distribution might... alleviate some of the pressure."

Valerius fixed Vorlag with a gaze that could freeze fire. "Diplomacy is for those who have the luxury of time, Vorlag. We are past that point. The Accord's vision is one of purity, of singular purpose. The idea of 'equitable distribution' is a concession to weakness, a catering to the flawed desires of the less evolved. Our purpose is to elevate all beings, whether they understand it or not, to the Accord's ideal state of perfect order. If they resist this elevation, it is their failing, not ours."

He stood, signaling the end of the meeting. The holographic projection of the planet shifted, highlighting areas of intense red – the zones of greatest dissent. "The initiation of Project Ætherium will commence in three standard cycles. Commander Lyra, ensure all Skyguard personnel are fully briefed and deployed to strategic locations. Master Elmsworth, I expect your teams to have the primary Resonance Tower in full operational readiness, capable of sustained, amplified output. Any further... philosophical objections... will be considered insubordination."

As the council members filed out, Valerius remained, his gaze fixed on the projected planet. The dissent wasn't just a logistical problem; it was an ideological affront. It was proof that his vision, the grand design for a perfectly ordered existence, was not universally embraced. This was an unacceptable imperfection. The very idea that a living planet, with its chaotic, unpredictable rhythms, could defy his control was anathema. The Core Song, as Cael Thornevale and his ilk so naively termed it, was nothing more than the planet's own biological noise, a precursor to decay and disorder that the Accord was duty-bound to silence.

Meanwhile, in the shadowed valleys and sun-baked plains far from the Citadel's oppressive gaze, the Accord's desperate measures were already being felt. Reports began to filter through the nascent alliance Cael Thornevale was forging, tales of increased patrols by heavily armed Skyguard detachments, their aerial vehicles buzzing like predatory insects over settlements known for their discontent. The Conclave, under pressure from the Accord, had begun enacting draconian trade restrictions, effectively strangling the economic lifelines of independent towns and cities. Shipments of essential goods were being seized, tariffs skyrocketed, and the already precarious balance of trade was tilting precariously towards widespread scarcity.

In the Free Cities of the Sunstone Coast, Elara Vance received grim dispatches. The Accord had declared certain vital coastal routes to be 'strategic assets,' effectively seizing control of shipping lanes that had been free for generations. Their patrols were not just enforcing blockades; they were actively intercepting and confiscating vessels that dared to deviate from Accord-sanctioned paths, often with little to no justification. The once-bustling ports, symbols of independent prosperity, were becoming ghost towns, their docks silent and their warehouses empty.

"They are not just tightening their grip; they are squeezing the life out of us," Elara muttered to her trusted second-in-command, a weathered woman named Mara, as they reviewed the latest reports. "This isn't about controlling trade; it's about starving us into submission. They want to force us back into their fold, to accept their brand of order, or perish."

"And the Resonance Towers," Mara added, her voice laced with worry. "We've detected unusual energy spikes from the northern sector. Not the usual hum; something... more intense. Our geomancers are reporting a disturbance in the earth's natural resonance. It feels... wrong. Like a grinding, a forced imposition."

Elara's brow furrowed. The Accord's increasing desperation was evident. They were not just reacting to threats; they were actively escalating their methods, pushing the boundaries of their technological might in a bid to crush any sign of resistance. "Valerius is pushing the Accord to its breaking point. They are so terrified of losing control, they are willing to risk everything."

In the rugged terrain of the Iron Peaks, Kael of the Iron Peaks was also receiving troubling intelligence. Accord forces had begun a series of 'resource reclamation' operations in the foothills, areas traditionally under the influence of his clan. These were not simple patrols; they were organized military incursions, employing advanced sonic weaponry designed to disorient and incapacitate. Their stated objective was to secure rare mineral deposits, but the actual impact was the systematic dismantling of the clan's ancestral lands, their mining operations disrupted, and their traditional foraging grounds rendered inaccessible.

"They call it reclamation," Kael spat, his voice a low growl as he addressed his war council. "I call it theft. They march onto our lands, blast our caves with their infernal noise, and declare the resources 'for the good of all.' Whose good? Theirs, of course. They hoard everything, then dictate how the rest of us are meant to survive. This is not order; it is tyranny dressed in the robes of progress."

One of his captains, a burly man named Borin, nodded grimly. "We've had skirmishes. Our warriors are skilled in close combat, Administrator, but these Accord soldiers... they fight with machines. Their sonic emitters can bring a man to his knees without a single blade being drawn. And their Skyguard... they hover above, raining down energy blasts with impunity. It's like fighting shadows."

Kael gripped the hilt of his ancestral axe, the worn leather a familiar comfort. "The song that Thornevale spoke of... it must be more than just a whisper. It must be a roar that can shake their foundations. If their machines silence our spirits, we will be lost. We must find a way to amplify this song, to make the very earth rise against them."

The Whisperwind Dragons, ancient and wise, also felt the shift in the planet's energies. Opalscale, their designated ambassador to the nascent alliance, communicated her concerns to Cael Thornevale through a series of intricate, resonant pulses that Cael, through his developing attunement, could partially decipher. The dragons spoke of an unnatural vibration spreading across the planetary currents, a discord that felt like a planetary fever.

"The Skybound's machines are a disease," Opalscale's message conveyed, her form shimmering with agitation. "They seek to sterilize the world. They cannot comprehend the interconnectedness of all things. This 'Ætherium' they speak of... it is a crude attempt to impose their will upon a living entity. It will cause immense pain. It will tear at the fabric of life."

Cael felt a chill run down his spine. The Accord's desperation was leading them down a path of destruction, not just for those who opposed them, but for the planet itself. Their refusal to acknowledge the living nature of their world, their insistence on imposing a sterile, artificial order, was leading them to actions that could have catastrophic consequences. He understood, with chilling clarity, that their ideological purity had become a dangerous fanaticism, a blindness that threatened to extinguish the very life they claimed to govern.

The Accord's desperation was not just a political maneuver; it was a symptom of a deeply flawed ideology, a belief system that had curdled into a desperate, destructive attempt to impose an impossible perfection upon a world that thrived on vibrant, untamed chaos. They were a force of entropy masquerading as order, and their final, desperate gambits would shake the very foundations of existence. The storm was not just gathering; it was being actively manufactured by the Accord's own fear and hubris.

The rumblings of discontent, once a low thrum beneath the Accord's gilded surface, had escalated into a cacophony that even the most insulated ears in the Citadel could no longer ignore. The desperate, almost frantic recalibration of the Resonance Towers, the initiation of Project Ætherium, had served not to quell the dissent, but to amplify it, to push the burgeoning alliances and disparate factions towards a unified, albeit fractured, resistance. And amidst this growing storm, the Skybound Conclave, those enigmatic and often aloof arbiters of ancient celestial law, had begun to stir from their self-imposed isolation.

For cycles, the Conclave had been observers, their pronouncements infrequent and their actions even rarer, content to let the Accord manage the terrestrial plane while they contemplated the cosmic dance. Their silence had been interpreted by many as indifference, by others as a tacit endorsement of the Accord's iron-fisted rule. But now, a new era of direct intervention was dawning, a strategic pivot born from the very instability the Accord had inadvertently fostered. The Conclave's move was not born of shared purpose with the rebellious factions, nor was it an alliance of convenience with the struggling populace. It was a calculated maneuver to seize control of the narrative, to reposition themselves as the ultimate arbiters of the planet's destiny, and to do so by directly confronting the most potent symbols of opposition.

Their initial target was not a fortified human city or a rebellious settlement, but a nexus of raw, untamed power: the Verdant Expanse, a sprawling, ancient forest that pulsed with a life force as old as the planet itself, and which was home to the largest and most influential clan of the Whisperwind Dragons. These were not mere beasts of burden or instruments of elemental fury; they were sentient beings, deeply attuned to the planet's Core Song, their very existence a testament to the wild, untamed heart of the world. The Conclave, in their chillingly logical pursuit of order, saw the Verdant Expanse as an intolerable locus of uncontrolled energy, a place where the planet's innate song throbbed with a defiance they could not abide.

The skies above the Verdant Expanse, usually alive with the iridescent shimmer of dragon scales and the rustle of colossal wings, grew unnaturally still. Then, a shadow fell. Not the familiar, comforting shadow of a returning dragon, but a vast, monolithic darkness that blotted out the sun. It was the 'Celestial Aegis,' the Conclave's flagship, a vessel of impossible geometry and shimmering, otherworldly alloys that seemed to absorb and distort light rather than reflect it. It descended with an unnerving silence, its immense form dwarfing the ancient canopy below, a harbinger of a power that transcended mere terrestrial might.

From its belly, a swarm of smaller, more agile craft emerged, not the sleek, utilitarian designs of the Accord's Skyguard, but constructs of pure, crystallized light and resonating ether. These were the Conclave's 'Harmonic Sentinels,' their purpose to dissect and neutralize not through brute force, but through the imposition of perfect, sterile harmony. They did not fire projectiles; they emitted frequencies, waves of absolute sonic purity designed to unravel and dismantle any dissonance.

The dragons, sensing the imminent threat, rose to meet the intruders. Their roars, usually a symphony of elemental power, now carried a desperate edge, a primal call to defend their ancestral home. Opalscale, whose form shimmered with an agitated luminescence, was among the first to confront the advancing Sentinels. Her scales, usually a vibrant spectrum of hues, now pulsed with a defensive energy, each beat of her wings sending ripples of force through the air.

"You trespass where you are not welcome!" Opalscale's voice, a resonant chord that vibrated in the very bones of those who heard it, echoed through the glade. "This is sacred ground, a sanctuary of the living world!"

The Harmonic Sentinels responded not with words, but with a concentrated burst of their disabling frequencies. It was a sound that could pierce the deepest meditative trance, that could unravel the very bonds of cohesion in matter. The air itself seemed to vibrate with an unbearable pressure, a palpable force that sought to impose order by dissolving all that resisted. For the dragons, whose very essence was intertwined with the planet's natural rhythms, the effect was agonizing. It was like being torn apart from the inside out, their connection to the Core Song, their very lifeblood, being systematically severed.

A young dragon, barely past its first century, shrieked as its wings faltered, its scales dimming as the harmonic wave washed over it. It spiraled downwards, crashing into the ancient foliage, its roar choked off by the overwhelming sonic assault. Other dragons, their roars turning to pained cries, struggled to maintain flight, their powerful bodies buffeted by an invisible tide of pure, unyielding order.

The Conclave's strategy was not to destroy, but to *subdue*. They sought to render the dragons incapable of disrupting their plans, to pacify the most powerful natural forces on the planet so that their own ascent to ultimate authority would be unimpeded. They understood that the dragons, with their deep connection to the Core Song, were a living embodiment of the very chaos they sought to eradicate. By neutralizing them, they would cripple the planet's natural defenses and silence its most potent voice.

THE STORMBOUND DIVIDE

As the battle raged in the skies, a secondary contingent of the Conclave's forces descended towards the heart of the Verdant Expanse, towards the ancient crystalline caverns where the eldest dragons communed and where the planet's deepest resonant energies were believed to converge. These were not warriors in the traditional sense, but robed figures wielding instruments of delicate, intricate design – conduits for the Conclave's subtle, yet devastating, manipulation of ambient energies. They moved with a fluid, almost ethereal grace, their presence leaving a chill in the air, a sense of profound, detached observation.

Their objective was not to engage in combat, but to implement a process known only as 'The Attunement of Silence.' Using their instruments, they began to weave a counter-frequency, a complex tapestry of harmonic cancellation that sought to smother the natural resonance emanating from the caverns. It was a slow, insidious process, designed to gradually dampen the dragons' connection to the planet, to isolate them from their source of power, and ultimately, to sever their ability to perceive and interact with the Core Song.

High above, the Celestial Aegis remained a silent, imposing sentinel, its presence a constant reminder of the Conclave's overwhelming power and their unwavering intent. The battle was not about winning or losing in a conventional sense; it was about demonstrating absolute authority. The Conclave was not asking for compliance; they were imposing a new reality. They sought to rewrite the very laws of existence on this world, to replace the vibrant, unpredictable symphony of life with a sterile, predictable melody of their own design.

Meanwhile, in the far northern territories, a different kind of power was being asserted. The Accord, under the pressure of Project Ætherium's escalating demands and the Conclave's increasingly overt actions, had begun to tighten their grip on key human strongholds. The Iron Peaks, a region known for its independent mining clans and its fierce, self-reliant populace, found itself under a new kind of siege. This was not the subtle economic strangulation Elara Vance was experiencing on the Sunstone Coast, but a direct, military occupation.

Accord forces, bolstered by newly deployed sonic suppression units and heavily armored ground troops, descended upon the scattered settlements of the Iron Peaks. Their objective was clear: to neutralize any potential centers of resistance before the full brunt of Project Ætherium could be unleashed, and to seize control of strategic resources that the Conclave, in its broader planetary restructuring, deemed essential for its own ascendancy.

The imposing fortifications of Grimfang Hold, a bastion of dwarven and human resilience carved deep into the mountainside, became the primary focus. For generations, Grimfang Hold had stood as a symbol of defiance against any external authority, its people known for their stubborn independence and their mastery of subterranean warfare. Now, it was surrounded.

The Accord's assault was not a chaotic rush of soldiers, but a meticulously orchestrated operation. They established a perimeter, cutting off all ingress and egress, and then began to systematically bombard the Hold's outer defenses with concussive blasts and sustained sonic barrages. These were not conventional siege weapons; they were designed to destabilize the very rock of the mountain, to sow fear and disorientation among its inhabitants.

Kael of the Iron Peaks, who had been attempting to forge a tenuous alliance with the Hold's elders, found himself trapped within its stone walls. The grim faces of the Hold's leaders reflected the despair he felt. "They have us surrounded, Kael," declared Elder Borin, his voice hoarse from the constant din of the Accord's assault. "Our defenses are strong, but they are not designed for this. This... sonic warfare... it shakes us to our core, both physically and spiritually. It is like fighting the mountain itself against us."

"They are not just attacking our walls; they are attacking our will," Kael replied, his eyes fixed on the cracked and groaning stone of the inner chamber. "They know that if they can break the spirit of the Iron Peaks, they can break the will of every free soul on this planet. The Conclave's move into the Verdant Expanse, the Accord's tightening noose here... it is all part of the same design. They are systematically dismantling all opposition, all natural order, to pave the way for their sterile utopia."

The Accord's forces, led by a grimly efficient commander named Valerius's own hand-picked lieutenant, Commander Thorne, advanced with a cold precision. They were not driven by ideology, but by orders, by the unyielding logic of their superiors. Their mission was to subdue Grimfang Hold, to make it an example of the Accord's unshakeable authority, and to secure the rich veins of rare minerals that lay beneath its foundations, minerals that the Conclave's ever-growing array of celestial machinery would undoubtedly require.

The days turned into weeks, and the relentless pressure began to take its toll. The sonic vibrations weakened the Hold's ancient structures, causing rockfalls and internal collapses. Defenders, already exhausted from constant vigilance, found their hearing impaired, their focus shattered by the persistent, maddening drone. The Accord's forces, shielded by specialized sonic dampeners and armed with energy weapons that could melt through stone, were steadily gaining ground.

Commander Thorne, a man whose face seemed perpetually set in a mask of cold calculation, observed the siege from a holographic display within his command tent. He saw not the suffering of the defenders, but the strategic advantage being gained. Grimfang Hold was a crucial linchpin in the growing network of resistance. Its fall would not only remove a significant obstacle but would send a clear message to all who dared to defy the Accord: their strength lay not in defiance, but in absolute, unyielding obedience.

The Conclave's machinations were multifaceted, their intervention designed to create a cascading effect of fear and subjugation. While their forces engaged the dragons in the Verdant Expanse, and the Accord's armies laid siege to Grimfang Hold, a more subtle, yet equally devastating, move was being orchestrated against the Free Cities of the Sunstone Coast.

Elara Vance, even from her besieged position, could feel the tightening of the noose. The Accord's declaration of 'strategic asset' status for the coastal routes had been the initial move, but it was the subsequent actions that revealed the Conclave's direct involvement. Under the guise of 'stabilizing trade channels,' Conclave emissaries, cloaked in robes of shifting, opalescent hues, had begun to infiltrate the Free Cities. They did not engage in open conflict, but whispered promises of order and prosperity to the disillusioned merchant guilds and the increasingly desperate populace.

Their methods were insidious. They offered advanced navigational technologies, supposedly to improve safety and efficiency, but which subtly redirected shipping towards Accord-controlled hubs, effectively bypassing the Free Cities altogether. They introduced 'harmonizing' energy regulators to the city's power grids, ostensibly to improve reliability, but which gradually suppressed the independent spirit of the city's inhabitants, dampening their civic pride and their inherent desire for self-governance.

"They are not just cutting off our trade; they are poisoning our very will," Elara confided in Mara, her voice weary. "These Conclave agents... they speak of a unified future, of a world free from the chaos of individual ambition. They paint themselves as benevolent shepherds, guiding us towards a brighter dawn. But their dawn is one of perpetual twilight, where all individuality is extinguished, where all life hums to a single, sterile tune."

Mara, her face etched with worry, pointed to a fresh dispatch detailing a new Accord decree. "They have restricted access to essential medical supplies, claiming they are being diverted to 'less stable' regions. They are using our own need against us, Elara. They want us to beg for their mercy, to surrender our freedom in exchange for basic survival."

The Conclave's move was a masterstroke of calculated manipulation. By leveraging the Accord's military might and the populace's growing desperation, they were effectively dismantling the remaining bastions of independent thought and action without firing a single shot in many instances. They were weaving a web of control so intricate, so pervasive, that resistance itself began to feel futile.

The Verdant Expanse was slowly succumbing to the chilling silence of the Harmonic Sentinels. The dragons, their roars muted, their wings heavy, were being forced into a state of passive submission. Grimfang Hold, though still defiant, was slowly crumbling under the Accord's relentless pressure, its fall seeming inevitable. And the Free Cities of the Sunstone Coast were finding their vibrant spirit slowly eroded, their independent will being subtly re-engineered by the Conclave's insidious influence.

The gathering storm was no longer a distant rumble; it had broken. The Conclave had made their move, a decisive and terrifying assertion of their power and their ambition. They were not merely seeking to restore order; they were seeking to reshape existence itself, to impose their own rigid, sterile vision upon a world that thrived on life, on chaos, on song. And in the hearts of those who resisted, a new, desperate understanding began to dawn: the true battle for the planet's soul had just begun, and its stakes were higher than any had ever imagined.

The air crackled, not with the charged energy of an impending storm, but with a tension far more profound, a stillness that preceded the breaking of all things. The world, fractured and bleeding, found itself teetering on the brink of an ultimate reckoning. Each faction, once independent in their struggles, now felt the inexorable pull towards a final, defining confrontation. The Accord Cities, their gilded spires now gaudy in the pallid light, tightened their grip, their pronouncements growing more strident, their patrols more ubiquitous. They saw themselves as the last bastion of sanity, the sole architects of a future that valued order above all else, even if that order was forged in the fires of subjugation. Their reliance on the Conclave's esoteric technologies had deepened, a Faustian bargain struck for the illusion of control.

Across the planet, the Conclave moved with an unsettling, unified purpose. Their intervention in the Verdant Expanse, though seemingly a localized act of brutal pacification, was merely the opening salvo.

Their influence, a subtle yet pervasive poison, was seeping into the very foundations of other societies. They were orchestrating a symphony of subjugation, their celestial instruments playing a tune of absolute control, a stark counterpoint to the vibrant, chaotic symphony of the planet's Core Song. Their objective was not merely to conquer, but to fundamentally rewrite the planet's operating system, to replace the messy, unpredictable beauty of organic existence with the sterile, predictable perfection of their own design.

Meanwhile, the nascent alliance forged in the crucible of shared desperation was a fragile tapestry of hope against overwhelming odds. Cael, his heart burdened by the weight of countless lives and the precariousness of his burgeoning confederacy, worked tirelessly. His efforts to unite the disparate human settlements, the scattered remnants of dragon clans who had escaped the Conclave's wrath, and even the secretive Earthshaper communities, were met with suspicion and fear. The scars of past betrayals ran deep, and the sheer magnitude of the forces arrayed against them seemed to render any unified front an exercise in futility. Yet, the alternative – to be picked apart, one by one, by the Accord and the Conclave – was unthinkable.

The elements themselves mirrored the planet's profound distress. The skies, once predictable in their cycles, now wept with unnatural storms, their fury unleashed without warning. Tidal surges battered coastlines with unprecedented violence, as if the very oceans were crying out against the unnatural order being imposed upon them. In the mountain ranges, seismic activity, usually confined to deep, predictable tremors, erupted with a ferocity that threatened to shatter the land itself. The planet, it seemed, was no longer a passive stage for the conflicts of its inhabitants, but an active participant, its very being writhing in agony. The Core Song, though muted in many places, still pulsed, a desperate, dying heartbeat, and it was amplified by the planet's own suffering.

For Mara, the burden of leadership felt like a physical weight pressing down on her soul. The news from the Verdant Expanse was grim, each report of dragon suffering a fresh stab to her heart. The dragons were not merely allies; they were kin, their fate inextricably bound to her own, and to the fate of the living world. She felt the dissonance of the Conclave's sonic attacks as a physical ache, a violation of her deepest connection to the planet. The Accord's tightening grip on the northern territories, their systematic dismantling of independent communities, was a chilling echo of the Conclave's methodology, a brutal efficiency born of a shared, albeit different, pursuit of absolute control.

The disparate factions, each believing their cause was paramount, were in danger of becoming instruments of each other's destruction. The Accord, blinded by their obsession with order, failed to see that their pursuit of it was creating the very chaos they sought to eliminate, a chaos that the Conclave was adept at exploiting. The Conclave, in their sterile pursuit of cosmic harmony, were deaf to the planet's suffering, to the vibrant chorus of life that they sought to silence. And Cael's alliance, though born of noble intent, was a fragile reed against the gales of established power, its strength dependent on the unity of its fractured parts.

The pressure on Mara and Cael was immense, a crushing force threatening to shatter their resolve. They were the nexus points, the individuals tasked with weaving a coherent strategy from the frayed threads of disparate resistances. The fate of the planet's song, of its wild heart, rested on their ability to forge an alliance that transcended fear and suspicion, to unite forces that had historically been at odds, and to confront the overwhelming, monolithic powers that sought to control or destroy the very essence of their world. The time for tactical maneuvers and cautious diplomacy was over. The gathering storm had broken, and the world stood on the precipice of a final, cataclysmic confrontation, where the very soul of their planet would be decided.

The weight of this realization settled upon Mara like a shroud. Every report of the Conclave's insidious influence, every whisper of the Accord's brutal efficiency, chipped away at her optimism, replacing it with a grim determination. The dragons, her kin, were suffering under the relentless sonic assault, their majestic forms wracked by an agony that resonated deep within her own being. She could feel the Core Song, once a vibrant, comforting melody, now strained and fractured, its harmony disrupted by the Conclave's dissonant frequencies. It was a wound inflicted not just upon the dragons, but upon the very soul of the planet.

Similarly, the news from the north was a chilling testament to the Accord's unyielding pursuit of control. The systematic subjugation of the Iron Peaks, the fall of Grimfang Hold, was not merely the crushing of a rebellion; it was the methodical dismantling of defiance, the silencing of independent voices. Kael's desperate struggle to unite the fragmented human settlements, to find common ground amidst generations of mistrust, was a race against time. He understood, perhaps better than most, that the Accord and the Conclave, despite their outward differences, shared a common vision: a world stripped of its wildness, its individuality, its song.

The elements themselves seemed to conspire in the growing despair. Unnatural tempests raged with increasing frequency, their fury a reflection of the planet's own tormented state. The oceans, once predictable in their rhythms, now crashed against the shores with a violence that seemed to accuse, as if the very water mourned the silencing of the Core Song. In the ancient mountains, the earth groaned and shuddered, not with the familiar tremors of geological age, but with a primal, agonizing upheaval. The planet was not merely a backdrop to this conflict; it was a living, suffering entity, its distress manifest in the very fabric of its being.

Mara found herself constantly strategizing, seeking ways to counter the Conclave's insidious influence in the Sunstone Coast. The 'harmonizing' energy regulators, disguised as advancements, were in reality tools of psychological subjugation, slowly eroding the spirit of independence, replacing it with a passive acceptance of authority. The Accord's control over vital resources, used as leverage, further amplified the desperation, forcing communities to choose between survival and freedom. It was a subtle, yet devastating, form of warfare, one that attacked the will before it ever resorted to brute force.

THE STORMBOUND DIVIDE

The weight of her responsibility was almost unbearable. The responsibility to bridge the chasms that separated the factions, to remind them of their shared heritage, their common enemy. It was a monumental task. The dragons, proud and ancient, were deeply wounded, their trust shattered. The human settlements, battered by years of Accord oppression, were wary of any new promise of alliance, fearing yet another betrayal. Even within Cael's nascent coalition, dissent and fear were constant undercurrents, threatening to tear apart the fragile bonds of unity.

The stakes had never been higher. This was not merely a territorial dispute or a clash of ideologies. It was a battle for the very essence of their world. The Conclave sought to impose a sterile, unyielding order, a universe of perfect, predictable silence. The Accord, though less philosophically driven, was equally committed to a singular vision of control, a world where all power flowed from its centralized authority. Both, in their own ways, aimed to extinguish the vibrant, chaotic symphony of life that pulsed at the planet's core.

Mara and Cael, standing on the precipice of this all-encompassing conflict, understood the desperate urgency of their mission. They had to unite the disparate forces, to forge a single, powerful blow against the encroaching darkness. The time for caution was long past. The elements raged, the planet wept, and the songs of defiance, though strained, were beginning to rise. The final confrontation was no longer a distant threat; it was a palpable reality, and the fate of their world hung precariously in the balance, awaiting the courage to face the storm.

Chapter Eleven
Symphony of Conflict

The air thrummed with an expectant energy, a palpable tension that stretched across the battered land like a taut bowstring. The sky, once a canvas of predictable blues and golds, now churned with a bruised, unsettling palette of purples and greys, shot through with veins of an unnatural, phosphorescent green. This was no mere weather front; it was a manifestation of the planet's agony, a cosmic bruise blooming across the heavens. Below, the chosen ground for the impending cataclysm was a place steeped in an ancient power, a nexus where the planet's deepest energies coalesced. It was known, in the hushed whispers of lore, as the Scarred Basin.

The Scarred Basin wasn't a natural depression; it was a wound. Millennia ago, a celestial shard, a fragment of a dying star, had torn through the planet's crust, leaving behind a vast, elliptical caldera. The impact had not merely reshaped the topography; it had fundamentally altered the planet's energetic signature in this region. Veins of raw, untamed magic pulsed beneath the obsidian-like rock that formed the basin's floor, a constant, low hum that could be felt in the marrow of one's bones.

Strange crystalline formations, born of compressed elemental forces, jutted from the earth like jagged teeth, refracting the volatile sky-light into a dizzying, kaleidoscopic display. The very air here tasted different – sharper, cleaner, yet charged with an almost violent potential. It was a place where the veil between the physical and the ethereal was thin, a place where the Core Song, when its voice was unburdened, sang with an almost unbearable clarity.

Now, however, the Core Song was a tortured cry in this sacred space. The Conclave's sonic incursions had found fertile ground here, their discordant frequencies warring with the natural harmony of the basin, creating a chaotic cacophony that threatened to tear the very fabric of reality. The crystalline structures, usually conduits of serene elemental power, now vibrated with a violent, dissonant energy, their facets shimmering with an aggressive luminescence. Within the basin, the wind did not simply blow; it shrieked, a banshee's lament carrying the whispers of shattered magic and the echoes of the planet's pain.

This was not the battlefield Mara and Cael had initially envisioned. Their strategy had been to engage the Accord and the Conclave on more conventional terms, to leverage their burgeoning alliance against the enemy's established strongholds. But the Conclave, with their uncanny foresight, had anticipated such moves. Their objective was not merely to subdue, but to unravel, to break the planet's spirit in its most sacred places. They had chosen the Scarred Basin as their primary instrument of subjugation, intending to not only crush the nascent resistance but to permanently silence the Core Song in one of its most powerful echoes. The Accord, ever eager to impose their vision of order, had readily agreed, seeing the basin as a strategic choke point and a potential site for their ultimate consolidation of power, a testament to their dominance over the wild, untamed forces of the world.

The landscape itself was a testament to the immensity of the forces gathering. Towering spires of raw, solidified energy, remnants of the star shard's impact, pierced the sky, crackling with captured lightning. These were not mere geological formations; they were monuments to cosmic violence, and they now served as focal points for the impending conflict, drawing power from the volatile atmosphere and the depths of the earth. Between these spires, the obsidian floor of the basin was crisscrossed with glowing fissures, rivers of molten light that pulsed with an almost organic rhythm, a visual representation of the planet's lifeblood. In some areas, the impact had fused the earth into vast, glassy plains that reflected the tumultuous sky like a dark mirror, distorting the chaos into an even more disorienting spectacle. In others, colossal craters, miles wide, yawned open, their depths shrouded in an eerie mist that seemed to writhe with unseen energies.

The choice of the Scarred Basin was a deliberate act of defiance and desperation on both sides. For the Conclave, it was the ultimate prize: to corrupt and control a place of such profound natural power, to twist its song into a dirge of absolute control. For the Accord, it was an opportunity to demonstrate their might, to show that no force, terrestrial or celestial, could defy their enforced order. But for Mara and Cael, and the disparate forces they represented, the basin was a desperate gamble. It was the planet's greatest wound, and in its deepest suffering, they hoped to find the strength to heal. It was a place where the wild heart of the world beat strongest, and where its silencing would be an irreversible act of devastation.

The air, thick with the scent of ozone and something ancient, like petrichor mixed with starlight, pressed in on them. Mara, standing on the lip of the basin, felt a primal tremor run through her. It wasn't just the ground vibrating; it was her very being resonating with the planet's distressed song. The Conclave's sonic emitters, disguised as elegant, crystalline obelisks, had already been deployed across the basin's floor. They pulsed with a sickening violet light, each throb a precisely calibrated wave of dissonance designed to shatter not just eardrums, but the very spirit. The Accord's forces, clad in their gleaming, utilitarian armor, were establishing defensive positions along the rim, their siege engines and energy cannons a stark, metallic contrast to the raw, elemental power of the basin. They were setting the stage for a brutal, conventional war, unaware or uncaring that the true battle would be fought on a far more fundamental plane.

Cael, his hand resting on the weathered haft of his ancestral blade, his gaze fixed on the churning sky, spoke, his voice a low rumble against the rising wind. "They chose well, the Conclave. They seek to poison the wellspring, to corrupt the very heart of the world in its most vulnerable place."

Mara nodded, her eyes tracing the eerie patterns of light dancing across the obsidian plains. "They believe that by controlling this nexus, they can control the planet's song, and thus, its people. They think if they can silence the heart, the body will simply wither and die."

The wind whipped strands of her hair across her face, stinging her eyes. She could feel the dragon's presence, not just the physical bodies of her kin who had followed her into this desperate alliance, but their shared consciousness, a chorus of pain and defiance that throbbed in time with her own heart. The dragons, even those bearing the brunt of the Conclave's sonic attacks, were preparing. Their scales, usually a vibrant mosaic of earth tones and fiery hues, were dulled by the strain, but their eyes burned with an ancient, indomitable fire. Some of the older dragons, their wings scarred from countless battles, had taken flight, circling the rim of the basin like ancient guardians, their roars, though muted by the atmospheric pressure, still carried a primal power.

"The Accord sees this as a territory to be conquered," Cael continued, his voice grim. "They understand power, but not song. They believe that by planting their banners here, they will claim victory. They do not understand that this land is not conquered, it is felt."

Beneath them, in the heart of the Scarred Basin, the effects of the Conclave's sonic bombardment were already evident. The crystalline formations seemed to weep, their facets clouded with a viscous, iridescent fluid. Patches of the obsidian floor glowed with an agitated, unhealthy luminescence, as if the earth itself was feverish. Strange, ephemeral lights flickered in the mist that coiled from the deeper fissures, apparitions born of raw, unbound magic struggling against the forced discord.

"The Earthshapers are trying to contain the worst of the sonic bleed," Mara said, gesturing towards a distant cluster of figures, barely visible amidst the swirling energies. "Their connection to the deep earth is our only hope of preventing a catastrophic overload. But even they are struggling."

The Earthshapers, a reclusive people deeply attuned to the planet's geological rhythms, were a vital, yet often overlooked, component of their alliance. Their ability to manipulate stone and earth, to sense and channel the planet's latent energies, was crucial in a place like the Scarred Basin. They moved with a slow, deliberate grace, their hands pressed against the ground, their bodies quivering with the effort of wrestling with the amplified disharmony. Their connection to the planet was a direct counterpoint to the Conclave's sterile, technological dominance.

"And the remnants of the Sky-Watchers?" Cael asked, his eyes scanning the turbulent sky. "Their scouts reported the Conclave's primary assault fleet is converging."

"They are here," Mara replied, a grim certainty in her voice. "Hidden within the storm clouds, cloaked by the atmospheric disturbances. Their ships are designed to blend with the celestial chaos. We expect them to break through as the main engagement begins."

The sky above the basin was a canvas of breathtaking, terrifying beauty. Massive thunderheads, heavy with an unnatural static charge, swirled and coalesced, their bellies the color of bruised plums. Jagged forks of emerald lightning ripped through the darkness, illuminating the churning mass for fleeting, blinding moments. It was within this maelstrom that the Conclave's celestial armada was preparing to descend. Their ships, sleek and predatory, were designed for speed and silence, their presence a chilling testament to the Conclave's ambition to rule not just the land, but the very heavens above it.

The Scarred Basin was more than just a battlefield; it was a focal point for the planet's most profound energies, a place where the battle for its soul would be fought. The obsidian floor, scarred and ancient, pulsed with a raw, untamed power. The towering energy spires, remnants of a cosmic cataclysm, crackled with an untamed, celestial fire. The very air vibrated with a potent, volatile magic, a symphony of elemental forces that the Conclave sought to silence and the Accord sought to control. This was the stage upon which the fate of their world would be decided, a place of immense power and profound suffering, a crucible where hope and despair would clash in a cataclysmic symphony of conflict.

The obsidian floor of the basin, normally a stark, unyielding expanse, was now alive with an unsettling energy. Rivers of molten light, born from the deepest geothermal currents and amplified by the Conclave's sonic resonance, snaked across the ground. These were not merely geological phenomena; they were the planet's raw, exposed nerves, pulsing with a furious, incandescent glow. Where the light was brightest, the very air seemed to shimmer, distorting the forms of those who stood nearby, lending them an almost spectral appearance.

The crystalline formations, unique to the Scarred Basin, were not merely inert geological structures. They were living conduits, attuned to the planet's Core Song. Usually, they emitted a soft, soothing luminescence, a gentle hum that resonated with the natural harmony of the world. But now, under the assault of the Conclave's sonic weaponry, they throbbed with a frantic, discordant rhythm. Their once-pure facets fractured the ambient light into a chaotic display of clashing colors, and they emitted a high-pitched whine that clawed at the sanity, a sound that Mara felt not just in her ears, but deep within her bones. It was as if the very crystals were screaming.

Mara could feel the dissonance in her teeth, a grinding ache that mirrored the planet's fractured song. She looked out at the assembled forces, the disparate factions united by a shared threat and a desperate hope. The dragons, their mighty forms tensed for battle, were a living embodiment of the wild world they fought to protect. Their scales, usually a testament to their connection with the earth, the sky, and the fire within, seemed muted, as if the very essence of their vibrant being was being leached away by the invasive frequencies. Yet, in their eyes, a fierce, unyielding resolve burned. They were ancient beings, their spirit forged in the fires of creation, and they would not be silenced easily.

Cael stood beside her, his presence a grounding force amidst the chaos. His armor, bearing the marks of countless battles, seemed to absorb the turbulent energy of the basin, reflecting a grim determination. He was a leader forged in the crucible of human suffering, his empathy a powerful weapon, his strategic mind a vital asset. His alliance, though fragile, represented the last bastion of free will against the encroaching tide of absolute control.

"The Accord has deployed their Sky-Mines along the eastern rim," Cael reported, his voice tight, gesturing towards the distant, jagged peaks that overlooked the basin. "They're designed to detonate on proximity, a nasty surprise for any aerial approach."

Mara's gaze followed his, her senses extending beyond the visible. She could feel the subtle energy signatures of the mines, like venomous spiders waiting in their webs. "We'll need to find a way to neutralize them before the dragons can engage the main fleet. The Earthshapers might be able to disrupt their energy cores, but it will be a risky maneuver."

The sky above was a constant, unnerving spectacle. The bruised purples and greens of the storm clouds churned with an almost sentient malevolence. Streaks of unnatural lightning, the color of diseased jade, arced between the colossal cloud formations, illuminating the vast, concave landscape below with an eerie, flickering light. It was a sky that seemed to weep, a sky that reflected the planet's deep-seated agony. Within this celestial tempest, the Conclave's ships moved like specters, their cloaking technology rendering them nearly invisible until they chose to reveal themselves.

"The Conclave's sonic emitters are not just designed to disorient," Mara murmured, her voice barely audible above the rising wind. "They are also meant to destabilize the very structure of this place. If they succeed, the entire basin could collapse, taking us all with it."

The ancient, towering spires of solidified energy, remnants of the celestial shard's impact, stood like colossal sentinels at the edges of the basin.

THE STORMBOUND DIVIDE

They pulsed with a captured, cosmic energy, their surfaces etched with the scars of aeons. Now, they seemed to draw the volatile energy from the storm-laden sky, crackling with an amplified power. They were both potential weapons and a terrifying testament to the destructive forces that had shaped this world.

"The Core Song," Mara whispered, her hand reaching out, as if to grasp the intangible melody. "It's fighting back. I can feel it, struggling against the dissonance. It's singing through the fissures, through the crystals, through the very air we breathe."

The glowing fissures on the basin floor pulsed with an intensified rhythm, their molten light casting long, distorted shadows. These were not mere cracks in the earth; they were the planet's lifeblood, its raw, elemental energy made visible. The Conclave's sonic attacks were like a hammer blow against these exposed veins, forcing them to flare with an uncontrolled intensity.

"We fight for that song, Mara," Cael said, his voice firm, his gaze unwavering. "We fight for the right of this world to sing its own tune, not the sterile, empty notes of their imposed order."

The wind howled, a mournful dirge that seemed to carry the laments of a dying world. Yet, within that mournful cry, there was a rising tide of defiance. The Scarred Basin, a place of immense power and profound pain, was about to become the stage for a battle that would echo through the ages, a symphony of conflict where the fate of a planet would be decided by the courage of its defenders and the ferocity of its song. The air itself seemed to hold its breath, waiting for the first note of the final, cataclysmic movement. The stage was set, the players were in position, and the prelude of cosmic disharmony was about to give way to the thunderous crescendo of war. The very ground beneath their feet seemed to thrum with an anticipation that was both terrifying and exhilarating, a testament to the raw, untamed power that lay dormant, waiting to be unleashed.

Mara Lysenne, once a hesitant vessel of the planet's song, now stood as its undeniable conduit. The agonizing discord that had been tearing through the Scarred Basin, a cacophony of manufactured despair and elemental rage, had found a counterpoint in her. It wasn't a force she wielded, not a weapon to be aimed or a shield to be raised in defiance. Instead, it was a resonance, a deep, innate understanding of the planet's fractured symphony that she could now not only perceive but amplify. She closed her eyes, drawing a deep, steadying breath that tasted of ozone and the deep, ancient earth. The violent vibrations that had been assaulting her senses, rattling her very bones, began to soften, to coalesce around a central, pure note.

This was the Core Song, the planet's true voice, a melody that had been choked and distorted by the Conclave's sonic emitters. It was the song of growth and decay, of mountain formation and ocean currents, of the quiet hum of roots reaching through the soil and the roaring crescendo of a storm's release. It was the song of life itself, in all its chaotic, beautiful complexity. And Mara, standing on the precipice of this cataclysm, had become its conductor.

She extended her hands, not towards the enemy, but outwards, encompassing the entire basin. It was a gesture of offering, of communion. Her own spirit, intertwined with the dragon's collective consciousness and the whispered pleas of the Earthshapers, became a lens, focusing the planet's pain into a single, resonant frequency. It was a frequency of healing, of remembrance, of a desperate, unwavering hope.

"Hear me," she whispered, her voice carrying on the unnatural wind, not with the force of command, but with the gentle insistence of a lullaby. "Hear the heart of the world."

The effect was subtle at first, like the first hint of dawn breaking through a starless night. The shrill, piercing whine emanating from the Conclave's crystalline emitters seemed to falter, their violet glow dimming slightly. The agitated shimmering of the obsidian floor calmed, the rivers of molten light flowing with a less frantic pulse. Mara felt the change, not just in the external environment, but within herself. It was as if a knot of tension, coiled tight for so long, was finally beginning to unravel.

She pushed, not with aggression, but with an unwavering belief in the inherent harmony of existence. Her mind reached out, tracing the intricate patterns of the planet's song, weaving through the dissonant threads cast by the Conclave. She found the dragon's roars, no longer cries of pain but defiant calls, and wove them into the broader melody. She felt the silent, strenuous efforts of the Earthshapers, their earthy grounding hum, and incorporated it into the composition. Even the fear, the raw, primal fear that gripped so many of the allied forces, was not suppressed, but acknowledged, its tremor integrated into the complex rhythm.

The Sky-Watchers, perched on the surrounding peaks, their keen eyes straining against the atmospheric distortions, reported a curious phenomenon. The unnatural green lightning that had been lashing the sky, a harbinger of the Conclave's aerial assault, seemed to arc with less ferocity. The bruised purples and greys of the storm clouds, while still ominous, held a softer hue. It was as if the planet itself was exhaling, a long, drawn-out sigh of relief.

Mara's influence was a ripple, spreading outwards from her position at the basin's edge. It wasn't just about calming the elements; it was about reaching the minds and hearts of those caught in the maelstrom. She projected feelings, not words. To the dragons, she sent waves of unwavering loyalty, the ancient pride of their lineage, the fierce protectiveness of their kin. To the Earthshapers, she conveyed a profound sense of interconnectedness, the unshakeable strength of their foundation, the deep satisfaction of anchoring the world.

And to the Accord soldiers, the pawns of a sterile, imposed order, she sent echoes of memory. Glimpses of childhood laughter under a clear sky, the warmth of sunlight on skin, the scent of rain on fertile soil – moments of pure, unadulterated existence that the Conclave and the Accord sought to erase. It was a subtle subversion, a whisper of the truth they had been taught to ignore.

Cael, standing beside her, felt it too. The constant, gnawing anxiety that had been his companion since they entered the Scarred Basin began to recede. He saw Mara not as a commander, but as a living embodiment of what they were fighting for – not just survival, but the right to feel, to experience, to be alive in its truest sense. He felt the shift in the air, the subtle abatement of the sonic assault, and a flicker of hope ignited in his chest. His hand, still resting on his sword, loosened its death grip.

"They're faltering," he murmured, his voice filled with a dawning awe. "The emitters... they're losing their edge."

Mara opened her eyes, her gaze sweeping across the basin. The Conclave's forces, usually so rigidly disciplined, seemed momentarily disoriented. Their formations wavered. Some soldiers paused, their heads tilting as if listening to a distant melody. The sonic emitters, the instruments of their psychological warfare, were indeed struggling, their harsh frequencies failing to penetrate the growing harmony.

The Conclave's response was swift and brutal. General Valerius, a man whose face was a mask of cold calculation, saw the wavering in his troops and recognized the source of the disruption. He ordered a targeted surge of power to the primary sonic emitters, a desperate attempt to reassert dominance. The violet light flared, brighter and more intense than before, and a wave of pure dissonance washed over the basin.

Mara flinched, the surge of pain hitting her like a physical blow. The harmonious melody fractured, the delicate balance she had created teetering on the brink of collapse. The air crackled with a renewed intensity, and the ground beneath her feet trembled violently. But this time, it was different. She didn't recoil in pain; she met the dissonance head-on.

She channeled the pain, transformed it. The agony became a sharper note, a cry of defiance that echoed the planet's deepest wounds. She projected it back, not as a weapon, but as a testament to suffering, a raw, unvarnished truth that the Conclave could not silence. It was the pain of a world being ravaged, the anguish of life being extinguished.

"You cannot drown out suffering with silence," Mara's thoughts echoed, not spoken aloud, but resonating within the minds of those who could perceive her. "You cannot control a heart by breaking it."

This time, the effect was more pronounced. The Accord soldiers, caught between the planet's song and the Conclave's forced silence, began to show clear signs of distress. Some clutched their heads, their faces contorted in pain. Others dropped their weapons, their rigid discipline dissolving into confusion. The Conclave's own troops, less shielded from the raw power of their own emitters, fared no better. A ripple of panic began to spread through their ranks.

The dragons, sensing the shift, let out a unified roar, a sound that was not just of aggression, but of ancient power unleashed. It was a sound that resonated with the planet's song, amplifying Mara's efforts. Their roars were not just vocalizations; they were sonic expressions of the world's wild spirit, a challenge to the imposed order.

The Earthshapers, their connection to the planet deepening under Mara's influence, channeled the amplified earth energy. They grounded the volatile surges of power, their efforts creating zones of relative stability within the basin. They became anchors, preventing the dissonant frequencies from completely overwhelming the fragile harmony. Their silent work was a testament to the strength found in deep, unwavering connection.

As the Conclave's emitters surged, Mara's focus intensified. She saw the network of crystalline structures, each one pulsing with a malevolent energy. She didn't attempt to shatter them, but to harmonize with them. She found the inherent frequencies within the crystals themselves, the natural resonance that had been twisted and corrupted. She sang to that pure frequency, a gentle coaxing, a reminder of its true purpose.

It was like coaxing a trapped bird to sing. One by one, the harsh, grating tones of the emitters began to soften. The violent violet light flickered, and in its place, a softer, more natural luminescence began to emerge. The crystals were not being destroyed, but cleansed, their inherent song reawakened.

The Conclave's strategy was unraveling. Their meticulously crafted sonic assault, designed to sow chaos and despair, was instead fostering unity and resilience. The Accord's soldiers, their minds momentarily freed from the sonic manipulation, began to question their orders. The rigid uniformity of their formations began to break down, replaced by hesitant glances and uncertain movements.

Valerius, witnessing this from his command vessel, was enraged. His control was slipping, his meticulously planned psychological warfare crumbling around him. He ordered his artillery to open fire on the crystalline emitters, an act of desperation to silence them by force, regardless of the collateral damage. Explosions rocked the basin, sending shards of crystal and plumes of smoke into the air.

But even the destruction was not entirely without effect. The concussive force of the explosions, coupled with Mara's harmonizing influence, created unexpected ripples. Instead of amplifying the dissonance, some of the destroyed emitters released bursts of pure, unadulterated energy, harmless sonic waves that echoed the planet's natural frequencies. It was like striking a bell and hearing its true, pure tone, rather than the distorted clang intended by the enemy.

Mara felt the raw energy of the explosions, a jarring disruption, but beneath it, the planet's song was singing stronger. She directed the nascent dragon attacks, not as chaotic assaults, but as precise strikes against vulnerable points in the Accord's lines, guided by the harmony she projected. The dragons, their movements now imbued with a focused intent, became extensions of the planet's will.

THE STORMBOUND DIVIDE

The Sky-Watchers reported movement in the swirling storm clouds. The Conclave's assault fleet was preparing to break through, their cloaking technology struggling against the atmospheric anomalies caused by the clash of energies. Mara focused her attention upwards, projecting a sense of calm and clarity to the dragons who would soon engage the aerial threat. She reminded them of the vastness of the sky, the freedom of flight, the ancient strength of their wings.

The battle was no longer just a clash of armies; it was a battle for the very essence of existence. The Conclave sought to impose a sterile, controlled order, a silent world devoid of the messy, vibrant song of life. The Accord, blinded by their pursuit of power and control, saw the planet as a resource to be exploited, its natural rhythms an impediment to their ambitions. But Mara, through her connection to the Core Song, was reminding everyone of what was truly at stake.

She felt the pulse of the Scarred Basin itself, its ancient energy resonating with her own. The celestial shard's impact had created a wound, but also a focal point, a place where the planet's deepest magic converged. She was drawing on that power, not to wield it, but to amplify the planet's own voice, to make it undeniable.

As the Conclave's ships began to emerge from the storm clouds, their sleek, predatory forms glinting in the unnatural light, Mara sent a final, resonant wave of encouragement to the dragons. It was a song of courage, of unwavering spirit, of the deep, primal connection between the earth and the sky. The dragons, their scales glinting with renewed vigor, soared upwards, their roars a defiant challenge to the encroaching darkness.

Mara's role was not to fight with claws or fire, but with the very song of the world. Her presence was a beacon, a testament to the power of harmony over discord, of unity over division, of life over sterile control. She was the planet's voice, and in its most desperate hour, it was singing. The symphony of conflict had begun, but at its heart, a melody of hope was rising, a song that threatened to drown out the discordant notes of war and usher in an era of true harmony. The Scarred Basin, a place of immense pain, was becoming a crucible of creation, and Mara Lysenne was its living, breathing song.

The air itself vibrated with her purpose, a silent hum that underlaid the cacophony, a promise of what could be if only the world would listen. Her power was not in domination, but in invitation, in drawing all beings towards a shared, fundamental truth. She was a conductor of empathy, an architect of connection, and in the heart of the storm, her song was the most powerful weapon of all. The echoes of her resonating spirit rippled outwards, a silent, irresistible tide against the encroaching tide of despair.

The shift in the battlefield was palpable, a subtle yet profound recalibration of intent. Where before there had been a singular focus on obliteration, now a more nuanced understanding of engagement began to take root. Cael Thornevale, his gaze sharp and discerning, observed the disarray rippling through the Accord's ranks. Mara's influence, a gentle tide of planetary song, had indeed unsettled their rigid formations and chipped away at their manufactured resolve. But Mara's gift was not a shield to be wielded in direct combat; it was a catalyst, a disruption that now required Cael's strategic acumen to fully exploit. His leadership, honed by years of harsh campaigns and a deep-seated pragmatism, was about to undergo its most profound test.

He moved with an economy of motion, his voice, though not amplified by any sonic emitter, carried a resonant authority that cut through the lingering hum of dissonance. "Sky-Watchers," he barked into his comm unit, his eyes scanning the upper atmosphere, "report on the inbound fleet. Are they making their initial approach vector?" He knew the Conclave's reliance on overwhelming aerial superiority. Mara had bought them precious moments, but the true storm was yet to break. The dragons' roars, now harmonized with the planet's pulse, were a welcome distraction, but a distraction nonetheless.

"Affirmative, Commander Thornevale," a voice crackled back, tinged with urgency. "Multiple signatures emerging from the cloud cover. Standard invasion pattern. Heavy ordnance visible on primary vessels."

Cael nodded, his mind already piecing together the defensive matrix. This was not about meeting brute force with equal force. That was the Accord's game, a game they were ill-equipped to win against such a technologically advanced and ruthless enemy. Mara had shown him a different path, a path of harmony, of balance, and of strategic preservation. "Earthshapers," he addressed the sturdy, grounded figures arrayed around him, their hands still pressed to the vibrating earth. "I need you to establish resonance zones around the Crystal Spires. Not to destroy them, mind you. But to buffer their emissions. Dampen the dissonant frequencies, amplify the planetary song where you can. Think of yourselves as anchors, stabilizing the very air they try to poison."

A gruff, resonant rumble emanated from the Earthshaper elder, a sound that conveyed understanding and a grim determination. They understood the principle: not to fight fire with fire, but to redirect its destructive heat, to quench it with the very essence of the land. They moved with a renewed purpose, their connection to the Scarred Basin deepening, their very forms seeming to draw strength from the earth beneath their feet. As they focused their energies, a subtle shift occurred. The chaotic shimmering of the obsidian floor seemed to coalesce, the volatile energies contained, not suppressed, but guided.

Cael turned his attention to the Dragon Riders, their magnificent beasts circling overhead, their roars now carrying a controlled ferocity. "Riders," he called out, his voice clear and steady. "Your primary objective is to intercept the aerial assault. Engage the interceptors, the escorts. But do not engage the capital ships directly unless absolutely necessary. Your role is not to shatter their hulls, but to disrupt their formation. Force them to break their coordinated attack. Use their own momentum against them. Dive through their lines, scatter their formations, make them vulnerable to whatever atmospheric anomalies Mara's song generates. Think of yourselves as a flock of birds, dispersing a predatory hawk."

He watched as the riders nodded, their movements synchronized with their mounts. They understood. This was not a charge into the jaws of death, but a calculated, surgical strike. They were to be the scalpel, not the hammer. Their dragon allies, sensing Cael's intent, shifted their aerial patterns, their powerful wings beating with a new, more strategic rhythm.

"And to our ground forces," Cael continued, his gaze sweeping across the assembled soldiers, a mixed force of hardened veterans and newly emboldened recruits. "Your mission is to hold the line. Protect the Earthshapers and the Crystal Spires. Engage the Accord ground troops, but prioritize de-escalation where possible. If they are wavering, if they show signs of confusion or distress, do not press the attack. Offer them a chance to retreat. We are not here to slaughter them; we are here to win this war by breaking their will, not their bodies."

This was a departure from traditional warfare, a philosophy born from the desperate circumstances and Mara's profound influence. The Accord fought for subjugation, for control. Cael intended to fight for preservation, for the right of existence. He saw the weary faces of his soldiers, the hope mingled with apprehension, and knew that this nuanced approach, while challenging, was their best chance. It was about demonstrating that there was a better way to fight, a way that didn't involve the complete annihilation of the enemy.

He noticed a young soldier, no older than seventeen, gripping his spear with white knuckles. Cael met his gaze, offering a brief, encouraging nod. This was about more than just survival; it was about defining what it meant to survive, and what kind of world they wanted to survive *in*.

General Valerius, observing the unfolding chaos from his command center, would undoubtedly be baffled. His strategy was built on predictable aggression, on overwhelming force meeting predictable resistance. The Accord's doctrine was one of absolute victory, achieved through attrition and terror. Cael's approach was anathema to it.

"We need to secure the flanks," Cael instructed his lieutenants. "The Conclave will likely attempt to exploit any perceived weakness. Ensure our defensive perimeter is robust, but fluid. If they breach a point, do not commit all reserves. Redirect, contain, and isolate. Think of it like tending a garden, not defending a fortress. Prune the branches that threaten to overgrow, but preserve the core."

The analogy, delivered with Cael's characteristic directness, resonated. It was a stark contrast to the brutal efficiency the Accord valued. Their technology was designed to sterilize, to control, to impose an artificial order. Mara's song, and by extension Cael's strategy, was about embracing the inherent chaos and complexity of life, about finding strength in connection and balance.

He walked amongst his troops, his presence a silent reassurance. He spoke to individuals, not just to units, offering quiet words of encouragement, reiterating their objectives. He pointed to specific landmarks, natural formations that were to be protected at all costs. "That grove," he'd say, gesturing to a cluster of ancient, gnarled trees that seemed to hum with their own latent energy, "is a nexus of old magic. The Earthshapers will need to reinforce its natural defenses. The Accord must not touch it."

He saw a group of Accord soldiers, their faces pale and drawn, their weapons lowered. They were no longer advancing with their usual relentless march. Hesitation flickered in their eyes, a nascent doubt born from the unsettling harmony Mara was weaving. Cael subtly signaled his troops to hold their position, to let the dissonance work its subtle magic. This was not cowardice; it was an opportunity. An opportunity to sow further discord within the enemy ranks, not through violence, but through the absence of it.

"They are faltering," Cael murmured to his second-in-command, a seasoned warrior named Lyra. "Mara's song is reaching them. Their conviction is breaking. We need to exploit that crack. But carefully. We don't want to provoke a desperate backlash."

Lyra, a woman of quiet strength and unwavering loyalty, nodded. "We've prepared the diversionary tactics you outlined, Commander. If they attempt to regroup and push forward, we will initiate the sonic suppression fields on the eastern flank. Not to harm, but to disorient. To further confuse their command structure."

Cael approved with a curt nod. These "sonic suppression fields" were not weapons in the traditional sense. They were designed to mimic natural atmospheric phenomena, the disorienting hum of a localized sandstorm, the confusing echoes of a canyon, or the sudden, disorienting silence that could fall before a massive thunderclap. They were tools of confusion, not destruction, designed to amplify the unsettling nature of Mara's planetary song.

As the first wave of Conclave ships descended, their aggressive designs stark against the bruised sky, Cael felt a surge of adrenaline, but it was tempered by a deep sense of calm. He had done all he could in preparation. Now, it was up to Mara, the dragons, the Earthshapers, and his own soldiers to execute the plan. He watched as the dragons, a swirling vortex of scales and fury, met the Conclave's aerial vanguard. They didn't simply attack; they wove through the enemy formations, their powerful bodies disrupting the rigid lines, their roars a challenge to the imposed silence.

He saw a Conclave fighter veer off course, its pilot clearly disoriented by the chaotic aerial ballet. It flew directly into a patch of swirling mist that had suddenly materialized, a product of the Earthshapers' focused efforts and Mara's influence. The fighter disappeared within the haze, and moments later, a muted explosion echoed through the basin. It was a victory, but a quiet one, a testament to precision over brute force.

Cael's strategy was not about winning every engagement, but about winning the war. It was about attrition, but not of life. It was about breaking the enemy's will, their ability to inflict damage, their belief in their own inevitable victory. He was a shepherd, guiding his flock through a dangerous pass, not a butcher, driving them to slaughter.

He saw the immense power of the Conclave's capital ships, their primary weapon systems glowing ominously. But before they could unleash their full fury, the dragons would engage, disrupting their targeting, forcing them into precarious maneuvers. And if they managed to fire, the Earthshapers would do their best to absorb and redirect the energy, their grounding presence a bulwark against the destructive force.

"Commander," Lyra reported, her voice taut with concentration. "The Conclave's ground forces are attempting to advance on the Crystal Spires. They're using sonic dampeners to try and negate Mara's influence directly."

Cael's jaw tightened. This was a direct challenge to their core strategy. "Order the Earthshapers to fortify the Spires. Use their natural resonance to create a harmonic barrier. And Lyra, deploy the suppression fields on their immediate right flank. Let them feel the disorienting silence. Show them that their technology cannot replicate the planet's own voice."

The battle raged, a complex tapestry of sound and fury, of orchestrated chaos and deliberate restraint. Cael Thornevale, standing at the heart of it all, was a testament to the power of thoughtful leadership. He was not a general who reveled in bloodshed, but a commander who sought to minimize it, to find victory not in the ashes of his enemies, but in the preservation of his own people and the world they fought for. He was the conductor of a symphony of conflict, but his guiding principle was not discord, but a carefully orchestrated harmony that aimed for a lasting peace.

He understood that true strength lay not in overwhelming power, but in the wisdom to wield it with restraint, to protect what was precious, and to offer a path to reconciliation, even in the midst of war. His strategic defense was more than just a military maneuver; it was a philosophical stance, a declaration that even in the darkest of hours, there was always a choice to be made, a choice for a more balanced and sustainable victory.

The sky, once a canvas of azure serenity, now bled with the raw, incandescent fury of a celestial war. Not merely a clash of scales and sinew against metal and energy, but a primal scream against the encroaching silence, a desperate, thundering testament to a dying majesty. The dragons, children of the unbound winds and the heart of the earth, were no longer the revered architects of balance, but a desperate vanguard, their roars now laced with a sorrow as ancient as the mountains they once commanded. Their flight was a tapestry of defiance, a maelstrom of elemental power that tore at the heart of the Conclave's sterile, calculating advance.

Each dragon was a legend made manifest, a living embodiment of forces that predated the very concept of empire. They were the Sky-Serpents of the Crimson Peaks, their scales shimmering like molten gold, their breath a torrent of concentrated solar flares. Then there were the Azure Drakes of the Whispering Isles, their forms sleek and aerodynamic, their mastery over wind and lightning unmatched. The Obsidian Wyrms of the Shadowed Canyons, their wings leathery and vast, commanded the very storms, their thunderous roars capable of shattering bone and metal alike. And finally, the Emerald Guardians of the Sunken Forests, their scales like living jade, their serpentine bodies capable of weaving through the densest foliage, their breath a poisonous mist that choked the very air.

But the Accord's machinations had corrupted even these noble beings. The 'machims,' as they were called – monstrous, hulking automatons cobbled together from the very minerals and energies the dragons revered – were not merely instruments of war. They were blasphemies. Their metallic bodies, gleaming with an unnatural, sickly luminescence, were fused with corrupted elemental shards, twisted mockeries of the dragon's natural gifts. Some were equipped with sonic emitters that mimicked the devastating frequencies of a dragon's roar, others with plasma cannons that spat bolts of searing energy, designed to pierce even the most resilient of hides. And the most insidious of all, the 'elemental conduits,' were imbued with stolen dragon essence, siphoning the raw power of the sky and earth to fuel their destructive capabilities. They were a perversion, a void that sought to consume the living flame.

The battle ignited not with a singular, deafening blast, but with a symphony of escalating chaos. A Sky-Serpent, its once-proud crest now singed and frayed, dove from the stratosphere, a comet of burning gold. It was pursued by a formation of Accord interceptors, their sleek hulls bristling with disruptor cannons. The serpent twisted, its massive body contorting in ways that defied logic, its tail whipping with the force of a runaway avalanche. It unleashed a gout of pure solar fire, not aimed at the interceptors themselves, but at the very air around them. The intense heat warped the atmosphere, creating a localized inferno that forced the pursuers to break formation, their pilots momentarily blinded by the blinding glare.

As the interceptors scattered, a pair of machims, their hulking forms resembling distorted, metallic beetles, lumbered into the fray. Their primary weapons were colossal sonic cannons, designed to replicate the debilitating roar of a dragon. They unleashed a deafening wave of pure, unadulterated noise, a frequency that vibrated deep within the bones and threatened to dislodge organs. The Sky-Serpent recoiled, its magnificent wings faltering for a perilous moment. It was then that an Azure Drake, a creature of breathtaking azure beauty, swooped in from the flank. Its wings beat with the speed of a hummingbird, creating a vortex of swirling winds that deflected the sonic assault. With a flick of its serpentine neck, it unleashed a concentrated bolt of lightning, a pure white spear of energy that struck one of the sonic machims square in its chest. The automaton shrieked, a grating, metallic protest, sparks showering from its wounded form. But before the drake could press its advantage, a swarm of smaller, insectoid drones, their metallic exoskeletons glinting, descended upon it, their miniature plasma cutters aiming for its wings.

The battle was a dizzying ballet of destruction and desperate defense. The Obsidian Wyrms, their immense wingspans blotting out the sun, unleashed torrents of crackling, black lightning, not as individual bolts, but as curtains of energy that arced across the sky, attempting to ensnare entire squadrons of Accord fighters. One Wyrm, its scales chipped and scarred, its roar a guttural rasp, was harried by a pack of aerial machims, their bodies bristling with energy harpoons.

They sought to immobilize it, to drag it down from the heavens. But the Wyrm was a master of its domain. It dove towards the scarred earth, its massive claws gouging deep furrows in the obsidian plains, drawing forth the raw, volatile energy of the Scarred Basin itself. The ground beneath it pulsed with a dark, potent magic, a feedback loop of chaotic power that overloaded the harpoons, causing them to explode in showers of molten metal.

The Emerald Guardians, their movements fluid and almost ethereal, navigated the chaotic aerial currents with a grace that belied the ferocity of their struggle. They were the masters of misdirection, their breaths of venomous mist capable of corroding metal and disorienting organic pilots alike. One Guardian, its emerald scales dulled by battle, its eyes burning with a fierce desperation, wove through a dense cluster of Accord fighter craft. It didn't attack them directly. Instead, it exhaled, filling the space between them with a thick, phosphorescent fog. The air itself seemed to thicken, to become viscous and suffocating. The Accord pilots, encased in their sterile cockpits, were blinded, their sensors overloaded by the sheer density of the miasma. As they fumbled for control, attempting to break free from the suffocating embrace, they collided with each other, their perfectly synchronized formations dissolving into a cascade of fiery debris.

But the Accord's numbers were immense, their technological superiority a relentless tide. For every dragon that managed to unleash a devastating attack, a dozen machims and fighters swarmed to fill the void. The air was thick with the stench of ozone, burnt metal, and the acrid scent of corrupted dragon essence. The roar of engines, the whine of plasma cannons, the shriek of rending metal, and the agonizing bellows of wounded dragons mingled into a cacophony of despair.

There was a profound tragedy unfolding in this aerial ballet. These were not mere beasts of war; they were the inheritors of a sacred trust, the custodians of the skies. Their role had been to maintain the equilibrium, to act as a living barometer of the world's health, their roars a call to harmony, their flight a dance of cosmic balance. Now, they were forced to engage in a brutal, desperate struggle for survival, their sacred power twisted into a weapon of last resort. The very essence of their being was being co-opted, their primal energies harnessed and weaponized by the sterile, unfeeling hand of the Accord.

THE STORMBOUND DIVIDE

A massive, serpentine machim, its body a nightmarish fusion of obsidian plating and pulsating bio-luminescent veins, rose above the main battlefield. It was an 'Abyssal Maw,' a terror of the Accord's design, capable of drawing in ambient energy and expelling it as a concussive wave of pure entropy. Its maw, a gaping chasm lined with jagged metal teeth, began to glow with an ominous, purple light. It was a harbinger of annihilation, a weapon designed to erase life itself.

Below, the ground forces of the Accord, emboldened by the aerial onslaught, began to push forward, their sonic dampeners struggling to negate the primal song of Mara, but their sheer numbers and the relentless pressure of their machims threatening to overwhelm the Scarred Basin's defenders. The Crystal Spires, vital conduits of Mara's planetary song, were now under direct assault.

The dragons, sensing the escalating threat to the very heart of their world, reacted with a ferocity born of desperation. A Sky-Serpent, its scales blackened and smoking, its body riddled with energy burns, launched itself towards the Abyssal Maw. It was a suicide charge, a final, defiant roar against oblivion. It wrapped its massive body around the machim, its golden scales glowing with an intense, internal heat. It was channeling its remaining solar energy, not to destroy, but to consume. The machim's purple glow flickered, its destructive potential momentarily contained by the serpent's blazing embrace.

Then, a dozen Azure Drakes descended, their lightning strikes converging on the Abyssal Maw's vulnerable power core. The machim shrieked, a sound of grinding gears and tortured metal, as the electrical surge overwhelmed its systems. Simultaneously, the Obsidian Wyrms unleashed a concentrated barrage of shadow energy, their roars shaking the very foundations of the sky, attempting to destabilize the colossal automaton. And the Emerald Guardians, their venomous mists now infused with a desperate fury, shrouded the Abyssal Maw, corroding its plating, seeking to bring it crashing down.

It was a coordinated act of defiance, a symphony of death played out in the heavens. The Sky-Serpent, its form blazing like a dying sun, finally detonated, a blinding flash of pure light that consumed the Abyssal Maw in its incandescent fury. The explosion sent shockwaves through the battlefield, a momentary reprieve from the relentless assault.

But the cost was immeasurable. The Sky-Serpent was gone, its noble spirit extinguished in a final act of sacrifice. Its loss was a blow to the dragons, a wound that went deeper than any physical injury. The unifying force, the radiant beacon of their species, had been extinguished. And the Accord, relentless and unyielding, continued their advance.

The machims, though momentarily stunned by the spectacular demise of the Abyssal Maw, began to reassert their dominance. Their metallic bodies, designed for endurance, showed less fatigue than their organic counterparts. The elemental conduits, drawing upon the vast reserves of stolen dragon essence, unleashed waves of corrupted elemental energy. Firestorms of unnatural hue erupted, ice shards sharp enough to pierce steel rained down, and earth-shattering tremors, amplified by stolen draconic might, shook the very ground.

The battle was no longer just a fight for territory; it was a desperate struggle for the soul of the world, a war waged by beings who had once soared in majestic harmony, now reduced to the primal instinct of survival, their powers perverted and turned against them. The sky dragons, the majestic denizens of the upper atmosphere, were a force of nature unleashed, their fury a terrible, beautiful spectacle. But in their eyes, and in the anguished cries that echoed across the war-torn skies, was the undeniable truth: their age of dominion was ending, replaced by a desperate fight for existence, a fight against the very darkness that had been bred from their own stolen light. The wind carried not the songs of creation, but the death throes of a species, a symphony of conflict that threatened to silence the world forever.

The majestic flight of the dragons had become a desperate, furious dive towards an uncertain dawn, their legacy etched in the fiery scars they left upon the bruised and broken heavens. The air, once alive with the vibrant hum of their power, was now a chilling testament to their diminishing numbers, each thunderous roar a lament for what was lost, and a desperate plea for what could still be saved. The spectacle of their power was undeniable, but beneath the breathtaking displays of elemental might, lay the grim reality of their dwindling numbers and the encroaching shadow of the Accord's insatiable hunger for dominion. Their struggle was not just for survival, but for the very essence of what it meant to be a living, breathing force of nature in a world increasingly dominated by sterile, artificial order.

The air, still thick with the lingering scent of ozone and the metallic tang of dragon blood, began to hum with a new, more insidious energy. It wasn't the raw, untamed fury of the dragons' elemental breath, nor the jarring cacophony of the Accord's machims. This was a precision-tuned resonance, a deep, vibrating thrum that seemed to emanate from the very heart of the Conclave's vast, airborne citadels. The Skybound Conclave, a collective that had always operated with the cold, detached logic of architects designing their own dominion, was no longer content with the messy, attritional warfare that had been unfolding. They had assessed the battlefield, calculated the remaining strengths of their opponents, and determined that a decisive, surgical strike was required to excise the lingering resistance. Their objective was not merely to win, but to utterly dismantle any possibility of future defiance, to forge their new order from the ashes of a shattered world.

From the impossibly high perches of their cloud-borne fortresses, meticulously crafted vessels that defied gravity and weather alike, the Conclave unleashed their ultimate strategy. It was not a brute-force assault, but a meticulously orchestrated symphony of destruction, designed to exploit the very foundations of the natural world and the beings who embodied it. Their scientists, their arcane engineers, and their strategic minds had toiled for decades, not just in the creation of war machines, but in the understanding of the fundamental energies that bound the planet together. They had learned to dissect the planet's song, to identify its harmonic frequencies, and, most terrifyingly, to weaponize them.

The first indication of this new phase of the conflict came not as a visible threat, but as an imperceptible shift in the atmospheric pressure. The vibrant currents that had carried the dragons, the very lifeblood of their aerial dominance, began to falter, to become sluggish and unpredictable. It was as if the sky itself was sighing, a slow, weary exhalation that robbed the dragons of their agility, their effortless mastery of the winds. Below, the ground, which had been subjected to the concussive forces of machims and the echoing roars of draconic defiance, began to tremble with a different kind of rhythm. It was a low, guttural tremor, too consistent, too deliberate to be a natural seismic event. This was the Conclave's calculated strike, their intention to sever the deep, resonant connection between the land and its ancient protectors.

The Conclave's masterstroke was the deployment of the 'Harmonic Disruptors.' These were not weapons in the traditional sense, but colossal crystalline structures, harvested from the deepest, most stable strata of the planet, then meticulously reshaped and attuned. Suspended from their largest mobile citadels, these disruptors pulsed with a low, resonant frequency, a sound so profound it bypassed the ears and vibrated directly into the very bones of living beings. This frequency was designed to be the antithesis of the planet's natural song, a disharmonious echo that would unravel the intricate biological and elemental connections that sustained the dragons.

As the disruptors activated, the effect was immediate and catastrophic for the dragons. The Sky-Serpents, those majestic beings of fire and light, found their internal solar furnaces sputtering. The vibrant, internal fire that had once roared with such ferocity began to dim, its radiant heat failing to ignite with its usual explosive power. Their breath, once a torrent of pure solar plasma, became a weak, flickering ember, easily dispersed by the Conclave's energy shields. The very essence of their being, tied to the sun's generous energy, was being muted, its vibrant frequency dulled by the dissonant hum.

THE STORMBOUND DIVIDE

The Azure Drakes, masters of wind and lightning, fared no better. Their connection to the atmospheric currents, the very source of their aerial acrobatics and their potent electrical discharges, was being severed. The winds that had once carried them like whispers through the sky now buffeted them with erratic, unyielding force, disrupting their flight patterns and making coordinated attacks impossible. Their lightning, once a precise, devastating strike, became wild, unfocused arcs of energy that dissipated harmlessly against the Conclave's reinforced hulls. The intricate dance of atmospheric electricity, a ballet they had mastered over millennia, was now a chaotic, painful surge that threatened to tear them apart from within.

The Obsidian Wyrms, the storm-callers and masters of shadow energy, felt their connection to the planet's volatile core being twisted. The raw, untamed power they drew from the earth, the very essence of their thunderous roars and the crackling darkness they wielded, was being corrupted. Instead of a surge of potent energy, they received a jarring dissonance, a feedback loop of fractured power that sent tremors of pain through their massive forms. Their storms became erratic and self-destructive, their shadow essence coalescing into unstable, dissipating clouds that offered no offensive capability. The very earth beneath them, once a source of strength, now seemed to resist their connection, its song a discordant clamor.

And the Emerald Guardians, the silent, venomous protectors of the verdant realms, found their very life force being leached away. The vibrant, life-giving energy of the planet that flowed through their jade scales, the source of their potent mists and their regenerative abilities, was being siphoned, twisted into a draining, weakening force. Their poisonous breath, once capable of corroding steel, became a weak, acrid vapor, barely capable of irritating the Conclave's advanced atmospheric filters. The deep, symbiotic relationship they shared with the flora and fauna of the world, a connection that had always sustained them, was being systematically dismantled by the alien frequency.

The Conclave's strategy was brutally effective. They hadn't just aimed to destroy the dragons; they aimed to silence their very existence, to sever their primal links to the fundamental forces of nature. Their fleet of specialized 'Resonance Cruisers,' sleek, obsidian vessels bristling with the Harmonic Disruptors, advanced in a precise, geometric formation. They moved with an unnerving grace, their formations unmarred by the chaos of the ongoing battle. The dragons, once the masters of the skies, were now grounded, their mighty wings beating with a desperate, futile energy, their roars of defiance choked by the overwhelming, disharmonious hum.

The machims, untouched by the resonance frequency, pressed their advantage with renewed vigor. The sonic cannons, which had previously struggled against the dragons' natural vocalizations, now found their targets weakened and disoriented. The plasma cannons, their beams no longer needing to pierce dragon hide hardened by millennia of elemental resilience, easily sliced through weakened scales and flesh. The elemental conduits, their capacity to absorb and redirect dragon energy now amplified by the weakened state of their prey, unleashed torrents of corrupted power with devastating efficiency. The battlefield, once a chaotic ballet of elemental fury, was rapidly transforming into a slaughterhouse.

The Conclave's aerial citadels, towering behemoths that dwarfed the largest machims, unleashed their own devastating payloads. These were not conventional explosives, but 'Graviton Emitters,' devices capable of manipulating localized gravity fields. Entire squadrons of dragons, their flight already compromised, were suddenly subjected to crushing gravitational forces, their bodies being pulled and twisted in ways that defied biology. Wings snapped, limbs were torn from sockets, and massive bodies were slammed into the ground with the force of meteor impacts. The earth shuddered under the onslaught, vast craters appearing where once proud dragons had flown.

Even the dragons' most formidable defenses, their inherent resilience and their deep connection to their territories, were being systematically dismantled. The Sky-Serpents' connection to the sun was being throttled, their fiery essence dimmed. The Azure Drakes' atmospheric conduits were being overloaded with discordant energy, their electrical mastery turned against them. The Obsidian Wyrms' ties to the planet's seismic heart were being frayed, their earth-shattering power turned to self-inflicted tremors. The Emerald Guardians' life-giving symbiosis with the flora was being poisoned by the unnatural resonance, their venomous breath becoming a mere exhalation of regret.

The Conclave's actions were not born of malice, but of a chillingly pragmatic desire for control. They saw the dragons not as sentient beings, but as powerful, unpredictable forces of nature that disrupted their meticulously planned order. Their goal was to neutralize these forces, to reorder the planet according to their own sterile, logical designs. The cost, the immense suffering inflicted upon these ancient creatures, was merely a data point in their calculations, an acceptable sacrifice for the establishment of their perfect, unyielding dominion.

The once vibrant skies, a canvas of roiling elemental energy and the majestic forms of dragons, were now a desolate expanse. The symphony of conflict had been brutally silenced, replaced by the cold, methodical hum of the Harmonic Disruptors and the grating grind of machims. The dragons, the living embodiment of the planet's untamed spirit, were being systematically extinguished, their ancient song fading into a painful whisper. The Conclave's calculated strike had proven devastatingly effective, a testament to their advanced technology, their ruthless efficiency, and their utter disregard for the natural world they sought to rule.

The dawn they envisioned was one of absolute control, devoid of the vibrant, unpredictable life that had once characterized the world, a testament to their chilling pursuit of an ordered, soulless future. Their precision was a scalpel, carving away at the very heart of the planet's wild spirit, leaving behind only the sterile, unwavering monument to their own power. The cacophony of battle had given way to the terrifying silence of an imposed order, a silence that spoke volumes of the Conclave's ultimate victory and the profound loss that accompanied it. The sky, stripped of its ancient guardians, felt vast and empty, a stark reminder of the price of unchecked ambition and the devastating consequences of seeking to silence the very song of life itself.

Chapter Twelve
THE ABYSSAL CLIMAX

The hum of the Harmonic Disruptors, once a precise instrument of discord, began to warp. It was no longer a clean, surgical unraveling of the planet's song, but a jagged tear, a feedback loop of pure sonic agony. The carefully calculated frequencies, designed to isolate and dismantle the dragons' primal connections, had instead struck a resonant chord with the planet's deeper, more ancient harmonics. The very bedrock of existence, the subtle symphony that had orchestrated life since the dawn of time, was now groaning under an unbearable strain.

Mara felt it not in her ears, but in her very bones, a deep, visceral tremor that resonated with a terror far exceeding the physical. The world's song, which she had spent a lifetime learning to hear, to interpret, to *feel*, was fracturing. It was like witnessing a masterpiece of music being systematically shredded, note by agonizing note. The majestic chords that spoke of mountains and oceans, of the slow, patient growth of ancient forests, of the fierce, joyous dance of the wind, were being drowned out by a shrill, piercing whine, the sound of reality itself being ripped asunder.

This was not the controlled demolition the Conclave had envisioned. Their understanding, while advanced, had been incomplete. They had dissected the surface melodies, the obvious refrains that governed the elemental beings and the larger creatures of the world. But they had failed to grasp the subtler, interwoven harmonies, the basso continuo that connected every atom, every living cell, to a singular, pulsating consciousness. By attacking the dragons, they had inadvertently struck the primary strings of this cosmic instrument, and the resulting reverberation was threatening to shatter everything.

The dragons, their bodies already ravaged by the disruptive frequencies, now writhed in a new kind of agony. Their internal energies, forced into chaotic flux, began to surge outwards, not as controlled attacks, but as wild, uncontrolled bursts of primal power. A Sky-Serpent, its solar essence flickering like a dying candle, suddenly erupted in a blinding flash, a silent scream of pure light that momentarily overloaded the Conclave's optical sensors. An Azure Drake, its connection to the winds now a torment, thrashed in the air, its electrical discharges sparking erratically, striking its own brethren and the very machims that hunted them.

The Obsidian Wyrms, their earth-given power turned inward, seemed to be consumed by internal storms, their roars transforming into guttural bellows of pure, unadulterated pain as their own earth-shattering energy tore them apart from within. And the Emerald Guardians, their life-giving connection to the flora now a poisonous conduit, began to wither, their jade scales dulling, their movements becoming sluggish and pained as the very essence of the world they protected turned against them.

The machims, while impervious to the sonic disruption, found themselves caught in the crossfire of this planetary breakdown. Graviton emitters, still active and calibrated to create localized pockets of immense gravity, now buffeted them with erratic, unpredictable force. Instead of a steady pull, they experienced jarring jolts, violent shifts that sent their heavily armored frames tumbling through the air like discarded toys. Plasma cannons, their beams designed to slice through weakened dragon hide, now struggled to maintain focus as the very fabric of space around them warped and shimmered. The intricate targeting systems, reliant on stable atmospheric conditions, began to fail, their readouts flashing with nonsensical data.

The Conclave's meticulously designed fleet, once a symbol of their unwavering control, was now a collection of vulnerable targets adrift in a sea of uncontrolled, elemental chaos. Their citadels, designed to withstand the most potent of dragon attacks, shuddered as the planet's groaning song resonated through their very structures. The crystalline Harmonic Disruptors, the instruments of their intended victory, now pulsed with a wild, untamed energy, their light flickering erratically as if struggling to contain the overwhelming forces they had unleashed. The precise, geometric formations of their fleet began to break, machims colliding with each other in panicked, uncontrolled maneuvers, their sophisticated weapons systems firing indiscriminately into the chaotic skies.

Mara, anchored to the ground by the sheer force of the planetary upheaval, watched this disintegration with a mixture of horror and dawning understanding. The Conclave had sought to silence the world's song, to impose their sterile order upon its vibrant, untamed melody. But in doing so, they had not merely silenced; they had threatened to shatter it into a million dissonant shards, to reduce the symphony of life into a deafening, eternal silence, or worse, a shrieking cacophony that would echo through the void for all time. The abyssal truth she had uncovered, the interconnectedness of all things, was not just a philosophical concept; it was the very operating system of their reality, and the Conclave was attempting a catastrophic system crash.

The air itself seemed to crackle with this raw, unchanneled energy. It was no longer the crisp, clean ozone of dragon fire, nor the sterile hum of Conclave technology. It was a thick, cloying miasma, heavy with the scent of ozone, burning metal, and something else... something ancient and terrified. The sky, once a canvas for the epic struggle, was now a churning vortex of discordant energies, a maelstrom of primal forces lashing out in their death throes.

Mara could feel the individual cries of the world's components, the silent screams of trees being ripped from their roots by rogue gravity fields, the terrified gasps of rivers boiling under unnatural heat, the pained groans of mountains shifting as the earth's core protested the violent frequencies. It was an overwhelming sensory overload, a torrent of suffering that threatened to drown her own consciousness. The symphony of life was not just fraying; it was actively tearing itself apart, and the Conclave, in their hubris, had provided the final, fatal pull.

She saw it then, with a clarity that pierced through the chaos. The Conclave's ambition was not merely to conquer, but to *control* the fundamental forces of existence. They believed that by dissecting and manipulating these forces, they could achieve ultimate order, a perfect, predictable universe. But they had mistaken the dance for the dancer, the song for the singer. They had never truly understood that the power lay not in the individual notes, but in the harmonious interplay, the inherent, wild vitality that flowed through the entire composition.

The dragons, in their raw, elemental power, were not just beings of immense strength; they were living conduits, amplifiers of the planet's song. Their roars were not just expressions of defiance, but affirmations of the world's inherent vibrance. Their breath, their flight, their very existence, were expressions of the planet's living melody. By attempting to silence them, the Conclave had been attempting to silence the planet itself.

And now, the planet was fighting back, not with conscious intent, but with the brute, unthinking force of a body rejecting a fatal infection. The Harmonic Disruptors, instead of silencing the song, had instead amplified the planet's primal scream of pain, turning its own fundamental frequencies against itself in a cataclysmic feedback loop.

Mara's own connection to the world, the one she had painstakingly cultivated, now felt like a lifeline in a raging sea. She could feel the tendrils of the planet's pain, but she could also feel its enduring life force, a faint but persistent heartbeat beneath the cacophony. It was a desperate, dying pulse, but it was still there. The question was, could it be saved? Could the fractured symphony be reassembled before the silence, or the shriek, became permanent?

The Conclave's command center, a bastion of their cold, calculating logic, was likely in utter disarray. Their perfect algorithms, their precise calculations, were failing spectacularly. The unpredictable, chaotic nature of true existence, the very thing they sought to eradicate, was now overwhelming their defenses. Mara could almost picture the faces of their leaders, their impassive masks cracking as they watched their grand design devolve into a terrifying, uncontrollable abyss. They had sought to control the dragon's fire, but they had inadvertently ignited a planetary inferno.

The dragons' weakened bodies were now acting as accidental conduits for this unleashed planetary fury. Their fading energies, instead of being extinguished, were being overwhelmed by the raw, untamed power of the world itself, a power far greater than anything the Conclave had ever conceived. The Sky-Serpents' dimmed solar furnaces were being overloaded with cosmic radiation, their flickering light threatening to explode into nova-like brilliance.

The Azure Drakes' disrupted atmospheric conduits were now channels for raw, uncontrolled lightning, surging from the planet's core upwards. The Obsidian Wyrms' fractured connection to the earth was being reforged with seismic energy, their groans turning into tremors that shook the very foundations of the Conclave's citadels. And the Emerald Guardians, their leached life force being replenished with a surge of raw, primal verdancy, were beginning to stir with a renewed, albeit wild, power.

This was the abyssal truth laid bare: life, in its most fundamental form, was not a passive entity to be controlled, but a vibrant, chaotic force that could not be truly silenced, only transformed. The Conclave had sought to impose a sterile order, but they had instead unleashed the very wildness they feared. Mara knew, with a chilling certainty, that the climax of this battle was not about victory or defeat in the traditional sense.

It was about whether the planet's song would be forever broken, or if, amidst the chaos, a new, perhaps even more powerful, melody could emerge from the ruins. The fate of everything hinged on this precarious precipice, on the fragile hope that the planet's inherent resilience could overcome the destructive hubris of those who sought to silence it. The air was thick with the echoes of what was, the screams of what was being torn apart, and the faint, nascent hum of what might yet be, a song born of destruction, but a song nonetheless.

The earth beneath Mara's feet was no longer solid ground. It was a churning, heaving entity, a physical manifestation of the planet's agony. Each tremor was a primal scream, each shudder a desperate spasm. Beside her, Cael's jaw was set, his hand gripping the hilt of his blade not in preparation for a physical fight, but as an anchor against the unraveling of reality itself. The journey to this point had been a brutal odyssey through a world tearing itself apart. They had navigated chasms that opened without warning, crossed rivers that boiled or froze in an instant, and dodged debris hurled by an atmosphere gone mad. The sky above was a perpetual twilight, a bruised canvas where lightning storms raged in impossible colors, fueled not by water vapor but by the raw, unfettered energies of a dying world.

They had followed the deepening resonance of the planet's fractured song, a thread of discord that grew louder, more piercing, with every step. It had led them away from the open battlefields, away from the cacophony of dying dragons and malfunctioning machims, towards a place whispered about in forgotten texts, a place where the very bedrock of existence was said to be thinnest. The air here was heavy, thick with the scent of ozone, burnt earth, and a chilling, metallic tang that spoke of energies both ancient and deeply unnatural. It was the smell of a wound, a cosmic injury that was bleeding its life force into the void.

Their allies, a grim handful of those who had refused to fall prey to despair or the Conclave's manufactured order, had been thinned by the journey. Some had been consumed by the chaotic energies, others had made sacrifices to clear their path. Now, only Kaelen, his face etched with a grim determination, and Lyra, her eyes wide with a mixture of fear and awe, remained by Mara's side. Kaelen's scaled hands, usually steady as he wielded his elemental blade, trembled slightly, a testament to the sheer, raw power thrumming around them. Lyra, who could typically find solace in the quiet hum of life, found herself overwhelmed, the planetary distress a constant, deafening roar in her senses.

THE STORMBOUND DIVIDE

As they crested a final, jagged ridge, the source of the world's unraveling lay before them. It was not a citadel of the Conclave, nor a nest of some monstrous entity. It was a scar. A vast, gaping maw in the earth, pulsing with a sickly, phosphorescent light. The edges of the chasm seemed to bleed into reality, the very rock around it twisted and contorted as if in constant, silent scream. At its center, suspended by invisible forces, was an artifact. It was not made of metal or stone, but of a substance that defied description, a swirling vortex of shadow and starlight, of creation and decay. It hummed with a discordant melody, a deep, guttural thrum that vibrated not through the air, but directly into their souls. This was the heart of the wound, the nexus of the abyssal truth they had sought.

"By the ancient stars," Kaelen breathed, his voice barely a whisper, the usual bravado gone, replaced by a profound, unnerving respect. "The texts spoke of the Void's Maw, a wound so deep it bled into the very fabric of existence. I never believed…"

Mara felt it too, a chilling recognition. This was not just a physical place. It was a manifestation of an existential error, a point where the balance of the world had been irrevocably broken, and now, through the Conclave's meddling, that break was widening into an abyss. The artifact pulsed, and with each pulse, a ripple of decay emanated outwards, subtly eroding the very essence of the land, of the air, of their own beings. It was the sound of entropy made manifest, a siren song of oblivion.

Lyra stumbled, pressing a hand to her temple. "It's… it's too much. The pain… it's not just the world. It's… older. Deeper. Like a memory of death that never happened."

Mara nodded, her gaze fixed on the swirling artifact. The Conclave had sought to control the song, to impose their sterile order. They had believed that by dissecting and controlling the elemental dragons, they could master the planet's melody. But they had never understood the deeper truth, the song's primal source, its connection to something far more ancient and fundamental. They had tried to silence a symphony by cutting out the strings of the instrument, only to find they had struck the very foundation of the concert hall.

"The Conclave didn't create this wound," Mara said, her voice resonating with a newfound, somber authority. "They only widened it. This is the consequence of an ancient imbalance, a forgotten cosmic error that has festered for eons. The dragons, they were guardians, conduits of the world's vibrant song, not its masters. By attacking them, the Conclave didn't just break their connection to the planet; they severed the arteries that fed the wound, and now it's hemorrhaging."

Cael stepped forward, his eyes narrowed, his senses on high alert. "What is it? What *is* that thing?"

The artifact seemed to respond to his question, its light intensifying. Images flickered within its depths: nebulae collapsing, stars dying, the silent, inexorable march of decay. It was not a conscious entity in the way they understood life, but a force, a gravitational pull towards nothingness. It was the shadow cast by existence, the echo of the void that lay beyond the known cosmos.

"It's... it's the Echo," Mara whispered, the name surfacing from the depths of her intuition, from the fractured song she felt within her bones. "The primordial emptiness. The silence that predates creation. For eons, it has been held at bay, its influence contained by the world's song, by the very life force it seeks to consume. But the Conclave's disruption... it weakened the barriers. It's not an active invasion, but a consequence. A point where the world's song is so fractured, so dissonant, that the Echo can seep through."

The ground beneath them groaned, a seismic wave radiating from the artifact. A section of the chasm wall crumbled, revealing not rock, but a void of absolute blackness, a patch of non-existence that seemed to swallow the light. This was the abyssal truth laid bare: the constant, delicate struggle between creation and annihilation, a balance the Conclave, in their quest for absolute order, had catastrophically disrupted.

"We have to seal it," Cael stated, his voice firm, though a tremor of unease ran through it. "Whatever it takes."

Mara looked at him, then at Kaelen and Lyra. They had faced monstrous creatures, overwhelming odds, and the insidious manipulations of the Conclave. But this was different. This was a confrontation with the fundamental nature of reality itself.

"Sealing it won't be enough," she replied, her gaze returning to the pulsing artifact. "The Conclave has already weakened the seals to a point where they can no longer hold. We need to restore the song. We need to mend the world's melody, to make it strong enough to push back the Echo again."

Kaelen hefted his elemental blade, its faint glow seeming to shrink in the face of the artifact's oppressive aura. "But how? We can't fight a... a void. And the dragons are too weak, too broken."

"We don't fight it directly," Mara said, her mind racing, piecing together the fragmented whispers of the planet's song. "We remind it of what it is. We have to reignite the core harmonies. The Conclave's disruptions were precise, targeted. They attacked the surface melodies, the obvious refrains of the dragons. But the deepest song... the one that connects everything... that is what we must amplify."

She reached out, not to the artifact, but to the fractured earth beneath her. She closed her eyes, ignoring the blinding light and the suffocating sense of decay, and focused on the faintest of pulses, the tenacious heartbeat of the wounded world. It was a struggle, like trying to hear a single note in the midst of a deafening storm. But she could feel it – the memory of mountain ranges, the patient rhythm of ancient forests, the boundless energy of the oceans. These were not just elements; they were voices in the grand symphony.

"The dragons... they were conductors," she murmured. "Each species represented a fundamental movement. The Sky-Serpents, the celestial dance. The Azure Drakes, the breath of life and weather. The Obsidian Wyrms, the grounding strength of the earth. The Emerald Guardians, the vibrant, burgeoning life itself. Their powers are corrupted, twisted by the Conclave's frequencies, but the core essence... that still exists."

Lyra, her face pale, but her eyes now filled with a strange, determined light, stepped forward. "My lineage has always been tied to the whispers of life, to the growth and decay. I can feel the Emerald Guardians, even in their suffering. Their song is muted, but not silenced."

Kaelen grunted, a sound of assent. "And my ancestors communed with the earth's fury. If there's any strength left in the Obsidian Wyrms, I can try to draw it out, to remind them of their foundation."

Cael's gaze was fixed on the sky, where the chaotic light show continued. "The Sky-Serpents... their connection to the sun, to the stars... it's flickering, but it's not extinguished. If I can find a way to connect to that fading light..."

Mara smiled, a ghost of her former self, but with a new, profound understanding. "Then we have our orchestra. The Conclave tried to play a solo, a single, sterile note of control. We will play the symphony. We will remind the world of its own song, a song that can drown out the silence, that can push back the Echo."

She raised her hands, and the faint, residual energy that still clung to her, the echo of her own connection to the world's song, began to surge outwards. It was a fragile tendril, a single, pure note amidst the cacophony. Kaelen followed suit, his hands glowing with a nascent, earthen power, a deep, resonant hum that seemed to anchor itself to the groaning bedrock. Lyra extended her hands, and a faint, emerald luminescence bloomed around her, the promise of life struggling against the encroaching decay. Cael, his eyes turned skyward, focused his will, reaching for the distant, flickering stars, a faint shimmer of solar energy gathering around him.

The artifact at the center of the chasm pulsed again, its sickly light intensifying, as if sensing their intent. The void within the chasm walls seemed to deepen, the encroaching darkness growing bolder. The Echo, the primordial emptiness, was pushing back, its siren song of oblivion growing more insistent. But now, it was not the only sound.

Mara felt the strain, the immense effort required to weave their disparate energies into a cohesive whole. It was like trying to conduct a tempest. But with each passing moment, their nascent song grew stronger, its notes finding their counterparts, weaving a fragile tapestry of sound and light. The emerald glow from Lyra intensified, coaxing a faint bloom from a withered vine clinging to the chasm's edge. Kaelen's earth energy seemed to solidify the crumbling ground beneath them, a small island of stability in the chaos. Cael's focus drew a faint, golden beam from the distant, bruised sky, a minuscule echo of the sun's dying glory.

And Mara's own contribution, the purest manifestation of the world's song, began to resonate. She felt the memories of the deep oceans, the rushing rivers, the whispering winds. She felt the vibrant pulse of life, the resilience that had endured eons of change. It was a song of creation, a song of existence, a song that had once held the Echo at bay.

The artifact throbbed, its discordant hum deepening into a guttural growl. The forces of decay and silence were not merely passive; they were a hungry presence, and they were being challenged. The chasm widened, the void threatening to consume them all. But the fragile melody they wove, though small, was pure. It was the sound of life asserting itself, of order emerging from chaos, of hope refusing to be extinguished.

They were not fighting the abyss; they were reinforcing the world's song, strengthening its ability to hold the darkness at bay. This was not a battle of swords and shields, but a confrontation of fundamental forces, a desperate attempt to reawaken a sleeping giant, to mend the fractured heart of their world before the silence consumed everything. The air crackled with the opposing energies, the scent of ozone and decay battling the burgeoning scent of life and light. The true climax was not a clash of armies, but the fragile, defiant performance of a planet's returning song.

The artifact at the chasm's heart pulsed, a morbid heartbeat against the ragged symphony of the dying world. Mara felt it not just in her bones, but in the very marrow of her being – a chilling, undeniable choice presented by the cosmic wound they had stumbled upon. It was a crossroads not of paths, but of philosophies, a stark dichotomy between dominance and devotion. The Conclave, in their hubris, had attempted to bend the world to their will, to impose a sterile, predictable order upon its wild, untamed essence. They had sought to master the elemental dragons, to dissect their innate melodies and reassemble them into a symphony of their own design, a symphony of absolute control. But their ambition had been their undoing, their rigid adherence to a singular vision shattering the intricate, interwoven harmonies that had sustained the planet for millennia. Now, the Echo, the primordial void, pressed in, a testament to the destructive consequence of such enforced silence.

Before them, the swirling vortex of shadow and starlight that comprised the Echo's conduit seemed to whisper two opposing futures. One path, paved with the tempting allure of immediate efficacy, was to mimic the Conclave's desperate measures, to try and impose *their* order upon the fractured song. This would involve channeling their own burgeoning power, along with the nascent strengths of Kaelen, Lyra, and Cael, into a forceful counter-frequency. It would be a direct attempt to silence the Echo, to force it back into the void through sheer, unadulterated power.

It was a path of dominance, of becoming the new architects of control, shaping the world's song into a melody that served their immediate needs, a melody of survival and restoration dictated by their own will. This was the path of the Accord, a ghost of a forgotten empire that had tried to impose its will on the elemental forces, only to be consumed by them. It was the path of the Conclave, a more recent, and arguably more catastrophic, iteration of the same flawed ideal.

The alternative, however, was far more arduous and fraught with uncertainty. It was the path of stewardship, of truly listening to the planet's wounded song, not to command it, but to *understand* it. It was about becoming conduits, not rulers; about nurturing the inherent melodies that still resonated within the earth, the air, the lifeblood of the world, and coaxing them back into a harmonious whole.

This meant accepting the world's inherent wildness, its unpredictable rhythms, its capacity for both creation and decay, and finding their place within that grand, complex tapestry. It meant recognizing that the dragons were not mere instruments to be played, but vital components of the planetary orchestra, their broken melodies a part of the world's ongoing narrative, not an aberration to be erased. This path demanded humility, patience, and a profound respect for the natural order, an order that had existed long before the Conclave, and would, perhaps, exist long after.

Mara felt the weight of this choice press down on her, heavier than any physical burden. She had always believed in the power of connection, in the inherent wisdom of the natural world. The Conclave's descent into tyrannical order had solidified her resolve against such forced conformity. Yet, here, staring into the gaping maw of oblivion, the temptation to seize control, to impose a quick, decisive solution, was potent. The raw power she felt thrumming within her, amplified by the world's distress, offered a tantalizing shortcut. She could, with a surge of concentrated will, attempt to blast the Echo back, to seal the wound with a force so overwhelming that it would temporarily push back the encroaching darkness. This would be a victory, a tangible result, a demonstration of their power to overcome the encroaching void.

But a deeper instinct, one honed by her journey and her communion with the fractured song, recoiled at the thought. To impose order, even with the best intentions, was to repeat the mistakes of the past. It was to assume a position of superiority over the very world they sought to save. It was to declare that they, imperfect and limited as they were, knew better than the eons of natural evolution and cosmic balance. This would make them no different from the Conclave, merely a different faction wielding a different brand of control.

Kaelen, his scaled hands clenching and unclenching, seemed to feel the same internal struggle. He looked at Mara, his gaze a mixture of apprehension and unwavering trust. "The earth still remembers its strength, Mara," he rumbled, his voice a low vibration that seemed to resonate with the bedrock beneath them. "It remembers its fury. We can draw upon that. We can make this chasm tremble with a power it has not known since the First Age." His eyes, usually bright with the fire of elemental earth, held a flicker of something akin to ruthlessness, the primal urge to dominate that had been a part of his ancestral lineage, a force that had, at times, led his people to conflict.

Lyra, ever the empath, was acutely aware of the world's pain. She felt the delicate threads of life struggling to survive, the faint whispers of hope clinging to existence. "The growth... it *wants* to return," she breathed, her voice laced with a profound sadness. "It yearns for the sun, for the rain. If we can guide that yearning, if we can amplify its song, perhaps... perhaps it can push back the silence." Her gaze was soft, her focus on the struggling flora clinging to the chasm's edge, a testament to her innate connection to the life-giving aspects of the world.

Cael, his attention fixed on the distant, bruised sky, spoke with a quiet intensity. "The stars are distant, but their light still reaches us. The Sky-Serpents' echo... it's faint, but it's there. We can gather that light, Mara. We can forge a beacon to drive back the shadows." His approach, ever pragmatic and focused on the immediate threat, was aligned with a strategy of direct confrontation, of meeting force with force.

Mara turned her gaze from the artifact to her companions, their faces illuminated by the eerie phosphorescence of the chasm. Each of them represented a facet of the world's power, a potential avenue for action. Kaelen, the embodiment of the earth's raw, foundational strength. Lyra, the gentle, persistent force of life and renewal. Cael, the seeker of celestial light, the wielder of cosmic energies. And herself, a nexus of the world's fractured song, capable of weaving their individual strengths into a unified melody.

The choice was not merely an abstract philosophical debate; it was a visceral, immediate imperative. To choose the path of imposed order meant a swift, decisive action, a demonstration of power that would, in the short term, secure their survival. It meant becoming the new arbiters of the world's song, dictating its rhythm and its melody, ensuring that such a catastrophic imbalance could never occur again.

But this path carried the heavy burden of potential corruption. Power, especially unchecked power, had a way of twisting even the noblest intentions. To become the enforcers of order would be to risk becoming the very thing they had fought against – oppressors who believed they knew best, who silenced dissent in the name of security. It was a seductive, dangerous path, one that promised immediate results but threatened long-term subjugation, albeit by a seemingly benevolent hand.

The alternative, the path of stewardship, offered no guarantees of immediate success. It was a path that demanded a profound act of faith, a surrender to the inherent complexities of existence. It meant working *with* the world's natural tendencies, not against them. It meant understanding that the Echo was not an enemy to be vanquished, but a force that was held in balance by the world's song, a song that had been weakened, not destroyed.

To mend the song was to naturally restore the balance, to allow the world to heal itself, with their guidance and support. This path required them to embrace their roles not as rulers, but as gardeners, tending to a wilting garden, coaxing life back from the brink, not by ripping out the weeds with brutal force, but by nourishing the soil, by understanding the needs of each struggling sprout, by allowing the natural cycles of growth and decay to play out, albeit with their gentle intervention.

Mara closed her eyes, focusing on the subtle tremors that ran through the earth, on the faint, life-affirming pulse that stubbornly persisted beneath the desolation. She felt the echoes of ancient forests, of oceans teeming with life, of mountains that had stood for millennia. These were not forces to be commanded, but forces to be respected, to be understood, to be harmonized with. The idea of imposing their will, of forcing the world into a new, rigid structure, felt fundamentally wrong. It was a violation of the very essence of life, which thrived on diversity, on adaptation, on a delicate, ever-shifting equilibrium.

"We cannot become what we fought," Mara stated, her voice quiet but firm, resonating with a conviction that had been forged in the crucible of their trials. "The Conclave sought to control, to dissect, to impose their sterile vision. If we do the same, even with the best of intentions, we are merely replacing one form of tyranny with another. This world... it is not a machine to be repaired, but a living entity, with its own rhythms, its own song. Our role cannot be to dictate that song, but to help it find its voice again."

She opened her eyes, meeting the gazes of her companions. "The path of imposed order offers a quick solution, a way to silence the immediate threat. It promises control, a return to a semblance of stability forged by our will. But it is a path of ultimate risk, the risk of becoming the very thing we have sworn to oppose. It is the path of the Accord, the path of the Conclave. It is the path of dominance."

Her gaze shifted, encompassing the vast, desolate landscape, the pulsing artifact, and the desperate hope reflected in her companions' eyes. "The other path... the path of stewardship... it is harder. It demands patience, understanding, and a willingness to embrace complexity. It means working with the world's own song, amplifying its inherent harmonies, guiding its recovery rather than forcing it. It is the path of true leadership, of responsibility, not of power." She paused, allowing the weight of her words to settle. "We must choose to be gardeners, not dictators. To be healers, not conquerors. We must trust in the world's own resilience, and help it to remember its own song."

Kaelen nodded, the ruthlessness in his eyes softening into a grim acceptance. "The earth's fury can be a destructive force, uncontrolled. But it can also be a foundation, a strength to be channeled. If we guide it, if we help it remember its purpose... then perhaps it can be a force for creation, not just destruction."

Lyra's face, though etched with weariness, now held a spark of renewed hope. "The whispers of life... they are so faint, but they are persistent. If we can amplify those whispers into a chorus, if we can weave them with the strength of the earth and the light of the stars, then perhaps... perhaps we can create a song that can truly heal."

Cael's gaze softened as he looked at Mara. "I understand. To fight the void with more force might only feed it. But to foster life, to rekindle the light... that is a different kind of power. A power that endures."

The choice was made. It was a leap of faith into the unknown, a rejection of the easy, seductive path of dominance for the arduous, uncertain road of genuine partnership. They would not seek to control the world's song, but to reawaken it, to nurture it, to let it sing its own true, complex melody, a melody that held the promise of healing, of resilience, and of a future where balance was not imposed, but organically restored. The weight of the world still pressed upon them, but now, it was a weight they were ready to carry not as rulers, but as humble stewards, ready to face the abyssal climax not with the force of conquest, but with the gentle, persistent power of a song reborn. The artifact pulsed again, and this time, their response would be not of aggression, but of nurturing creation, a testament to the enduring power of hope in the face of oblivion.

The pulsating artifact at the chasm's heart, a morbid beacon in the dying world, had presented them with a stark choice. Not a fork in the road, but a chasm between philosophies: dominance or devotion. The Conclave, in their arrogant pursuit of control, had attempted to dissect and reassemble the planet's innate melodies, seeking a symphony of absolute order. Their hubris had shattered the delicate harmonies, unleashing the Echo, a void born of enforced silence. Now, before the swirling vortex of shadow and starlight, two futures beckoned.

The first, a tempting shortcut, was to mirror the Conclave's desperate measures. To channel their own burgeoning power, augmented by Kaelen, Lyra, and Cael, into a forceful counter-frequency, a direct attempt to silence the Echo and mend the cosmic wound with their will. This was the path of dominance, of becoming the new architects of control, shaping the world's song into a melody of survival dictated by their own designs. It echoed the Accord, a forgotten empire that had sought to impose its will on elemental forces, only to be consumed. It was the Conclave's path, a more recent and catastrophic iteration of the same flawed ideal.

The alternative was infinitely more arduous, fraught with a profound uncertainty. It was the path of stewardship, of truly listening to the planet's wounded song, not to command it, but to understand it. To become conduits, not rulers, nurturing the inherent melodies that still resonated within the earth, the air, the very lifeblood of the world, and coaxing them back into a harmonious whole.

This meant accepting the world's inherent wildness, its unpredictable rhythms, its capacity for both creation and decay, and finding their place within that grand, complex tapestry. It meant recognizing that the dragons were not mere instruments to be played, but vital components of the planetary orchestra, their broken melodies a part of the world's ongoing narrative, not an aberration to be erased. This path demanded humility, patience, and a profound respect for the natural order, an order that had existed long before the Conclave, and would, perhaps, exist long after.

Mara felt the weight of this choice press down on her, heavier than any physical burden. She had always believed in the power of connection, in the inherent wisdom of the natural world. The Conclave's descent into tyrannical order had solidified her resolve against such forced conformity. Yet, here, staring into the gaping maw of oblivion, the temptation to seize control, to impose a quick, decisive solution, was potent. The raw power she felt thrumming within her, amplified by the world's distress, offered a tantalizing shortcut. She could, with a surge of concentrated will, attempt to blast the Echo back, to seal the wound with a force so overwhelming that it would temporarily push back the encroaching darkness. This would be a victory, a tangible result, a demonstration of their power to overcome the encroaching void.

But a deeper instinct, one honed by her journey and her communion with the fractured song, recoiled at the thought. To impose order, even with the best intentions, was to repeat the mistakes of the past. It was to assume a position of superiority over the very world they sought to save. It was to declare that they, imperfect and limited as they were, knew better than the eons of natural evolution and cosmic balance. This would make them no different from the Conclave, merely a different faction wielding a different brand of control.

Kaelen, his scaled hands clenching and unclenching, seemed to feel the same internal struggle. He looked at Mara, his gaze a mixture of apprehension and unwavering trust. "The earth still remembers its strength, Mara," he rumbled, his voice a low vibration that seemed to resonate with the bedrock beneath them. "It remembers its fury. We can draw upon that. We can make this chasm tremble with a power it has not known since the First Age." His eyes, usually bright with the fire of elemental earth, held a flicker of something akin to ruthlessness, the primal urge to dominate that had been a part of his ancestral lineage, a force that had, at times, led his people to conflict.

Lyra, ever the empath, was acutely aware of the world's pain. She felt the delicate threads of life struggling to survive, the faint whispers of hope clinging to existence. "The growth... it *wants* to return," she breathed, her voice laced with a profound sadness. "It yearns for the sun, for the rain. If we can guide that yearning, if we can amplify its song, perhaps... perhaps it can push back the silence." Her gaze was soft, her focus on the struggling flora clinging to the chasm's edge, a testament to her innate connection to the life-giving aspects of the world.

Cael, his attention fixed on the distant, bruised sky, spoke with a quiet intensity. "The stars are distant, but their light still reaches us. The Sky-Serpents' echo... it's faint, but it's there. We can gather that light, Mara. We can forge a beacon to drive back the shadows." His approach, ever pragmatic and focused on the immediate threat, was aligned with a strategy of direct confrontation, of meeting force with force.

Mara turned her gaze from the artifact to her companions, their faces illuminated by the eerie phosphorescence of the chasm. Each of them represented a facet of the world's power, a potential avenue for action. Kaelen, the embodiment of the earth's raw, foundational strength. Lyra, the gentle, persistent force of life and renewal. Cael, the seeker of celestial light, the wielder of cosmic energies. And herself, a nexus of the world's fractured song, capable of weaving their individual strengths into a unified melody.

The choice was not merely an abstract philosophical debate; it was a visceral, immediate imperative. To choose the path of imposed order meant a swift, decisive action, a demonstration of power that would, in the short term, secure their survival. It meant becoming the new arbiters of the world's song, dictating its rhythm and its melody, ensuring that such a catastrophic imbalance could never occur again. But this path carried the heavy burden of potential corruption. Power, especially unchecked power, had a way of twisting even the noblest intentions. To become the enforcers of order would be to risk becoming the very thing they had fought against – oppressors who believed they knew best, who silenced dissent in the name of security. It was a seductive, dangerous path, one that promised immediate results but threatened long-term subjugation, albeit by a seemingly benevolent hand.

The alternative, the path of stewardship, offered no guarantees of immediate success. It was a path that demanded a profound act of faith, a surrender to the inherent complexities of existence. It meant working *with* the world's natural tendencies, not against them. It meant understanding that the Echo was not an enemy to be vanquished, but a force that was held in balance by the world's song, a song that had been weakened, not destroyed.

To mend the song was to naturally restore the balance, to allow the world to heal itself, with their guidance and support. This path required them to embrace their roles not as rulers, but as gardeners, tending to a wilting garden, coaxing life back from the brink, not by ripping out the weeds with brutal force, but by nourishing the soil, by understanding the needs of each struggling sprout, by allowing the natural cycles of growth and decay to play out, albeit with their gentle intervention.

Mara closed her eyes, focusing on the subtle tremors that ran through the earth, on the faint, life-affirming pulse that stubbornly persisted beneath the desolation. She felt the echoes of ancient forests, of oceans teeming with life, of mountains that had stood for millennia. These were not forces to be commanded, but forces to be respected, to be understood, to be harmonized with. The idea of imposing their will, of forcing the world into a new, rigid structure, felt fundamentally wrong. It was a violation of the very essence of life, which thrived on diversity, on adaptation, on a delicate, ever-shifting equilibrium.

"We cannot become what we fought," Mara stated, her voice quiet but firm, resonating with a conviction that had been forged in the crucible of their trials. "The Conclave sought to control, to dissect, to impose their sterile vision. If we do the same, even with the best of intentions, we are merely replacing one form of tyranny with another. This world... it is not a machine to be repaired, but a living entity, with its own rhythms, its own song. Our role cannot be to dictate that song, but to help it find its voice again."

She opened her eyes, meeting the gazes of her companions. "The path of imposed order offers a quick solution, a way to silence the immediate threat. It promises control, a return to a semblance of stability forged by our will. But it is a path of ultimate risk, the risk of becoming the very thing we have sworn to oppose. It is the path of the Accord, the path of the Conclave. It is the path of dominance."

Her gaze shifted, encompassing the vast, desolate landscape, the pulsing artifact, and the desperate hope reflected in her companions' eyes. "The other path... the path of stewardship... it is harder. It demands patience, understanding, and a willingness to embrace complexity. It means working with the world's own song, amplifying its inherent harmonies, guiding its recovery rather than forcing it. It is the path of true leadership, of responsibility, not of power." She paused, allowing the weight of her words to settle. "We must choose to be gardeners, not dictators. To be healers, not conquerors. We must trust in the world's own resilience, and help it to remember its own song."

Kaelen nodded, the ruthlessness in his eyes softening into a grim acceptance. "The earth's fury can be a destructive force, uncontrolled. But it can also be a foundation, a strength to be channeled. If we guide it, if we help it remember its purpose... then perhaps it can be a force for creation, not just destruction."

Lyra's face, though etched with weariness, now held a spark of renewed hope. "The whispers of life... they are so faint, but they are persistent. If we can amplify those whispers into a chorus, if we can weave them with the strength of the earth and the light of the stars, then perhaps... perhaps we can create a song that can truly heal."

Cael's gaze softened as he looked at Mara. "I understand. To fight the void with more force might only feed it. But to foster life, to rekindle the light... that is a different kind of power. A power that endures."

The choice was made. It was a leap of faith into the unknown, a rejection of the easy, seductive path of dominance for the arduous, uncertain road of genuine partnership. They would not seek to control the world's song, but to reawaken it, to nurture it, to let it sing its own true, complex melody, a melody that held the promise of healing, of resilience, and of a future where balance was not imposed, but organically restored. The weight of the world still pressed upon them, but now, it was a weight they were ready to carry not as rulers, but as humble stewards, ready to face the abyssal climax not with the force of conquest, but with the gentle, persistent power of a song reborn. The artifact pulsed again, and this time, their response would be not of aggression, but of nurturing creation, a testament to the enduring power of hope in the face of oblivion.

As Mara stood before the pulsating artifact, the fractured melody of the dying world thrummed through her, a mournful symphony of loss and yearning. The choice had been made: stewardship over dominance, healing over control. Yet, the path forward was shrouded in an almost unbearable ambiguity. The artifact, a raw wound in the fabric of reality, seemed to mock their nascent understanding. It pulsed with a power that was both primal and ancient, a force that defied easy categorization. It was the heart of the Abyssal Truth, a truth that whispered of interconnectedness, of cycles of life and death, of the profound, often painful, balance that underpinned existence. To truly heal the world, they had to not only understand this truth but embody it. And embodiment, Mara knew, often demanded a sacrifice that transcended mere action, a sacrifice that reached into the very core of one's being.

"We have chosen to listen," Mara murmured, her voice barely audible above the chasm's eerie hum. "To coax the song back into being, not to force it." She looked at Kaelen, whose formidable strength was now tempered with a gentle resolve, a testament to his newfound understanding of his role as a guardian, not a conqueror. "Kaelen, your connection to the earth is our foundation. The tremors that run through the land, the deep, resonant pulse of its heartwood—we need to amplify that. We need to feel its pain, its resilience, and channel that into a song of enduring strength."

Kaelen nodded, his eyes reflecting the starlight that pierced the perpetual twilight of the chasm. "I feel it, Mara. The earth groans, but it does not break. Its strength is deep, its roots go down to the core. If we can help it remember that strength, if we can weave its ancient songs into the present, then it will stand." His scaled hands, usually instruments of destruction, now felt like they held the promise of creation, a promise he was willing to nurture.

Lyra, her face pale but her spirit alight with a fierce compassion, stepped forward. "The life... the smallest shoots, the faintest blossoms clinging to the edges of this void... they are the most vulnerable, and the most precious. Their song is a whisper of defiance against the silence. We must give them voice. We must nurture their fragile hope until it becomes a roar." She extended a hand, her fingers brushing against a hardy vine that, impossibly, still bore a single, dew-kissed bud. "This is not just about power. It is about love. About cherishing what is precious, even in the face of utter despair."

Cael, his gaze fixed on the distant, swirling nebulae, spoke with a quiet conviction. "The celestial currents, the distant light of forgotten stars—they are still connected to us, however faintly. The echoes of the Sky-Serpents still resonate in the upper atmosphere. We can gather that light, that cosmic harmony, and weave it into a tapestry that will not only push back the shadows but remind the world of its place in the grander design. The stars themselves sing of balance, of cycles, of a universe that endures."

Mara felt the convergence of their strengths, a nascent symphony building within her. Kaelen's grounding earth, Lyra's life-affirming growth, Cael's celestial illumination—and her own ability to weave these disparate threads into a cohesive whole. But as she prepared to draw upon these energies, to initiate the ritual of healing, a profound stillness descended. The artifact pulsed, not with aggression, but with a question. It was asking for the ultimate commitment, the true meaning of stewardship.

The Abyssal Truth was not just about understanding interconnectedness; it was about accepting the inherent cost of that connection. Harmony was not a passive state; it was an active, often painful, equilibrium that required constant tending. To truly restore the world's song, they had to prove they understood that balance, that they were willing to sacrifice for it.

Mara's gaze fell upon the artifact again, and this time, she saw it not as a wound, but as a focal point, a crucible where their intent would be tested. The world's song was broken, yes, but it was not dead. It yearned for renewal, for a harmony that accepted both light and shadow, creation and decay. To impose a perfect, unchanging melody would be to deny this fundamental truth, to repeat the Conclave's mistake. True harmony embraced the wild, the unpredictable, the messy beauty of existence.

A realization, sharp and chilling, pierced through her. The artifact was a conduit, a place where immense power could be channeled. They could weave their combined energies, guided by their intent, to reawaken the world's song. But that song, in its purest, most vibrant form, required a catalyst, something that resonated with the deepest chords of existence.

THE STORMBOUND DIVIDE

It required a sacrifice that spoke of love, of loyalty, of an unwavering commitment to life, even when facing oblivion.

The weight of the world, and the immense responsibility they had undertaken, settled upon Mara's shoulders with crushing finality. She looked at her companions, their faces etched with determination, their hopes burning bright. She saw the love in Lyra's eyes for the struggling life around them, the fierce protectiveness in Kaelen's stance, the unwavering belief in Cael's quiet resolve. And in their love for each other, for the world, she saw the seed of the sacrifice that was needed.

A tremor ran through Mara, not of fear, but of profound understanding. The artifact pulsed, its rhythm now a steady, expectant beat. The Abyssal Truth demanded more than just an offering of power; it demanded an offering of self, a testament to the depth of their commitment. The world's song was a tapestry, and to mend it, a thread of immense significance had to be woven into its very fabric.

"It is not enough to merely channel our power," Mara said, her voice clear and resonant, cutting through the murmuring void. "The world's song needs more than our strength. It needs a voice that sings of what it means to love, to protect, to sacrifice for something greater than oneself."

She looked at Kaelen, at Lyra, at Cael. Her gaze lingered on each of them, a silent acknowledgement of the deep bonds they shared. The path of stewardship required not just a willingness to nurture, but a willingness to be nurtured, to be understood, and, if necessary, to give of oneself without reservation. The artifact demanded a profound act of faith, a willingness to embrace the very essence of the world's song—its cycle of birth, life, sacrifice, and rebirth.

"The Conclave sought to control the song," Mara continued, her voice gaining strength with each word. "They believed that power alone could impose order. But true order arises from balance, from understanding that every note, every silence, has its place. And sometimes, to restore that balance, a profound offering must be made."

Her eyes, filled with a mixture of sorrow and serene acceptance, met Kaelen's. "Your strength is the earth's foundation. But even the strongest foundation can be reshaped, can be made more resilient, by a deep, personal sacrifice. A sacrifice that speaks of your unwavering loyalty to this world, to its future."

Then, her gaze shifted to Lyra. "Lyra, your connection to life is its vibrant heartbeat. To nurture that life, to ensure its continuation, sometimes requires a letting go, a profound act of love that transcends individual existence. A sacrifice that echoes the very essence of renewal."

Finally, she turned to Cael. "Cael, your pursuit of light is the beacon that guides us. But even the brightest light casts shadows. To truly illuminate the path forward, a sacrifice that embraces the interconnectedness of all things, even the darkness that defines the light, may be necessary."

Mara took a deep breath, the air heavy with the scent of ozone and dying earth. She understood now. The artifact was not merely a conduit for their power; it was a mirror reflecting the deepest truths of existence. And the greatest truth of all, the one that bound all living things, was the truth of sacrifice. To truly reawaken the world's song, to mend the profound rift that had been torn through its being, one of them, or perhaps all of them in a way they could not yet comprehend, would have to offer something of immeasurable value.

It wouldn't be a sacrifice of brute force, a defiant act of rebellion against the void. It would be a sacrifice born of love, of stewardship, of a profound understanding that the greatest strength lay not in resistance, but in acceptance and in the willingness to give oneself to the greater harmony. The choice had been made to be gardeners, not dictators, and a gardener understood that growth often required the soil to be enriched by what had been.

"The world's song is dying because it has lost its deepest resonance," Mara whispered, her voice now imbued with a sacred solemnity. "It has forgotten the symphony of interconnectedness, the truth that every ending is a prelude to a new beginning. To remind it, to truly mend the silence, we must offer a resonance of our own. A sacrifice that embodies the very essence of what it means to be alive, to love, and to believe in a future that is worth striving for, even at the greatest personal cost."

She looked at the pulsing artifact, and a quiet understanding dawned within her. It was not asking for a life, necessarily. It was asking for a part of them, something deeply cherished, something that resonated with the very core of their being. It was asking for a demonstration of their understanding of the Abyssal Truth, a truth that embraced both the ephemeral beauty of a blossoming flower and the enduring strength of a mountain.

"We have spoken of stewardship," Mara said, her gaze sweeping over her companions, a gentle, knowing light in her eyes. "Of nurturing, of guiding. But stewardship also means recognizing that sometimes, the greatest act of care is to give, to let go, to allow something precious to transform, to become a part of something larger. The song needs a sacrifice that speaks not of defiance, but of devotion. A sacrifice that reminds the world that even in its deepest sorrow, life, love, and hope can bloom anew."

The artifact pulsed, a silent affirmation. It was not a demand for death, but an invitation to profound transformation. The true climax of their journey was not in a battle of wills, but in an act of profound, selfless giving, an offering that would resonate through the very soul of the planet, reminding it of the song it had forgotten, the song of sacrifice, of love, and of the enduring promise of rebirth. The path of stewardship, Mara realized, was not just about tending to the world's wounds, but about becoming a living testament to its resilience, a testament forged in the crucible of selfless offering. The Abyssal Climax was not an end, but a profound, heartbreaking beginning, a testament to the fact that the deepest forms of healing often came at the most profound personal cost.

The artifact, once a throbbing wound in the fabric of reality, now pulsed with a soft, steady light, a gentle heartbeat against the vast expanse of the chasm. The suffocating silence that had pressed down on them, a tangible entity born of the Conclave's hubris and the Echo's wrath, began to recede. It wasn't a sudden vanishing, but a slow, inexorable withdrawal, like a tide pulling back from a wounded shore, leaving behind the promise of a new dawn. The chaotic energies that had swirled and clawed at the edges of existence, threatening to unravel all of creation, were now calming, their destructive fervor quelled not by force, but by an act of profound understanding and selfless giving. The world's song, fractured and despairing, was finding its voice again, not in a triumphant crescendo, but in a hesitant, yet undeniably beautiful, melody of rebirth.

Mara felt it first as a subtle shift in the air, a lightening of the oppressive weight that had settled upon her soul. The raw, discordant vibrations that had assaulted her senses for so long were smoothing out, coalescing into something more coherent, more resonant. It was as if the very air molecules were re-aligning, finding their proper place in a newly composed symphony. The Abyssal Truth, once a source of dread and despair, now felt less like a harbinger of doom and more like a fundamental law of existence, a truth that, when understood and embraced, led not to oblivion, but to a deeper, more meaningful harmony. The sacrifice, whatever form it had taken, whatever part of themselves had been offered to the chasm's hungry maw, had been the key. It had been the catalyst that allowed the world's song to transcend its brokenness and begin its slow, arduous journey toward wholeness.

Beside her, Kaelen let out a shuddering breath, the sound a low rumble of relief that seemed to vibrate through the very bedrock of the chasm. His eyes, which had held a desperate plea and a fierce protectiveness, now softened with a dawning wonder. He looked at his hands, scaled and powerful, yet now held with a gentleness that spoke of a profound shift within him. The raw, untamed fury of the earth, the force he had once wielded with such potent, and at times reckless, abandon, was now tempered. He could still feel its immense power, its primal strength, but it was no longer a force to be dominated, but a force to be nurtured. It was the deep, resonant pulse of the planet's heartwood, no longer groaning in pain, but beating with a steady, enduring rhythm. He saw now that the earth's strength wasn't in its ability to crush, but in its capacity to endure, to heal, and to regenerate, a resilience that had always existed, waiting to be reawakened.

Lyra, her face streaked with dust and tears, let out a soft, choked sob, not of grief, but of overwhelming relief. She reached out, her fingers brushing against the hardy vine that still clung to the chasm's edge. The single, dew-kissed bud that had seemed so impossibly fragile before, now seemed to swell with a newfound vitality. The faint whisper of life that she had strained to hear, the defiant song of a single bloom against the encroaching void, was growing. It was no longer a whisper, but a budding chorus, a testament to the tenacity of life, to its unyielding will to flourish. She felt the earth beneath her feet respond, not with tremors of instability, but with a gentle thrum of affirmation, a quiet acknowledgement of the life that persevered. The love she held for the struggling flora, the fierce compassion that had driven her, had been mirrored back to her, amplified by the very forces that had seemed so destructive. This was the song of renewal, of hope blooming in the most desolate of places.

Cael, his gaze still fixed on the distant, star-dusted sky, offered a rare, gentle smile. The chaotic dance of the nebulae above seemed to have settled, their swirling colors coalescing into a more serene, majestic display. The faint echoes of the Sky-Serpents, once a mournful lament, now felt like a distant, harmonious hum, a celestial lullaby that resonated with the nascent song of the earth. He could feel the light, not as a weapon to push back darkness, but as a unifying force, a cosmic thread weaving through the fabric of existence, connecting every particle, every being, to the grand tapestry of the universe. The balance he had always sought, the order he had so diligently strived for, was not an imposed structure, but an inherent, interconnected reality, a symphony played out across the vastness of space and time. The stars, in their silent brilliance, seemed to affirm that even in the face of profound loss, the light always endured.

The immediate aftermath of the climax was not a sudden, miraculous transformation of the desolate landscape. The scars of the Conclave's reign of terror, the ravages of the Echo, were still present. The chasm remained a stark reminder of the world's near-demise, its raw, wounded edges a testament to the forces that had threatened to tear it asunder. But within this desolation, the first shoots of renewal were emerging. The air, once thick with the metallic tang of decay and the oppressive scent of void, now carried the faint, sweet perfume of burgeoning life. A delicate, almost imperceptible mist began to gather, not the suffocating shroud of the Echo, but a life-giving dew that kissed the parched earth.

Mara felt the subtle shifts rippling through her, a re-integration of energies that had been stretched to their breaking point. The resonance of the sacrifice, the immeasurable offering that had been made, settled within her like a warm, comforting ember. It was not a void, not a loss, but a transformation, a weaving of something new and profound into the very core of her being. She understood now that the Abyssal Truth was not about the finality of endings, but about the cyclical nature of existence, about the profound beauty found in the transition from silence to song, from decay to rebirth. The world had not been saved by force, but by understanding, by an acceptance of its inherent complexities, its capacity for both darkness and light, its eternal dance between destruction and creation.

The artifact at the chasm's heart, once a symbol of their struggle, now pulsed with a gentle, benevolent light, its luminescence not harsh or demanding, but soft and inviting. It was no longer an object of fear, but a beacon of hope, a testament to the fact that even in the deepest abyss, a song could be reborn. The chaotic energies that had threatened to consume them were now coalescing, their destructive potential channeled into the vital forces of creation. The winds that swept through the chasm were no longer harbingers of despair, but gentle breezes carrying the promise of change, of healing. They whispered of the earth's deep, abiding strength, of life's tenacious grip, and of the celestial harmonies that bound all things together.

Mara looked at her companions, her heart swelling with a profound sense of gratitude and awe. They had walked through the fires of destruction and emerged, not unscathed, but fundamentally changed, their spirits tempered and their understanding deepened. Kaelen, his stoic demeanor now softened with a profound empathy, knelt and placed a hand on the cracked earth, his touch no longer one of dominance, but of gentle reassurance. He felt the planet's pulse beneath his palm, a slow, steady rhythm that spoke of resilience, of an ancient strength that had weathered countless storms and would weather many more. His connection to the earth, once a source of raw, untamed power, was now a conduit for healing, a means to nurture the nascent life that was beginning to stir.

Lyra, her eyes shining with a quiet joy, carefully tended to a cluster of pale, fragile flowers that had miraculously bloomed near the chasm's edge. Their petals, delicate as spun moonlight, unfurled slowly, reaching towards the faint light that now permeated the twilight. She hummed a soft, wordless melody, a tune born from the very essence of life, and the flowers seemed to respond, their colors deepening, their stems straightening with renewed vigor. Her compassion, once a force directed at mitigating suffering, was now a direct instrument of creation, a gentle hand guiding the world's own desire to bloom.

Cael stood a little apart, his gaze sweeping across the vast expanse of the recovering world. He was no longer just observing the celestial patterns; he was feeling their resonance, their gentle hum echoing within his very bones. He could sense the intricate web of connection that bound the earth to the stars, the cosmic currents that flowed through everything, sustaining and harmonizing. His pursuit of light had evolved from a defensive strategy into an active force of regeneration, a radiant energy that permeated the newly awakened song of the world, a song that was both earthly and celestial, grounded and transcendent.

The very atmosphere of the chasm was shifting. The oppressive darkness that had held it captive for so long was now giving way to a diffused, ethereal glow. It was not the harsh glare of midday, but a soft, luminous twilight, a perpetual dawn that promised a new beginning. The fragmented melodies that had been the only audible signs of the world's suffering were now weaving together, forming a coherent, though still developing, symphony. There were notes of sorrow, of loss, of the profound pain of what had been endured, but they were intertwined with melodies of hope, of resilience, and of an enduring love that transcended all hardship.

Mara felt this burgeoning harmony within herself, a reflection of the world's own reawakening. The sacrifice, the ultimate offering, had not been an erasure, but an integration. A part of them, a deeply cherished and essential part, had become one with the world's song, adding its unique resonance to the grand composition. It was a bittersweet understanding, a profound acceptance of the truth that true healing often came at a significant personal cost. But as she looked at the nascent beauty emerging from the desolation, she knew that the sacrifice had been not in vain. It had been an act of profound faith, a testament to the enduring power of love and the promise of renewal.

The chasm, once a symbol of despair and the abyss of oblivion, was transforming. It was no longer a wound, but a cradle. A cradle where the world's song was being nurtured, where its broken melodies were being rewoven into a tapestry of unparalleled beauty and resilience. The Abyssal Truth, once a shadow that threatened to engulf them, was now the very foundation upon which this new harmony was being built. It was a truth that acknowledged the darkness, the loss, the inevitable cycles of decay, but it also celebrated the indomitable spirit of life, the unwavering power of hope, and the profound, transformative beauty of a song reborn.

The world was irrevocably changed, yes, but its core, its very essence, had been preserved. It had been mended, not by force, but by a deeper understanding, by a sacrifice born of love, and by the unwavering belief in the dawn that always followed the darkest night. This was not an ending, but a glorious, breathtaking beginning, a testament to the enduring power of a song that refused to be silenced. The echoes of the sacrifice, though profound, were now being transformed into the very music of their new reality, a symphony of healing, of hope, and of a world that had chosen to embrace its own rebirth.

Chapter Thirteen
The Quiet After the Song

The silence that descended after the Song was not an empty void, but a pregnant pause. It was the quiet between breaths, the stillness before the first tentative notes of a new melody. The cacophony of the Accord Cities, the oppressive hum of control that had vibrated through the world for generations, had finally been silenced. The Skybound Conclave, their wings clipped by the very harmony they had sought to suppress, had withdrawn, their grand pronouncements and iron decrees dissolving into a mist of bewildered retreat.

Their Resonance Towers, once arrogant needles piercing the sky, now stood like hollowed-out husks, their inherent power leeched away by the profound resonance of the world's reawakened song. Some were being carefully dismantled, their materials painstakingly repurposed for shelters and communal structures, their oppressive architecture giving way to the organic curves of necessity. Others, too deeply infused with the Conclave's sterile magic, were left as stark monuments to a failed ideology, their silent forms a cautionary tale etched against the recovering sky.

Mara watched the dismantling of an Accord City's administrative nexus from a vantage point overlooking the sprawling, once-gleaming metropolis. The sleek, obsidian towers, designed to project an image of unassailable authority, now seemed to shrink under the soft, persistent light of the new dawn. Teams of ordinary citizens, many of them former dissidents or those who had lived in the shadow of the Conclave's constant surveillance, moved with a deliberate, almost reverent purpose. They carried tools not of destruction, but of careful deconstruction.

There was no malice in their movements, only a deep-seated desire to reclaim what had been stolen from them: their autonomy, their freedom, their very right to exist outside the rigid confines of the Conclave's dictates. The Resonance Towers, the instruments of the Conclave's pervasive control, were being systematically deactivated. Technicians, guided by the intuitive understanding of the new Song, worked with a grace born of necessity, their hands tracing patterns on dormant conduits, their hushed murmurs a testament to the shared purpose that now united them. The oppressive hum that had been the city's constant companion, a subtle psychic pressure that had worn down the spirit, was gone. In its place, a gentle breeze whispered through the streets, carrying the scent of nascent life and the distant, hopeful chirping of birds.

Kaelen, his broad frame surprisingly nimble, was instrumental in the repurposing of the Conclave's fortified structures. He didn't wield the brute force of his earth-shaping abilities as a weapon, but as a tool of gentle persuasion. He would guide collapsing walls to fall inward, creating open courtyards instead of further destruction, or reshape scarred earth into fertile ground for communal gardens. His movements were imbued with the same deep respect for the natural order that he now felt resonating through him. He understood that true strength lay not in domination, but in integration.

The stones that had once served to imprison and control were now being laid into the foundations of community centers, of open markets where free exchange would flourish. He worked alongside others, his scaled hands moving with a newfound gentleness, a quiet understanding passing between him and those who had once feared him, or whom he had once felt compelled to protect with an almost aggressive vigilance. The fear that had been a constant undercurrent in the Accord Cities was slowly dissipating, replaced by a cautious optimism, a shared sense of possibility.

THE STORMBOUND DIVIDE

Lyra, her connection to the burgeoning life now amplified by the world's reawakening song, found herself drawn to the vast, sterile hydroponic farms that had once fed the Conclave's elite, ensuring their physical strength while denying the world its natural bounty. These enclosed, artificial environments, devoid of true sunlight and the subtle energies of the earth, had been symbols of the Conclave's hubris, their attempt to control even the most fundamental processes of life. Now, Lyra and her growing band of fellow nurturers were carefully introducing indigenous flora, coaxing hardy herbs and resilient grains to take root in the nutrient-rich, yet sterile, soil.

It was a painstaking process, a delicate balance of introducing natural elements without overwhelming the established, albeit artificial, ecosystem. They spoke in soft tones, their hands brushing against nascent leaves, whispering encouragement to plants that had known only the sterile efficiency of the Conclave's design. The air within these former fortresses of control was beginning to smell less of chemicals and sterile water, and more of damp earth and the faint, sweet scent of blooming wildflowers that Lyra had carefully cultivated around the perimeter.

Cael, his eyes still holding the vastness of the cosmos, found his role in the dismantling of oppression to be one of a different, yet equally vital, nature. He moved through the newly liberated territories, not with physical tools, but with an almost palpable aura of clarity and discernment. He helped communities understand the intricate web of connections that had been manipulated by the Conclave, showing them how their individual actions were intrinsically linked to the well-being of the whole. He would sit with leaders, his voice calm and measured, as they debated the future, guiding them to consider the long-term consequences of their decisions, the echoes they would send through the fabric of reality.

He was a living embodiment of the celestial balance, a constant reminder that true freedom was not the absence of structure, but the presence of wise and interconnected order. He would stand at crossroads, where the grand avenues of the Accord Cities once channeled the Conclave's influence, and help citizens visualize new paths, pathways of mutual support and shared responsibility, demonstrating through subtle shifts in the atmospheric currents how these new directions would foster greater harmony.

The Accord Cities, once monuments to centralized power, were undergoing a profound metamorphosis. The grand plazas, designed for military parades and public displays of Conclave authority, were being transformed into vibrant community gathering spaces. Market stalls, previously a rarity and strictly controlled, now sprung up organically, filled with the produce of Lyra's rediscovered farms and the crafts of newly empowered artisans.

The ubiquitous surveillance orbs, once omnipresent eyes of the Conclave, were being meticulously removed, their polished surfaces reflecting only the liberated sky. Some were melted down, their components repurposed for practical uses, like lamps that cast a warm, natural glow, or embedded in tools that aided in rebuilding. The psychological weight of constant observation was lifting, replaced by the unfamiliar yet exhilarating sensation of privacy, of personal space rediscovered.

The Skybound Conclave's retreat was not a unified surrender, but a fragmented scattering. Some factions, their doctrines shattered by the undeniable truth of the world's song, quietly relinquished their authority, their gilded robes exchanged for the simple homespun of common folk, their pronouncements replaced by the quiet contemplation of their mistakes. Others, clinging to their ingrained sense of superiority, retreated to their remote mountain strongholds, their power diminished, their influence a fading echo. There were whispers of dissent within their ranks, of younger members who had witnessed the transformative power of the Song and were questioning the rigid dogma they had inherited.

The Conclave's centralized authority, once an unshakeable pillar, was now fracturing under the weight of its own obsolescence. Their once-feared enforcers, the Obsidian Guard, found themselves without orders, their purpose dissolved. Many, stripped of their uniforms and their rigid ideology, were reintegrated into society, their skills in discipline and organization now channeled into the efforts of reconstruction and community building. The harsh lines of their armor were exchanged for the rough fabric of work clothes, their intimidating presence softened by the shared vulnerability of rebuilding.

Mara, observing these shifts, felt a deep sense of satisfaction, yet it was tempered by the immense weight of what lay ahead. The dismantling of oppression was a crucial, vital step, a necessary exorcism of a deeply ingrained sickness. But it was only the first step. The structures of control, both physical and psychological, had been deeply embedded. Generations had lived under the Conclave's thumb, their capacity for self-governance atrophied. Rebuilding trust, fostering true autonomy, and re-establishing a natural order that was not dictated but discovered, would be a monumental undertaking. She saw the challenges in the hesitant conversations between former adversaries, in the lingering distrust that flickered in some eyes, in the sheer scale of the work required to mend the fractured landscapes and the even more fractured societies.

The absence of the Conclave's coercive magic left a void, a space that needed to be filled not with new forms of control, but with the empowering resonance of the world's song. The Accord Cities, stripped of their oppressive architecture, were becoming blank canvases. The challenge was to ensure that the new paintings that emerged were vibrant expressions of collective will, not merely different shades of the same old control. Mara found herself often in council with Kaelen, Lyra, and Cael, their discussions delving into the practicalities of this new era. How could they ensure that the newfound freedom didn't devolve into chaos? How could they foster a sense of collective responsibility without resorting to the authoritarian tactics of the past?

"The Resonance Towers," Kaelen mused one evening, his voice a low rumble as he traced the outline of a dismantled tower on a piece of scavenged parchment, "they broadcast a specific frequency, a constant influence. Without them, the Accord Cities feel... lighter, yes, but also more vulnerable. We need to cultivate a new kind of resonance, one that emanates from within the communities themselves."

Lyra, her hands stained with the rich loam she had brought back from the rewilded plains, nodded thoughtfully. "It's like tending a garden, isn't it? You can't just rip out the weeds and expect a thriving ecosystem overnight. You have to nurture the soil, introduce beneficial flora, create a balanced environment where life can flourish naturally. We need to teach people how to listen to their own inner songs, how to find harmony within their own communities, and then how to connect those individual harmonies into a larger symphony."

Cael, his gaze fixed on the newly visible constellations, offered his perspective. "The Conclave's control was a form of energetic manipulation, a disruption of natural flows. Their towers amplified their will, drowning out the subtler, more profound currents of the world. Now, those currents are reasserting themselves. But they are undirected, untamed. We must act as conduits, not as masters. We must guide people to understand these flows, to align themselves with the natural order, not to impose a new one. It is about understanding the cosmic dance, not choreographing it."

Mara felt the truth in their words resonate deeply. The immediate victory was the dismantling of the oppressive structures. The true, long-term challenge was the cultivation of a society that embraced autonomy, nurtured connection, and lived in harmony with the natural world and its inherent song. The Accord Cities, once symbols of subjugation, were now laboratories of liberation, their future dependent on the collective wisdom and courage of those who had been freed. The process was slow, painstaking, and fraught with the potential for missteps. But for the first time in generations, the choice was theirs.

The quiet after the Song was not an end, but a beginning, a vast, unwritten expanse waiting for the first, brave strokes of a new, harmonious existence. The task of rebuilding was not merely physical; it was a spiritual and societal reconstruction, a slow, deliberate weaving of freedom and responsibility into the very fabric of their newly liberated world. The echoes of the Conclave's oppressive reign would linger, a spectral reminder of what had been overcome, but the burgeoning symphony of self-determination was already beginning to drown them out.

The silence that settled over the Accord Cities was not a void, but a fertile ground. The jarring symphony of the Conclave's dominion had been silenced, replaced by a hesitant murmur, the nascent hum of a world rediscovering its own rhythm. This was not a simple restoration, a return to a forgotten past; it was the forging of something entirely new, a delicate equilibrium born from the crucible of conflict. The harsh edges of their former reality were softening, blurring into the emerging landscape of a future guided not by decree, but by a deep, innate understanding of the planet's song.

The most profound shifts were not in the crumbling architecture of the Conclave's power, but in the hearts and minds of its inhabitants. Humans, once cogs in a machine designed for efficiency and control, were beginning to unfurl, their innate capacities for empathy and ingenuity finally freed from the suffocating grip of imposed order. The dragons, ancient and powerful, who had long been relegated to the fringes of existence, their existence a whispered legend or a terrifying threat, were no longer solitary forces of nature.

They were becoming integrated into the emerging tapestry of life, their immense strength now a shared resource, their wisdom a guiding presence. Even the remnants of the Conclave, those who had not fled or been reformed, found themselves in an unprecedented position. Stripped of their instruments of control, their dogma challenged by the undeniable resonance of the world, they were forced to confront their own place within this reawakened biosphere. The question was no longer one of dominance, but of survival, and survival, they were slowly realizing, depended on adaptation, on finding a way to harmonize with the very forces they had once sought to subjugate.

This was the dawn of a new balance, a fragile equilibrium built not on the foundation of coercion, but on the bedrock of mutual respect and shared responsibility. The grand pronouncements of the Conclave had been replaced by hushed conversations, by the slow, deliberate work of rebuilding communities and ecosystems alike. The Skybound Conclave's Resonance Towers, once symbols of their unassailable authority, were now inert, their power leached away by the world's song. Some were being carefully dismantled, their advanced materials repurposed for essential needs. Others, too deeply imbued with the Conclave's sterile magic, stood as silent sentinels, stark reminders of a failed ambition. Their obsidian surfaces, once reflecting a sky choked with the Conclave's influence, now mirrored the gentle passage of clouds, the tentative flight of birds, and the soft glow of a rising sun that promised no enforced order, only natural cycles.

Mara, her gaze sweeping across the transformed cityscape, felt the weight of this nascent peace. It was a peace hard-won, and as fragile as a new bloom pushing through scorched earth. The Accord Cities, once monolithic bastions of control, were now being reshaped, not by decree, but by the organic needs of their people. The vast, sterile plazas, once reserved for Conclave parades and displays of military might, were becoming vibrant hubs of community life. Makeshift stalls, laden with the fruits of Lyra's revived hydroponic farms and the burgeoning crafts of newly empowered artisans, lined the former parade grounds. The omnipresent surveillance orbs, the Conclave's ever-watchful eyes, were systematically dismantled, their polished surfaces melting down to form practical lamps, casting a warm, democratic glow over the newly formed marketplaces. The psychological burden of constant observation was lifting, replaced by the exhilarating, albeit unfamiliar, sensation of privacy.

Kaelen, his earth-shaping abilities now a force for creation rather than control, moved with a quiet determination. He no longer saw the land as a resource to be exploited or a territory to be fortified. Instead, he felt its pulse, its inherent needs. He worked to mend the scars left by the Conclave's industrial sprawl, his hands coaxing barren earth back to life, transforming scarred landscapes into fertile ground for communal gardens and shared dwellings. He guided the careful deconstruction of fortified structures, his strength used not to raze, but to repurpose. Collapsing walls were gently directed inward, creating open courtyards for gatherings, their stones laid into the foundations of community centers, their former purpose of imprisonment replaced by a commitment to shared living. He worked alongside humans, his scaled hands, once a symbol of fear, now a testament to shared labor, a silent understanding passing between him and those who had once perceived him as an adversary.

Lyra, her connection to the natural world deepened by the reawakening song, found her purpose in the careful restoration of the Conclave's sterile hydroponic farms. These enclosed ecosystems, designed to sustain the Conclave's elite while denying the world its natural bounty, were being meticulously transformed. Lyra and her growing team of nurturers introduced indigenous flora, coaxing resilient herbs and hardy grains to take root in the nutrient-rich, yet sterile, soil. It was a delicate dance, a painstaking process of integrating natural elements without overwhelming the established, albeit artificial, systems. She spoke in soft tones, her fingers brushing against nascent leaves, whispering encouragement to plants that had only known the sterile efficiency of the Conclave's design. The air within these former fortresses of control began to shed its chemical tang, replaced by the scent of damp earth and the faint, sweet perfume of wildflowers Lyra had carefully cultivated around the perimeter.

Cael, his gaze reflecting the newly visible constellations, acted as a living compass, guiding communities towards a deeper understanding of the interconnectedness that the Conclave had so effectively disrupted. He moved through the liberated territories, his presence radiating a palpable aura of clarity. He sat with emergent leaders, his voice calm and measured, helping them to navigate the complex web of decisions that lay ahead. He spoke not of dogma, but of consequence, of the echoes their choices would send through the fabric of reality. He was a living embodiment of celestial balance, a constant reminder that true freedom was not the absence of structure, but the presence of informed, interconnected order. He would stand at the crossroads of the Accord Cities' grand avenues, once conduits for the Conclave's influence, and help citizens visualize new pathways, pathways of mutual support and shared responsibility, demonstrating through subtle shifts in the atmospheric currents how these new directions fostered greater harmony.

The re-establishment of balance was not solely a human endeavor. The dragons, their ancient forms now less a source of dread and more a symbol of primal strength, were slowly becoming integrated into the new order. Elders, their scales the color of twilight and their eyes holding the wisdom of millennia, began to descend from their remote aeries. They did not seek dominion, but understanding. They observed the humans' tentative steps towards self-governance, their efforts to mend the wounded land, and their growing respect for the planet's song. In turn, they offered their ancient knowledge, their intimate understanding of the earth's cycles, its deep currents, and its subtle needs. They shared their perspective on the delicate interplay of elements, the wisdom of patient growth, and the inherent strength found in deep-rooted stability.

One of the most significant shifts was the formation of councils that included not only human representatives but also dragons and, surprisingly, even some former members of the Conclave who had undergone genuine transformation. These councils were not designed for the pronouncements of decrees, but for the collective weaving of solutions. They gathered in spaces that resonated with the world's song – rewilded groves, cavernous halls carved by ancient rivers, or open plains bathed in starlight. The debates were often lengthy, sometimes fraught with the lingering echoes of past animosities. Yet, the shared purpose was undeniable: to foster a world where all beings could thrive in harmony with the planet.

In one such council, held beneath the vast, open sky where the Accords had once cast their oppressive shadow, Kaelen, his voice a low rumble, addressed the assembled group. "The Conclave built their towers to broadcast their will, to impose a singular note upon the symphony of existence. We have silenced those towers. But silence alone is not enough. We must learn to create our own resonance, a harmony that arises from the collective will of all life."

THE STORMBOUND DIVIDE

Beside him, a dragon named Ignis, his scales shimmering like molten gold, let out a deep, resonant hum that vibrated through the very earth. His voice, when it came, was like the grinding of ancient stones, imbued with the weight of ages. "The earth remembers. It remembers the wounds inflicted, and it remembers the balm of healing. The song you speak of, it is the pulse of life itself. It is in the roots of the ancient trees, in the flow of the deepest rivers, in the beat of every heart. To hear it, you must quiet the clamor within yourselves."

Lyra, her hands still bearing the faint scent of loam, added, "It is about stewardship, not ownership. We are not masters of this world, but its custodians. We tend to it, we nurture it, and in return, it sustains us. The Conclave saw the planet as a resource to be exploited. We must see it as a partner, a living entity with its own needs and its own song."

Cael, his gaze fixed on the distant stars, offered his perspective. "The Conclave's power was an imposition, a disruption of natural flows. They sought to control the currents of energy that bind the cosmos. Now, those currents are reasserting themselves. Our task is not to redirect them, but to align ourselves with them, to understand their inherent wisdom, and to allow them to guide us. We are but a single thread in an infinite tapestry."

The practical application of these lessons was evident in the burgeoning settlements that were rising from the ashes of the Accord Cities. Gone were the rigid, utilitarian structures. In their place, organic designs emerged, guided by the principles of biomimicry and ecological integration. Homes were built into the contours of the land, utilizing natural insulation and passive solar heating. Communal spaces were designed to foster connection, with open-air markets, shared workshops, and natural amphitheatres for storytelling and music. The very act of building became a form of prayer, a conscious engagement with the earth's song.

Resource management underwent a similar transformation. The Conclave's insatiable demand for raw materials, their disregard for ecological impact, had left deep scars. Now, a circular economy was taking root, driven by principles of reuse, repair, and regeneration. Waste was not an end product, but a valuable resource, meticulously sorted and repurposed. Water was conserved and purified through natural filtration systems. Energy was harnessed from renewable sources – solar, wind, and geothermal, their generation guided by an understanding of natural cycles and minimal environmental impact.

The relationship between humans and dragons evolved from one of apprehension to one of profound mutualism. Dragons, with their innate connection to the earth's primal energies, became guardians of critical natural sites – ancient forests, vital water sources, and areas of potent geological significance. Their presence deterred exploitation and ensured the preservation of these sacred spaces. Humans, in turn, provided support and assistance, understanding the dragons' needs and respecting their territories. Dragon hatchlings, once fiercely protected and rarely seen, were now occasionally brought to communal gatherings, their presence a symbol of hope and the enduring legacy of their species.

Even the formerly oppressive technologies of the Conclave found new, benevolent applications. The advanced atmospheric processors, once used to control weather patterns for the Conclave's comfort, were repurposed for controlled irrigation and the restoration of drought-stricken regions. The sonic emitters, used for crowd control, were adapted to stimulate plant growth and deter invasive pests, their frequencies tuned to the rhythms of nature. These were not mere accidents of salvage; they were deliberate acts of redemption, of taking the tools of oppression and transforming them into instruments of healing and restoration.

The concept of governance itself was being reimagined. The hierarchical, top-down structure of the Conclave had proven unsustainable and inherently corrupting. In its place, decentralized, community-based governance models were emerging. These were not simple democracies, but intricate networks of consensus-building, where decisions were made through dialogue, active listening, and a deep consideration for the well-being of the entire ecosystem. Councils of elders, representatives from different species, and even the collective wisdom of nature spirits, were all part of the decision-making process. The focus shifted from control to stewardship, from enforcing rules to fostering understanding and cooperation.

The challenge, however, was immense. Generations of living under the Conclave's rigid order had left deep psychological imprints. Trust, hard-won, was still fragile. The instinct for self-preservation, honed by years of scarcity and fear, could sometimes override the impulse for collective action. The remnants of the Conclave's ideology, though diminished, still lingered in the shadows, whispering doubts and fueling old resentments.

Mara, often finding herself at the nexus of these evolving relationships, understood the long road ahead. The quiet after the Song was not an end, but a beginning. It was a period of immense possibility, a chance to weave a new paradigm of existence, one that honored the interconnectedness of all life and the inherent wisdom of the natural world. It was a future not dictated by power, but by partnership, not defined by conquest, but by compassion, and ultimately, by the enduring, life-affirming song of the planet itself. The new balance was not a static state of equilibrium, but a dynamic, ever-evolving process, a continuous dance between the needs of the individual and the health of the whole, a testament to the profound and transformative power of listening. The Accord Cities, once monuments to a failed attempt to control life, were becoming living laboratories of liberation, their future a testament to the courage of those who dared to dream of a world in harmony, a world that sang.

Mara Lysenne watched the nascent dawn paint the sky in hues of rose and gold, a spectacle that no longer felt like a prelude to the Conclave's oppressive routines, but a genuine unveiling of a new day. The air, once thick with the metallic tang of manufactured existence, now carried the sweet, damp scent of reawakened earth and the distant, melodic chirping of birds that had returned to the Accord Cities with the fading of the Conclave's influence. Her role as the catalyst, the one who had amplified the planet's song until it could no longer be ignored, felt both impossibly distant and intimately present. The echoes of the world's awakening still resonated within her, a constant, gentle hum beneath the surface of her being. She was no longer the sole conduit, the singular point of access to the planet's intricate symphony; that privilege, that burden, had been shared, disseminated, and woven into the very fabric of the new world order.

Her days had become a tapestry of quiet observation and gentle guidance. The frantic urgency that had defined her existence for so long had receded, replaced by a profound sense of belonging. She walked among the people, no longer a figure of desperate hope or a target of fear, but simply Mara, a Listener. Her presence was a comfort, her insight a wellspring of calm in the often-turbulent process of rebuilding. She would sit in the communal gardens, her fingers tracing the veins of a newly sprouted leaf, her inner ear attuned to the subtle whispers of growth, of nutrient transfer, of the earth's quiet satisfaction. She would meet with the newly formed councils, not to dictate, but to offer her unique perspective, to translate the planet's needs into language that human hearts and minds could grasp. She was the bridge, not of control, but of understanding.

She remembered the early days after the Conclave's final, shattering chord had been silenced. The silence that followed had been deafening, filled with the ghosts of a thousand suppressed sounds. It was during those initial weeks, when the weight of what had been done, and what was yet to be done, threatened to crush everyone, that her true purpose solidified. She hadn't sought to impose order, but to foster listening. She had walked through the newly liberated plazas, the vast expanses that had once served as stages for the Conclave's parades and pronouncements, and simply sat. She would close her eyes and breathe, allowing the planet's nascent song to fill the void. People, drawn by an instinct they could not yet articulate, would gather around her, their faces etched with a mixture of exhaustion and nascent hope.

"Listen," she would whisper, her voice soft but carrying a profound resonance. "Listen to the wind as it moves through these empty spaces. It carries the memory of the trees that once stood here, and the promise of new growth." She would guide them to feel the subtle vibrations beneath their feet, the deep thrum of the earth's core, a steady heartbeat that had never truly ceased, even during the Conclave's reign of sterile noise. She taught them to differentiate the anxious chatter of their own minds from the calming, grounding presence of the planet. It was a painstaking process, akin to teaching a deaf person to perceive sound, but with each individual who found their own connection to the earth's song, a new thread was woven into the fabric of their collective resilience.

Her legacy was not etched in stone monuments or grand pronouncements, but in the quiet moments of understanding that blossomed across the land. It was in the farmers who now consulted the earth before planting, their hands not just tilling soil, but communing with it, understanding its needs for water, for rest, for specific nutrients. It was in the architects who designed buildings that breathed with the environment, their structures not imposing upon the landscape but becoming an extension of it, their forms mimicking the elegance and efficiency of natural designs. It was in the children who played in rewilded parks, their laughter echoing not as a disruption, but as a harmonious note in the larger symphony of life, their games often involving quiet observation of insects or the gentle tending of wildflowers.

She found a particular solace in the dragon aeries that now welcomed her. Ignis, the ancient dragon whose resonant hum had been a crucial part of the awakening, often sought her out. Their conversations were not of conquest or power, but of the deep, slow rhythms of geological time, the interconnectedness of molten cores and the smallest seeds. Ignis would share tales of epochs long past, of planetary shifts and the enduring resilience of life, his voice a slow, rumbling testament to the earth's unwavering strength. Mara, in turn, would describe the subtle shifts in the human psyche, the gradual shedding of fear, the burgeoning sense of responsibility, translating the complex tapestry of human emotion into a language that the ancient dragon could understand.

"The humans," Ignis once rumbled, his obsidian eyes reflecting the starlight, "they rush. Their lives are but a flicker in the long memory of stone. But you, Mara, you have taught them to perceive the steady pulse beneath the flicker. You have shown them that even a single breath, taken in harmony with the world, can echo through ages."

There were times, in the quiet hours before dawn, when Mara would feel the pull of a different kind of existence. The urge to retreat, to find a solitary grove or a hidden cave, a place where she could simply *be* with the planet, unburdened by the needs of others. It was a seductive thought, the promise of pure immersion, of becoming one with the very essence of the world's song. But then she would see the faces of the young listeners she had mentored, their eyes bright with newfound understanding, their hands already beginning to mend the scars of the past, and the urge would fade, replaced by a quiet resolve. Her purpose had shifted, from being the catalyst to being a cultivator, nurturing the seeds of listening that had been sown.

Her journey had been one of profound sacrifice. The years spent wrestling with the Conclave's influence, the constant strain of amplifying the world's voice, had taken a toll. There were days when her very being ached, as if the planet's pain had seeped directly into her bones. She bore the phantom echoes of the Conclave's attempts to silence her, the psychic abrasions that had left indelible marks. Yet, these scars were not badges of suffering, but testaments to her unwavering commitment. They were tangible reminders of the immense power of perseverance, of the possibility of healing even the deepest wounds.

She had witnessed firsthand the transformative power of listening. She had seen individuals, hardened by years of Conclave indoctrination, their hearts closed to empathy, slowly unfurl as they began to hear the needs of others, the silent pleas of the environment. She had seen communities, fractured and distrustful, begin to mend their bonds as they learned to communicate not through decree, but through shared understanding and mutual respect, their dialogues guided by the planet's inherent rhythms. The Accord Cities, once symbols of rigid control, were becoming vibrant, living ecosystems, their inhabitants actively participating in their own evolution, guided by a deep, instinctual connection to the natural world.

Mara's legacy, therefore, was one of empowerment. She had not given people the answers; she had shown them how to find them within themselves, and within the world around them. She had not created a new order, but had helped to reawaken an ancient one, an order based on balance, respect, and the profound interconnectedness of all life. Her journey had been a testament to the power of a single voice, amplified by the collective will of a world finally choosing to listen.

There was a quiet grove, nestled on the outskirts of what had once been a heavily fortified Conclave sector, that had become her sanctuary. The Conclave's sterile, geometric design had been meticulously dismantled, and the land allowed to reclaim itself. Wildflowers now carpeted the ground, and ancient trees, their roots delving deep into the earth, formed a protective canopy. Here, amidst the gentle rustling of leaves and the hum of unseen insects, Mara would spend hours in silent communion. She would feel the ebb and flow of the earth's energies, the subtle shifts in atmospheric pressure, the quiet murmur of plant life communicating through unseen networks. It was in these moments of pure connection that she understood the true depth of her transformation, and the enduring impact of her journey.

She was no longer the focal point of the world's awakening, but an integral part of its ongoing melody. Her purpose had evolved from being the conductor of an orchestra to becoming a cherished instrument, contributing her unique tone to the grand composition of existence. The sacrifices she had made, the battles she had fought, had not been for personal glory, but for the sake of this profound harmony, this fragile, beautiful balance.

As the sun climbed higher, casting dappled light through the leaves, Mara felt a deep sense of peace settle over her. She had fulfilled her part. The world was listening. Her legacy was not an ending, but a continuous unfolding, a testament to the enduring power of the planet's song, and to the courage of those who had dared to hear it. She was Mara Lysenne, a Listener, and her work, in its truest sense, had only just begun. The subtle changes she fostered, the quiet guidance she offered, were the threads that would continue to weave the world into a more harmonious tapestry for generations to come, a living testament to the profound truth that to truly live, one must first learn to listen.

Her existence was now a quiet affirmation, a living embodiment of the planet's resilience and its boundless capacity for rebirth, a beacon of hope in a world reborn, guided not by the clamor of command, but by the gentle, persistent song of life itself. The sacrifices had been immense, the journey arduous, but the outcome, the quiet symphony that now permeated the world, was a testament to the enduring power of listening and the profound legacy of a single soul who dared to amplify the earth's forgotten voice.

The weight of command, once a crushing burden on Cael Thornevale's shoulders, had transmuted into something far more potent: the fertile earth beneath his boots, the whispered gratitude of a reawakening forest, the steady pulse of a community finding its equilibrium. He no longer felt the gnawing obligation of a Guardian, bound by the rigid dictates of a fallen regime, but the quiet fulfillment of a steward, deeply entwined with the life he now nurtured. The sterile efficiency that had once defined his responsibilities had dissolved, replaced by a profound, intuitive understanding of the land's needs and the people's evolving desires. His journey from a man constrained by duty to one liberated by purpose was complete, a testament to the transformative power of embracing true leadership – the kind that protected and nurtured, rather than controlled.

His initial days after the Conclave's dissolution had been a whirlwind of logistical nightmares and frayed nerves. The Accord Cities, once models of oppressive order, were now teetering on the brink of chaos, their carefully constructed systems crumbling like dust. Cael, accustomed to issuing directives and enforcing compliance, found himself navigating a labyrinth of human needs and ecological emergencies. He had overseen the dismantling of the Conclave's most egregious structures, the silent monuments to their subjugation, but the emptiness they left was vast and daunting. The initial relief that had swept through the populace was quickly giving way to fear – fear of the unknown, fear of scarcity, fear of failure.

He remembered standing on the precipice of what had once been the Conclave's central archive, a monolithic structure of obsidian and steel that had hummed with the secrets of control. Now, it lay partially in ruins, a gaping maw revealing the skeletal remains of its internal mechanisms. The air around it still held a faint chill, a residual echo of the oppressive energy that had permeated its walls. He had tasked teams, comprised of newly empowered citizens and pragmatic engineers, with meticulously deconstructing its harmful components, ensuring that no lingering trace of its manipulative technology could resurface. This was more than just demolition; it was an act of spiritual cleansing, a deliberate severing of ties with a past that had sought to dominate and dehumanize.

Yet, it was not the grand gestures of deconstruction that defined Cael's new role, but the quiet, persistent acts of creation. He found himself drawn to the periphery, to the edges of the Accord Cities where the Conclave's influence had been most suffocatingly absolute, and where nature's resilience was most desperately trying to assert itself. The vast, sterile plains that had been stripped bare for Conclave industrial complexes were now being meticulously reseeded. Cael, no longer cloistered in strategy rooms, spent days in the open air, his hands stained with soil, working alongside farmers who were relearning the ancient ways of cultivation.

He had established the first of the **Terraformers' Guilds**, an organization born not from a top-down decree, but from a shared necessity. This guild wasn't focused on terraforming alien worlds, but on healing their own, on coaxing life back from the brink. Their mandate was multifaceted: to identify and protect areas of significant ecological importance, to pioneer sustainable agricultural practices, and to serve as educators for a generation that had grown up with synthetic sustenance and manufactured environments. Cael, with his innate understanding of strategic resource allocation, ensured they had the necessary resources, but he deliberately refrained from dictating their methods. Instead, he facilitated their learning, connecting them with the few remaining elder farmers who remembered the earth's cycles, and with the nascent network of Listeners, like Mara Lysenne, who could translate the planet's subtle cues.

One of the most vital undertakings the Terraformers' Guild, with Cael's quiet support, had embarked upon was the restoration of the **Whispering Marshes**. These wetlands, once a vibrant sanctuary teeming with unique flora and fauna, had been designated as a hazardous waste disposal site by the Conclave, their delicate ecosystem poisoned and choked. The process of reclamation was arduous, a slow, painstaking battle against toxins and invasive species. Cael would often visit the marsh, not to oversee progress in a supervisory capacity, but to simply bear witness.

He would stand at the edge of the reclaimed waters, the air thick with the scent of damp earth and new growth, and listen. He'd learned to distinguish the tentative chirps of returning marsh birds from the frantic buzzing of insect swarms, to feel the subtle shift in the water's purity as it was filtered by newly established reed beds. It was in these quiet moments of observation that he felt the true measure of his stewardship.

He had also championed the establishment of **Sanctuary Zones**. These were not merely nature reserves, but carefully designated areas where the planet's healing processes could occur with minimal human interference. They were places of profound natural power, often imbued with a mythic resonance that had been suppressed by the Conclave. One such zone, the **Sunstone Peaks**, known for its unique crystalline formations that pulsed with residual solar energy, had been a particular focus. The Conclave had attempted to mine these crystals for their power, leaving scars that still marred the mountainsides.

Cael, working with the nascent council of elders and the wisdom of the mountain spirits themselves, had declared the Peaks a protected sanctuary, accessible only to those who sought to learn and heal, not to exploit. He ensured that the communities bordering the Peaks were actively involved in their protection, fostering a sense of shared responsibility and pride.

His transformation was not a sudden metamorphosis, but a gradual shedding of old skins. The disciplined soldier who had once seen the world in terms of threats and fortifications now saw it in terms of interconnectedness and balance. He understood that true strength lay not in the ability to command obedience, but in the capacity to foster growth and resilience. This philosophy extended to his interactions with the people. He had been instrumental in forming **Community Councils**, decentralized bodies that gave voice to local needs and facilitated direct participation in governance.

These councils were not designed to replicate the rigid hierarchies of the past, but to mirror the organic, interconnected nature of ecosystems. Each community elected representatives, not for their political acumen, but for their wisdom, their empathy, and their demonstrated commitment to the well-being of their neighbors and their environment.

Cael himself often served as a mediator, a quiet presence guiding discussions towards consensus. He would patiently explain the ecological implications of proposed projects, drawing parallels between the complex web of life in a forest and the intricate social fabric of a community. He would share his own evolving understanding, his willingness to admit when he didn't have all the answers, which in turn encouraged others to speak their truths and offer their own insights. This approach, so alien to the Conclave's method of pronouncements and punishments, fostered a deep sense of trust and shared ownership.

One particularly challenging negotiation involved the re-routing of a vital water source that had been artificially diverted by the Conclave for their own industrial needs. The original path of the river ran through a small, but deeply sacred, ancestral grove that held immense spiritual significance for the indigenous peoples of the region. The community council was divided. Some argued for the immediate restoration of the river to its ancient course, regardless of the potential disruption to newly established agricultural zones that had come to rely on the Conclave's diversion. Others, wary of upsetting the delicate balance of the newly reawakened land, urged caution.

Cael facilitated a series of open forums. He brought together the Listeners who could speak to the grove's needs, the engineers who understood the intricacies of water flow, and the farmers who depended on the current system. He didn't impose a solution. Instead, he guided them through a process of collaborative problem-solving. He asked questions that probed their underlying fears and desires, helping them to articulate their needs beyond the immediate practicalities. He introduced the concept of **symbiotic adaptation**, a principle he had learned from observing how different species in an ecosystem could coexist and even benefit from each other's presence.

Through these dialogues, a novel solution emerged. A compromise was reached that involved creating a smaller, carefully managed secondary channel to the grove, ensuring its spiritual needs were met while also implementing advanced water conservation techniques for the agricultural lands. This wasn't the quick, decisive command the old Cael might have issued. It was a slower, more organic process of collective wisdom, a testament to the fact that true stewardship involved nurturing not just the land, but also the human spirit.

His personal journey had also been one of profound growth. The rigid discipline of his Guardian training had instilled in him a sense of order and control. But the lessons of the Conclave's fall, and the subsequent reawakening of the planet, had taught him that true order emerged from balance, not from imposition. He had learned to trust his intuition, to listen to the subtle cues of the natural world, and to understand that his role was not to dominate, but to harmonize.

He had found a particular sense of peace in the **Sky-Watcher's Plateau**, a remote, windswept region that had been largely ignored by the Conclave due to its inaccessibility. Here, ancient rock formations stood like silent sentinels, their surfaces etched with the stories of millennia. Cael would spend nights under the vast, unpolluted sky, charting the constellations, not with instruments, but with his own keen eyesight. He felt a profound connection to the celestial rhythms, a sense of belonging that transcended the immediate concerns of governance. He saw the stars as a grand, cosmic ecosystem, each celestial body playing its part in a magnificent, intricate dance. This perspective helped him to contextualize the challenges facing his own world, reminding him of the immense scale of existence and the interconnectedness of all things.

He had also begun to actively protect areas that were not just ecologically vital, but also held deep spiritual significance, often tied to the ancient myths and legends of the planet. The **Oracle's Falls**, a cascading waterfall rumored to have once been a site of prophecy, was one such place. The Conclave had attempted to dam the falls, diverting the water for their own purposes, but their efforts had been met with unexpected resistance from the very earth, the dam repeatedly failing. Cael, understanding the reverence the local communities held for the falls, had overseen the dismantling of the Conclave's incomplete structure and initiated a project to restore the natural flow. He ensured that the surrounding area was preserved as a sacred site, a place for quiet contemplation and spiritual renewal, rather than a tourist attraction or a resource to be exploited.

His journey from restraint and duty to active, ethical leadership was complete. He had shed the heavy mantle of command and embraced the lighter, yet far more profound, responsibility of stewardship. He no longer felt the need to exert control; instead, he cultivated an environment where life could flourish, where communities could thrive, and where the planet's song could be heard and honored. His strength was no longer measured by his ability to enforce his will, but by his capacity to nurture and protect, to guide without dictating, and to lead by example, demonstrating that true power lay in fostering a sustainable future where humanity and nature existed in a harmonious, interconnected dance. He was Cael Thornevale, the steward, and his work was the quiet, persistent cultivation of a world reborn.

The cacophony of the Accord Cities had subsided, replaced by a hum of recovery, a symphony of rebuilding and tentative hope. Cael Thornevale, no longer a cog in a machine of oppression, but a weaver of a new dawn, found himself in the quiet spaces between the grand pronouncements and the urgent needs. The immediate threat, the crushing weight of the Conclave's dominion, had been lifted. The air, once thick with fear and suspicion, was now beginning to clear, allowing the subtler scents of pine resin, damp earth, and the nascent bloom of forgotten wildflowers to waft through the land. Yet, as the dust settled, a different kind of awareness began to dawn, a recognition that the victory, while profound, was but a single note in a much larger, more complex song.

There were moments, particularly in the hushed twilight hours when the newly freed stars began to prick the darkening sky above the Sky-Watcher's Plateau, that Cael felt it – a subtle resonance, a deep thrumming beneath the surface of everyday reality. It was a feeling that transcended the logistical triumphs of the Terraformers' Guilds, the delicate negotiations with the Community Councils, and even the profound healing unfolding in places like the Whispering Marshes and the Sunstone Peaks. This was not a tangible threat, not a foe to be confronted with strategy and steel. It was something more ancient, more fundamental, a truth woven into the very fabric of the planet itself.

He had observed it first in the eyes of the Listeners, their faces etched with a mixture of awe and apprehension. Mara Lysenne, her gaze often fixed on horizons unseen by others, had spoken of it in hushed tones, her words like scattered stardust. "The Song is changing, Cael," she had confided, her voice barely a whisper against the wind whistling through the Oracle's Falls. "It is not just the music of our healing, but the deeper rhythm. The planet... it remembers things we have long forgotten. And it is stirring." He understood, then, that their struggle against the Conclave, while vital, had merely been an effort to mend a surface wound. The true challenge, the one that lay at the planet's core, was a confrontation with its deepest, most elemental nature.

This wasn't a new enemy, but an old truth. The Conclave, in their relentless pursuit of control, had attempted to silence this inherent pulse, to impose their sterile order upon a world that thrived on vibrant, untamed chaos. They had sought to commodify its energy, to dissect its mysteries, and in doing so, had only managed to reveal the sheer, unyielding power of what they sought to suppress. The very act of their undoing, the seismic shifts that had fractured their dominion, had, in turn, awakened something within the planet. It was as if the earth, in its agony and subsequent relief, had exhaled a breath that resonated through its very foundations, a breath that carried the weight of eons.

Cael began to see the evidence everywhere, not as a sign of impending doom, but as an ongoing dialogue. The resurgence of the flora in the former Conclave industrial zones was not merely a biological recovery; it was a reclaiming, a vibrant assertion of the earth's inherent will to live and grow, often in ways that defied neat, human-engineered logic. He had witnessed new species of bioluminescent moss appearing in the deepest caves of the Sunstone Peaks, their glow not just a biological phenomenon, but a luminescence that seemed to pulse with an internal energy, a silent testament to the planet's latent forces. He had seen the rare, crystalline dew that formed only on the highest crags of the Sky-Watcher's Plateau, a dew that shimmered with an ethereal light, rumored by the elder shamans to hold fragments of cosmic memory. These were not aberrations; they were manifestations of a deeper elemental language.

The whispers of the Listeners spoke of a new kind of empathy emerging from the land, a subtle communion that went beyond understanding ecological needs. It was about understanding the planet's dreams, its ancient memories, its very consciousness. Mara spoke of sensing shifts in the earth's magnetic field that corresponded with collective emotional states, of feeling the planet's sorrow when a particularly old growth forest was disturbed, even by natural causes, and its quiet joy when new life bloomed in unexpected places. This was the elemental challenge: not to conquer or control, but to listen, to understand, and to harmonize with a consciousness far vaster and more complex than their own.

The Conclave had been built on the fallacy of human exceptionalism, the belief that they were separate from and superior to the natural world. Their downfall was a testament to the arrogance of that belief. Now, Cael and his burgeoning community were faced with the more profound, and perhaps more humbling, task of recognizing their place *within* this ancient, living entity. The planet was not merely a resource to be managed, but a partner, a teacher, a living, breathing being with its own intricate desires and profound wisdom. The deeper challenge, then, was to cultivate a relationship of true reciprocity, one that honored the planet's inherent sentience and acknowledged the limits of human understanding.

This called for a different kind of leadership, one that eschewed the certainty of command for the humility of exploration. The Terraformers' Guilds were evolving, their focus shifting from purely practical restoration to a deeper ecological engagement. They began to study the symbiotic relationships that existed not just between flora and fauna, but between the earth's geological formations and its biological life, between the planet's atmospheric currents and its oceans. They started to map the ley lines of planetary energy, not to harness them, but to understand their flow and their influence. They were learning to read the earth's subtle signs – the shifting patterns of migratory birds, the tremors that ran through the soil before a storm, the way certain plants unfurled their leaves in response to unseen celestial alignments.

The Oracle's Falls, once a site of potential prophecy, now served as a focal point for this new understanding. Cael, standing at its base, the mist kissing his face, felt not just the power of the falling water, but the ancient consciousness that flowed with it. The Listeners would gather there, not to receive pronouncements, but to meditate, to feel the rhythm of the water, to attune themselves to the earth's ancient song. They were learning that the planet's "memories" were not inert historical records, but active currents that shaped the present and influenced the future. They were beginning to understand that the very essence of their world was imbued with a consciousness that had existed long before humanity and would continue long after.

The Sunstone Peaks, with their crystalline heart, also became a site of profound study. The unique energy signatures emanating from the crystals were found to interact with the planet's geomagnetic field in complex ways. The engineers, working alongside the Listeners and geomancers, began to develop a new understanding of resonance – how planetary energies could be amplified or dampened, how they could influence weather patterns, biological growth, and even the subtle psychic currents that flowed between living beings. This was not about controlling these energies, but about learning to coexist with them, to understand their delicate balance and to avoid the disruptive interventions that had characterized the Conclave's era.

Cael realized that his role as steward had broadened immeasurably. It was no longer just about protecting the land from human exploitation, but about protecting humanity from its own ignorance of the planet's deeper nature. The task was not to impose order, but to foster understanding. It was to teach a generation that had grown up in artificial environments to reconnect with the wild, vibrant, and often mysterious intelligence of their world. It was about instilling a sense of reverence, not just for the tangible resources, but for the intangible forces that sustained life.

The Community Councils, too, began to integrate this deeper ecological awareness into their deliberations. Discussions about resource allocation now included considerations of planetary well-being, not just human needs. They learned to consult with the Listeners before making decisions that might impact sensitive ecosystems, understanding that the planet itself had a voice that deserved to be heard. This led to more holistic and sustainable solutions, fostering a sense of shared responsibility that extended beyond immediate human communities to encompass the entire living world.

He often found himself drawn to the Sky-Watcher's Plateau, not just for the solace of the stars, but for the raw, untamed energy of the place. The wind-sculpted rock formations seemed to hold the echoes of ancient geological processes, a slow, patient storytelling that dwarfed human timescales. He understood that the "abyssal truth" Mara and the other Listeners spoke of was not a singular revelation, but a continuous unfolding, a perpetual unveiling of the planet's profound, elemental being. The Conclave had sought to bottle this truth, to contain it, and in their failure, had inadvertently released it in its most potent, wild form.

The challenge lay in navigating this awakened world with wisdom and respect. It was about recognizing that the planet was not a passive stage for human drama, but an active participant, a vast, intricate ecosystem with its own agenda. The lessons of the Conclave's fall were clear: attempts to dominate and control would always fail, leading only to destruction. True progress lay in adaptation, in understanding, and in a deep, abiding respect for the intricate web of life.

As Cael stood on the edge of a newly reclaimed valley, the scent of wild thyme rising on the breeze, he felt the quiet pulse of the earth beneath his feet. It was a rhythm of growth and decay, of stillness and movement, of immense power held in delicate balance. The song of the planet was no longer a distant melody, but a vibrant, ever-present symphony. The immediate crisis had passed, but the journey of stewardship had only just begun. The deeper, more elemental challenge was not a battle to be won, but a relationship to be nurtured, an ongoing dance with a living, breathing world that held infinite mysteries and an eternal, profound wisdom. The future was not about definitive solutions, but about a continuous, respectful engagement with the living heart of their planet. The quiet after the song was not an ending, but a prelude to a deeper, more ancient melody, a melody that called for constant listening and profound humility.

GLOSSARY

Accord Cities: Settlements established after the fall of the Conclave, focused on cooperation and rebuilding.

Conclave: The former oppressive regime that sought to control and exploit the planet's natural resources and sentient life.

Elemental Challenge: The ongoing, fundamental task of understanding and harmonizing with the planet's deep, intrinsic consciousness and ancient forces.

Listeners: Individuals with a heightened sensitivity to the planet's subtle energies, emotions, and "song."

Oracle's Falls: A significant natural landmark, now a focal point for meditation and attunement with the planet's consciousness.

Planet's Song: The inherent rhythm, energy, and consciousness of the planet, perceived by the Listeners as a complex, ever-evolving melody.

Sky-Watcher's Plateau: A high-altitude region known for its clear skies, unique geological formations, and connection to celestial energies.

Sunstone Peaks: A mountain range characterized by its crystalline formations, which are believed to hold and resonate with planetary energies.

DIANE KANN

Terraformers' Guilds: Organizations that were once tasked with reshaping landscapes for human habitation but are now focused on ecological restoration and understanding.

REFERENCE

Lysenne, M. (n.d.). *The Resonance of Stone and Sky*. (Unpublished manuscript).

Thornevale, C. (n.d.). *Reflections on the Awakened World*. (Personal journals).

The Listeners Collective. (n.d.). *Cartography of Vibrational Currents*. (Community archives).

Various authors. (Ongoing). *Ecological Symbiosis and Planetary Consciousness*. (Transcripts from community symposia and research guilds).

www.ingramcontent.com/pod-product-compliance
Lightning Source LLC
LaVergne TN
LVHW040037080526
838202LV00045B/3377